PRAISE FOR THE LADY DARBY MYSTERIES

"[A] history mystery in fine Victorian style! Anna Lee Huber's spirited debut mixes classic country house mystery with a liberal dash of historical romance."
—Julia Spencer-Fleming, *New York Times* bestselling author

"Riveting . . . Huber deftly weaves together an original premise, an enigmatic heroine, and a compelling Highland setting." —Deanna Raybourn, *New York Times* bestselling author

"[A] fascinating heroine . . . A thoroughly enjoyable read!"
—Victoria Thompson, national bestselling author

"Reads like a cross between a gothic novel and a mystery with a decidedly unusual heroine." —*Kirkus Reviews*

"Huber deftly evokes both [Sebastian and Kiera's] attraction and the period's flavor." —*Publishers Weekly*

"[A] clever heroine with a shocking past and a talent for detection." —Carol K. Carr, national bestselling author

"[Huber] designs her heroine as a woman who straddles the line between eighteenth-century behavior and twenty-first-century independence." —New York Journal of Books

"[A] must read . . . One of those rare books that will both shock and please readers." —Fresh Fiction

"Fascinates with its compelling heroine who forges her own way in a society that frowns upon female independence. The crime itself is well planned and executed. The journey to uncover a killer takes many twists and leads to a surprising culprit." —*RT Book Reviews*

"One of the best historical mysteries that I have read this year." —Cozy Mystery Book Reviews

As Death Draws Near

ANNA LEE HUBER

BERKLEY PRIME CRIME, NEW YORK

BERKLEY
PRIME
CRIME

An imprint of Penguin Random House LLC
375 Hudson Street, New York, New York 10014

This book is an original publication of Penguin Random House LLC.

BERKLEY® PRIME CRIME and the PRIME CRIME design are trademarks of
Penguin Random House LLC.
For more information, visit penguin.com.

Library of Congress Cataloging-in-Publication Data

Names: Huber, Anna Lee, author.
Title: As death draws near : a Lady Darby mystery / Anna Lee Huber.
Description: New York : Berkley Prime Crime, 2016. | Series: A Lady Darby mystery ; 5
Identifiers: LCCN 2016007702 (print) | LCCN 2016013169 (ebook) |
ISBN 9780425277720 (softcover) | ISBN 9780698181779 () |
Subjects: LCSH: Serial murder investigation—Fiction. | Scotland—Social life
and customs—19th century—Fiction. | BISAC: FICTION / Mystery & Detective /
Historical. | FICTION / Mystery & Detective / Women Sleuths. | GSAFD:
Historical fiction. | Mystery fiction.
Classification: LCC PS3608.U238 A93 2016 (print) | LCC PS3608.U238 (ebook) |
DDC 813/.6—dc23
LC record available at http://lccn.loc.gov/2016007702

PUBLISHING HISTORY
Berkley Prime Crime trade paperback edition / July 2016

PRINTED IN THE UNITED STATES OF AMERICA

Cover illustration by Larry Rostant.
Cover design by Emily Osborne.

Penguin
Random
House

For my father,
for showing me that a good man treats women with care and respect,
and that actions sometimes speak louder than words.
With love and gratitude.

ACKNOWLEDGMENTS

As always, I have so many people to whom I'm extremely grateful for making this book possible. Much thanks to my fabulous editor, Michelle Vega, and all of the team at the Berkley Publishing Group for their extraordinary expertise. To my agent, Kevan Lyon, for providing guidance and support. To my cousin, Jackie Musser, and my friend Stacie Miller for their camaraderie and impeccable critiques. To all those who assisted in my research, including the talented Hazel Gaynor and the archivists at the Institute of the Blessed Virgin Mary and Irish Province of the Loreto Sisters Archives.

Much thanks to all of my author friends who encourage and bolster me in innumerable ways, especially Marci Jefferson and Rebecca Henderson Palmer (who helped me find my way out of a very sticky plotting situation), and my fellow Sleuths in Time Authors. To my amazing readers who have reached out to ask me questions and tell me how much they enjoy the Lady Darby books. None of this would be possible without you. I would also like to give a special shout-out to reader Angie Baugh, who won the right to name a character in this book last year during my online release party for *A Study in Death*. Homer turned out to be a perfect addition to the cast.

I also want to express my appreciation for my many family members and friends for all of their care and support, particularly my parents, who do so much for me. Boundless love and thankfulness to my husband and daughter. You are my heart. And immeasurable gratitude to God for all of His many blessings.

CHAPTER ONE

For my soul is full of troubles: and my life
draweth nigh unto the grave.

—PSALM 88:3, BIBLE, KING JAMES VERSION

JULY 1831
KESWICK, ENGLAND

It began with a letter. Or perhaps, more accurately, a messenger. Though I suppose it's pointless to quibble over such a triviality.

My new husband, Sebastian Gage, and I had been enjoying a delightful picnic at the top of a hill overlooking Derwentwater in the thick of the Lake District of Cumberland. Our mutual friend, Lord Keswick, had offered us the use of his home, Brandelhow Manor, for our wedding trip while he and his family were in London for the season, and we had happily accepted. After a rather tumultuous ten months, filled with murderous inquiries, an uneasy courtship, my sister's difficult childbirth, our rushed marriage, and the grim court trial from a recent investigation, we had both longed to escape the clamor and bustle of daily life for a time.

Fortunately, the Lake District was everything we'd hoped. Relative privacy, breathtaking scenery, and plenty of room to ramble whenever we needed fresh air. After more than four blissful weeks of such idyllic contentment, I was thoroughly enchanted with both my new husband and this northwest corner of England.

Having filled our stomachs with smoked mackerel, quark

cheese spread on crispy bread, and luscious little strawberry tarts, we reclined in the dappled sunshine beneath the branches of the ash tree at Gage's back.

"Do you think we could convince Lord Keswick to sell us his estate?" I murmured with a drowsy sigh.

He glanced fondly down at me, where my head rested against his shoulder. The wind rustled the leaves above and ruffled through the golden curls resting against his forehead. His hair had grown a bit overlong since our wedding two and a half months prior, but I didn't mind. "I think it's likely entailed. And I wager he would sooner see us disappointed than sell his young son's inheritance." His gaze strayed back toward the view unfolding before us. "But you're right, Kiera. It is lovely."

I smiled. "Darling, I think the word 'lovely' is rather a profound understatement."

Below the grassy slope on which we lounged, the shimmering blue expanse of Derwentwater rippled with life. Tiny skiffs with bright white sails darted across its surface, most having departed from Keswick village to our right and aimed for one of the small islands dotting the lake's center, or the lush green hills and spectacular fells of the far shore. The round, slightly curved heights of Catbells arched over the other fells like a crooked finger, as if to nudge the downy clouds chasing each other across the brilliant sky. From our vantage, we could watch their shadows racing over the landscape below, from the scorched celadon of the exposed bluffs, down through the green forest of trees, and across the rich canvas of blues which made up the water of the lake. The air was pungent with life— with earth, and moss, and sunbaked skin—yet softened by the swirling breeze.

This was the first opportunity I'd had to visit the Lake District of Cumberland, but I vowed it would not be the last. I well understood Lord Keswick's attachment to the place. The scenery was breathtaking. I couldn't recall seeing colors so vivid. The depths of the blues and greens were so rich and intense that I could not even begin to guess how to re-create them. It was impossible. Though the artist in me had been determined to try.

Landscapes had never been of particular interest to me, nor were they my forte. My gift was for portraiture. But in light of the views surrounding Brandelhow, I had been determined to make the effort, with mixed results. My attempt had been mediocre at best, but I would always cherish the painting simply for the memories it evoked. Particularly the smudges in the bottom right corner which attested to Gage's powers of persuasion and the tight confines of my makeshift studio.

"Oh, then what word would you have me use? *Stunning? Exquisite?*" Amusement shone in his eyes. "I'm not exactly Wordsworth."

"And well I know it," I teased back.

A shout of laughter escaped him, rumbling up from his chest. I lifted my head to look up at him just as he lifted his hand to cradle my jaw.

"You minx."

His voice was warm with affection, and I tilted my face upward for his kiss.

Which was when we heard the sounds of a galloping horse approaching. His eyes strayed over my shoulder, and I turned to watch as the rider of a bay stallion rounded the bend in the dusty path at the base of the hill. Upon catching sight of us, he reined in his horse, bringing the steed to an almost sudden stop. Anderley, Gage's dark-haired valet, stood from his seat halfway down the slope of the hill next to a Brandelhow footman to intercept the man before he could charge up the hill. He'd vaulted from his horse as if to do just that.

"Who is it?"

Gage sat up straighter. "A messenger of some kind."

We watched as the rider conferred with Anderley and then somewhat reluctantly passed him something. The valet spoke to him again and then swiveled to begin climbing the hill toward us.

"With a letter," I guessed, seeing the folded square in Anderley's hands. "But from whom?"

I considered all the natural possibilities—family, close friends—but there was really no way to know until we read it. My stomach tightened with apprehension. One thing was for certain. Whoever had sent it had been anxious for us to receive it. Even from the top of the slope I could see that the horse was winded and glistening with sweat from a hard ride.

"I'm not expecting anything," Gage said. "At least, not delivered like this. Though I suppose it's always possible . . ."

I glanced at him as he fell silent, trying to understand what he'd been about to say. His mouth flattened and his face grew taut, erasing the carefree expression of a moment ago. I eyed the missive Anderley carried with misgiving, somehow knowing, whatever the contents, our honeymoon was at an end.

"An urgent message from London, sir," Anderley told his employer as he passed him the letter.

I blinked in surprise, briefly meeting the valet's gaze as he turned to move a short distance away to give us privacy while Gage read the missive. The same tightly controlled expression ruled his face.

Gage flipped the missive over in his hand as he sat forward and braced himself by wrapping an elbow around the knee of one of his long legs encased in buff riding pantaloons and dark leather Hessians. He hesitated a second, as if recognizing the same thing I had, before finally breaking the seal and unfolding it.

I tried not to stare at him while he read, reaching for my glass of lemonade. It had grown tepid in the sunshine, and my mouth puckered at the sour warmth. However, it was impossible to ignore him completely. So I pretended to observe the progress of a small boat as it glided across Derwentwater toward the tall, dark pines studding the expanse of one island, while out of the corner of my eye I studied him.

It was clear almost from the start that the contents of the letter were not altogether welcome or unexpected. In fact, he seemed to review the words with a resigned acceptance coupled with intense irritation. He gazed at the bottom of the page for a moment after he'd finished before lowering it with an aggrieved sigh that was also part grunt. "It's from my father."

My eyebrows shot skyward. As far as I knew, Gage had not heard from his father since our wedding. Lord Gage had returned to London almost immediately following the ceremony, which he had attended only under threat. The haughty war hero had not been pleased by his son's choice for a bride, having already selected a charming and politically advantaged debutante for him. Knowing he believed me to be a shameless, scandalous woman, and that Gage would be hurt by his father's failure to attend our wedding, I elected to use my unfairly earned reputation to my advantage, threatening to forbid Lord Gage access to any future grandchildren if he did not appear. A bluff that turned out to be effective as he'd thought me heavy with his first grandchild at the time since Gage and I had pushed forward our wedding date.

I had not told Gage about my gambit, and I assumed neither had his father, but I had to wonder for a moment whether the jig was now over. My eyes strayed toward the hasty scrawl on the foolscap. "What does he say?"

"He wants us to investigate something."

My spine stiffened. This was a surprise. At least, to me. After the amount of trouble he'd given us during our last murder inquiry, and the number of derogatory comments he'd made about both of our investigative skills, I had never expected him to request his son's assistance with an inquiry ever again. But to apply to us both . . .

"Both of us? He actually said that?"

His pale blue eyes focused on me. "Yes. But here. You can see for yourself."

I took the letter from him gingerly, a bit hesitant to read Lord Gage's acerbic commentary.

Sebastian,

I trust this letter finds you well and adequately rested. I need you to go to Ireland posthaste, to the village of Rathfarnham, south of

Dublin. A Miss Harriet Lennox, now a nun at the Loretto Abbey there, has gotten herself murdered. The matter is of some importance to His Grace, the Duke of Wellington, seeing as the chit is his distant cousin. We cannot allow the murder of his relative, foolish and disgraceful papist though she may be, to go unchecked.

Obviously the matter is delicate, and of some urgency, otherwise I would have handled it myself. As you are already hundreds of miles closer, I recommended to His Grace that you should be sent in my stead. I also suggested that your wife might be of some assistance, as she is of the same irrational sex as these nuns, and certainly not above pressing them should the inquiry require it.

I shall expect word from you upon your arrival, and upon the discovery of any crucial piece of information.

The letter went on to inform Gage of the accommodations his father had arranged for us with an acquaintance who owned a cottage in the same village as the abbey, but such details were of little import at the moment. As were the two letters of introduction included inside from the duke, one addressed to the Reverend Mother Mary Teresa Ball; the other to a Sir John Harvey, Inspector-General, and others to Whom It May Concern.

I narrowed my eyes. "The same irrational sex?"

"The letter is from my father. What did you expect?"

"A bit more courtesy. He does realize he's summoning us from our honeymoon, does he not?"

Gage draped his arm over his raised knee, the sleeves of his shirt rolled up to his elbow exposing his forearms, which were now bronzed by the sun, and chuckled mirthlessly. "Oh, I'm certain of it. I'm sure this timely interruption was just a perquisite."

I frowned, glancing down at the missive one more time, and then set it aside. "A nun murdered in a convent? This sounds like the beginning of some ghastly Gothic novel. One expects a mad monk or a poorly disguised ghost to appear next."

His mouth quirked. "And what does that make me? The righteous and thoroughly dull hero of this tale?"

I arched a single eyebrow. "That's far better than being the girl who goes about shrieking and fainting all the time. And being kidnapped by the villain, not once, but twice."

"Oh, but I've been so looking forward to catching you mid-swoon."

I angled him a quelling look, but it only made his smile broaden.

I shook my head, and then tapped the letter with my finger. "In all seriousness, what do you wish to do?"

He didn't answer immediately, instead turning to stare at the variegated peaks of the fells in the distance. His father had placed him in a difficult situation. How does one say "no" to the Duke of Wellington, or allow a young woman's murder to go unpunished? For if we declined to go, by the time the missive reached his father telling him so, the trail would have grown even colder, and that much harder to investigate.

That being said, I also knew neither of us was eager to end our honeymoon, to abandon our arcadia and return to the dangers and difficulties we sometimes faced as private inquiry agents. We had planned a slow journey south, stopping where and when we wished, enjoying the long days of summer in the countryside before we reached London. Jeffers, the eminently capable butler we had poached from the brutish husband of the victim of our last murder inquiry, had already been sent ahead of us to prepare Gage's town house for our arrival. After setting to rights the Edinburgh town house Gage had purchased me for a wedding present within a week, I had no doubt Jeffers could manage what Gage sheepishly described as his "rather bachelor abode." What that had meant precisely, I didn't know, but I'd suspected it had more to do with his choice in colors and conveniences than the possible presence of half-naked female statues.

Now that leisurely trek seemed altogether unlikely.

Anderley shifted his feet in the grass, recalling our attention to him and the rider standing next to his horse below. The man chatted with the footman from Brandelhow, who had descended the hill to join him, while sending us restless glances.

"Give the messenger some coin for his trouble, and send him on his way," Gage instructed his valet.

"I can't," Anderley surprised him by saying. "He says he's come all the way from London and must wait for a reply."

Gage scowled at his dark-haired servant, but I knew his displeasure was not directed at the valet, but at his father.

"I hope he hasn't ridden that beast all the way," I proclaimed, staring down at the lathered bay below. "It's a wonder the horse is not dead if he's ridden him this hard at every stage."

Anderley pivoted to face me, his handsome face betraying no emotion. "I'm sure he's been trading out his mount every so many miles, my lady. Says he made the journey in three days." His eyes flicked down toward the base of the hill and his mouth tightened. "Though I suspect he's ridden this particular horse a bit longer than is strictly good for him."

"Then tell the footman to take him back to Brandelhow and see that he's fed and given a bed while the stable lads see to his horse," Gage instructed him. "I'm sure between the two of us we can manage the picnic hampers and blankets. We'll wake the rider when I have a reply for him."

Anderley nodded. "Very good, sir."

Gage sat silently, watching as his valet descended the hill out of earshot, but even then he didn't speak. He wore a contemplative frown, as if still trying to decide what to do about his father's abrupt and rather rude directive. I suspected part of his worry was that he would disappoint me in some way, allowing his father to disrupt our wedding trip, but I remained quiet, waiting for him to speak first.

The footman and rider guided the horse back toward Brandelhow, soon rounding the bend in the path and disappearing beyond the high grasses. Anderley settled onto a large rock near the edge of the trail, facing out toward the lake to wait for us.

Unexpectedly, Gage chose that moment to tip me backward flat on the blanket and lean over to kiss me fiercely, stealing my breath. "Blast my father," he growled as he lifted his head to look down at me. "And blast this bloody girl for getting murdered."

I smiled gently, recognizing the true source of his frustration. "I doubt she wished for such an outcome."

"I know." He heaved a sigh and then scowled. "Listen to me. I'm as bad as my father."

"No, you aren't." I brushed my hands over the silk of his silver blue waistcoat and up over his collarbone. "You have a legitimate reason for being irritated. I don't relish the interruption of our wedding trip any more than you do." I quirked a single eyebrow. "Your father, on the other hand, is simply being a jackass."

This startled a smile out of him, softening the sharp lines of his face. "Yes, well, jackass or no, what do we do?" His fingers lifted to toy with the strands of my hair near my neck that had fallen from my upswept chignon and now rested against the blanket. "The truth of the matter is, I don't think my father would have requested our assistance if he wasn't desperately in need of it, loath as he would be to admit that."

"I had the same impression," I confessed, trying to remain focused on what he was saying and not the brush of his fingers against my skin. His father's low opinion of me and my investigating abilities had been made abundantly clear.

"So he and Wellington must truly be in a pickle." He scowled. "Which puts *us* in a pickle."

His too-long hair flopped over his eyes as he hovered above me and I reached up to push it aside. "What will happen if we decline?" I ventured to ask for the sake of thoroughness.

He didn't reply at first, but from the tightness around his eyes, I could tell he was working through the implications himself.

"Your father won't go, will he?"

"Not if he can avoid it. And if he does, the inquiry will be rushed. Some Irish peasant will be charged with the crime. Or perhaps worse, a Catholic politician it would be expedient for the government to be rid of."

"Your father won't be impartial?" I asked in surprise.

He looked away. "Maybe. Maybe not."

His uncertainty was unsettling. I knew what it was to be charged with a crime I hadn't committed, to be tried and condemned in the eyes of the public if not the law. It was not something I could idly sit by and allow to happen to someone else.

I also knew, no matter the truth, if we declined to go, Lord Gage would blame me. He would consider his son's refusal yet another example of my unfortunate influence on him, and one more reason to disapprove of our marriage. Little as I cared for Lord Gage or his opinion of me, I cared greatly how they affected Gage, and anything I could do to smooth matters between them was for the better. There was also an element of challenge to Lord Gage including me in his request, almost as if he'd thrown down a gauntlet, daring me to prove him wrong. I had to admit, I wanted to meet and exceed it, and then flaunt my success in his face.

I pushed Gage away from me, so that I could sit up. The beautiful scenery surrounding us was unchanged. The colors were still brilliant, the sky scattered with down-soft clouds, the breeze lazy and alluring, and yet nothing was the same. Our idyll was over.

I could feel his eyes on me, waiting for my reaction, perhaps for my blessing. I knew he didn't want to make this decision alone, to dictate where we needed to go, as his father so often tried to do to him. His willingness to not only listen to but oftentimes heed my opinion meant much. In fact, it was one of the reasons I had agreed to marry again, despite the unhappy memories of my first marriage.

I picked up a blade of grass that had fallen on the skirts of my russet brown walking dress and tossed it aside. "I suppose Lord and Lady Keswick will be returning from London soon anyway. The season usually draws to a conclusion before the heat of mid-July arrives."

"True." His hand captured mine where it rested on the blanket between us. "Does that mean you think we should go to Ireland?"

I allowed myself one more moment of indecision before

nodding my head once determinedly. "Yes. If not us, then who? Besides, we'll still be together."

"Yes." He drew me closer, wrapping his arm around my back. "I'm not sure I'll be able to let you out of my sight, wife."

I smiled at his playful protectiveness. "I must admit, I'm also somewhat intrigued by the whole thing. Who murders a nun? And why? Aren't they normally sequestered away in some dank abbey? Singing, and praying, and absorbed in silent contemplation of God and His holy word."

"I suspect they still fall prey to the same sinful thoughts and emotions we do, just to a lesser degree. They may have cloistered themselves away from the world, but they are still of this world, no matter their vows."

I tipped my head, resting it in the crook of his neck with a small sigh. "I'm sure you're right. Either way, we shall find out soon enough."

Gage held me closer, as if feeling just as acutely as I how our time was suddenly slipping away. It left a bittersweet ache in my chest recalling how much I had enjoyed this place, and yet knowing tomorrow our time here would be over. I supposed it wasn't uncommon for people to experience this after a particularly lovely holiday, but I was unfamiliar with the emotion. It was almost akin to loss, which I had experienced plenty of. The similarities rattled me.

It was on the tip of my tongue to tell Gage I'd changed my mind. That I didn't want to go to Ireland. But the moment passed, like a cloud's shadow scuttling across the landscape. There was nothing to fear. Whether we went to Ireland or not, we would have to leave the Lake District soon anyway. It might as well be on an adventure, doing what we did best.

If only I'd recognized then exactly what that chilling sense of dread had meant, perhaps I wouldn't have dismissed it so readily. Perhaps the distress that followed might have been mitigated.

CHAPTER TWO

That evening I sat before the dressing table, watching Bree in the mirror as she plaited my hair. Though, I didn't know why I let her bother. I woke each morning with my tresses spilling across my pillows in a tangled mess, courtesy of Gage's wandering fingers. My maid must have known it was not an accident that my braids came undone, for they had rarely done so in the months prior to my marriage, but she never mentioned it.

It was long past time that I should have said something, but I rather enjoyed the soothing bedtime ritual, the feel of my maid's deft fingers weaving through my hair. It was comforting somehow. Perhaps because my most vivid memories of my mother were of me resting my head on her shoulder while she reclined in bed, her fingers combing through my unruly chestnut curls while my siblings bounced on the counterpane around us, telling her about their day. She died when I was eight, but if I closed my eyes, I could almost imagine it was her fingertips brushing across my scalp and not Bree's.

However, I must also admit I was a bit self-conscious. Gage and I were too recently married, and nothing from my first marriage had prepared me for the startling intimacy of being alone with Gage. Sir Anthony Darby had been cold and distant at the best of times, and outright cruel at the worst. Gage was nothing like that. In fact, he was nearly my first husband's opposite in every way. What happened between us—what was spoken and done in the privacy of our own chamber—meant too much. It was all too fresh and new for me to speak of it elsewhere, even with Bree. I'm not sure I could have put it into words had I tried.

So I didn't. Instead, I chose to focus on more mundane things. Such as our upcoming trip.

"Have you been able to finish the packing?"

Her gaze flicked up to meet mine briefly in the mirror. "Aye, m'lady. All 'cept what you'll be needin' in the morn."

I would have nodded except for the tight grip she had on my hair. "Thank you. I'm sorry for giving you such short notice." My eyes dropped to the remaining brushes left on the table, and I absently reached out to straighten them. "I suspect this may not be an uncommon occurrence, given the manner of my and Gage's business."

Bree's eyes lit with a smile. "No' to worry, m'lady. If e'er there were a lady equipped for expediency, it would be you. I wager it takes longer to pack your art supplies than it do your dresses and such. An' you willna let anyone help you wi' that."

I knew she was just teasing me. That no servant in their right mind wishes to be given more work, to be given responsibility for packing their employer's fragile and specialized art implements, as well as the pigments and the potentially volatile chemicals involved. But I felt a twinge of embarrassment all the same. It was probably past time I entrusted her with such a delicate task, and one day soon I would. Just not today. Not for this journey.

I studied Bree's dark eyes as she concentrated on the ends of my hair and finished the braid, wondering how she felt about our trip the next day. Perhaps I should have asked when I told her of our plans earlier that day. I'd already experienced the difficulties an anxious, unwilling maid could wreak when traveling. Though a well-meaning girl, my maid before Bree, a young lass named Lucy, had been ill suited to life away from my brother-in-law's Highland estate. I did not think Bree suffered from any of the same naïve flaws of character, but it still seemed best to ask.

"Bree, do you have any qualms about going to Ireland?"

She glanced up in some surprise as she reached for a pale ivory ribbon to secure my hair. "Nay, my lady. Though I do thank ye for askin'. If ye remember, I told ye my granny was Irish."

"I do," I replied. It was not difficult to recall, as one of my grandmothers had also been born in Ireland. "Which part of the country did you say she came from?"

"County Mayo. In the west."

"So nowhere near Dublin."

"Nay." She hesitated almost imperceptibly before adding, "Though I do have a brother who lives in Dublin. Works at the docks."

"Do you?"

"Aye, m'lady."

I swiveled to look at her, wondering at the note of uncertainty I heard in her voice. "Well, you should write to him then, to let him know you shall be so nearby. I would be more than happy to give you an extra day or two off so you can visit him. It must be some time since you last saw him."

Bree's face did not brighten as I'd expected. "Three years, m'lady. And I thank ye, m'lady. I'll think on it."

She must have been able to read the furrow of confusion between my brows, but she made no move to explain, so I did not press her. I knew as well as most how complicated family could be. Should she wish to tell me anything, she would.

In any case, Gage had rapped on the door from the connecting chamber he used to dress before entering. Bree gathered up my clothes from the day and left us with a soft "Good night."

I stared after her a moment longer, still puzzling over her reaction, before I turned to Gage with a shake of my head.

He stood next to the bed with his hands tucked into the pockets of his burgundy silk dressing gown. "What is it?"

"Nothing," I replied, brushing the matter aside. "Has everything been made ready for tomorrow?"

"Yes. I told the staff we would be leaving at first light."

"And Anderley? How did he react?"

Gage's eyebrows lifted at the question. I was well aware that I had always been a bit too familiar with servants, too concerned with their opinions, but it was a difficult habit to break, especially when I did not care to do so.

"He didn't object," he said, as if that were answer enough. Which I supposed it was.

He smiled, crossing over to where I sat. "Do not look so troubled. I assure you that should Anderley not wish to do something, he would make it known. Our traveling trunks would have suddenly gone missing, or an inkwell would have been accidentally knocked over on my travel documents."

My eyes widened. "Is he truly so underhanded?"

Gage chuckled. "Undoubtedly. Though his hands always come out looking immaculate. But rest assured. He is loyal to me. To us," he amended, reaching out to toy with the end of my braid, which trailed over my shoulder. "And at times I find his clever underhanded ways to be useful."

I narrowed my eyes, curious whether I had already encountered the valet's deviousness. "My gray serge painting dress. Is he responsible for it going missing?"

Gage would not meet my eyes. "He did mention how atrocious he thought it on you."

"It wasn't meant to be fashionable," I snapped. "What does he think I should paint in? A demure white morning dress? The thing will be streaked with paint and ruined within an hour."

"I know."

A thought occurred to me. "Oh, no. Poor Bree. She was terribly upset, thinking she'd misplaced it. I told her it was of no concern, but I knew she still felt horrible."

"Well, I wouldn't worry about her," he murmured obliquely.

I paused to look at him, waiting for him to elaborate.

"I'm fairly certain she uncovered the truth." His mouth

creased into a grin. "At least, the manner in which Anderley was twitching the next day, desperately trying not to fidget and scratch himself, suggests so."

I pressed a hand to my mouth. "What did she do?"

"Put itching powder in his shirt, I'd wager."

I couldn't help but laugh. "Oh, poor, Anderley."

"He deserved it."

"I know, but still." I shook my head. "How dreadful."

"Don't pity him too much. He's also the one who informed Lady Westlock's maid of your involvement in our inquiry at Gairloch Castle." Our first investigation together. "And the maid undoubtedly told Lady Westlock, not her husband." Whom we had blamed.

I gasped in outrage. "Why, of all the rotten . . ."

"Yes." Gage pulled me to my feet. "At the time, he thought he was helping me. But, of course, he only made matters worse." He spread his fingers through my hair at my scalp. "And pushed me closer to you."

It was only then that I realized he'd already pulled out the ribbon Bree had used to secure the ends of my hair.

"Sebastian," I protested weakly as he leaned in to kiss me. I sighed as he brushed his fingers down through the intertwined strands, loosening them. At the sound, he deepened the kiss, interpreting it as encouragement, and I didn't correct him. Because, of course, it was.

The next morning as dawn crept over the eastern fells, painting pink and yellow streaks through the clouds and tinting the dark water of the lake lavender and mauve, we set out for the coast. There was no direct route to the town of Whitehaven through the western fells, so we were forced to go around. Though the road north and then west was by no means an easy one, bouncing and jarring us inside the carriage, so that it was impossible to sleep. Fortunately, the spectacular sights more than made up for the discomfort. In this more rural part of Cumberland there were few villages, and little to interrupt our view of the gorse-strewn hills, tumbling rock formations, and sparkling streams.

As we neared the coast, the road swung south again. The land gradually flattened into fields of wheat and barley, and homes and shops began to dot the roadside. Even with such an early start, by the time we reached the port of Whitehaven, the sun was well on its way to its zenith. So while Bree and I refreshed ourselves at a dockside inn and purchased a few additional provisions for the journey, Gage and Anderley went to see about chartering a boat to take us across the Irish Sea. We were seated at a corner table in the front room, nursing small glasses of ale, when they returned.

"We're in luck," Gage proclaimed. "I've managed to hire the crew of a fishing schooner. Normally they would just be returning with the day's haul, but they had some trouble with their equipment and had to remain in port last night. They said they'd welcome the extra wages, and still have the chance to bring back a catch with them when they return." He leaned over to pick up my still half-full glass, nearly draining it in one swallow. He offered the glass back to me, but I shook my head. "They said the seas are favorable, so if you both are ready." He arched his eyebrows in question as he finished the ale.

"Yes." I rose to my feet, smoothing down my straw yellow and rose striped silk carriage dress. "I believe we have everything."

Before we could take a single step toward the door, a familiar voice drawled from across the room near the stone hearth. "It *is* you. I thought it might be, but it was difficult to tell with your head tucked up primly beneath that bonnet, and your maid guarding you like some Scottish terrier. But now that I see Sebastian Gage, I realize it must be Lady Darby."

For a moment, I stared in surprise at the man lounging in his chair, his foot propped on the bench opposite as he smirked in satisfaction. Until I remembered how much he enjoyed inciting just such a reaction from people. Particularly me, for some reason. I flattened my expression as best I could.

"Marsdale," Gage replied tightly. "What on earth are you doing here?"

It was a legitimate question. The Marquess of Marsdale was the dissipated son and heir of the Duke of Norwich, and had played a somewhat unsavory role in our first inquiry at Gairloch Castle during a house party my sister was hosting. From what I'd gathered, he spent most of his life trawling between London and various house parties, drinking, gambling and bedding numerous women. Because of his title and his dark good looks, he was allowed to behave so without being entirely ostracized from society. A portside inn in the small town of Whitehaven seemed as dubious a place to find him as I could imagine. Though, the fact that he was seated in the tavern area, drinking a pint, was somehow less astonishing.

"I could ask you the same thing." He slanted us a sly look. "Running off to Ireland, are we? Don't tell me you mean to elope?"

Considering the fact that I had been a widow, and we were both well beyond the age of consent, the question was absurd. But I suspected that had been his intention. Marsdale loved nothing so much as tweaking our noses.

"Actually we're already wed," I told him. "Two months past. So I'm Mrs. Gage now."

I expected to see some sort of reaction from him, but he barely gave us one. His smile merely deepened. Either he was better than I realized at hiding what he did not want to be seen, or he already knew.

"Well, well," he murmured, rising to his feet. "I suppose congratulations are in order then." His steps did not yet weave, but his sallow skin was flushed, making me suspect this glass might not have been his first.

He reached out a hand to Gage, who reluctantly accepted it. "May I kiss the bride?" He flashed his teeth in a wolfish grin, which made it clear he would not be aiming for my cheek.

"Only if you want your lip split," Gage warned.

He shrugged. "Ah, well. Can't blame a man for trying with such a lovely lady." He tilted his head. "And you *are* still

Lady Darby, you know. Perhaps not by right, but by courtesy. Everyone will still address you as such."

This was not news to me. I was aware of the idiosyncrasies of the correct forms of address among the British aristocracy. Even so, it stuck like a burr in my side. Society would think it a snub to take away the higher rank I'd been accorded from my first marriage by addressing me as a mere missus, but I was more than eager to shed Sir Anthony's name. However, I knew that would not happen permanently until Lord Gage passed away and Gage inherited his title, making him higher ranked than my first husband.

I flicked a glance at Gage, curious how he was reacting to Marsdale's words. He appeared annoyed, but not upset. After all, this wasn't the first time we'd encountered this unwanted courtesy, and it wouldn't be the last.

"All the same, I prefer Mrs. Gage," I said.

Marsdale shook his head. "I'm sure you do. But you know how society is. Such a stickler for tradition."

I arched a single eyebrow. "And we all know how important you hold society and tradition."

He smiled. "Ah, Lady Darby, I have missed you."

I didn't dignify that with a response, instead turning to gather up my reticule and beckon Bree forward.

"Good to see you, Marsdale," Gage remarked, making it clear he meant the opposite. "But we really must be going." He wrapped his hand around my elbow to guide me forward.

"Wait." Marsdale's voice grew more earnest. "Did I hear you say you were sailing to Ireland?"

Gage hesitated. "Yes."

"Might I sail with you?"

This stunned both of us into silence. We stood stiffly staring at him for so long that the noises of the tavern surrounding us began to filter into my consciousness—the clink of glasses and the scraping of chairs. I watched as the amusement Marsdale ordinarily displayed at having shocked us began to fade to strain. His left eye even twitched, making me realize he was serious.

"To Ireland? You want to come with us to Ireland?" Gage tried to clarify.

"Yes." When Gage didn't reply, he added, "I'm more than happy to help defray the cost. In fact, I'll pay for half the charter fee . . ."

Gage cut him off with a shake of his head. "Why?"

Marsdale's tongue seemed uncustomarily tied.

"Why do you wish to go to Ireland?" Gage's eyes narrowed. "What sort of trouble are you in?"

He tried to laugh off the suggestion, but I could tell Gage was right. "I know my reputation precedes me, but really, Gage. I think you've been dabbling in inquiries for too long. Such suspicion."

Gage didn't rise to his bait or release him from his glare.

He must have realized he was going to have to be forthright if he wished to persuade Gage to let him join us, for he heaved an aggrieved sigh. "It's nothing. Just a small misunderstanding."

"What misunderstanding?"

Marsdale's mouth flattened into a petulant line. "Some chit decided to crawl into my bed at Kendal's house party."

Which explained his presence in Whitehaven, fifty or so miles to the west.

"Which chit? Do you mean a debutante?" Gage asked, his voice rising in outrage.

"Yes," he snapped. Then he mumbled, "The Earl of Skipton's daughter."

My eyes widened. Even *I* knew about the earl's notorious temper. About his younger days spent as a pugilist, until after a series of tragic deaths the earldom fell to him.

I glanced up sharply at Gage as a bark of laughter erupted from him.

"And she entrapped you?"

It was not an uncommon worry among gentlemen with wealth and titles. More than one young lady had succeeded in forcing a marriage by arranging to be caught in a highly prized lordship's bed.

Gage's humor at Marsdale, of all men, finding himself in such a predicament slowly died. "Or did you coax her there?"

His scowl blackened. "I know better than to dandle with the virginal young misses, especially Skipton's kitten. No, the girl and her friend arranged it all."

Knowing Marsdale, I somehow doubted this. "And you didn't encourage her?"

"Well, of course, I encouraged her. But I never expected she'd actually sneak into my room, the cheeky minx."

I lifted my eyes heavenward. At least, he was honest. Inappropriately so. I didn't dare ask him whether he'd ignored Skipton's daughter's invitation once she was in his bed. I didn't want to know.

Neither did Gage, apparently, who continued to glare at the marquess. "So you fled."

"What else was I to do? Marry the chit? Refuse? If I did that, Skipton would have served me my bollocks for breakfast."

"Marsdale, mind your tongue. There is a lady present."

He huffed in annoyance. "You grasp my dilemma? It would be best if I left Jolly Old England for a while."

"Best for whom?" I scolded. "This girl's reputation will be ruined."

"That's not my fault."

Oh, it was, but I could see he didn't think so. I turned away in disgust. Perhaps it was for the best. After all, what woman in their right mind wants to be wed to a man like Marsdale? Despite the scandal, I had to believe Skipton's daughter would be happier in the long run. So long as Skipton didn't disown her, or worse.

Gage must have been able to divine my thoughts, for he touched my arm to gain my attention. "Lord Skipton has a temper, but he's a reasonable man, and devoted to his family. I suspect his daughter will suffer no harm from him." His eyes hardened as they lifted. "Marsdale, on the other hand, is another matter."

Our interloper jumped at this opening. "Precisely. So help a gent out. Save yourself the bother of another inquiry.

Or better yet, add soothsaying to your abilities and prevent a murder."

Gage stared at him in irritation.

He smiled hopefully, as if sensing his opponent was yielding. "Come on, Gage. What say you?" His dark eyes glanced toward me. "I can help protect your lady wife."

At this, Gage growled. "If you wish to speak with the captain of our ship and arrange passage to Ireland, that's your own affair, Marsdale. I won't naysay you. But I won't help you either. We leave as soon as we board, so if you think to wait for your valet to pack . . ."

"My valet is following behind with the luggage. I'll leave a message. He can catch another boat."

I blinked in surprise. For a self-indulgent fop like Marsdale to willingly flee the country without his servant and his belongings must mean he truly did fear for his life.

Gage moved a step closer, exploiting the few inches of height he had over the marquess. "However, if you trouble me or mine, I will not hesitate to dump you overboard." He stepped back as Marsdale jerked a nod, cupping my elbow with his hand. "As for my wife, I wouldn't bother trying to 'protect her,' if I were you. She carries a pistol."

Marsdale looked at me with new interest as Gage ushered me forward, and I smiled viciously.

CHAPTER THREE

We hurried along the docks, weaving around crates, fishing nets, and dockworkers loading and unloading cargo. I guessed Gage intended to test the marquess's resolve, hoping he would fail to keep pace with our quartet, but Marsdale gamely followed. It was only when I stumbled that I realized Gage was so preoccupied with his own thoughts that he hadn't noticed how fast we were moving. He slowed his steps, guiding me up a narrow gangplank onto the schooner.

He nodded to a man I guessed to be the captain as we boarded. "We're ready to sail as soon as you and your men are." Our trunks must have already been loaded and taken below.

Soon enough, we were pushing away from the quay and gliding out toward the open sea, with Marsdale in tow. What exactly he had told the captain, I never knew, but he easily negotiated his passage. What was one more when you were carrying four?

In port, the ship had smelled strongly of fish, as was to be expected, but once the sails caught the wind, thankfully, the stench began to dissipate. I stood at the rail, watching in some trepidation as the coast of England drifted farther away until it was a speck on the horizon. I decided then that perhaps it would be best if I joined Bree belowdecks in the cabin that had been offered for our use. At least then I wouldn't see the last sight of land disappear.

Unlike Gage, I had done little sailing, and none out on the open sea. I wasn't certain what to expect, or how to prepare myself. So I tried to ignore the tiny little flips my stomach was making whenever I thought of the water and the waves. The last time I had been in a boat, I had been at the mercy of a killer and almost drowned. I fought back my quavering nerves and threw myself into helping Bree to prepare our luncheon.

The cabin was by no means fresh or well appointed, but it was relatively clean, and likely the best accommodations they had on the ship. A pair of narrow bunks were attached to one wall, while a hammock swung across another corner. It brushed Bree's strawberry blond curls as she sat in one of the chairs pulled up to a battered wooden table nailed to the floor in the center of the room.

We unpacked some of the food from the hamper they had sent with us from Brandelhow and settled in to enjoy a modest meal. The men would join us soon enough. However, halfway through luncheon, the sea beneath us became choppier, and the churning I had felt in my stomach earlier returned with a vengeance. I began to wonder whether I should have skipped food altogether.

My struggle must have been obvious, for Gage took one look at my face when he entered the cabin and advised me to come back up to the deck with him.

"I don't think that's such a good idea," I protested.

"It's the best place for you if you're feeling ill," he cut in gently. "The sea air will help."

I swallowed against the urge to wretch and allowed him to take my hand and pull me from the room. Without saying a word, we passed Anderley and Marsdale waiting in the narrow corridor.

He guided me to the rail and pressed a steadying hand to my back. "Pick a point on the horizon and fix your gaze on that," he instructed me, raising his voice to be heard above the sharp wind.

"But there's only water. And it's constantly moving."

"Yes, but that far in the distance, where the sea meets the sky, that point remains fixed. Keep your eyes on it, and it will trick the rest of your body into thinking the sea is more steady."

I inhaled the salty breeze and followed his advice, focusing on that narrow slice of the world. The sea between the ship and the horizon was a slate green, rolling up from the deep to lash out at the boat like a petulant child, while overhead the sky was misty gray, much like the sky in the Highlands after it rained. I could feel the heavy dampness against my cheeks, but far from being unwelcome, it was actually quite comforting. Like having a cool moist cloth pressed to my forehead by the hand of God Himself. Between the wind and the wet, I knew my hair must look a riotous mess, but at that particular moment I didn't care. The untidiness was well worth it if it would help settle my stomach.

True to Gage's assertions, in a mere matter of minutes, the queasiness lessened. By no means did it disappear, but at least it was manageable. I loosened my grip on the railing, flexing my fingers, and lowered my shoulders from where they had crept up around my ears. But I kept my gaze pinned to the horizon, for every time I looked away, I felt my stomach flounder.

"Better?" Gage asked.

"Yes. Thank you. But am I supposed to stand here the entire voyage?" I could hear the strain in my voice. After all, we had only just set out. The majority of the journey lay ahead of us, and already I was feeling a bit desperate to reach land. "What am I going to do overnight?"

He rubbed reassuring circles on my back. "The captain told me we should pass out of the wake of the storm that caused these rough seas as we near the Isle of Man, and then the waters should be calmer."

I glanced swiftly to my left, catching sight of several members of the crew working with a length of rope, before I returned my gaze to the horizon. Between gusts of wind, I could catch snatches of conversation and laughter as they completed their tasks of which I knew nothing about. "And how far is it to the Isle of Man?"

"Oh, a few hours."

I could tell he was lying. I knew my geography well, and if we weren't going to reach Dublin until the following morning, we certainly weren't going to skirt the south of the Isle of Man in only a matter of hours. Before nightfall, perhaps, on these long summer days, but not before dinner.

I didn't argue. It was clear he was only trying to bolster me, and telling a frazzled person, barely keeping their sickness at bay, that they had six to ten more hours before they might find relief seemed rather cruel. Instead I inhaled a deep breath of the brisk sea air and tried to distract myself by categorizing the shades of pigment I would need to depict the scene before me.

Anderley appeared for a short time, passing Gage one of the cold roast beef sandwiches the staff at Brandelhow had prepared and packed for us, a wedge of sharp cheese, and a cup of cider. I felt I should excuse him to go below to eat his midday repast out of the wind, but I was not yet feeling well enough to stand there on my own. Besides, I knew the words would be wasted. Gage would refuse to leave me to shift for myself in such a situation.

I was glad of his continued presence when Marsdale suddenly decided to join us at the rail. I had expected him to huddle below in one of the cabins, snoring blissfully as we crossed the Irish Sea. A swift glance at his face told me he wasn't ill. At least, no more ill than normal. His complexion was always somewhat sallow and strained from the life of overindulgence he led.

Then he opened his mouth and surprised me again. "Gage, go on below with that. I'll keep Lady Darby company while you eat."

Gage seemed just as startled as I was by his courteous offer. And just as mistrusting. "Thank you, but I'm quite content to eat here."

Marsdale studied him, as he juggled his sandwich and wedge of cheese in one hand, and drink in the other. He shrugged. "Do as you please."

We stood quietly, each of us examining the willful sea as its waves tussled with one another and slapped against the boat, and the gray horizon sat veiled and smoky like a men's parlor, but I knew the silent contemplation could not last long. Not with Marsdale present.

"So why are you headed to Ireland?" he asked as casually as I supposed was possible when springing such a question out of nowhere. Then he added with mocking horror, "Don't tell me that's where you intend to honeymoon."

I frowned.

"No," Gage replied. "We've been asked to conduct an inquiry there."

I suppose he thought this would squash the marquess's interest, as it did not touch on our personal lives, but if so, he had forgotten the man's irreverence when it came to matters of murder and death. I flicked a glance upward to find his eyes were already glittering with curiosity.

"I should have suspected as much. Another murder? Who got crashed?"

Risking my stomach's contents, I turned fully to glare up at him. Before I could speak, Gage touched my shoulder. I bit my tongue, and turned back to the horizon.

"This isn't a lark, Marsdale," he chided more calmly than I could have managed. "A woman has been killed, her life brutally blotted out while her murderer roams free. It's a travesty to justice."

Marsdale straightened his shoulders, seeming to sober himself. "Quite right. My apologies."

Gage eyed him a moment longer, as if to be certain of his earnestness, and then turned away to take another bite of his sandwich.

"Who was she?" Marsdale queried. "I mean, I suppose she must have been someone important, or meant something to someone important; otherwise you wouldn't be undertaking such a journey."

The comment stung somehow, as if we only took the time to investigate the crimes of the wealthy and influential. But in a way, he was right. Lord Gage would never have asked us to conduct an inquiry into the death of some nun at a convent in Ireland if she had not been related to the Duke of Wellington. I knew Gage's inquiries in the past had largely been done on behalf of members of high society, because they wished for discretion, and they expected their crimes and inconveniences to be solved. The lower classes simply trudged along, knowing it was doubtful anyone would care what misfortunes befell them. The authorities were as likely to cause trouble for them as to help.

That realization was discomforting and somewhat discouraging, and it distracted me from being mindful of whom I was speaking to. "A Miss Harriet Lennox. She's a nun at the abbey in Rathfarnham, where we're headed."

Marsdale made a sound at the back of his throat as if he was choking. I swung my head around, trying to understand the bright look in his eyes.

"A nun?" he managed to gasp.

I narrowed my eyes. Was he struggling not to laugh? "That girl's death is not a trick for your amusement. How would you feel if she was *your* relative? Your sister, or mother, or cousin?" He started to cough and I loomed closer, lowering my voice in threat. "How do you think Wellington would react should we tell him how hilarious you found his cousin's murder?"

In the face of this threat, Marsdale seemed to regain control of himself, latching on to my last statement. "She was Wellington's cousin?"

I paused, worried I'd said too much. "Yes."

"Oh, well. My apologies." His manner was stilted, almost uncertain, though perhaps it only appeared that way because he was suddenly quite serious and I had never seen him so. "My brother served with Wellington. Thought highly of the man. It's simply not crack for one of his relatives to be murdered, even if she was a papist."

My stomach roiled and I turned to scowl at the sea in annoyance. I realized how little the majority of the members of British society thought of Catholics, but that did not make it any easier to hear how little they cared for their lives. However, something else he had said also caught my attention.

"Your brother served with Wellington?"

I didn't understand how that could be. The Battle of Waterloo had been fought sixteen years ago, ending the Napoleonic Wars. Even accounting for the lines a life of dissipation had wrought on his face, I knew Marsdale to be younger than Gage, and Gage had been seventeen when the wars ended. If Marsdale was his father's heir, then any brothers he had would be younger than him.

Marsdale leaned against the rail, raising his face to the breeze so that it almost lifted his hat from his head. "Yes. My father's first son. You didn't know I was the spare, did you?" he remarked with a wry twist to his lips. "My brother was a decade older than me. And when his mother died of some strange illness, our father worried her son might carry the same weakness. So he wed my mother and got me on her as swiftly as possible." The careless way in which he spoke only made his blunt, sharp words more disquieting. "It's why Lewis joined the Army. Our sire thought it would toughen him, root out the weakness. But he died at Waterloo. Shot and crushed by his horse."

I was too stunned to stammer more than a weak apology. "I . . . I'm sorry, Marsdale. That must have been awful for you."

"No more than death is for most people," he replied briskly, but I could see the way his hands were gripping the wooden railing, as if to tear it in two. "How did the nun die?"

I recognized avoidance when I saw it, and knew the matter was closed, for now. But I had trouble discarding the pain I'd heard in his voice as rapidly as he seemed determined to do.

Fortunately, Gage was not so affected. "We don't know," he replied in frustration. "Lord Gage didn't see fit to tell us."

"He didn't see fit to tell us much of anything," I added, flicking a glance at my husband. "What sort of situation do you suppose we'll be walking into?"

He chewed and swallowed the final bite of his sandwich before answering. "I honestly can't say. From what I gather, Ireland isn't like England, or even Scotland. The divide between classes is wide in Britain, but it's even wider in Ireland. And there is a great deal of unrest and unresolved animosity between Protestants and Catholics."

"But I thought the latest Catholic Relief Act was supposed to alleviate some of that?"

Gage's eyebrows arched tellingly. "In some ways it only made it worse."

Passed only two short years earlier after a long, contentious fight, the Catholic Relief Act had granted near political equality to Roman Catholics, allowing them to become members of Parliament and hold a limited number of government offices. It was the final act in a series of legislative reforms which began fifty years before with the repealing of some of the harshest penal laws affecting Catholics and ended in 1829 with emancipation. However, not everyone had been happy with this outcome. I clearly recalled my first husband Sir Anthony's outrage that the Duke of Wellington, who was prime minister at the time, and his government were supporting the bill. He, like many in Britain, believed it was an affront to the British way of life, a threat to the Crown and the English Constitution.

I had been conflicted about the issue. But when Sir Anthony had died of an apoplexy just a few short days before the relief act was passed and then the scandal over my involvement with his human dissections had broken, any thoughts of Catholics and their emancipation were forgotten. I had more pressing matters to contend with, including being brought up on charges of unnatural tendencies and desecrating the dead, all of which were summarily dismissed.

"What does that mean for us?" I asked, trying to decipher the reticence I saw in his gaze whenever I snatched a glance at him.

"It means we'll have to tread carefully. As outsiders, everyone will be suspicious of us. The Catholics simply because we're Anglican. The Anglicans and Protestants because I don't intend to toe the mark when it comes to any biased behavior." He sighed heavily. "It will be a fine balancing act getting any of them to trust us."

"I thought you'd never been to Ireland."

"I haven't. But I began a correspondence with Lord Anglesey a number of years ago." He turned to meet my gaze. "When I was in Greece."

Knowing what I did about his time spent fighting in the Greek's War of Independence from the Ottoman Empire, I understood the sudden solemnity behind his eyes. He had only recently shared with me some of the horrors he'd witnessed, both private and public, but it had been enough to give me nightmares.

"I went to school with Anglesey's son, so we were already acquainted, and he wanted to be kept apprised of the situation in Greece," he explained. "In particular, there were a number of Irishmen who joined the fighting, sympathizing with the Greeks' cause—slaving under the yolk of their Turkish oppressors." He arched his eyebrows. "Much as Ireland is under the thumb of Britain."

"I see," I replied, not seeing at all. I kept my eyes trained on the horizon, lest Gage see my doubt. "So you played informant."

"When it suited me. Other times I conveniently forgot what some of my fellow British subjects were involved in."

I smiled at his droll admission. This sounded more like the man I married.

"And so you continued your correspondence, even after Lord Anglesey became Lord Lieutenant of Ireland?" I guessed.

"It has proven useful. And the man *is* a diverting letter writer." His mouth twisted in suppressed amusement. "Though he does have a tendency to revise his own history."

Marsdale pivoted to face him. "That bit about when his leg was hit with a canonball at Waterloo and he was standing close to Wellington? 'By God, sir, I've lost my leg!'"

"'By God, sir, so you have!'" Gage replied, continuing the script. His eyebrows arched skeptically. "I imagine there was a great deal more screaming involved."

"He certainly sounds like a character," I said, being unfamiliar with the man.

Of course, I knew who he was. He was a war hero, after all, like the Duke of Wellington and Lord Gage, who had served as a captain in the Royal Navy. But I did not often converse in such lofty circles, even with an earl for a brother-in-law. I had never wished to. Though I had known Gage was well connected, through his father if nothing else, he had rarely spoken of his high-placed friends. Perhaps because he didn't consider them friends, but acquaintances. Either way, I was beginning to feel quite out of my depth.

"He most certainly is. And enamored of the ladies."

"Much like myself, he's left rather a long string of broken hearts," Marsdale interjected.

I scowled at his conceit.

"Including his first wife," Gage pointed out dampeningly.

Marsdale grimaced. "Yes. There is that." Apparently, even the marquess had standards, and that included not running off with your friend's wife, forcing your own wife to sue you for divorce.

The boat crested a large wave at an awkward angle, dropping us down harshly. I gripped the rail as the rocking propelled us back, feeling the dip in my stomach. The men seemed less affected. Needing only one arm to hold himself upright, Gage even pressed a hand to my back to steady me. I swallowed, hoping this wasn't a sign of worse seas to come.

"Do you think Lord Anglesey will be able to assist us?" I managed to ask.

"Perhaps, should we need it. With any luck, the county

constabulary will be able to inform us of all the particulars and provide support."

"Will they have investigated?"

"One hopes. Though I gather they're more often employed to keep the peace and execute warrants. I don't know what sort of experience they have with this kind of inquiry, or how seriously they will have taken it. I suppose it depends on the man in charge." He paused. "And whether they're interested in capturing a nun's killer."

"Well, someone informed the Duke of Wellington."

"Yes, but that might have been the mother superior."

I hadn't thought of that. I supposed if she were head of her religious institution, she must have some connections. After all, even clergy, even Catholics, were beholden to some politics and secular traditions.

I frowned as my annoyance with Lord Gage grew. Could he not have taken ten more minutes to write down some of the details of the crime and the people involved rather than sending us into this inquiry blind? He hadn't even told us how the girl died. After all, there were any number of ways she could have "got herself murdered."

Another wave threw us back from the rail, nearly making me lose my grip. Nausea or no, I was beginning to wonder if maybe I would be safer below. The wind, which before had been reviving, now seemed to stab icy fingers through the fabric of my carriage dress. I shivered and lowered my chin, grateful I'd left my straw crape bonnet in the cabin, for it surely would have been ripped from my head. As it was, Marsdale was having to wrestle with his own hat.

Gage moved closer, trapping me between his arms where his hands clasped the railing. I didn't know whether it was because he'd noticed my chill or he was worried I would be knocked off my feet, but I was glad of it. I breathed easier with his warm, solid presence at my back, even though my hair, which had been ripped loose from my coiffure by the gusts of wind, must have been whipping in his face.

"We shall find out all soon enough," Gage murmured into my ear. "For the moment, it is enough that we are on our way. And Lord willing, we shall make good time and reach Rathfarnham by nightfall tomorrow."

I stared out at the crashing waves, which seemed to surge upward even to the horizon. "Yes, Lord willing."

CHAPTER FOUR

Ultimately, the captain was proven right. The sea did calm as we passed to the south of the Isle of Man sometime in the hours just before nightfall. However, we first had to pass through a squall, which tossed the boat about like a piece of driftwood.

Soon after our conversation had ended, I'd been forced to go belowdecks or risk being soaked to the skin and possibly flung overboard. Not surprisingly, because of this combination of unfortunate elements, I was soon quite ill. I spent the next few hours on the bottom bunk, moaning and begging for the world to stop moving. It was then that I missed my cat, Earl Grey, most.

I had decided to leave the mischievous gray mouser in the care of my nieces and nephews at my sister's town house in Edinburgh. It had seemed unfair to drag him on such a long carriage ride to the Lake District in Cumberland and then on to London, when he could be happily ensconced in the nursery with the children, whom he adored with the indifferent fervency that only a cat can manage. Besides, I knew my niece Philipa would have been distraught to see him go, even more so than the others. She had begged to pay me and Gage a visit in our new town house every day after our wedding, but I knew it had not been me she was missing, but Earl Grey. So it seemed best to leave him behind.

After learning we would be traveling by boat to Ireland, I had been all the more glad he'd not made the journey with us. Until now. I missed his warm, rounded weight on the bunk beside me, the rumble of his purr, the comfort of stroking his fur. Bree sent the men away and cared for me as best she could, but she simply wasn't Earl Grey.

It took several hours for my insides to stop churning even after the rough waves had ceased to do the same to the boat. I could not stomach dinner, but I did manage to sleep, tucked in close to Gage's long body in our small bunk. Bree occupied the bunk above us while Anderley wrangled with the hammock in the opposite corner. Where Marsdale slept, I never knew, nor did I care.

By morning, I felt blessedly more like myself, and even able to enjoy a meager breakfast. The skies overhead gleamed a crystalline blue with scarcely a cloud in sight as the green shores of Ireland came into view. My spirits lifted with each mile we traveled toward land, eager to escape the waves, not trusting the fair weather to last.

We docked at the port of Howth, northeast of Dublin, around midmorning, pausing only long enough to transfer our trunks before we climbed into a hired coach and set off south along the Dublin Road. Marsdale somehow charmed his way into joining us, though Gage told him we would not be traveling into Dublin, but taking the Circular Mail-Coach Road around. He insisted his destination was along our route, and offered to pay half the cost of the carriage, so Gage relented.

The only person who was truly inconvenienced by the marquess's continued presence was Anderley, who was forced to ride up top with the coachman. Given the fair weather, I thought he might not mind, but seeing the furtive looks he sent Marsdale's way, it was clear I was wrong. Knowing what I did now about Anderley's penchant for making his displeasure known and felt, I couldn't help speculating on how he would manage that in this case.

I didn't have long to wait. After our first stop at a coaching inn to stretch our legs and use the necessities, Marsdale spent half an hour squirming fitfully. I bit my lip, trying to work out the source of his discomfort. When finally he coaxed Bree, who was seated next to him, to check the back of his cravat, she pulled out a burr which had become buried in the folds.

"How the devil did that get there?" he remarked.

None of us responded, though I heard Gage clear his throat, and when Bree turned toward the window, I could see she was suppressing a smile.

Much of the rest of the journey passed without incident, though it was warm and not altogether comfortable, even with Gage's shoulder to lean on. Because Gage had elected to take the Circular Road, we traveled through several swaths of open country where the view from our windows was quite lovely— green hills, and fields of wheat, and clear rippling streams. West of Dublin, we passed several artillery barracks, the dreaded stone block of Kilmainham Jail, and the Royal Hospital with its tall central spire. Then the road crossed over and ran alongside a wide canal, busy with barges, before sweeping away to the north toward the city. Soon after, we finally turned to the south, crossing the canal once again and plunging deeper into the impossibly green, wooded landscape for which Ireland was so well known.

Just when I began to wonder how much farther we had to go before we reached Rathfarnham, the sound of the carriage wheels changed as we rolled across the stone surface of a bridge. Over the clatter of the wheels, I could hear the rushing waters of the River Dodder, and leaned forward to stare out through the branches of the ash and alder trees overhanging it, largely blocking our view of the tributary. Our coachman had informed us in his lilting tongue that the river was the boundary of Rathfarnham village and the old Rathfarnham Demesne. Here the roadside gradually gave way to more homes and businesses. Next to the river on the right stood the sprawling wooden structures of a mill, and then the stolid block of a gray stone manor house. The imposing walls of a gate lodge which, no doubt, led to some other manor rose up to our left, before the beginning of a tidy row of shops that stretched along either side of the lane.

Our carriage slowed to a crawl, giving us a better glimpse of the town, as well as its people, bustling to and fro in the afternoon sun. The villagers barely spared us a glance. I supposed because our carriage wasn't the only coach and six on the street, though there were far more single-horse carts and buggies, pulled just as often by mules and donkeys, as black town coaches. An arched opening in an otherwise plain stone wall on the right marked the entrance to a graveyard blocked by black iron gates, I presumed to separate the living from the dead.

Only two shops stood between this sober reminder of mortality and the barracks of the county constabulary, situated at the corner of a narrow lane. Several horses were tethered at the front of the billet, their heads buried in troughs. With the street in front of the building so occupied, our coachman guided the carriage toward the opposite corner, where the parish church stood in all its Georgian splendor. Its tall spire reached up as if to pierce the sky, towering above everything around it. We slowed to a stop next to a swath of manicured shrubs and bright flowerbeds buzzing with bees.

I glanced at Gage, expecting him to issue some sort of instructions before we alighted, but his gaze was focused on the scene outside my window. I could tell from the pucker between his brows that something was troubling him, but before I could ask what, he suddenly reached for the door. "Wait here," was all the explanation he offered as he stepped out.

We heard him conferring softly with the coachman, though Bree and Marsdale gave no indication they could make out his words any better than I could. A moment later, he climbed back into the coach and we set off down the road again.

"I thought you wished to consult with the chief constable," I queried, confused by this sudden change in our plans.

"I did. But upon seeing how many people would witness our first stop in Rathfarnham being at the constabulary, I decided that might not be in our best interest, or that of our investigation."

I turned to peer out the window at the villagers again, several of whom now paused to take note of our passing carriage. Their heads tilted together in speculation.

"Aye. An' the other half o' the village would ken ye went to the Peelers by sundown." Bree shook her head. "The Irish dinna trust the guard."

"True enough." Gage's eyes looked a question, but he did not ask it.

"Her grandmother was Irish," I explained. And then, lest Bree feel awkward, I added. "As was mine."

"I'd forgotten that," he remarked. "Your mother's mother?"

"Yes. She was born north of Dublin, but she moved to Scotland to live with an aunt and uncle when she was young." I turned to look out the window as the road swerved to the east, and the tall trees lining the road thinned enough to provide a glimpse of a square white tower. "She didn't often speak of Ireland. Though I was only five when she died. So it's possible I simply don't recall."

My grandmother, Lady Rutherford, had been a formidable and fascinating woman. Even as a young child, I had seen the way others watched her. With her white hair, and bright lapis lazuli eyes—the same shade as mine—and her musical voice, she had still possessed the ability to charm men half her age, though it had been obvious she had adored only my grandfather until the day she died. There had been some scandal over their marriage because of her lineage. It was ridiculous. Yes, she could trace her ancestors back to the ancient Irish kings, but she also claimed blood from English nobles, part of the Ascendancy who had been granted Irish land confiscated by the Crown during one of Ireland's unsuccessful seventeenth-century revolts. As far as I could tell, it was pure snobbery, possibly because my grandmother refused to hide the lilt that still colored her voice. The lilt my grandfather so loved.

"So you have relatives here in Ireland?" Gage persisted, unaware of my thoughts.

I glanced back at him. "I suppose. But I'm afraid I don't know where or even who they are." The truth was, it had been a long time since I'd thought of the Irish branch of my mother's family. I didn't even know for certain how my grandmother had felt about her relatives, though I had a very vague sense that she was happy to leave them in the past.

"So where are we going?" I asked, returning to the matter at hand. "The cottage where we'll be staying? The Priory?" At least, that was what Lord Gage had called it.

"I thought we'd pay a visit to the abbey first. We'll be passing it anyway, and I'd like to speak with the mother superior to find out what details she can tell us as soon as possible." Gage's eyes cut to mine. "Besides, didn't you say time was of the essence in regards to certain pieces of evidence?"

I knew he was speaking of the body. We'd not been given the exact date of the murder, and I'd expressed worry over the amount of decomposition the nun's corpse might have already undergone, particularly in the summer heat. At a guess, I estimated at least a week had passed, and I was already bracing myself for the level of putrefaction I would be forced to confront.

I swallowed and turned away. "At this point, another hour won't make much of a difference. It's still going to be extremely unpleasant."

Out of the corner of my eye, I saw Marsdale wince, guessing correctly what evidence we were referring to.

"Well, regardless, I'd like to visit the abbey first," Gage declared before giving him a hard glare. "Marsdale, would you like me to have the carriage stop at this tavern?" He tipped his head toward the window, where outside we were passing a thin, three-story building painted the shade of ochre with brown trim. "The Yellow House" was emblazoned above the door and windows in gold letters.

We'd waited the entire trip for Marsdale to tell us where

to convey him, but since we'd turned on the road leading south, I'd begun to have a sneaking suspicion we were not going to be rid of him so easily. Though why he should wish to linger with us was beyond my fathom. Surely the marquess would enjoy whatever entertainments could be found in Dublin city far more than those here in the countryside. To be fair, he had been surprisingly quiet much of the journey, and he'd kept the majority of his ribald humor to himself, but I didn't trust this good behavior to last.

"No. I know a fellow who lives nearby. I'm sure he'll be quite happy to take me in." His voice was lighthearted enough that I wanted to believe him, but I couldn't, not until he'd actually been delivered to this friend.

Evidently, Gage felt the same way. "Then the coachman can deliver you to this friend while we speak to the mother superior."

"No need for that. I can join you and have the carriage take me once you're settled at this Priory you mentioned." He smiled his most amiable smile. "I wouldn't wish to inconvenience you."

Bree scoffed at this last comment, continuing to stare out the window.

I pressed my lips together to hide my amusement. However, Gage was focused on something I'd missed.

"You are not entering the abbey with us, Marsdale."

Some of his nonchalance began to slip. "Why not? I could be of assistance."

Gage arched an eyebrow at the absurdity of that statement. "How exactly? By questioning the nuns?" His voice was flat, suggesting nothing overtly, but I felt my cheeks heat at the hidden implication.

Marsdale's teeth flashed in a wide grin. "I bet I could charm them out of quite a lot. But no. That's not what I meant."

"Regardless, I'm not going to allow you to make a nuisance of yourself." His mouth twisted. "At least, not any more than you already have."

"Oh, come now," he wheedled. "I'm quite capable of behaving myself when the situation warrants it. In fact, I've been very well mannered this entire carriage ride. You know I have."

I rolled my eyes heavenward. He sounded like nothing so much as a little boy trying to persuade us he deserved a special treat.

Gage was equally unimpressed. "That may be so, but that doesn't mean I trust you to keep a civil and courteous tongue while we're at the abbey."

"Oh, for heaven's sake!" Marsdale snapped. "I'm not going to seduce the nuns."

"I should hope not." Gage turned to stare out the window in a bored manner. "Regardless, you're not going to be given the opportunity."

Marsdale's mouth turned down in frustration, but he made no further arguments. It seemed the matter was dismissed.

We continued past the Yellow House following the line of trees and shrubbery which separated us from the tall white tower I'd seen earlier. A short distance from the tavern there was another gap in the vegetation. This one revealed a tiny stream or mill race which had run under the road and emptied into a large pond. Beyond that stood the white tower, one of four matching turrets that projected symmetrically from each corner of a large four-story square building. I decided this must be Rathfarnham Castle. Our coachman had told us about it at our last stop when I'd asked him how much he knew about our intended destination. His knowledge was limited, but he was aware of there being a castle which the village had initially been established to serve.

A short distance later, the road ended abruptly at a cluster of small cottages that appeared to have seen better days. We were forced to turn either left into almost a leafy tunnel or right in the direction our driver guided the carriage, heading south again for another quarter mile. Here on our left stood a black wrought iron gate flanked with gray block pillars. As the carriage slowed and turned onto the gravel before the gate, I had a brief glimpse of the black and gold seals hanging from the center of each which read "Loretto Abbey."

We had been waiting for about a minute for someone inside the grounds to come open the tall gates for us to enter, when Marsdale suddenly spoke from the corner where he sat silently stewing. "She's my cousin."

All three of us turned our heads sharply to look at him.

Marsdale glowered at us when we didn't reply. "Miss Lennox. The girl you say was murdered. She's my cousin."

I didn't know whether to think this was some peculiar trick to convince us to let him join us inside the abbey or the truth.

"She's *your* cousin?" Gage attempted to clarify.

"Yes. Though on her father's side. I'm no relation to Wellington." Who was related to her through her mother.

Gage and I shared a look, communicating our mutual mistrust and suspicion.

"I see." Gage settled deeper into the squabs, clasping his hands in his lap as he studied the marquess. "And you didn't think to inform us of this until now?"

Marsdale's eyes cut to the window, where a bee buzzed about the frame and then flew away. "Yes, well. It seemed a dashed awkward thing to discuss."

"Is that really why you were in Whitehaven?" I asked.

"No. I told you the truth about that. I didn't know your voyage to Ireland had anything to do with my cousin until you mentioned her on the boat." His mouth twisted in self-deprecation. "Didn't even know she had entered a convent, let alone that she was dead."

"Then you weren't close?"

"I don't think I can even tell you the last time I saw her." He shot me another wry glance. "We didn't exactly run in the same circles." His brow furrowed and his voice softened. "But I was rather fond of her, in my own way."

I watched the play of emotions across his face and realized they were genuine. They made the boorish and selfish marquess somehow more likable, though I was sure he would have hated to hear me say so. "That's why you sounded like you were choking. On the boat. You weren't holding back laughter but shock and distress."

Marsdale didn't reply. He didn't need to. I already knew it was true.

"You could have told us then that she was your cousin," Gage pointed out.

"I could have. But I didn't. And then it seemed it would be better if I kept it to myself, so I didn't have to explain why I kept quiet. As you're making me do now."

Gage was not swayed by this display of frustration. "You're only telling us now so that we'll let you join us in our interview with the mother superior, but I still don't think that would be a good idea."

His dark eyes flashed. "Dash it, Gage! She's my cousin. I have every right to hear how she died and why."

"Perhaps. But that's not what I meant." The lines around Gage's mouth had grown tight, and I shifted uncomfortably, knowing of what he spoke. Bree's hands clenched in her lap.

Marsdale seemed intent on arguing, but then comprehension dawned in his eyes. He swallowed before speaking in a flat voice. "I could remain in the parlor."

Gage shook his head as he replied, not ungently. "Today's visit is going to be unpleasant for a number of reasons. You do not want to join us. I assure you. Your cousin would not want it."

Marsdale's shoulders slumped and he nodded, turning his eyes blindly toward the window.

We all fell silent, brooding on what was to come. It was as if a shadow had fallen over our carriage even though the sun still shone bright on the stone and gravel outside.

We waited what seemed like a quarter of an hour for a nun to walk down the long front drive to open the gate. I saw her standing to the side in her black habit, watching as we passed. The grass on either side of the lane was trimmed and evenly spaced with short evergreens no more than a dozen years old, except for one which stood tall in the distance, casting its shade over a small building with a cross above its door.

The abbey itself was nothing like what I'd expected. Rather than the cold, stolid stone and the soaring heights to be found in the ruins of abbeys like Dryburgh and Kelso, which stood near my childhood home in the Borders region of Scotland and England, here sat a quaint Georgian manor house. Built of warm red brick seven bays wide, it better resembled the home of a prosperous country squire than that of a religious institution. This was clearly not a medieval structure, but a far more modern establishment, and as such, the melodramatic Gothic scenarios which had played in my head since I heard of the nun's death fled.

At the center of the building, a double stair built with the same stone as the gateposts swept up to form a small terrace with a white balustrade before the main door. This door was fashioned of a warm oak, and topped by a classically inspired pediment. Below the terrace, at ground level, stood another door painted gray to blend in with its surroundings, which likely led into the kitchens and old servants' quarters. It was this door that opened first and then swiftly shut again before another sister emerged onto the terrace above. Her hands were tucked inside the black linen serge sleeves of her habit.

As Gage climbed out of our conveyance, I turned to Bree. "Will you join us?"

She seemed to falter for a fraction of a second before answering, though it was clear from the look in her eyes when she did that she knew what I was really asking. "Aye, m'lady."

I studied her a moment longer, wondering at that hesitation. Perhaps she was unsettled by our earlier conversation with Marsdale, but that was unlike Bree. She had iron nerves, forged from her past—some of which I knew, and some that I only guessed at. In the few months she'd been employed as my maid, she normally seemed quite eager to help with an investigation. I supposed it was wrong for me to presume that would always be the case, but in this instance, I didn't think that's where the uncertainty lay.

Bree's mouth curled into a questioning smile, and I brushed my curiosity aside, to be contemplated later. With a swift nod to Marsdale, I accepted Gage's proffered hand to help me down.

While he assisted Bree, I took a moment to glance around more fully at our surroundings. The grounds on which the abbey stood were quite expansive—lush, and green, and bursting with flowers. The lawns must have been freshly cut, for the scent of grass and hay was strong, overpowering that of the pine trees and sunbaked gravel. To the south, I could see the undulating green hills of the Dublin Mountains rising away from us, their eastern slopes sliding into shadow as the sun began to sink to the west.

It seemed the last place on earth someone would be murdered, and yet Miss Lennox had.

That one may smile, and smile, and be a villain . . .

It was a quote from *Hamlet*, spoken about the villain Claudius, but somehow it seemed oddly apropos. That the sun might shine, the flowers might bloom, even though something quite terrible had happened here. Something that had not yet been explained to us.

And never would be if we did not go inside.

I heard Gage shut the carriage door with a decisive click before speaking to Anderley up on the coachman's box. "See that Lord Marsdale is taken to his friend's residence and then return for us."

"With pleasure, sir."

My mouth twitched at the valet's cheek as the carriage slowly rolled forward. Marsdale had made no ally there. I began to turn back toward the others when something caught my eye.

It was a trio of girls, no more than twelve or thirteen years old, all dressed in drab gray dresses with white collars at the neck and wrists, and white pinafores. It was the uniform of a school girl, and I realized with a shock as more such girls of varying ages came into view, that this wasn't any normal abbey. It was also a boarding school.

The girls all eyed us with unabashed curiosity even as they continued plodding ahead on some known course. I suspected this was their afternoon constitutional. My own governess had made me take one each day at the same time.

I glanced behind me in horror, wondering if Gage had seen them, and apprehended the same thing I had. He stood watching them for a moment as I had, and then he reached a hand out to draw me forward, tucking my arm through the crook of his elbow. Bree fell in step close behind us as we moved toward the stairs, our soles crunching on the gravel, and I spoke softly over my shoulder to her.

"You'll be all right belowstairs?"

"Aye, m'lady. I ken what to do," she replied evenly.

I nodded and she separated from us to move toward the gray door through which servants had once come and gone. I was unfamiliar with life in an abbey, but I suspected that there was still some form of caste system among nuns, and that if there were not enough sisters to manage the day-to-day life of an order—the cooking, and cleaning, and other such tasks—they must hire outside assistance. If this was the case, I knew those sort of domestics were far more likely to speak to a fellow servant such as Bree than a lady like me.

Even so, I disliked sending my maid off alone in an unfamiliar place such as this, where we knew a murder had taken place. Surely she would be safe surrounded by these women of faith. Unless somehow faith had been the motive for Miss Lennox's murder.

The nun who had emerged as our carriage drew to a stop on the drive still stood next to the door waiting for us as Gage and I climbed the stairs. Her posture was as impeccable as any debutante, making me wonder if the nuns wore corsets under those voluminous black habits. I couldn't imagine why they would, unless it was some form of penance.

As we drew closer, I could see that her eyes were a brilliant shade of sapphire blue, made all the more startling because of her austere garments. They seemed to glint and sparkle as she watched us, as if unable to quite contain the vigor and curiosity bubbling inside her though it had been tightly leashed elsewhere.

"I am Mother Mary Paul. Welcome to Loretto Abbey." She spoke softer than I'd expected, still carefully restraining that energy. "You must be Mr. Gage and Lady Darby. The reverend mother has been expecting you."

CHAPTER FIVE

I felt Gage's arm tighten under my own.

"She's been expecting us?"

Mother Mary Paul gave a single nod. "She had a letter from His Grace, the Duke of Wellington." Her head tilted to the side as she studied Gage's furrowed expression. "This displeases you in some way?"

Gage swiftly masked his thoughts about the duke and his father's presumptions. "No. I'm merely surprised by how swift the post runs." Apparently, that letter of introduction they sent us would not be needed.

The nun nodded in easy acceptance, but I could see her eyes evaluating, perceiving more than perhaps he wished. "It only arrived today." Her gaze shifted to meet mine, and I could tell she was aware I had observed her assessment. Her face softened in a smile for the first time. "But the reverend mother can tell you what you wish to know. If you will please follow me, I shall take you to her."

She led us through the door into the entry hall with polished mahogany floors and trim, white walls, and rather minimal decoration. However, the parlor we entered through the first door on the left was far from simple. It was a large room divided into seating arrangements—one before the hearth, another two grouped around each of the front windows, and a third surrounding the far corner—and yet there seemed to be an acre of floor space between them and their Aubusson rugs. The same polished mahogany ran through this room, though the walls were covered in embossed leather wallpaper. The walls were handsomely preserved and probably original to the house, as much of the furniture seemed to be, but they also added a weight to the room that it did not need. It was far from inviting, and I found myself wishing that a fire would be lit in the fireplace even on this warm summer day just to give the room a bit of a human touch.

As Mother Paul guided us toward the pair of settees facing each other across the hearth, a door on the opposite side of the room opened and a slight woman of middling height entered. Even without the gold pectoral cross hanging from a chain around her neck, I would have known she was the mother superior by sight alone. There was something in the way she walked, the manner in which she held herself. It was almost queenly. Her posture was just as beautiful as Mother Paul's, perhaps even more so because it was not stiff or restrained, but seemingly natural. I did not know how much effort it cost her to make it appear so, or if it was innate to her being.

"May I present the Reverend Mother Mary Teresa of the Institute of the Blessed Virgin Mary," Mother Paul said, and then turned to the mother superior and bowed. "Reverend Mother, this is Mr. Gage and Lady Darby."

Reverend Mother opened her arms, offering us a gentle smile. "You are most welcome. Please have a seat."

Gage and I sat side by side on one of the settees upholstered in a stiff goldenrod velvet with walnut trim while she instructed Mother Paul to have tea brought in. Then she settled across from us with a well-practiced swish of her habit, so that it did not get caught beneath her and pull in the back, much as any gown. She was a very striking woman. Perhaps not beautiful with her rather pointy nose and high forehead, but arresting. She looked young to be a mother superior, but then I had expected a wrinkled old woman, not someone still possessed of a rosy, almost luminescent complexion. In truth, it was difficult to tell her and Mother Paul's ages accurately, dressed as they were in their black habits. She could have been far older than I realized. The wisdom and solemnity in her dark eyes as she regarded us certainly suggested it, though maybe that was only a manifestation of her recent trials.

"I wish I could be welcoming you here under different circumstances, but the situation being what it is, I am glad the Lord has brought you to us now." She spoke both earnestly and directly, setting me at ease, while also somehow making me anxious not to disappoint her. "What can I tell you? What do you wish to know?"

Gage and I shared a glance before he spoke. "To be honest, we haven't been informed of many of the details."

Reverend Mother's eyes flickered in surprise.

"We were not in London when your letter reached the Duke of Wellington," he hastened to explain. "May I assume it was you who wrote to His Grace?"

"It was. Being Miss Lennox's mother superior, I was, of course, aware of her connection to His Grace. She made it known to me when she applied to be admitted to our order. Though as a general rule, I don't believe she made it known to many here at the abbey."

"Why do you say that?" I asked, curious why the girl would hide such an auspicious connection. "Because she was raised Anglican?"

Reverend Mother spoke with care. "I suppose that may have been part of it. Though she did not hide her recent conversion. After all, she was not our first convert here at Rathfarnham." This was said with a glance at Mother Paul as she entered the room carrying the tea tray. The other woman merely nodded in confirmation, swiftly deducing what we were discussing. "It was nothing to be ashamed of, but rather rejoiced. No, I think it more likely that with the state of unrest about Ireland, she felt it best not to publicize her connection lest it upset someone."

"Or that someone might try to take advantage of it?" Gage pressed, not unkindly, but we needed complete honesty.

Reverend Mother hesitated and then gave a single bob of her head. "Just so. As a postulant, she was preparing herself to let go of all worldly things, to seek the Lord's will, but the world does not always let go easily."

The conversation paused as Mother Paul prepared each of our teas as skillfully as any gentleman's daughter, before settling in a chair a short distance away with a cup of her own. These two women definitely didn't come from inferior families. I reckoned their fathers had been prosperous tradesman, at the very least, or perhaps landed gentry. They had obviously been given an education, including proper elocution, for while their voices both held traces of that musical Irish lilt, it was faint. Reverend Mother sounded quite English at times, and at other times not, making me wonder whether she'd spent any significant period in Britain.

She took a drink of her tea before replacing it in her saucer. "Now, you said you had not been informed of many details. What precisely do you know?"

Gage shifted forward to set his cup on the table between us and the nun. "That a young lady named Miss Harriet Lennox, a distant cousin of the duke's, has been murdered here at the abbey, and that the matter was to be handled with discretion and urgency."

Reverend Mother stared at him expectantly until she realized, with a furrowing of her smooth brow, that this was all he could tell her. "Well, that *is* very little information. And yet you came."

This was not spoken as a question, but I knew it was one regardless.

"Because we were needed," I replied.

Her eyes met mine again, that wisdom I had noted earlier somehow sharpening. "Yes." She sighed. "Yes, you most certainly are." She set her own cup aside. "Let me start at the beginning then, shall I?"

Miss Harriet Lennox had arrived at the abbey some four

months earlier and had seemed to settle in easily enough to life at the convent. She was perhaps quieter than most new postulants, but Reverend Mother had sensed this was because she had become used to keeping things to herself as a necessity. She was a quick learner and dedicated to her prayers and study, and the students seemed to gravitate toward her. This was not uncommon. The postulants were often younger and closer to the girls in age as well as temperament, still struggling with some of the same anxieties and uncertainties of youth.

There had been no indications of trouble until one evening about a week before her death. Miss Lennox had been caught returning to the grounds of the abbey through a portion of the garden wall that had been removed because of work being done to fix some drainage issues in the orchard after a particularly wet spring. Loretto sisters, including postulants, were not allowed to leave the property of the abbey without special permission and dispensation. She claimed she had become absorbed in following the flight of a gray heron and wanted to see whether it nested near the large pond beyond the abbey proper. This behavior was not entirely out of character, for Miss Lennox had often been observed watching the swans, and other birds and animals which populated the abbey gardens and small pond. She had even been the person to first note a den of red foxes below a beech tree at the southern end of the property. Her manner had been properly contrite, and she had done her penance without complaint, so the reverend mother had thought little more of it.

However, a week later when Miss Lennox failed to appear for evening prayers and then the meal that followed, she couldn't help but wonder if there had been more to the girl's absence from the abbey than she had confessed. As the dinner hour stretched out, she began to feel uneasy about the missing girl. It was unlike her to behave in such an inconsiderate and neglectful way. She asked several of the sisters to search the abbey grounds, particularly the orchard and the area beyond its tumbled walls to see if Miss Lennox could be located. It was possible the girl had suddenly fallen ill or met with some sort of accident and needed help.

Unfortunately, by the time they reached her, she had been beyond their earthly assistance.

"I informed the county constabulary," Reverend Mother explained. "But as soon as I witnessed the way they were treating the sisters, frightening the students, and bullying the gardeners, I ordered them to leave. I knew they would never uncover the truth. Not like that. Then I immediately wrote to the Duke of Wellington for assistance."

"I'm surprised the chief constable bowed to your wishes with a murder happening on your grounds," Gage remarked.

Her gaze turned shrewd. "Ah, but the murder didn't happen on the abbey grounds, but just over the wall, about ten feet to the north. I can't keep them away from there, but I can keep them from entering the abbey. For now."

Clearly she was a woman who possessed a strong backbone and some powerful connections.

"They also wanted to examine Miss Lennox's body, beyond what could be seen cursorily outside her clothing, but I would not allow it. It would have been entirely improper. Even if Miss Lennox had not yet professed her vows, she was still intent on becoming a bride of Christ. For any man to have touched her would have been a sacrilege."

I had anticipated as much, guessing that one of the reasons Lord Gage had recommended his son bring me was because I was one of the few people who possessed both of the traits this investigation required. I was a woman and I possessed a detailed knowledge of anatomy, reluctantly accrued at the hands of my late anatomist husband, but acquired all the same. I knew this, and yet I hesitated to say what must be said, unsettled as always by this familiarity and what I was expected to do with it. Given the occupation my second husband had adopted, which I had decided to join him in, this skill had proven to be a useful asset. I could not dispute that. But I still had not grown comfortable with it being so.

Gage, for his part, did not force the issue on me, but I could see from the look in his eyes he was waiting for me to say something all the same. I wondered how long it would be before he became exasperated with me for dithering over the examination of a dead body during our murder inquiries.

I screwed up my courage, offering Reverend Mother a tight smile. "Would you allow me to examine her?"

Her eyes showed no surprise, only increased interest. "So it's true then? You assisted Sir Anthony Darby with his dissections?"

That wasn't precisely how I would have phrased it, but few people listened when I tried to explain, so I simply nodded. "Yes. In a manner of speaking."

I wasn't sure how she would react to this. Some people, especially those who held to a rather strict interpretation of the Bible, believed dissection was evil, and desecrating a corpse in such a manner would mean that body could not fully rise from the dead on the Day of Judgment. Others accepted it rather calmly, distancing themselves from the act by their belief that it would never happen to them.

Reverend Mother seemed to fall somewhere in the middle. She considered me, and I must have somehow passed muster, for she dipped her chin in affirmation. "Yes. I believe I would have." She lifted her hands in a gesture of futility. "But I'm afraid now it's quite impossible."

"What do you mean?"

"Miss Lennox has been dead for almost ten days. I postponed the burial a few days longer than normal on the chance something could be done, though at the time I wasn't certain what. But the fact is, it simply couldn't be put off any longer. The body, you understand, it was . . . returning to dust. And the smell . . ." She shook her head. "It would not have been right to deny her the comfort of the grave."

"Yes. Of course," I hastened to reassure her. "I understand entirely." After a week, the decay and decomposition would have been well advanced, and the scents of putrefaction would have been intolerable for anyone inexperienced with such things. Even as accustomed as I had been with it at one time, I had never grown a strong enough stomach to tolerate the stench for long. I had not been looking forward to examining Miss Lennox's body, particularly considering how much time I knew must have passed, and the realization that now I would not need to do so felt like a reprieve.

Reverend Mother appeared equally relieved by my ready acceptance of her decision. "We noted any details as best we could, but I'm afraid there wasn't much. Though perhaps we did not know what to look for." She glanced at Mother Paul, who appeared just as unsure. "I asked our infirmarian, Sister Mary Bernard, to take special note when she washed Miss Lennox's body and prepared it for burial, so you will wish to speak with her as well."

"Thank you," I replied, grateful she had thought to do as much. "Could you at least tell how she died?"

"She was bashed in the back of the head." She reached up to press a hand to her black crape veil on the right side. "Here." She lowered her hand quickly into her lap, clenching it so that it almost disappeared inside the pure white weepers of her cuffs. "At first I thought she might have tripped and fallen, striking her head. But there were no stones or other hard objects near enough to where she lay. And . . . the fabric on her shoulder was torn. Ripped," she clarified.

"Oh." The word left me on an exhale. I had not considered the possibility that the girl might have suffered another crime. One she might have lived through, for a short time anyway.

Reverend Mother's expression had grown grimmer as we talked, her face pale from the strain, but she never flinched from the truth. "From what I could see, I don't believe it was taken that far. I asked Sister Mary Bernard to see if she could tell anything further, though I don't know that she knew what to make of her observations. You might be able to draw a more decisive conclusion from the things she has to share."

"Of course." I hoped she was correct. That the girl, at least, had not suffered that pain and indignity.

Her eyes appealed to Gage. "But you understand why I felt compelled to think this wasn't merely an accident? That someone had harmed Miss Lennox?"

"I do," Gage replied solemnly. "Based on what you've been able to tell us, I'm inclined to agree. But until we've investigated the matter thoroughly, we can't accurately speculate on what happened."

"You must do what you think is best in order to get to the truth. It is why I wrote to the duke." Her perfectly straight back somehow straightened further. "I only ask that you proceed with kindness and fairness. Many of our sisters, students, and staff are deeply troubled by what has happened. They do not know any better but to cower from harsh questions."

I couldn't help but wonder how unpleasant and severe the local constabulary had been to make this woman feel like she had to warn us.

Gage's voice warmed with reassurance. "We will do our best not to unduly upset anyone. That is never our intention. But murder is a nasty business, and by its very nature disturbing. I'm afraid we cannot avoid distressing people entirely."

"I understand." She inhaled wearily. "Then, would you like to begin tomorrow? You should speak with Sister Mary Bernard, and I also think you should talk to Mother Mary Fidelis. She is our mistress of postulants, and would have acted as an advisor to Miss Lennox. If anyone would have known about something that might have been worrying Miss Lennox, it would be her."

"Thank you." I turned toward Mother Paul, who had observed our conversation in silence. "Would it be possible to speak with Mother Mary Paul as well?"

Reverend Mother turned to glance at the other woman, who only looked mildly surprised. "Of course. You must speak to whomever you like. Our abbey is open to you, Lady Darby."

"Please, call me Mrs. Gage." I smiled. "At least in private, if you're not comfortable doing so elsewhere. I know you are simply extending me courtesy, but I would prefer it if you called me by my newly married name."

"Certainly," she replied, her eyes traveling between Gage and me, reconsidering whatever she had already decided about us. "It was only how His Grace referred to you, so I assumed."

"I know. It's one of those perplexing rules of society that I don't entirely understand."

"Of course. But, Mr. Gage, I'm afraid I shall have to ask you to venture no further than this parlor when you return," Reverend Mother cautioned. "You understand? This is a convent and a girls' boarding school. It would not do to allow a man to wander about the building, no matter how good his intentions."

He nodded in easy acceptance. "May I be allowed to view the orchard through which Miss Lennox walked to reach the gap in the wall?"

"You may visit any part of the gardens and grounds you wish. It's only the buildings that I must restrict you from entering."

"For the sake of thoroughness, would it also be possible to have a list of everyone who had access to the abbey or its grounds at any time during the days surrounding Miss Lennox's murder? Nuns, boarders, gardeners, staff, workmen? And any callers who might have visited the abbey for any reason, be they guests of those living here or delivering supplies?"

"I can do that. I gave something similar to Chief Constable Corcoran, but who knows what the man has done with it."

Though she didn't say so, I could tell by the restrained tone of her voice that the reverend mother was not fond of Mr. Corcoran, and if that had not been clear, the brief flattening of Mother Paul's mouth would have been indication enough. Both women were careful with their criticism, but it was obvious they were not pleased with their local constabulary, or else there would have been no need to request our assistance. I only hoped the chief constable had accepted their banning him from the abbey with grace; otherwise we might have an angry constabulary to contend with as well as a murder to solve.

CHAPTER SIX

A nderley and Bree were standing next to our hired carriage, deep in conference, when we emerged from the
abbey. They both turned as we approached, and Anderley
nodded to the unspoken query in Gage's eyes.

"Marsdale's settled then?" Gage confirmed.

"Yes, sir."

"Good."

Neither man hid his satisfaction at that fact, and Bree
and I shared a long-suffering look.

Evening had begun to settle in, thinning the piercing blue
of the sky. Birds soared and dived overhead, seizing the
opportunity to frolic in the dying rays of sunshine before they
were forced to search out their nests for the coming night. I
could hear a thrush singing in the trees that bordered the
southwest corner of the abbey, perhaps chiding her fledglings
as they fluttered and tussled across the sky nearby.

Once we were all seated inside the coach and had set off
back down the lane, I turned to Bree.

"I dinna have much to tell," she replied with a shake of her
head. "All the sisters and the other staff I spoke wi' seemed to
like Miss Lennox, and were saddened by her death. Even
sayin' her name set one scullery maid to whimperin' as she
scrubbed oot a pan. But Sister Pip, who runs the kitchens,
said no' to mind her, she was merely simple."

"Sister Pip?" Gage asked, voicing the same thought that had struck me. "Was that truly her name?"

"Nay. 'Twas Sister Mary Philippa. But all the students call her Sister Pip—apparently, they have nicknames for all the sisters—and she says that suits her just fine."

I nodded distractedly. "But she didn't have anything to say about Miss Lennox's death?"

The corners of Bree's lips curled in the beginnings of a smile. "Oh, she had plenty to say. They dinna say the Irish are blessed wi' the gift o' the gab for no reason. But none o' it was much to do wi' Miss Lennox or her death, 'ceptin' how awful it was." She paused, tilting her head. "Though she did mention she thought the undergardener may have been sweet on her, even hopeless as that was."

"Did she tell you why she suspected that?"

"Nay. But she did say Miss Lennox was uncommonly pretty, so it may have been just that."

Gage's expression was doubtful. "Could he truly tell that with her draped in one of those voluminous habits?"

"But she weren't."

We all turned to her in confusion.

A little vee formed between Bree's eyes and she hesitated, as if deciding how to explain. "Miss Lennox was still a postulant, which means she wore a simple dress, similar to what those schoolgirls were wearin'. Nuns dinna cut their hair and start wearin' a habit and veil until aboot a year after they enter the convent and become a novice."

Clearly Bree knew much more about nuns and convents than any of the rest of us did, and I couldn't help but wonder how. Had her grandmother been a Roman Catholic? I could tell from the wary look in her eyes that this was not something she wished to discuss now.

Gage appeared to have intuited the same thing. "So she would have been dressed as any normal woman, if plainly." He rubbed his chin in thought. "This changes things perceptibly." He flicked a speaking glance at me.

"Her body was found just outside the abbey's property,

which means it's possible that whoever murdered her didn't even know she was a nun," I said, putting into words what he was thinking. "He, or she, could have believed her a member of the staff, or even a student." That thought was somehow more upsetting. I rushed on to say, "Or perhaps he didn't even know she was connected to the abbey in any way." I frowned. "Though the proximity of where she was found to the abbey does make that doubtful."

Gage turned toward the window, deep furrows grooving his forehead. "Another possibility we have to consider is that Miss Lennox did, in fact, trip and strike her head."

"But what of the ripped dress?"

"Maybe she wasn't alone. Maybe her companion tried to move her, tearing the shoulder of her dress in the process."

"Then why haven't they come forward to say so?"

"I don't know. Maybe they're worried about being blamed. Or perhaps they have something to hide. Something they'll be forced to reveal by admitting their presence there."

"One of the other nuns?"

Gage shrugged.

I supposed the theory had merit. If it were true, it might be the kindest outcome all around. No murder would have been committed, only a terrible accident.

But perhaps that's precisely what the killer wanted us to think.

I squeezed the bridge of my nose between my fingers, trying to alleviate the pain pressing behind my eyes. The past few days had been long and tiresome, and a bit of rest would do us all a world of good.

Even as I thought it, our hired carriage slowed and turned into a long drive, which passed between the solid stone pillars of an old entrance gate standing open before winding between groves of beech and chestnut trees. The shade of the trees was so complete in the deepening twilight that I couldn't help but lean forward to peer out the window, trying to catch a glimpse of what lay ahead. Then the tunnel suddenly ended, and a small yard spread before us. The coach slowed again, this time inching forward between another small white gate set between a massive stand of beech trees on the left and a great dark cedar on the right. Holly trees and briar patches crowded against the fence, blocking the sights beyond from casual view.

As we rounded the carriage sweep of the inner yard, the rather plain but substantial edifice of the Priory finally came into view. Why it was called the Priory, I did not know, for it certainly didn't look like one. Though to be fair, Loretto Abbey also had not looked like an abbey. I was beginning to sense a pattern, which perhaps began and ended with my antiquated medieval expectations.

The stone manor house was covered with ivy, kept well trimmed and away from the doors and windows, which stared out at us like large eyes, gleaming with expectation in the setting sun. I knew such thoughts were fanciful, but there seemed a melancholy watchfulness about the house, as if it were waiting for something, something it was not sure would ever come. Maybe it was the silence of the air, for the tall trees surrounding it on all sides seemed to block the wind, cocooning the house in a shell of stillness.

Several other buildings clustered around the manor, including a barn and stables. I could smell the freshly cut hay which the animals had been bedded down with, along with the crisp scent of the coming evening, and the soft perfume of crushed violets peeking through the green undergrowth at the edge of the gravel yard. When the door to the house did not open upon our arrival, Gage gestured for Anderley to proceed us down out of the carriage. He crossed the short distance to rap on the door while the rest of us descended to stare up at the slumbering façade. Even so, it took far longer for someone to answer the door than was customarily acceptable, and the shabbily dressed man who did so merely gasped and stared out at us with a rather dazed expression.

"This is the Priory?" Gage queried when Anderley's prodding was met with more astonished silence. "The home of Mr. Curran?"

"Yes. Yes, of course," another man bustled forward to say.

This servant was at least clothed in appropriate livery, though his sandy hair needed straightening. He must have caught my glance, for he reached up to smooth it down as he pushed the other man out of the way. "Con, what are ye doin' answerin' the door? Get belowstairs." He turned back to us with a tight smile. "My apologies. How can I be assistin' ye?"

The man seemed too young to be a butler, but the manner in which he'd taken control of the situation suggested he must be. However, his failure to recognize us or even to invite us inside was not in the least reassuring.

Gage moved a step closer, pulling me along with him into the light spilling from the doorway. "I am Mr. Gage, and this is my wife. My father, Lord Gage, informed us that Mr. Curran had made arrangements for us to stay . . ."

There was no need for him to finish his statement, for his words had elicited such a reaction in the butler as to be almost comical. His eyes widened in alarm, and his hand clutched at his coat pocket where I heard paper crinkle. "Mr. Gage! And . . ." He turned to me and paused in confusion. "Are ye not a lady of some kind?"

"Lady Darby," I replied. "But I much prefer . . ."

"My sincerest apologies. Please, please come in." He ushered us inside, guiding us toward the first door on the left. Then he swiveled to snap at two maids peering around a corner. "You, light the candles in the parlor. And you, fetch Mrs. Shaughnessy." He turned back toward us with another smile. "My name's Dempsey. We only just received Mr. Curran's letter today, and we believed we still had several more days before yer arrival. The family has been absent for nearly six months, so we've been keepin' many of the rooms closed up."

We paused just inside the doorway, staring at furniture covered in sheets to keep the dust off. They hovered like pale ghosts at the edges of the gloomy room as the maid moved from table to table, lighting what candles were there. Many of the sconces and holders stood empty. If this was any indication of what we would find in the rest of the house, it was a disappointing arrival indeed, particularly to my travel-weary bones.

"So you are, in fact, not ready for us," Gage murmured in a voice almost as fatigued as my own.

"'Tis but the work of a moment," the butler assured us. "We'll whisk the cloths away and . . ."

"What of dinner? I suppose there is nothing prepared." His voice was not accusatory, only matter-of-fact; however, Dempsey stammered as if he had been berated.

"Well . . . there . . . we haven't . . ." He swallowed and finally gasped, "I'm sure somethin' can be done."

It was evident now we should have come here instead of going to the abbey first. Then at least the staff would have had several hours' notice in which to clean and air the rooms we would most need and arrange dinner. There was no way such a thing could be done in a matter of a half an hour, and our standing about watching them would only make it worse.

My stomach grumbled and I put an embarrassed hand to it. This action seemed to galvanize Gage's decision.

"Does the Yellow House serve food?"

"I . . ." Dempsey began to protest, but then seemed to realize Gage was giving us all an easy escape from this awkward situation. "Why, yes, sir. Might I recommend their lamb stew. 'Tis quite delicious."

"Then we shall go there for our meal. See that our bedchamber, just one, is made ready before our return. The rest can be addressed tomorrow."

"Aye, sir. Very good, sir."

I allowed Gage to lead me back out into the growing dusk, where our trunks were being unloaded. Bree and Anderley insisted on remaining behind to see that our room and our things were handled properly. Whatever deficiencies Gage and I had detected in the staff, it was clear that Bree and Anderley were even less impressed.

So Gage and I set off for the Yellow House and whatever sort of meal we could avail ourselves of there. I was of half a mind to request merely a bit of bread and broth, feeling too tired to stomach much more. However, once we entered the tavern lit brightly by candles and bubbling with colorful voices and the notes of a lively reel played by a small group of musicians on the far side of the crowded room, I felt my spirits revive. The room smelled of yeast, ale, and some kind of meat stew mixed with the general stench of humanity clustered together. The sweat I could ignore when there was the promising aroma of that stew.

People stopped to look at us as we wove our way through the crowd trying to find an empty table, but I suspected this was because we were strangers, not because we actually stood out. There was a mixture of classes, some dressed in clothes as finely made as mine and Gage's, while others appeared as if they'd come straight from the fields, the grime of a hard day's labor staining their collars. The accents I heard were predominantly Irish, but there was also more than a few crisper English voices. One in particular made my spine stiffen.

"Gage! Kiera!"

We turned as one to see Lord Marsdale waving his free arm to capture our attention. The other arm was wrapped around the waist of a rather pretty, and rather buxom, Irish lass perched on his knee. I felt Gage's hesitance. I was no happier to see the roguish marquess than he was, and slightly irritated by his use of my given name, but given our crowded surroundings, also reluctantly grateful he hadn't yet exposed me as a lady.

"He has a table to himself," I pointed out, noting it seemed improbable we would find an empty one in this crush.

Gage relented with an aggrieved sigh, gripping my elbow to help me thread through the people between us and Marsdale.

He grinned up at us, taking a swig from his glass. "Fancy meetin' you here." He gestured with his head. "Take a seat."

As Gage helped me into my chair, Marsdale swiveled about to see us better, nearly dislodging the woman from his leg. From her appearance and the way one of the men behind the bar was barking at her across the room, I surmised she was one of the barmaids. She shrieked a response back at the man, but I could not for the life of me understand what she'd said. Something impertinent, clearly, for those listening nearby laughed.

"What brings ye to this fine establishment?" Marsdale slurred.

"We could ask you the same thing," Gage replied with a sharp glance.

"I thought ye woulda been tucked in cozy at the Priory by now," Marsdale continued as if he hadn't heard him.

"They weren't ready for us. So we took ourselves away to give them some time."

He nodded. "Same. Dashed Hodgens wasn't home, and his staff didn't know when to expect him." He eyed the dark-haired lass on his lap with half-lidded eyes. "So I decided an evening enjoying the pleasures at the local tavern wouldn't be remiss."

I barely refrained from rolling my eyes when the barmaid giggled, pressing her ample chest against his arm.

Unfortunately for her, Marsdale seemed to have only part of his attention fixed on her. "Then ye haven't eaten. Colleen, love, be a dear and fetch my friends a bowl of that splendid stew and some ale."

"'Course, *a mhuirnín.*"

He watched her appreciatively for a moment as she strolled away swaying her hips, before leaning forward to rest his elbows against the rough wood of the table. "So tell me. What did you find out about my cousin?"

I studied Marsdale's eyes, realizing he wasn't quite as foxed as I'd assumed, and wondering for whom he'd been pretending.

Gage, for his part, was surreptitiously glancing around us, trying to gauge who, if anyone, had heard what Marsdale had said. "A little more quietly, if you please."

Marsdale's back straightened. "My apologies. But surely you can tell me something." His voice dropped even lower. "Do you know how she died?" His eyes were earnest behind their intoxicated sheen.

I shook my head. "We don't know."

His mouth opened as if to argue, and I reached out a hand to forestall him.

"No, truly. She almost certainly died from a blow to the head, but whether she was struck with something from behind or fell and hit her head, we cannot say for sure."

"But they must believe she was struck; otherwise they wouldn't have asked you here."

His mind was quick. And his voice loud. Several curious onlookers glanced our way, their eyes gleaming with interest.

"Yes, there's more. But we're not going to discuss it here." Gage arched his eyebrows toward the people clustered around the table over my shoulder.

It was clear from the mutinous line of his mouth that Marsdale wanted to object, but he must have recognized the foolishness in doing so. Gage would not be budged. Besides, the fewer people who knew the details about his cousin's death, the better chance there would be that a killer might slip up and reveal too much. So instead he nodded begrudgingly and took another deep swig of his ale.

Colleen returned then with our food and drinks, but had to dash off again to do her job, I imagined. I was pleased to discover Marsdale was right. The stew was delicious—warm, and thick, and perfectly seasoned. I sighed in contentment and glanced up to find both men watching me with gentle amusement. Ignoring them, I reached for my glass and turned the conversation back on Marsdale.

"Maybe you can help us."

His eyebrows lifted in query as I took a drink of my ale. It had a roasted, almost burnt, flavor and a bitter fullness to it, which was actually quite pleasant with the heartiness of the stew.

I glanced at Gage, who I noticed had already drained half of his glass. "What can you tell us of your cousin's life before she came to the abbey? What was she like?"

Marsdale sat back in his chair, tipping his glass to stare

at the last two fingers of its mahogany-colored contents. "Harriet? She was . . . well, I suppose we all thought of her as a little mother. The other cousins and me." His eyes lifted to meet mine. "You know the type. Responsible and patient. Ever standing to the side, watching indulgently as we played our childish games and got into mischief, as if waiting for us to finally grow up. But she was a pip, Harriet was. Never ratted us out and, more often than not, helped us clean up whatever mess we'd gotten ourselves into."

"And knowing you, I imagine that was no mean feat," I muttered under my breath.

His eyes sparkled in agreement.

"You said you hadn't seen her in some time?" Gage prodded. His own eyes had taken on a lazy glimmer as he emptied his first glass and reached for the second, which Colleen had slipped by to bring him, pausing only long enough to toss him a saucy smile. As she walked away, her green eyes narrowed at Marsdale, who was no longer paying her any mind.

"Yes. Her family lived in Dublin. And when they visited London, I was too busy to bother with them." He tipped his glass back, draining the remainder of his ale. Whatever his true feelings about his cousin, one thing was clear. He was trying very hard to make us think he didn't care.

He set his glass back on the table with a thunk. His brow furrowed as if maybe he'd had a sudden thought and then smoothed out again. "As you've undoubtedly already gathered, I'm not a man who cares much for kith and kin. But the last time I heard anything of Harriet was perhaps a year ago, and somehow I'd gathered the impression she was engaged to be married."

I looked up in surprise, glancing briefly at Gage, who had also stilled.

"I can't remember why. I likely wasn't attending well to whatever relative was speaking to me, and it's almost certain I've mixed her up with another of my benighted cousins. But all the same, you can see why I was more than a little shocked to hear she'd joined a convent." He flicked his hand. "Well, that, and the whole papist thing."

Gage's eyes met mine across the table, and he gave an almost imperceptible shake of his head. I knew he was right. That line of inquiry was almost certain to be a waste of our time. After all, Marsdale was not the most reliable of men, even when he wasn't slumping in his chair, half bosky. It would be better to wait and see if Miss Lennox's parents mentioned it in their reply to the letter Gage had posted from Howth when we reached port.

In any case, it seemed wise for us to leave before we started any trouble, whether intentional or not. I'd already noticed a cluster of rowdy men pushing and jostling each other near the bar in not an altogether friendly way, and more than one of our table neighbors had overheard Marsdale's last comment. I felt their stares. As eager as I was to gather information, I knew that tonight was not the time to be asking questions, not when Marsdale was a trifle disguised and Gage, swallowing his third pint, was growing drowsy. My wits might have been slowed by fatigue, but I recognized the wisdom of retreat when nothing could be gained from the field. We left Marsdale brooding in his chair, hoping he was astute enough to either retire to some private room with Colleen or return to his friend's lodge before he spoke out of turn and got himself pummeled.

I had my hands full enough dealing with Gage, who had the tendency to become rather amorous when he'd had a significant amount to drink. Prude or not, I was not about to let this lead to its inevitable conclusion in a hired carriage with barely a mile and a half to travel. It would have been embarrassing enough to emerge rumpled and pink-cheeked from our own conveyance with our dependable John Coachman in the box, let alone a stranger. As it was, my coiffure and gown's integrity did not quite withstand Gage's rather persuasive embrace entirely intact.

I passed the Priory's butler with as much dignity as I

could muster, and allowed one of the maid's to lead me up the stairs to the bedchamber Gage and I had been assigned. Bree was there waiting for me, and from the twinkle that entered her eye at the sight of me, I was quite certain she knew how we had been diverting ourselves between the tavern and here. Gage had paused to speak to the butler, so I sat down on the padded silk bench before the dressing table and allowed her to begin pulling pins from my hair.

Everything was arranged as usual across the oak table's surface, a bit of familiarity in otherwise strange environs. In the reflection of the mirror, I could see the room was not large, though it was more than enough space to suit our purposes. A simple four-poster bed covered in a crisp white counterpane speckled with lace held pride of place in the middle of the wall directly behind me between two tall windows draped in layers of powder blue and sheer white curtains. With the shade cast by the trees crowded around the manor, I suspected heavier drapes were not necessary to block out the early morning light. A massive wardrobe stood in one corner next to a washstand and dresser, while on the opposite side of the chamber a fireplace sat empty and swept clean. Blocks of peat were stacked in a basket to the side, ready to be lit. I had no desire for a fire now, but I had felt the chill in the air as I scampered from the carriage into the house, and I knew by morning I should wish one.

Bree had just finished untangling my hair, and I'd ordered her to forgo the usual braid and pull it back in a simple queue, when Gage suddenly entered. He barely spared us a glance, crossing the room to sit on the edge of the bed to pull his traveling boots off. Bree paused in the midst of her task, perhaps a bit disconcerted by his failure to knock as he usually did before he entered. This *was* a strange house, and so our routines were unsettled, but it was unlike him to forgo such a politeness. However, when he collapsed back into the bedding with a groan of contentment, still dressed in his clothes, Bree smiled knowingly to herself.

Her gaze lifted to meet mine in the reflection of the mirror, telling me she'd guessed at the source of his befuddlement. "Did ye enjoy yer meal and yer ale, m'lady?"

"Yes. As did Gage." I flicked my eyes toward where he still rested with his eyes closed and his hands clasped over his abdomen.

But apparently he was still conscious and knew me well, for he mumbled, "Don't look at me like that. 'Twas only two glasses."

"Three," I corrected him without condemnation. Normally three glasses of ale on a night should not have mattered, but he was tired and he had drunk them rather quickly.

His only response was a muffled, "Oh."

"Aye, well, I'd take care." There was laughter in Bree's voice. "The Irish brew their ale like everythin' else. Strong. And you bein' a foreigner and a man, they willna wait for ye to finish yer glass afore they bring ye another. They consider that hospitality."

I rose from my seat and allowed Bree to begin unfastening the buttons down the back of my dress. "I believe we may have more need of you than even we realized," I told her over my shoulder, thinking of all the things she'd already explained to us. "The difference between a postulant and other nuns, for example."

I felt Bree's fingers fumble for a fraction of a second on one of the buttons before continuing their deft work. "Yes. I s'pose I ken more aboot the Irish from my granny than the rest o' you do."

Gage hadn't moved, but I could tell he was listening from his position on the bed, and I hesitated over whether to say more or wait until Bree and I were alone. But I knew he must have formed the same questions, and I would almost certainly tell him whatever she said regardless, so I voiced the suspicion that had been nagging at my mind.

"Is that all?" I asked gently.

With my back to her and being turned away from the

mirror, I couldn't see her face, but if it were possible, I could hear her thinking furiously. I didn't press, knowing that if what I suspected was true, it would be no small thing for her to admit. A clock I hadn't even realized was there ticked softly away on the mantel.

When Bree reached the bottom of the tiny row of buttons, she inhaled deeply, as if facing the inevitable. "I was raised Roman Catholic, if that's what ye mean."

It was indeed. "By your granny?"

She reached in to begin tugging at the laces of my corset. "Aye. An' my mam."

I allowed my posture to sag as the pressure holding my spine upright was released. "Are you still?"

Another slight hesitation. "I s'pose so."

"But you've always attended St. Cuthbert's in Elwick with the other servants and my family. And St. George's in Edinburgh," I argued, trying to understand.

"Because it wasn't possible to attend mass. All o' the mass houses were too far away. And it simply became habit to go wi' the family once we moved to Edinburgh."

I pulled my arms from the sleeves of my carriage dress and corset, allowing the gown to pool on the floor as Bree whisked away my corset, and I pivoted to look at her. Her expression was tight, her cheeks flushed with chagrin.

She shrugged. "I ken it goes against what I was taught, but I reckon the Lord dinna mind where I go, so long as I does."

She turned away to deposit my corset on the table and retrieve my nightdress, shaking the folds loose. I knew how I was supposed to react, that I should be shocked and horrified that my maid was a Catholic, but I couldn't seem to summon such a response. I knew Bree. I knew her heart—or at least, I thought I did—and it was good.

Ever since I was a child, we had been taught that Catholics needed to be saved from themselves. That they were superstitious and beholden to immoral traditions, and loyal only to the Pope. That the only way they could be a good

British subject was to convert. But Bree had never seemed any less loyal or more superstitious than most of the Anglicans and Protestants I knew. And neither had the reverend mother or Mother Paul.

Perhaps I was supposed to berate her, to scold her for her sinful ways and demand she convert or else be dismissed. I knew any number of ladies who would have done so, that their husbands would have insisted upon it. But I simply couldn't bring myself to do it. Maybe this was a failing on my part. Maybe it was a fault I would be taken to task for at heaven's pearly gates. But it was a risk I was willing to take seeing as the alternative option seemed far more harmful. I would certainly have difficulty embracing the faith of a people who rebuked me and then forced my conversion, and I couldn't imagine Bree was any different.

I remembered how our cook at Blakelaw House used to harangue me and my siblings with Bible verses whenever she witnessed or heard of us misbehaving. As a young child, I was made to feel horribly guilty, but when I grew old enough to recognize some of the verses and the manner in which she was misusing them, I all but ignored her. She'd done no good but to rile us and make us determined not to become sanctimonious hypocrites.

That memory brought me up short as Bree dropped my fine linen nightrail over my head, making me recall something else my maid had confided in me. "Is that one of the reasons Cook beat you?" I asked softly.

Dark recollections swam through the depths of Bree's brown eyes. "Aye."

I clenched my teeth against the desire to curse. Bree had worked as a kitchen maid at Blakelaw House for several years before being promoted to upstairs maid and then my lady's maid half a year ago. Unbeknownst to my father and me—when I had still lived there before marrying Sir Anthony—the cook had tormented her, eventually almost beating her to death with a rolling pin. My father had fired the cook and seen that Bree's injuries were taken care of, but the damage had been done, despite Bree's assurances to the contrary. I had seen the way she shrank from quick movements, much the way I did, but for a different reason. The sound of a shrill woman's voice almost visibly sent the hair bristling down her back.

She stooped to gather up my dress and shoes, tossing the former over her arm before she swiveled back toward the dressing table to slam shut the lock box with my necklace and earrings nestled inside. She wedged this into the bottom right drawer.

"Well, under the circumstances, I'm glad of your upbringing." I told her as she straightened, knowing I had to say something. "Neither Gage nor I have the slightest notion about Catholics, or abbeys, or what troubles they might face, and I suspect we shall need your expertise if we are to solve Miss Lennox's murder." I pressed a hand to my brow wearily. "If it's murder at all."

She stood staring at me with a rather flustered expression on her face.

"Have you had a chance to write to your brother?" I asked, wondering if our discussion might have dredged up memories of her earlier life.

"I . . ." She paused and then bent over to collect something she'd dropped. "Not yet."

"Did they assign you adequate accommodations somewhere?" I knew she must be as tired as, if not more so, than I was, and here I was keeping her.

She nodded. "Aye. I'm to share a room wi' one o' the maids. Far as I can tell, the girl is quiet and tidy, so it'll do."

"Then I should let you seek your own bed. Good night."

She picked up the candleholder by the door. "Good night, m'lady."

I waited until the door shut before crossing the room to crawl into bed next to Gage. His long body weighted the covers down so that I had wriggle my legs to slide underneath. Before I blew out the candle beside the bed and lay down, I turned to find him watching me with somnolent eyes.

I think I half expected him to chide me for not taking issue with Bree's Catholicism, but instead he murmured in a drowsy-deep voice. "You're right. We do need her." He grunted as he tried to roll himself toward the edge of the bed. "I think I know more about steam locomotives than I do Roman Catholics."

"Steam locomotives?" I asked in amusement as I pushed him, helping him to gain his momentum.

He managed to hoist himself upright, perched at the edge of the mattress. At first he didn't attempt any further movement, and I wondered if perhaps his head was spinning from the drink. Then he reached up to tug at his cravat, pulling it from around his neck and tossing it on the floor like a little boy. I'd noticed it was one of his more lamentable habits, and was glad I wasn't the one forced to pick up after him. That was Anderley's job.

"Yes. Your brother is simply mad about them. Jabbered my ear off about them at Dalmay and Lady Caroline's wedding breakfast. Declares they'll revolutionize the way we travel. And they just might."

"Then you'd best invest in them," I proclaimed with a yawn, too tired to continue to follow this conversation. Instead, I lay back and tried to keep my eyes open to watch him continue to divest himself of his clothes. He had a very fine back, did my husband. Smooth and well muscled. I had been admiring it and various other parts of his body with my artist's eye since our wedding night. Or perhaps it was with the appreciation of a rather smitten wife. Either way, he was thoroughly distracting.

"I already have." He shifted the mattress as he reached down to remove one of his stockings. "There are proposals to link the Liverpool and Manchester Railway with Birmingham."

I yawned, closing my eyes as I gave a disinterested hum.

I felt him lift the covers, letting in a draft of cool air, and then he rolled toward me, hovering over me as he pressed against my side. "Poor Kiera," he crooned. "Hauled across rough seas and all over Rathfarnham, and then forced to listen to her husband yammer about locomotives when she only wants to sleep."

"Sebastian."

"I know." He kissed my brow before leaning forward to blow out the light.

CHAPTER SEVEN

True to my expectations, the air the following morning was crisp and cool, and I shivered as I bathed and dressed in my walking dress and matching deep sapphire blue redingote with belt. The woods and rolling fields surrounding the Priory were steeped in low-hanging mist, which promised to burn off in the brilliant sun piercing through the haze. Our hired carriage and driver had returned to Howth, and the Priory did not possess a town coach or a landau, or employ a coachman, but there was a lightly sprung four-wheeled yellow phaeton stored in the carriage house that the butler said Mr. Curran sometimes used about town. So we set off down the lane with Gage handling the reins of the open carriage and Bree perched on the footman's seat behind us. Anderley rode alongside on the back of a beautiful roan gelding.

Gage and I had both agreed our first visit that morning should be to the constabulary to confer with the chief constable and find out what he could tell us about the matter of Miss Lennox's death. It still being rather early, the streets of Rathfarnham were not yet busy. Most of the shops were only just opening their doors, their proprietors sweeping the walks and polishing the front windows. The bell in the church steeple chimed, sending a flock of crows that had been roosting in the oak trees flanking the front walk wheeling into the air.

Their black bodies circled the sky, swooping downward toward the rooftops on the opposite side of the street only to rise upward again.

"A storm's a comin'," Bree leaned forward to say.

I glanced over my shoulder at her.

"'Least, that's what my granny always said when the crows wheeled aboot like that." She nodded at the sky.

I studied the black fluttering mass and then turned to Gage. His brow was furrowed in displeasure, though I didn't know if this was because of Bree's superstitious comment about the crows or the pair of uniformed men standing in front of the constabulary with their arms crossed in a rather unwelcoming manner.

"Go slowly," Gage leaned over to murmur as he pulled the horses to a stop.

I knew this meant he wanted me to follow his lead, and I was quite content to do so.

Anderley had ridden ahead so he could tie his horse to the hitching rail at the front of the building and be ready to take the reins for the phaeton from Gage. He did so now after helping Bree down. I knew she intended to run a few errands while Gage and I spoke to the chief constable. So I was surprised when I looked up to find her standing rigidly, staring at the constabulary as if she'd seen a ghost. Then without a word, she abruptly pivoted and hurried away. I glanced back over my shoulder at her retreating figure as Gage took my arm and guided me toward the door.

"Good morning," he greeted them. "We're here to speak with Chief Constable Corcoran."

Neither of the men moved aside. Attired in dark green coats and trousers with black braid and epaulets on their shoulders, they wore uniforms that appeared very similar to that of the light cavalry of the British Army, even down to the swords strapped at their sides, and the light carbines draped over their shoulders. Why they needed such weaponry while guarding the entrance to their constabulary, I had no idea, but I suspected it was as much a factor of vanity as anything.

Gage's eyes hardened. "I've a letter of introduction, should that be necessary." He paused for effect. "From the Duke of Wellington."

The man on the left, who sported a thick mustache, visibly stiffened, while the pale-haired man on the right only narrowed his gaze. "The duke, eh?" His brown eyes snapped. "An' why would he be sendin' ye here?"

The corners of Gage's mouth curled upward scornfully. "I believe that's an explanation I'll be addressing to your superior. So please, be kind enough to show us to him."

But the man still did not budge, even as his cohort shifted from foot to foot beside him.

"It's all right, Casey," a tired voice behind us said. "Let dem pass."

We swiveled to see who the newcomer was, deducing from the amount of braid and decoration on his uniform that this was, in fact, Chief Constable Corcoran. His dark hair was liberally dusted with gray, including his neatly trimmed mustache and thick side hairs. Combined with his red-rimmed eyes and florid complexion, he presented quite a colorful appearance.

Gage reached out his hand to introduce himself, but Corcoran was still staring at Casey. His expression creased into a fierce scowl. "I told ye to let dem pass."

Casey finally stepped to the side, but with the least amount of grace, fairly glowering at Corcoran and then us as we passed him through the door. Gage maintained eye contact with him until he could no longer comfortably do so, perhaps to make certain Casey did not intend to take his thwarted frustration out on Anderley. However, we soon had more pressing things to worry about, including keeping up with the chief constable's ground-eating stride as he led us down a long hallway.

"Murphy!" he barked as we encountered a trio of men clustered about a desk. "Get yer manky hide upstairs an' don yer uniform properly or I'll be stripin' ye."

I assumed he was speaking to the man still in shirt-sleeves, his uniform coat missing.

He turned right, crossing through an outer office and then into a room at the far back corner of the building. It appeared to look out on a garden of sorts, and beyond that stood an old stone wall. Through a gap in the vegetation surrounding it, I could see a thin slice of a graveyard with its rows of leaning graves, likely the same graveyard whose gates I had viewed from the road when we entered town just the day before. A rather morbid situation for one's office, but I supposed it was better than having no window at all. It was propped open to let in a soft breeze and a few dappled rays of the sunshine which had finally pierced through the morning haze.

He cleared away a stack of papers from the hard ladder-back chair set in the corner and pulled it nearer to his desk at the center of the room before sitting in another chair set behind it. "Ignore Constable Casey," he told us with a careless swipe of his hand as I took my seat across from him and Gage moved to stand at my back. "He's got a head full o' bees at the moment, he does." He clasped his hands in front of him on his desk. "Now, what can I be doin' for ye, Mr. . . ."

"Gage." He reached into the inner pocket of his midnight blue frock coat and extracted the second letter of introduction we'd been given—the one addressed to Corcoran's superior, Sir John Harvey, that had been meant to smooth our way with any rank of authority. Gage passed the missive across the desk to Corcoran.

He read it swiftly with almost no discernable reaction other than a brief lifting of his eyebrows, before refolding it and handing it back to Gage. "So yer here about the matter at the abbey." He seemed to be assessing us both, but then realized what he thought didn't matter. He'd been given his orders, from no less than Wellington himself. "Well, yer welcome to it," he declared, sitting back with the air of a man who was relieved to wash their hands of this case.

"Why do you say that?" Gage asked.

"Because it don't be makin' any sense. And those nuns . . ." He shook his head. "They'll not give a straight answer. Starin' at the ground, pretendin' to be too pious to know of such earthly tings." He leaned forward suddenly, lifting his finger. "You mark my words. They be hidin' something. I don't know what, but ye can be sure o' it."

I wasn't sure how to respond to such an assertion, and it was clear neither did Gage. What exactly had this man and his men been asking them?

"I see," Gage murmured. "Well, what can you tell us of the facts of the case, as far as you know them?"

His chair creaked as he sank back into it again. "As far as I knows dem, one o' the caretakers who lives in one o' the small cottages near the abbey came to the constabulary to tell us a lass there had been murdered. So my men fetched me an' we set off for the abbey. The mother superior's second-in-command met us herself at the gate an' guided us round the buildin', an' true the orchards to the spot where the girl was found." There was a wry twist in his voice that suggested he thought this might not be true.

"Where was that?" Gage asked.

"Just outside the abbey walls in a plot of open land. Part o' the wall was bein' repaired, so some of the stones were dislodged or missin'. But ye can see dat for yourself." It was becoming obvious that Corcoran valued efficiency, in word and action, and he had no desire to waste time discussing that which was unnecessary. "'Twas clear her head had been bashed by a fall or a blow."

"*Could* she have simply tripped and hit her head?"

I noticed he had not told the chief constable we had visited the abbey and spoken to Reverend Mother Mary Teresa. I supposed he wanted to hear what the man had to say without him wondering what we'd already heard from the nuns.

Corcoran's mouth flattened, nearly disappearing beneath his mustache. "Maybe. There was no rock nearby for her to 've fallen on, and the sisters swore they hadn't moved her, but . . ." he shrugged ". . . who's to say."

"But why would they lie?" I asked in confusion, not understanding why he would suspect such a thing.

His eyes dropped to meet mine. "I don't know, sure I don't. But I learned long ago not to be trustin' everything dem Catholics say, 'specially if there be religion involved."

"And the Anglicans?" I could hear the tension at the edges of Gage's voice, though it was clear he was trying to mask it.

Corcoran's eyes glittered, meeting his challenge. "Oh, they be just as quick wit a lie as all the rest. But they've less to lose."

I felt some of the tension leave Gage's hand where it rested against my shoulder, and I suspected he felt the chief constable's answer was satisfactory enough. This was a man with the same long-seated prejudices as most Anglo-Irishmen, but he did not seem to be grinding an ax to them.

He exhaled heavily, pushing a stack of papers farther toward the corner of his desk. "I'll not be mincin' words. I don't know whether to make heads nor tails of dis Miss Lennox's murder. The mother superior barred us from her convent afore we could discover much about the lass or her death, and she knows enough people up in Dublin over my head to keep me away. The Balls are a powerful family in their own right. Built their fortune in shippin' when Catholics were still barred from other trades." His eyes lifted from the blotter where he'd been staring. "I've no wish to challenge her in dis, and dat's the truth. So yer welcome to it. I'll help ye however I can, but my hands are full enough at the moment wit the Catholics an' their blasted tithe protest, and these bletherin' secret societies."

I had no idea what he was talking about, but it seemed Gage did. "They're active here, then?"

"Aye," he grunted. "Active enough. An' a benighted scourge they are. I've not enough men to deal wit dem and dis murder." His lips pursed. "An' truth be told, I don't know dat I've a man wit the wits to solve it. They're good men, they are. But not the sharpest o' the lot, dat's for sure."

Plainly the county constabulary was not the most respected of professions here in Ireland. In fact, I suspected they were more often than not viewed as the enemy, and whatever pay the men were given, it was unlikely to make up for the hostility they faced. I imagined the general laborers without land would prefer to find jobs at the mills and farms nearby rather than sign on to help police their own people for meager pay and living quarters in the crowded barracks above.

"Well, we appreciate your cooperation," Gage said, and I could tell he meant it. This was one less thing to worry over. "I didn't know if the local men would feel I was stepping on their toes."

"I cannot speak for everyone, but I'll not be quarrelin' wit ye."

"What of Casey?"

One corner of Corcoran's mustache twitched upward in chagrin. "Dat one's a bit pigheaded, to be sure. But I've none better at coaxin' his fellow Catholics to be reasonable, so long as the reasoning's sound."

Somehow that did not seem the least reassuring.

"Is he going to give us trouble?" Gage asked.

Corcoran sat forward as if to rise. "I'll see dat he doesn't. An' so long as ye appear to be fair to all, he'll see it's best not to bother ye."

A thought occurred to me. "Was he acquainted with Miss Lennox?"

He seemed slightly taken aback by this question. "Not so far as I know. But yer free to ask him."

Gage's hand gently squeezed my shoulder. "Thank you."

"If you've nothin' else to be askin' me, den . . ."

But Corcoran never got to finish his sentence, for one of his men rapped once before peeking his head through the door. He cringed, clearly prepared for a dressing-down. "Sorry to be disturbin' ye, sir. But Mr. LaTouche insists he speak . . ."

"Corcoran, what's this I hear about you abandonin' the

inquiry." The man in question didn't even bother to let the cadet finish his sentence, but barged through the door past him. His steps came up short at the sight of me and Gage.

Mr. LaTouche was a tall and imposing man, made all the more so by the expert fit of his clothing, clearly London-tailored. In fact, his appearance rivaled Gage's for sophistication, though the fact that Gage wore his attire so effortlessly only made LaTouche look as if he was trying too hard. I supposed the ladies would describe him as dashing, but any appreciation I might have felt was soured by his resemblance to Gage's father. However, where Lord Gage was light, LaTouche was dark, with raven black hair just beginning to turn to gray at the temples, except for a pair of piercing Irish blue eyes. These he turned to me with what I suspected was normally a devastating effect on the women of his acquaintance. Or so his arrogant smile seemed to say.

Corcoran, I noticed, had risen to his feet, but I elected to use my prerogative as a lady to remain seated. It irked me somehow to see how everyone seemed to cater to this Mr. LaTouche, though it was only to be expected. He was evidently a man of some importance here in Rathfarnham. People in every village in Britain acted the same way toward men of higher rank or consequence. Why should this one instance bother me?

Ah, but I knew the answer to that, and it was no fault of the man himself. I tried to push Lord Gage from my thoughts and listen as Corcoran performed the introductions and explained our presence.

Mr. LaTouche owned a sizable estate a short distance south of the Priory, where we were staying. It was what would be termed a gentleman's country residence, the place where he and his family would retire to from the overcrowding and stench of the city of Dublin. I gathered he was not the typical land-holding member of the gentry, for he owned two of the local mills, as well as several shipping ventures.

"Lady Darby," he murmured, bowing over the hand I offered him. "I'm enchanted."

"Please, call me Mrs. Gage," I replied, ignoring the flattery.

To his credit, he didn't even blink at my request. "But, of course." He stood tall again, taking us all in. "As I'm sure you've gathered, I'm here to find out what's bein' done about dat girl's death. But now dat I see you are here, well, I suppose dat's answer enough."

I smiled tightly, wondering just how much of our reputations had preceded us, and how much he was reacting to Corcoran's proclamation that Wellington himself had sent us.

"You *are* here to investigate the death of Miss Lennox, are ye not?" he pressed, clearly angling for information. "Not some other matter wit which I'm unfamiliar?"

Somehow I doubted this man was unfamiliar with much that mattered in this community.

"Yes, we're making inquiries into her death on behalf of the family," Gage replied, crossing one ankle behind the other to lean more casually against the back of my chair. "Were you acquainted with Miss Lennox?"

"Wit the family? Certainly. Hard not to be in a town as small as Dublin." By which he meant the good society of the Protestant Ascendancy, not the city itself; that was clear. "'Twas unexpected enough to hear of her conversion to Catholicism, but den to hear of her murder. Well, ye can imagine the shock. Such a ting simply cannot be allowed to happen. Even to a Catholic girl."

I frowned. It seemed I was to be perpetually caught off guard by the way these people thought of and chose to speak about Catholics. It was something I imagined I'd hardly noticed when people referred to them in the past, but now that the matter was forefront in my mind, I couldn't help but feel unsettled. This dislike and distrust was something British Catholics dealt with from the cradle, and yet I'd almost taken no note. It's never easy to discover you've been willfully ignorant of the struggles of others when you've experienced struggles of your own.

"Yes. They are, after all, still human," Gage drawled.

"Precisely," Mr. LaTouche declared, either unaware of his

sarcasm or choosing to ignore it. "Whether one believes in the wages of sin or not, such a murder is unacceptable."

I stiffened.

He flicked a glance at Corcoran. "If, in fact, it was murder."

It appeared he was almost as well acquainted with this inquiry as we were.

"Well." He smiled disarmingly at us. "I feel much better knowin' Wellington has sent his best people to handle this investigation."

I forced an answering smile to my face, though I now felt certain he was aware of exactly who we were, and was familiar with my scandalous reputation. It was there in the speculative gleam in his eyes, the avid scouring of my figure, as if he would find some clue written there. An extra limb perhaps? Or a forked tail?

I changed my mind about my earlier assessment. I still disliked him, but not because of his resemblance to Lord Gage. No, he had earned my enmity all on his own.

But I had learned from Gage when it was best to play nice. That you caught more flies with honey than vinegar. People most often let their secrets slip when they were least vigilant.

So we genially took our leave of Mr. LaTouche and Chief Constable Corcoran. Though, truth be told, I let Gage do most of the talking. I was afraid my tone of voice would reveal more than I wished.

Gage was quiet as we strolled down the hall toward the front of the building, ignoring the curious looks sent our way. He waited until we reached the door, which I noticed no longer boasted guards, before he spoke, mumbling almost under his breath, "The wages of sin. Now where have I heard that before?"

"It's from the Bible," I replied hollowly. "In Romans, I believe. 'For the wages of sin is death.'"

I felt his eyes on my face, perhaps better understanding my reaction now when Mr. LaTouche had quoted it. Then he surprised me. "'But the gift of God is eternal life through Jesus Christ our Lord.'"

I turned to meet his gaze, blinking against the brightness of the sun.

His mouth quirked in chagrin. "My grandfather rather strictly encouraged the memorization of Bible verses."

From the little he'd told me of his maternal grandfather, this did not shock me.

"Yes, well, I suspect Mr. LaTouche forgot that was the rest of the verse," I muttered.

His brow furrowed. "I suspect a lot of people do."

CHAPTER EIGHT

The phaeton still stood where we had left it, with Anderley holding the reins to the matching pair of Friesians. His mouth creased in the momentary flicker of a smile at something Bree had said while she absently stroked the shiny dark coat of the steed on the right. I'd not realized she was so comfortable with horses, but then again, I'd had little opportunity to view her in such a setting. I was starting to think there was a great deal I didn't know about my maid.

They both looked up as we approached, and something of my vexation must have been evident for Bree's freckled complexion blanched. "Did they no' wish yer help?"

"No. They were actually quite receptive," Gage replied, and then sighed. "If not predictably intolerant." He turned to his valet then, asking an unspoken question which Anderley seemed to understand, for he nodded down the street toward the river.

"They strolled that way, sir. The rude, towheaded one dipped into that gate, while the other continued down the street and crossed to the other side before making his way back toward town. Making his rounds, I suppose."

The gate in question led into the graveyard, of which we'd had a decent view through Chief Constable Corcoran's window. Given the lively and illegal body-snatching trade still occurring throughout Britain, I supposed it was common for the police to patrol cemeteries and other secluded places looking for possible disturbances or the presence of undesirables, but we had never seen Casey pass by. If his task had been to search the churchyard, he'd done a rather poor job of it.

Or had he slipped into the graveyard for another reason? Maybe to stand next to his superior's open window to hear what was said?

I could tell by Gage's lowered brow that he'd had a similar thought.

"Did you see him leave again?"

Anderley shook his head and Gage turned to stare at the ornamental gate some thirty feet away. I wondered if he was considering entering the graveyard himself, perhaps to confront Casey, but then he seemed to discard the idea, ushering me toward the carriage.

I waited until we passed the rows of shops before raising my voice to be heard above the clattering of the wheels. "Is that why you squeezed my shoulder to stop me from asking more questions about Casey? Did you know he was outside the window?"

His eyes flicked toward me before focusing on the horses once again. "No. But I was worried Corcoran might ask Casey about Miss Lennox himself, and then by the time we had a chance to question him, he would have his answer prepared."

Bree made a sound behind us like a hiccup, and I pivoted to look over my shoulder at her, but her gaze was trained on the side of the road. She raised her hand to a child standing there who appeared to be waving to us in greeting, and I did likewise. "I hadn't thought of that," I admitted. "He seemed so happy to pass the investigation on to us."

"Yes. But that doesn't mean he would be best pleased to hear secondhand how one of his own men could be a suspect. He might think it better to be diligent enough to see that doesn't happen."

I frowned. "Then I may have spoiled our chances of seeing his honest reaction."

Gage smiled. "Maybe. But I suspect there's more than one way to rile Constable Casey. If he thinks we're interested in him, he might save us the trouble and come to us."

It was plain to see that the gardens and grounds of the abbey were the true jewel of the property. I had yet to explore beyond the front hall and parlor inside, but I had a difficult time believing anything inside could rival the parklands, even knowing the house was formerly a gentleman's manor. A wide central walk lined with tall chestnut trees led down through the gardens, with narrower paths leading off in several different directions. There was the expected herb garden, and a rather large vegetable patch, but also a beautiful flower garden, bursting with blooms. I caught sight of a pond in the distance, with the pale white blur of Miss Lennox's swans floating across the surface. At the end of the walk stood a summerhouse overlooking a tiny stream, which trickled merrily over a small cascade of rocks as it made its way toward the pond.

We turned left just before the summerhouse, following the course of the stream for several more yards before it veered away. I suspected it joined the larger pond beyond the abbey property—the one Miss Lennox had claimed she was visiting when she was caught outside the walls—with the abbey pond. Mother Paul guided me and Gage through an arch shaped from twisted vines, carefully pruned and overgrown with brambles, their berries plump and ripe, ready to be picked.

Which, in fact, was exactly what a young man with a coppery head full of shaggy hair was doing. He'd propped a large basket against his hip to catch the berries he reached up to pluck with dexterous fingers. He glanced up as we passed, giving us a glimpse of his ruddy, freckled complexion and whiskey brown eyes, which widened at the sight of us. He was broad of shoulder, tall, and whipcord lean, making him appear at least as old as I was. Until his hand slipped and clamped down, bursting one of the blackberries.

He thoughtlessly swiped it down the side of his linen trousers like a little boy with fingers sticky from jam, and I began to suspect he might actually be a few years younger.

Mother Paul continued into the orchard with us trailing after her as we wove through the trees planted in uniform straight lines toward the far wall. The air was sweet with growing fruit—apples and pears and figs—and buzzing with the activity of bees, which zipped from branch to branch. High in the branches of one mulberry tree, a blackbird perched singing, her sharp tweets overloud in the peace and stillness. This truly was a quiet corner of the abbey, far from the house and the more populated gardens. The summer-full trees shielded you from sight, and the dense leaves absorbed much of the sound.

It was no wonder no one had heard cries of distress or witnessed a confrontation. Even if Miss Lennox had been found inside the abbey walls, she would still have been as far from the manor as possible. Which made me wonder if the first time she'd been caught outside the abbey walls had truly been the first time she'd ventured there. It also called into question her excuse that she'd been watching the flight of a gray heron and unthinking clambered through the wall. The missing portion of the wall was too far out of the way, too well hidden for someone to stumble upon. She had to have known it was there and deliberately set out for it.

When we finally reached the wall, I could better understand what the reverend mother had been trying to explain. It was a very old construction of mud and stone, and it was clear that at some point the ground around it had been flooded, loosening the joints and causing a two-foot-wide section to collapse. Some of the stones had been moved since then, and stacked neatly to the side, while others had been left to lie where they had fallen.

Through the gap I could see that the ground sloped upward and then leveled out into the soft green expanse of a field scattered with wildflowers. A small flock of sheep dotted the horizon just beyond the blue-green water of the pond Miss Lennox had supposedly gone to visit. At the right edge of the pond stood a beech tree, which towered over the open landscape, the tallest point in sight.

Mother Paul stood aside as Gage and I climbed through the rough opening of crumbled masonry into the field beyond. Here, more stones littered the ground, though most of them were clustered close to the wall.

"Has anyone moved these since Miss Lennox was found?" Gage swiveled to ask her as she leaned out through the wall, watching our search.

She glanced to the left and to the right. "Not that I'm aware of. But then the constables are free to come and go from the land outside the wall. They might have been here shifting things later. But . . ." she paused, scouring the grass again ". . . no. I don't think so."

Gage nodded and paced farther out into the field, the tall grass swishing against his leather boots. I hovered near the wall, watching him, fairly certain if there'd been anything to find, they would have uncovered it the evening Miss Lennox died. If not, it must have been dropped or thrown far from the abbey wall, and there was little chance of us locating it now in the tangle of this overgrown field.

I pressed closer to the cool stone of the wall, trying to escape the warm rays of the sun high overhead. My sapphire blue redingote with gigot sleeves had been quite comfortable in the chill of morning, but now I could feel the heat gathering beneath my stays. I couldn't imagine how warm the sisters must feel in their heavy black serge and crape veil, not to mention all the other intricate pieces of their attire—the petticoats, caps, tippets, and girdles. It was no wonder they began cutting their hair close to the head the moment they were clothed in their habit. How else could they bear it?

Mother Paul and I both turned at the approach of footsteps, watching as the dark shapes of two nuns emerged from behind the trees. The first sister was quite tall, her high stature aided by the fact that she seemed to glide across the ground, her feet barely touching the earth hidden beneath her habit. Her complexion was smooth as alabaster, and her expression serene and calm. It was a countenance to rival any of the saints I had seen painted on murals and triptychs.

In marked contrast, the other nun was short and slight, her fingers fidgeting with the ebony beads hanging at her side. She tried to feign a tranquil demeanor, but her dark eyebrows gave her away, shifting up and down, quivering as her forehead flexed. She was some years younger than the sister beside her, some years younger than even my twenty-six years, which might have accounted for her restlessness.

Mother Paul swiftly made the introductions as Gage joined us. My interest heightened as we learned that Mother Mary Fidelis, Miss Lennox's advisor, was this tall, serene nun, and Sister Mary Maxentia was the anxious younger one. Sister Maxentia was also still a novice.

From quizzing Bree earlier, I had learned that this was the second stage of becoming a nun. First, one became a postulant for about a year. After that, one could apply to become a novice, being clothed in the habit and given a new name. This stage lasted for about two to three years, before one finally made their profession, taking their vows and becoming fully a bride of Christ. But even that wasn't so simple. There were levels of vows—temporary, simple, solemn, perpetual—and the level of the vow you had taken, as well as the consideration of whether you had brought a dowry with you to be given to the convent, determined whether you were titled Sister or Mother. It was somewhat confusing for someone who had never reflected on the lives of nuns until a few days prior.

"Ye wish to know where we found Miss Lennox dat night?" Mother Fidelis asked softly.

"Yes," Gage replied carefully. "But if I may, can I ask how you came to look here in the first place?"

"Because Reverend Mother asked us to search the grounds for her, and I knew she'd gone dis way before." Mother Fidelis's voice was easy, almost emotionless, and yet not cold.

"And what did you find when you reached the wall?"

"'Twas nearly dark, so 'twas difficult to see much at a distance. I'd brought a lantern, but kept it shuttered, as at dat hour 'twas more of a hindrance yet than a help. We'd been callin' her name as we approached, but not heard a word in response." At this, she glanced sideways at Sister Maxentia, who nodded briskly, content for Mother Fidelis to do the talking.

"We paused at the wall—much as we're standin' now— and tried to peer out through the gloom. Reverend Mother hadn't given us permission to search beyond the abbey grounds, so I was hesitant to go much further. But den I thought I heard somethin'. A sort of whimper."

"Miss Lennox was alive when you reached her?" I gasped in surprise, not having expected this.

Mother Fidelis shook her head. "No. So perhaps I'm wrong. Perhaps what I heard was merely the sound of a small animal, or the wind." A small furrow formed between her eyes, the first indication of any uncertainty I'd seen in her, before being smoothed away. "But whatever the case, it made me decide a search outside the wall was warranted. Once I'd moved a few steps toward the pond, I could see her lyin' in the grass just there." She pointed behind us, and Gage crossed the space.

"Here?"

"A few steps more. Aye, dat's it."

Gage slowly turned, making a precursory examination of the area before dropping to his haunches to stare more closely into the patch of wild thyme. It seemed evident now. I could see how trampled the grass was in that expanse. But after nearly two weeks' growth, rain, and the footsteps of both the helpful and the curious, it would have been difficult to figure out exactly where in the trodden grass she'd rested.

"How was her body positioned?" I asked, trying to picture it.

Out of the corner of my eye I could see that Sister Maxentia had turned away, as if Miss Lennox were still lying out in the field. Mother Paul reached out to press a comforting hand to her shoulder.

"She was lyin' on her stomach, but tilted slightly to the side, wit her head toward us, her face turned to the east, an' her feet pointin' toward the pond."

"And her hands?"

At this, Mother Fidelis paused again, but when I glanced back, I could tell this was only because she was thinking. "One was beneath her an' the other was bent out to her side."

"Could you tell she was dead?"

"Not immediately. I tink I saw the torn fabric on her shoulder first and thought she'd been attacked. I rolled her over, tinking I might find she was cowerin', tryin' to hide her shame, but she didn't resist. 'Twas den I searched for a pulse, but couldn't find one."

I looked over to the other nun, needing to know what she was thinking even though it would undoubtedly upset her to recount the details. "And you, Sister Maxentia? Did you go to Miss Lennox?"

Her voice was as thin as a frayed thread, and it took her several attempts to get the words out. "I . . . I followed Mother Mary Fidelis. And I . . . kneeled beside Miss . . . Miss Lennox. And when she didn't respond to our words even when we rolled her over, I reached for her head to . . . to comfort her."

Her words suddenly stopped, and I knew then what so distressed her. "And you found blood?"

She nodded, her head turned to the side, her eyes shut tight.

"Her hair was sticky wit it," Mother Fidelis told us, sparing the novice from having to share any further details. "An' her skin was not as warm as, well, as I would've wished, to be sure."

"But it wasn't cold?" I clarified.

"No." Her eyes met mine squarely in understanding. "I don't think she could've been dead for long."

"Did you notice, was there much grass or dirt in her hair?"

"Some. But den, we'd rolled her over."

Yes, that would complicate matters. But perhaps that was a better question for the infirmarian, who had hopefully taken a closer look at the wound.

Gage rejoined us then, wiping his hand with his handkerchief. He indicated with a swift shake of his head that he hadn't found anything to assist in our investigation, before turning his attention to the sisters. "Mother Fidelis, can you tell us if there were any stones nearby that aren't where they rested that night? Does this field look the same?"

She scrutinized the land before her through narrowed eyes, but still did not move through the gap in the wall. It was somewhat frustrating, and almost comical, watching the three nuns crowded around the opening. Surely the reverend mother would allow them to step out into the field for this.

"Aye. I tink so. They were scattered there and there." She pointed to the rocks he had inspected earlier.

He folded his handkerchief and tucked it back into his pocket. "Once you realized she was dead, then what happened?"

"I sent Sister Mary Maxentia for help. Though by dat time others had begun makin' their way through the orchard, so she hadn't needed to go far. Reverend Mother came herself to see Miss Lennox, and den she told us not to touch anything else, and sent Mr. Scully for the constable."

"Mr. Scully?"

"He's the abbey's gardener and man of all work. His wife also lends us assistance, as we're still a rather small branch of the order. Only nine years old. And not enough sisters yet to handle all dat needs done."

I looked to Mother Paul, who had been observing our conversation solemnly. "Was he the young man we passed picking brambles?"

"No. That was our undergardener and Mr. Scully's assistant, Davy Somers. He's a local lad, and an orphan."

The boy who Sister Pip had believed was sweet on Miss

Lennox. Well, he was certainly someone we should talk to, along with the Scullys, but for the moment that could wait.

"I suppose we've asked all the obvious questions then," Gage quipped with a self-deprecating smile I knew was meant to both soothe and disarm. "But is there anything else you think we should know? Anything you noticed that seemed strange or out of the ordinary? A person who shouldn't have been there, or someone who was acting strangely? A pair of muddy shoes? A grass-stained sleeve? Anything, anything at all."

"There was one ting," Mother Fidelis said. Her eyes were troubled when she lifted them from where they'd been fastened on the ground. "Her simple veil. She wasn't wearin' it. 'Twas loosely clutched in her hand."

This obviously didn't strike me as strongly as it did her. "I didn't know postulants wore veils," I admitted.

"A short, white covering beginning at the crown of their heads."

"And I take it, she was not supposed to remove it."

"Not in public. Not without good reason."

I could tell that Mother Fidelis had more to say on the matter, but I decided that could wait until we were alone and able to discuss whatever Miss Lennox might have confided in her as an advisor.

"Didn't you want to see the pond more closely?" I asked in a low voice as Gage and I hung back from the others and returned through the orchard. Mother Paul and Mother Fidelis strolled sedately a few yards in front of us, but Sister Maxentia had long since disappeared, fleeing as if the hounds of hell were at her heels. Which, perhaps, we were. A rather sobering thought.

He shook his head. "I don't think the pond matters. I seriously doubt it had anything to do with why Miss Lennox was leaving the abbey grounds or why she was killed."

I sighed. "I don't either. It was a silly excuse, and I think she knew it."

"Which was why it worked. Who would believe she would make something like that up?"

I eyed the back of one of the figures in front of us. "Mother Mary Fidelis."

Gage turned to look at me. "You think so?

"I think she suspected. Maybe she'll tell me why."

CHAPTER NINE

As Gage and Anderley were not allowed inside the abbey, we elected to take a divide and conquer approach. Anderley rode off with the roan gelding to settle himself at the Yellow House and see what he could learn listening to the patrons, while Gage took the phaeton and the list the mother superior had compiled for us and set off to visit as many of the locals connected to the abbey as he could, including Dr. O'Reilly, the convent's attending physician, and Father Sullivan, the chaplain. He also intended to stop and speak to the workmen renovating a building at the edge of the abbey grounds to be used as a day school for local children. The reverend mother explained this was the reason the wall had not yet been repaired. All of their focus had been on finishing the day school before the fall term would start. He planned to return later to speak with the Scullys and Davy Somers at the end of their workday, and if I was available, I hoped to join him.

For my and Bree's part, we spent the remainder of the day at the abbey, she belowstairs and me above. I decided my first stop should be to the abbey's infirmary, which was situated in a large, airy room on the ground floor. I suspected it had once been a sort of billiard room and men's parlor, for even underlying the strong stench of camphor and lye, I could smell the decades' worth of cheroot and pipe smoke which had seeped into the wood paneling and moldings. Fortunately, the outer wall of the room was lined with tall Georgian windows, which were open to let in the sunshine and the summer breeze.

Whether as a consequence of her time spent in this room or a natural physical trait, Sister Mary Bernard spoke with a rather nasal voice in sharp, short bursts. It was as if what she had to say must be said quickly, and in as economical an amount of words as possible. At first I found myself taken aback, until I realized she meant no offense, and that, in fact, I should welcome her straightforward approach.

She ushered me toward the interior corner of the room, near a pair of tall cabinets and a small table, and far from where her single patient rested on a narrow cot near the windows. "Reverend Mother said you'd have questions. What do ye wish to know?"

"You examined her?"

She nodded. "Best I could. I don't know much."

"I understand," I assured her. "What can you tell me of her head wound?"

"'Twas a gash. A deep one. Dented her skull and bled someting fierce."

"Where was it located?"

She lifted her hand to illustrate. "Just here. At the back, but a little to the right."

That corroborated what the reverend mother had told us. "And what about the rest of her body? Did you notice any other injuries, even small cuts and bruises?"

She scrunched her nose as if it itched. "Two small bruises on her arm. One on the inside, and the other on the outside."

From someone grabbing her?

"And another larger one on the outside of her thigh, just below the hip," she added.

I studied her, trying to decide how best to ask what I next needed to. Sister Bernard appeared to be telling me the truth, but only as far as she might recognize it.

"Was her skin overly red or abraded anywhere? Or did you happen to find blood anywhere else on her body?"

"No, m'lady. Just the head."

I decided that was as close to a definitive answer as I was going to get without asking her whether she had examined Miss Lennox intimately, and I certainly wasn't going to do that. In any case, it told me what I wanted to know. Without the evidence of blood or bruises or even abrasions on the inside of her thighs or marks that suggested she'd been held down or restrained, it was unlikely Miss Lennox was assaulted.

"Thank you. You've been very helpful. If I could ask but one more question. Her hands, how did they appear? Was there anything underneath her nails? Were any of them broken?"

She nodded vigorously and my breath quickened, thinking this might be a bit of evidence we could use. But her answer was not what I'd expected.

"She'd bitten 'em all to the quick. Gnawed at a bit of the skin, too. They weren't pretty."

"I see." So it seemed Miss Lennox had not fought off an attacker, which told us nothing, as we'd already deduced that if she'd been murdered, she'd been struck from behind, either by surprise or while she fled. The only thing that was clear was that Miss Lennox had been anxious about something. Anxious enough to bite her nails down to painful nubs. But why?

I knew Sister Bernard would not have the answers I sought, so I thanked her again and asked whether she still had in her possession the clothes Miss Lennox had been wearing.

She turned to open the cupboard on the right, pulling a small box out from the bottom shelf and thrusting it into my arms. "Here."

Frowning, I carried this over to the table and carefully began to extract the contents. On top lay a drab gray dress with a white collar and cuffs. The collar and the gray serge at the right were stained with blood, while on the opposite shoulder I could see where the cloth had been ripped at the seam. The right shoulder of her chemise was also stained, but the rest of her clothes, including the short veil, appeared unmarred except for general wear and tear. The sides and backs of her shoes, particularly near the heel, were coated in dried mud, making me wonder where the muck had come from if the rest of her clothing was not also in a similar state. Had Miss Lennox been down to the edge of the pond? I couldn't think where else she would have . . .

I paused, catching a faint whiff of some earthy scent. Leaning forward, I sniffed the shoes. My nose wrinkled, recoiling from the stench. There was definitely a hint of fresh manure there. From the sheep we had seen beyond the pond?

Where on earth had Miss Lennox gone that fateful day? And why had she been so anxious about it? What sort of trouble could the postulant have possibly gotten herself into?

At the midday meal, the mother superior addressed everyone assembled, both her fellow sisters and the boarding students, on my behalf, asking them to please cooperate with us and to come forward with any information they thought might be helpful. At first, this proved to be a fruitless effort. Oh, I spoke to a number of well-meaning sisters, but they only wished to tell me they would pray that the Lord would grant me wisdom and guidance in my task. As much as their prayers were appreciated, after the fifth time a nun's approach raised my expectations and hopes, it was difficult not to feel somewhat flattened. I tried not to let my disappointment show, but it must have been obvious enough, for Mother Fidelis, seated across the table, offered me a gentle smile.

"Lady Darby, perhaps ye would join me as I prepare for my next class?"

"Of course," I replied, jumping at the opportunity to speak with her and escape the refectory. There was only so much of the students' wary glances and hushed voices, and the other sisters' well-wishes, I could endure.

She led me through a side door, which blocked much of the noise from the refectory as it shut behind us. Not that the room had been overly loud. Nowhere in the abbey was. That was one thing I couldn't help but notice. The sisters certainly preferred and commanded quiet. It was restful, if a bit unexpected at first, to see the students shuffle from class to class in silence.

I began to speak, and then wondered if I was to be quiet, too, as we traversed the corridors. Fortunately, Mother Fidelis put an end to that internal debate.

"Say what ye wish. As a guest yer not beholden to the same rules as the students."

I turned to her with a start. "How did you know that's what I was thinking?"

Her gently amused smile returned. "'Tis what all the visitors wonder when they first come here." Her eyes cut sideways at me, almost shrewdly. "The truth is, we order their silence as much for our own ears as for the students' spiritual discipline."

This admission surprised a grin out of me. "Well, I can't say I blame you. As loud as my four nieces and nephews can be, I can only imagine what dozens of adolescent girls would sound like."

She shook her head. "Don't try. 'Twill give ye a megrim just from the effort."

I laughed at that, and then stifled it with my hand, lest one of the students hear. Mother Fidelis only continued to smile.

Her classroom proved to be nearby, and I couldn't withhold a gasp as we entered to discover it was a studio of sorts. A cluster of easels sat on one side of the room, each with a canvas at the ready and a small table set beside it, cluttered with paint supplies. The other side of the studio, nearest to the door, was packed tight with tables and chairs, all facing another table at the front where a still life made from religious articles had been arranged. A gold chalice, a black-beaded rosary, and a small cross gleamed in the sunlight shining through the windows behind them.

"I didn't realize you taught drawing and painting."

"I try. I'm no master, but we've no one nearby whom we can coax to instruct such classes, so I make do."

"Do you often bring in outside instructors to teach the girls?" I asked, crossing to the wall at the back, where a number of fairly accomplished drawings hung—the best from past projects, I guessed.

"Not so often as we used to now dat we've more sisters. Mrs. Sherlock comes once a week to teach deportment and elocution. And until a few months ago, a man from the village helped to teach some of our music classes. But Sister Mary Xaveria has since taken dat over."

I nodded, having glimpsed Mrs. Sherlock's name on the list the mother superior had given Gage, but there had been no notation about other teachers. Perhaps this music tutor had already gone by the time Miss Lennox arrived.

"I'm sure the reverend mother will give ye a list of all the people Miss Lennox might've encountered, if she hasn't already."

"She has," I told her, not sure whether I should feel amused or unsettled by her ability to divine my thoughts. I understood what made her such a good advisor to those young postulants entering the abbey. Even now she was standing there patiently allowing me to sort through my impressions and decide what to ask next, though I was certain she already knew. I suspected few things slipped her notice.

"You were Miss Lennox's advisor," I prompted.

"I was."

I waited, hoping she would choose to elaborate, but she didn't. "The reverend mother said she believed you knew her better than anyone here at the abbey." She neither confirmed nor denied this, and I felt a twinge of annoyance. Perhaps if I phrased a direct question. "Could you tell me your impressions of her? Did she confide in you why she decided to convert to Catholicism and become a nun?"

Her eyes dropped from mine, as if deciding how much to say. "Miss Lennox was, I think, more complex than most gave her credit for. Aye, she was studious, gentle, and observant. But she was also conflicted and doubtful." She turned to stroll between the tables toward the windows and I followed. "If I were to speculate, I would say her heaviest burden may've been dat she was overly reflective. Always carefully considerin' her thoughts and words, weighin' every option, calculatin' the odds. I know for certain it was her biggest struggle—the temptation to live too much in her head, until dat which she had ne'er doubted, she suddenly did." She paused to adjust something in the still life on the table. "Dat and tryin' too hard to please others."

I had been contemplating what she was telling me, trying to form a better impression of Miss Lennox, but this almost offhanded pronouncement at the last stunned me. "Wait. 'Trying too hard to please others'?" How was that possible? The girl had completely ignored what I was sure her family had wanted for her.

But Mother Fidelis was either not listening or chose to ignore me. "As to why she converted and decided to become a nun, I don't know dat her professions on either o' dose subjects are pertinent."

I blinked, feeling knocked out of kilter with her calm assertions. "At this point, we don't know what is pertinent and what is not," I reminded her. "Her reasons for being here seem perfectly relevant to me, considering the fact that they may hold the key to why someone would wish to murder her."

"I understand," she replied with composed detachment. "But I'll still not share dat wit ye. Not yet anyway."

"Surely this isn't a matter of the sanctity of the confessional? As I understand, that only applies to priests. And I can't imagine Miss Lennox wouldn't want you to share what she told you if it would help bring her killer to justice."

"Whose justice?" she asked.

I stared at her, once more caught off guard by her words, though this time it might have been the tightening in her voice—the first sign of real emotion I'd seen her exhibit during this entire conversation—that disconcerted me.

"Because ye must realize dat sometimes what society views as justice might not be the same ting as what the Lord does."

"And you're only interested in the Lord's justice?" I guessed.

The corner of her mouth quirked. "Ah, but I didn't say dat now, did I?"

"But as a nun . . ."

"I'm to seek the Lord's will and righteousness? Aye. And I do. Dat's why I said I wouldn't share Miss Lennox's professions *yet*. First, I must pray."

I watched as she turned to pick up a stack of sketchbooks from the shelf of a bookcase, and began to stroll through the tables, laying them out. For her, it seemed the matter was closed, at least for the moment, but not for me. I fisted my hands in frustration, deciding to try a different tactic.

"It bothered you that Miss Lennox's veil had been removed, didn't it? I could see it in your eyes."

She did not look up from what she was doing, but her mouth pressed into a line. "Yes."

"Why? It somehow seemed quite significant to you."

"I was wishin' I knew whether she'd removed it herself, or if someone had removed it for her." Her eyes lifted to meet mine. "Either would be significant, but for different reasons."

I could see what she meant. If Miss Lennox had removed it, it could mean she was having second thoughts about her calling to be a nun, or more puzzling, that she had been trying to conceal her position as a postulant. But if someone else had done it, their motives were just as suspect. Were they trying to remove this reminder of who she was, and what her intentions were? Did they believe her unworthy? Or was it snatched away by accident, ripped from her hair as they grabbed for her when she ran?

Mother Fidelis was right. It could be significant. If nothing else, it might give us insight into the emotions roused just before the murder took place. Unfortunately, there was no way for us to know. Not short of a previously unknown witness coming forward or the killer confessing.

Two students entered the classroom then, stumbling to a halt at the sight of me next to Mother Fidelis. From the look in their eyes, you would think I was planning to force confessions out of them of their darkest sins.

"Find yer seats, girls," the sister said.

They hurried to comply, but never took their eyes from me, memorizing every detail to recite to their classmates later, no doubt.

"I should take my leave," I murmured, lowering my voice so that we could not be overheard. "But if I may, do you believe Miss Lennox told the truth about why she left the abbey grounds?" It was a rushed question, blunt and to the point. I'd asked it that way on purpose, as I'd hoped Mother Fidelis, being unprepared for it and half distracted by the students, would give me an honest reaction.

In her own infuriating way, she did, barely blinking an eyelash as she stood tall and still, staring down at me. "I shall pray on dat, too."

The students seemed to make it a game to dodge my gaze whenever I caught them looking at me as I encountered them in the corridors hurrying to class, as if by meeting my eyes they might suddenly come down with the plague. I knew much of it was adolescent nonsense. After all, I had been their age once, too. I recalled the anxiety and uncertainty, the fascination with that which was different.

However, with these girls there was something more. I detected genuine apprehension beneath some of their furtive glances and hurried walks. It was possible that one of them had discovered my scandalous history and reputation. That would explain some of it, but not all. Some of these girls' faces were stamped with near dread. Why? Did they know something they were afraid to share, something pertaining to Miss Lennox's death? Or were they worried I would ferret out another infraction, something they didn't want the sisters to know about? All I could do was try to look reassuring and hope that if whatever they were hiding had to do with Miss Lennox, eventually they would come forward.

Of course, there was one brazen girl—there always was—who approached me purely for the purpose of solidifying her reputation among her friends. I recognized the tactic, for it had been used often enough among the debutantes during the months I'd spent in London both before and after being wed to Sir Anthony. Speaking with me was some sort of dare, some sort of challenge to be met to prove their mettle, their refusal to bow completely to their mothers' authority, who warned them away from me. It was ridiculous and tiresome, and in a London ballroom I could have walked away. But here at the abbey that wasn't an option if I ever wanted the other girls to trust me.

Mother Paul witnessed the end of my exchange with the girl before stepping in. "Miss Walsh, you're late for French, are you not? And don't think I don't see you as well, Miss Donnelly and Miss Burke."

The girls stiffened where they stood, hiding in the shadows at the bottom of the staircase.

"Get yourselves to class, and do not bother Lady Darby again unless you have something worthwhile to inform her of."

They hurried to scamper off, but her next words, spoken in the same steady voice, momentarily brought their feet to a halt so they could hear them.

"I'm sure Mother Mary Aloysia will wish to discuss your tardiness later today during your study hours."

The students' shoulders deflated, but they did not argue as they disappeared from sight.

Mother Paul turned to me with a small smile, clearly accustomed to adolescent behavior. "Reverend Mother asked me to invite you to join her for tea in an hour."

"Of course. Thank you."

She nodded, tilting her head. "In the meantime, is there anything I can do for you?"

"Actually, yes. Would it be possible to see Miss Lennox's room?"

"Of course. I'll take you up myself." She turned to usher me toward the carved staircase. "Besides, I believe you wished to speak with me."

"I did," I replied, grateful she had remembered. "I wondered if you might have some insights into how Miss Lennox was feeling since you yourself are also a convert to Catholicism."

A small pleat formed between her eyes as we climbed the stairs side by side. "Well, I cannot speak directly for Miss Lennox. But I do know that religion is a very contentious thing." She glanced at me sideways. "Especially here in Ireland, you may have noticed."

"I have."

We followed the staircase around, resuming our climb to the next floor as I waited for Mother Paul to gather her words. "It isn't easy leaving one's family and turning your back on the way of life to which you were raised. I was brought up in a strict and prejudiced Anglican household, and for many years I was as intolerant as all the rest. But then I met a friend who made me begin to see differently, and after a great deal of study and reflection, I realized I had been wrong."

"What made you decide to become a nun? If that's not too impertinent of me to ask," I hastened to add, worried I'd overstepped myself.

She smiled softly, almost in amusement, and I suspected this wasn't the first time she'd been asked such a question, probably by a curious student. "It was less a matter of choice, and more of a . . . giving in to the Lord's calling, His plan for me."

Her answer surprised me. Of course, I'd heard the Bible verses about God making plans for us preached in church on Sunday, but they were presented as if we should each follow the prescribed procedure for our station, not that we had a particular plan intended specifically for each of us. "Is that how all the sisters came to become nuns?" I asked.

"I cannot speak for everyone, but the majority of us, yes. It is not an easy undertaking without one's absolute conviction that it is what the Lord intends."

I nodded, wondering if I'd ever felt that same sort of courageous certainty. I wanted to ask her more about this conviction, but now was not the time. Not if I wished to find out the truth about Miss Lennox's death.

"And Miss Lennox?"

"I don't know how or why Miss Lennox came to the same conclusion," Mother Paul said. "But I would presume it was something similar. Were her family and friends angry at her for converting? Undoubtedly. But angry enough to follow her here and kill her? That is far more difficult to answer. If they were like my family, they washed their hands of her and now pretend she doesn't exist."

She spoke without emotion, as if her family's rejection did not concern her, but my heart squeezed in sympathy all the same.

"I'm sorry," I told her, though the words seemed wholly inadequate.

"There's no need," she turned to say, forcing a smile that allowed me to see she wasn't completely unaffected, even if she thought she should be. "Their actions are not yours. In the end, we are only responsible for ourselves, no matter how much we might wish otherwise."

I suspected she was thinking of her family again, and I decided to move beyond them. "What of the local Protestants? Would any of them be enraged enough by her conversion to harm her? The chief constable said there's been a great deal of unrest between Catholics and Protestants."

"I do not know much about the recent struggles outside this convent, except where it touches on our students or the abbey's well-being, but I do know that it has always been so. Perhaps Catholic emancipation, and O'Connell's election to Parliament, and now this matter of the tithes has riled even the more modest of men. It is possible. But to attack a young woman simply because she has chosen to become a nun? That is quite extreme."

"I agree. But until we understand more, I don't think we can say it's outside the realm of possibility."

"No. I suppose not," she admitted cautiously as we reached the top floor and turned left.

I had not been able to tell from the outside, but I could see now that the top floor was a new addition to the house.

What had been carefully disguised on the exterior was not so well hidden inside. The floor and walls were built from different materials, and the bare stairway and hall still smelled of new construction. The space had been divided into tiny bedrooms, barely large enough for a small bed and dresser, similar to the arrangement of servants' quarters, except I knew from Bree that those were belowstairs. Some of the nuns were lucky enough to be assigned a room with a window. Miss Lennox had not been so fortunate.

Her tiny cell, as Mother Paul called it, was situated down a side corridor which stretched toward the back of the building. What possessions she'd had were meager, and seemed all the more stark being lit only by candlelight. The bed had already been stripped; the sheets washed, refolded, and placed on the bare mattress. Two more dresses exactly like the one she had been wearing when she died hung on a small hook on the wall behind the door. The dresser contained a few sets of undergarments and nightclothes, as well as a Bible and one or two other books, whose titles suggested they'd come from the abbey's library. I thumbed through all three, but found nothing. There were no letters or loose pieces of paper or even page markers.

"Are the sisters allowed to receive correspondence?"

Mother Paul's voice was humored behind me. "Yes. We live in a convent, not a prison. Though as I understand it, even prisoners are allowed to write and receive letters."

"Do you recall whether Miss Lennox ever did?" I asked, hoping that would be explanation enough for my previous query.

She fell silent, and I glanced over my shoulder to see if she was considering the matter. "I don't know. If her family and friends repudiated her, then, of course, it's possible no one ever wrote to her. Mother Mary Fidelis might be a better person to speak to about that."

I bit my lip, wondering if that was something else Mother Fidelis would need to pray about before she could answer.

The top drawer contained a few more personal items—a

hairbrush with strands of light brown hair still woven through the bristles, a toothbrush, a simple bar of soap—but nothing of real interest. I searched behind the drawers to see if anything had fallen through or been stuck behind, and under the mattress, but I didn't expect to find anything. There were no other places in which to hide something, so I abandoned the effort.

"I'm sorry you did not find what you were looking for," Mother Paul said as she closed the door behind us.

I glanced up at her distractedly. "What? No, it's not that. I only wish there had been something there to tell me more about the type of person Miss Lennox was. Some indication of her thoughts and feelings and hopes. Even a suggestion that she preferred lavender instead of roses."

"Well, I should think the fact that she was willing to live a life with so few possessions should say something in itself."

It was not spoken in scolding, but perhaps it should have been, I realized with chagrin.

"Yes. Yes, you're right. It does."

She smiled gently, as if to remove any sting I might be feeling. "I've always believed actions speak more loudly than words. Perhaps, in regards to Miss Lennox, that shall be your guide, as she has not left many words behind to assist you."

Truer words may never have been spoken.

Since many of the sisters and students were in various classes, I elected to settle myself in the parlor to wait for tea with the mother superior. As it was, I needed a few moments to myself, to collect my thoughts and sort through my impressions from the day. At least, that was my plan, but I had not realized until I sat down how tired I was. Between the soft cushions and the warm breeze softly rustling the curtains as it blew through the open windows, I was fighting a losing battle to keep my eyes open.

I must have dozed for a short period, for when next I looked up after what I thought had merely been a long blink, it was to find the reverend mother smiling down at me, her hands folded before her.

"*A leanbh*, you are exhausted," she crooned, sitting down on the settee across from me.

I offered a weak smile of apology, blinking my eyes wider. "I'm fine. Just a bit drowsy in this summer heat."

She shook her head in gentle chastisement. "My dear, you traveled a great distance, and have been running to and fro since you arrived. Of course you're tired."

"Yes, maybe a little," I relented with a soft laugh.

"Do not drive yourself too hard. The Lord does not wish us to toil without ceasing. He did create the Sabbath after all."

"I won't," I assured her, and she nodded in approval.

"Now, I know I promised you tea, but I think perhaps you would be best served by having a rest. We will still be here when you return."

I smiled at her jest, but when I opened my mouth to demur, she stopped me.

"I insist." Her eyes were kind, but I could tell she meant what she said.

I sighed in resignation. Who was I to argue? What she said was true. None of the sisters were going anywhere, for they could not, and if someone local had committed the crime and not yet fled, they weren't likely to. It would draw too much attention. On the other hand, if the killer was not local, they were already long gone, and so there was no urgency there. The same was true of the evidence. There was little risk of it disappearing in the next few hours. If it still existed, we probably would have already found it. There could be no harm in saving the remainder of my questions for the next day, except to our peace of mind.

"You are frustrated," she added in sympathy.

"Only because we still have far more questions than answers." My lips twisted wryly. "Trust me. It's not an altogether uncommon state to find myself in at the beginning of an inquiry."

Her eyes sparkled, appreciating my attempt at levity. "It

is not a comfortable way of life you have chosen. But then again, comfort does not often best serve the Lord."

I did not hear condemnation, only commiseration, in her voice, but her words pressed heavily on my chest all the same. Whether or not she'd realized, she was probing far too close to a topic I was not prepared to talk about.

The clatter of a carriage on the drive outside the window saved me from further conversation. She tipped her head to listen. "Ah, and I suppose this is your husband."

She was a very perceptive woman, and I knew she must have sensed my disquiet, but she let me go easily. "We will discuss whatever we need to in the morning, and then see what is to be done. The rest will keep 'til then."

If only that had been true.

CHAPTER TEN

It did not require a great deal of my skills of perception to realize Gage's morning had been fruitless. Lines of irritation creased his forehead and the corners of his mouth. Lines so tight that even the exhilaration of galloping steeds and the phaeton's swiftness could not dash them away.

"No luck?" I murmured, reaching up to straighten his windblown hair.

"Absolutely none," he grunted, taking my arm to escort me down the steps. "And you?"

"Limited. I did learn some interesting things from Sister Bernard and Mother Paul." I relayed the pertinent details of both discussions, including the bruises on Miss Lennox's arm and the mud and manure on her shoes, as well as what I found, or rather didn't find, in her room.

He paused next to the horses, their heads bent to chomp on the stray tufts of grass growing between gaps in the gravel, and turned back to stare up at the edifice of the abbey. "Yes, I suppose that is something."

I ran a hand down the flank of one of the Friesians, grateful to have a moment alone with Gage before Bree joined us. Particularly with what I had to relay next. "What might be most interesting, however, is what Mother Mary Fidelis refused to tell me."

Hs gaze turned to meet mine. "What do you mean?"

I explained about my frustrating interview and her serene lack of emotion. "I don't know whether she truly does feel the need to pray about what she reveals to us or if she's being deliberately evasive." I scowled. "But either way, I'm certain she knows something."

He leaned one arm against the phaeton and glanced toward the abbey door, his eyes narrowed in thought. "Do you think you can persuade her to tell you? Or ask the mother superior to convince her?"

"I don't think any amount of threats or coaxing is going to make Mother Mary Fidelis talk unless she wants to. She's strong, self-possessed, and extraordinarily perceptive." So much so that I could only surmise she'd suffered her own interior trials for her to be able to so quickly read them in others.

"Yes. I observed something similar earlier when she told us about finding Miss Lennox."

I glanced at him, having forgotten for a moment he had already met her. "She is not someone I would care to challenge to a game of piquet. Not that she would ever play such a heathen game."

"Oh, don't sell yourself short, my dear." His voice was warm with affection. "I would back your keen eye any day."

I knew he was offering me a compliment, but there were days when I would have traded my observant nature for an ounce of his charm. I wondered if Miss Lennox had ever felt the same way. Thus far, I'd heard many people describe her kindness and sweet spirit, but never her charisma and wit. Kindness and sweetness were all well and good, but they also seemed to be easily overlooked.

I lifted a hand to finger my mother's amethyst pendant, which she had given me just before she died, thinking of all that Mother Paul and Marsdale had said. "She must have been very lonely."

Something in my voice must have alerted him to the seriousness of my contemplation, for he turned to search my face. "Who? Miss Lennox?"

"Having to keep all those doubts to herself, away from her

family and friends. Or most of them. Presumably someone introduced her to Catholicism. One's faith and religion are not easy things to grapple with. But to do so alone, and then make the astonishing decision to not only abandon the beliefs of her family, but also to give up the possibility of marriage and children, everything she'd been raised to hope for, and join a convent." I shook my head in admiration. "That takes courage, conviction, and audacity."

"Yes, I suppose it does. Especially knowing the religion one is choosing is rather belittled if not outright despised among your peers." His left eyebrow arched in mocking. "Though, at least as a Catholic, she would be worshipping the same God, studying the same scripture. Or nearly. I can't imagine what her family would have done had she chosen to turn Turk."

I remained silent. I knew next to nothing about the Turkish people or their religion, but Gage had spent time in Greece fighting for their independence from the Ottoman Empire, so I suspected he knew a great deal more than most. In any case, he didn't elaborate, instead returning to the matter at hand.

"But wouldn't Miss Lennox have found herself among friends here, like-minded women devoted to God?"

"Perhaps, but that doesn't mean it was any easier to confide in them. It's not always easy to unlearn the habits one has adopted for one's survival." I felt his eyes on me, and turned to meet them. He would recognize I spoke from experience. "She might have felt more welcome to unburden herself, but that does not mean she was able to do so. Remember, the reverend mother told us she was quieter than most."

"Some people are naturally quiet."

"That's true. And I assume she was." I narrowed my eyes up at the top floor of the abbey, where the nuns' cells were located. "But I think this was more. I think this was very deliberate. I think she was keeping a great deal locked inside her when she was supposed to be purging all and becoming one with Christ." I turned to Gage suddenly. "Why? I can't imagine she made the drastic choice to join a convent without doing a thorough amount of research. She can't have been unaware of what was involved. So why the odd behavior? Why the secrecy?"

"Maybe she was having a change of heart," he suggested. "After all, imagining something is never the same as actually experiencing it. Perhaps she was worried she'd made a mistake."

I frowned, admitting he could be right. But somehow I felt there had to be more to it. The question was, what? And had it had anything to do with her death?

I was still considering this as Bree emerged from the door below the stairs. She shook her head to our looks of query, so we did not waste further time with discussion. If she had anything to share, she did not want it done here. We all climbed into the carriage to set off down the drive. We'd been given permission to come and go as we pleased from the abbey, so there was no need to trouble any of the sisters to let us out of the gate.

Gage slowed as we neared it and leaned closer. "Are you still willing to pay a visit to the Scullys?"

I assured him I was and he passed me the reins as he jumped down to manage the gate. Once we were through, and Gage took control of the horses again, he turned the phaeton back toward the village. A short distance up the road, he turned into a narrow lane which led along the outer perimeter of the abbey's wall.

A grove of dark cedars hid what lay beyond, but once we passed the trees, we emerged into a small clearing which sheltered two cottages—a larger one near the road and a smaller one tucked back near another line of trees. It was a charming little spot, and for a moment I felt I had stumbled into a German fairy tale. There was the woodcutter's cottage, and the tree stump with its ax sunk into it. The small plot of a garden over which a woman toiled. Except for the stone wall of the abbey running along its southern flank, grown thick with moss in places, we could have been deep in the Bavarian forest.

The woman in the garden turned to stare at us as we disturbed her pleasant idyll in our smart yellow phaeton. It was no stretch of the imagination to think this was the first time she'd ever had visitors such as us, and she seemed momentarily stunned. Gage took his time as he set the break, climbed down, and turned to help me and then Bree out, giving her a chance to recover and make her way toward us.

He offered her his most appealing smile. "Mrs. Scully, I presume?"

She bobbed her head, her dark eyes watchful as she wiped her hands on an apron tied about her waist. Her gaze met Bree's, and it was clear they were familiar with each other, probably from belowstairs at the abbey, where Mrs. Scully helped out.

"May I say what a lovely prospect you have? One expects to see the seven dwarves emerge at any moment."

I glanced sideways at him, not surprised he'd had the same impression of this little glade.

But it was clear Mrs. Scully had no idea to what he referred, though her pink cheeks proved she wasn't immune to his allure or good looks. "No dwarves here," she replied uncertainly. "Though we do be visited from time to time by a pair o' troublesome fairies."

For a moment he seemed nonplussed, unable to form a reply, but then he beamed brighter. "Yes, I can imagine."

Bree's head bowed, hiding a smile. If we had forgotten we were in Ireland, here was all the reminder we needed.

Gage cleared his throat. "We've come from the abbey, and we wondered if you and your husband might have a moment to speak with us."

"Yer here about Miss Lennox?"

"Yes."

She nodded her head briskly, the brim of her floppy hat bobbing before her. "Then come an' settle yourselves. Mr. Scully'll be up shortly."

The creak of a hinge alerted us to the presence of someone else, and we turned to see there was an actual wooden door nestled among the moss and overhanging ivy covering the stone wall. It had opened to emit a man with stooping shoulders and a craggy face, followed by the redheaded lad we'd seen picking brambles earlier. This was Mr. Scully, I presumed. He barely spared us a glance. Davy Somers, however, was obviously flustered, for he allowed the door to slip from his fingers and slam shut. The sound was overloud in the quiet clearing filled with birdsong. The older man gave him a sharp glare.

Introductions were made by Mrs. Scully, as her husband seemed incapable of emitting any sounds beyond grunts and Davy remained mute. A more welcoming pair I'd never met. I noted that from time to time Davy would also cast longing glances toward the smaller cottage on the other side of the glade, which I quickly surmised must be his own dwelling. That he did not, in fact, live with the Scullys. This seemed to be proven when Mrs. Scully ushered him after us toward their cottage.

"Why don't ye join us, Davy? Ye knew Miss Lennox, too."

"Not well," he murmured, but followed us without further argument.

The first floor of the cottage was divided into two rooms separated by a set of stairs. The door opened into a spotless kitchen, which smelled of herbs, onion, and the scent of meat cooking for their dinner. We were hurried through into the parlor and offered the few cushioned seats spaced about the room, while Mr. Scully and Davy carried in chairs from the table in the kitchen. Because of the shade of the overarching cedar trees outside, very little light filtered in through the small windows, which necessitated Mrs. Scully ordering Davy to light a few of the candles in the room.

We made awkward small talk, or rather Gage did, while Mrs. Scully bustled about in the kitchen, toasting bread and making tea. I didn't even think of refusing her hospitality, even though I would rather not have partaken of their meager resources. It would have been unconscionably rude to rebuff their kindness, so we all endured the discomfort of

Mr. Scully's and Davy's limited conversation, and then fell on Mrs. Scully's offerings with an enthusiasm that made the old woman's eyes gleam with pleasure.

Once everyone was settled, cradling their cups of warm, watery tea, as there was only one table in the room positioned between me and Bree, Gage decided it was best not to waste any more time with idle chitchat. "As I'm sure you know, my wife and I are investigating the matter of Miss Lennox's death, and we'd like to ask you a few questions. I assume you were all acquainted with her?"

I studied each of their faces as they glanced at one another, perhaps uncertain who should answer first.

"More or less," Mr. Scully replied gruffly. Upon entering the house, he'd removed his hat to reveal thinning gray hair that stuck up in little clusters about his head, a bit like a tufted titmouse.

"As I understand it, the reverend mother sent you to the constabulary after Miss Lennox's body was discovered," Gage asked, urging him to say more.

"I was snorin' here afore the fire wit the missus when they come a-knockin'. Would've sent Davy." He turned his glare on the undergardener. "If he coulda been found."

Davy flushed, his already pink complexion turning to red.

"Oh, now, ye can't be blamin' the lad for goin' to have a pint on an evenin'," Mrs. Scully protested more forcefully than seemed warranted. "You'd have been up at the Yellow House yerself, if'n ye hadn't fallen' asleep, sure ye would."

It was clear she felt some responsibility for the boy, motherly or otherwise, perhaps because he was an orphan. But it was just as apparent, Mr. Scully did not.

"The lad's never around when I've need of him," he groused.

"Dat's not true."

He leaned forward to yell at her. "Don't be tellin' me ye forgot about dat great branch fallin' on the roof? You was yellin' like a banshee den."

"One other time," she scoffed. "Dat doesn't mean never."

This was plainly an argument they'd had a time or two

before, and within Davy's hearing if the way he was staring at his lap was any indication. I glanced at Gage in bewilderment, wondering how we could bring this unhelpful dispute to an end.

Mercifully, Mr. Scully did so for us. "Well, he wasn't here for us den, an' he wasn't here for Miss Lennox neither," he declared with a bit more relish than the situation warranted.

Davy's face paled.

"Hush now," Mrs. Scully scolded, and then lowered her voice as if Davy wouldn't be able to hear her. "Can ye not see the lad feels bad enough about Miss Lennox's death? Ye don't need to be addin' to it."

Mr. Scully harrumphed.

"Were you close to Miss Lennox?" I asked Davy gently, speaking into the strained silence that had descended.

The question was innocent enough, but he blushed again as if I'd meant something quite different. That flush was the curse of his red hair. He couldn't hide anything with a complexion like that. "Not really." He glanced at Mrs. Scully as he spoke in a voice far softer than either of the Scullys and she nodded in encouragement, her hands clasped tightly in her lap as if to restrain herself.

"But you liked her?" I guessed. "Because she was kind?"

He shrugged, still not looking at me. "All the sisters are kind. But Miss Lennox, well, she didn't know how to ignore people. I don't tink she could."

And Davy, whether by accident or choice, was often ignored, I guessed.

"Did she spend a great deal of time in the gardens?" I asked both men.

Mr. Scully grunted and shrugged, making me suspect he didn't pay much attention to who came and went through his domain, so long as they didn't interfere with his work.

Davy was more thoughtful. "I suppose so. I saw her often enough. Usually watchin' the birds. Dat's why she liked the orchard. Some fancy bird o' hers nested there."

I nodded. So perhaps it was true enough that Miss Lennox

liked birds, but I still didn't believe that was the sole reason she'd left the abbey grounds.

Neither did Gage, if the pensive gleam in his eyes was anything to judge by. "Did you ever see her leave the abbey through that hole in the wall in the orchard?"

Davy hesitated and then shook his head. I noticed Mrs. Scully was twisting her napkin in her lap as she watched him.

"Truly?" Gage asked doubtfully.

Davy's eyes flicked to his and then dropped to the floor. "I never saw her leavin', but . . . I saw her standin' next to the wall once, just starin' out across the field."

"Did you ask her what she was doing?"

He shook his head again. "But she saw me. An' she said . . . she said how she wished she could get closer to dat beech tree by the pond. Dat there was a fisher king dat kept flittin' just out o' her reach."

"Fisher king?"

"I tot she was speakin' o' Christ in some fancy way. But she laughed an' told me they must've nested in the tree. Den I knew she meant birds." His voice had gone hoarse near the end, and I wondered if he'd ever spoken so long before in his life.

"She must've been talkin' about the kingfishers," Mrs. Scully chimed in helpfully, her voice sounding almost shrill compared to Davy's low, somber tones.

Davy nodded. "Dat's the one."

"'Cept kingfishers don't nest in trees. They make burrows in the riverbanks."

And if Miss Lennox had been as much of a bird lover as she portrayed, she would have known that. After all, kingfishers were plentiful enough in Ireland, and the brilliant blue feathers of the males made them one of the first birds a young enthusiast took an interest in.

Davy looked up at this pronouncement. His pale eyes swimming with sudden distress.

Sensing the lad needed a moment before being pressed further, Gage turned to Mrs. Scully. "What of you? Did you have much interaction with Miss Lennox?"

"Nay," she replied, her concerned gaze on Davy. "But in what little I did, she was always kind. Davy was right about dat." Her mouth curled upward as if in remembrance. "Had a real sweet smile, she did." Her voice broke at the end, and she reached up to dab at her eyes with a napkin.

Which was all well and good, but it wasn't getting us anywhere with our investigation. From all indications, *someone* had harmed Miss Lennox. Someone had killed her, whether on purpose or by accident. We couldn't know which until we figured out who and why. And hearing about her sweet smile was not getting us any closer to knowing either.

"The field where she was found, with the pond beyond," Gage remarked. "How difficult is it to get to that spot?"

"Not very," Mrs. Scully said. "Ye can approach it from any number o' directions." She gestured toward Davy's cottage. "Follow the abbey wall on down the lane past the trees an' ye can reach it in ten or fifteen minutes."

"Do many people know of its existence?"

"I should say so." She sounded almost offended. "'Tis famous. Least in dese parts."

"Famous? What do you mean?"

"'Twas the sight of a skirmish at the outbreak o' the 1798 Uprising. Don't be tellin' me you've not heard of it? Grove Cottage used to stand just over dat rise beyond The Ponds, an' dat's where they used to plan . . ."

"Moira," Mr. Scully hissed.

Her words stumbled to a halt as she turned to glare at him, but upon seeing the black look in his eyes, her irritation quickly turned to chagrin. Gage and I shared a look of our own.

"Well, I'm sure you understand," she explained with a careless wave of her hand. "'Tis long ago, an' though famous in local lore, mayhap not elsewhere."

Gage passed me his teacup, which I set on the tray on the table at my opposite elbow. "Has it seen any more recent use?"

"What? For meetings an' such? Nay. 'Tis all but been forgotten," Mrs. Scully scoffed.

Did she not realize she couldn't have it both ways? From the glare he sent her under his eyebrows, it was clear her husband had caught her slip. A place could not be both famous and all but forgotten, so which was it? Had she been exaggerating the importance of the site, or was she now trying to moderate its significance?

"What about by Ribbonmen?"

Unfamiliar with this term, I turned to look at Gage where he leaned forward in his chair and almost missed the Scullys' reactions. Mrs. Scully's knuckles turned white where she clasped them in her lap and Mr. Scully's brow turned thunderous.

"Don't know what yer talkin' 'bout," he growled. "We've no Ribbonmen here."

"Are you sure?" Gage's voice fairly dripped with skepticism.

Mr. Scully sat taller, flexing his shoulders. "Aye, I'm sure. Do ye tink I don't know me own neighbors?"

Davy watched this confrontation with interest, waiting until both men fell silent before attempting to speak. "But I've seen men in dat field," he declared, and then cowered under the look Mr. Scully threw his way.

"When?" Gage hurriedly asked, trying to keep him talking before the gardener bullied him into silence.

"Off an' on for years. But . . . but a few weeks ago, I saw a gent in fancy clothes, like yours." He nodded toward Gage's buff trousers and midnight blue frock coat.

"You saw a gentleman? Out in the field?"

He nodded again.

"Where exactly? What was he doing?"

Davy's eyes dropped and he shrugged. "By the pond. 'Twas lookin' toward the abbey. Don't know why."

"Could you see what he looked like?"

"Not well. 'Twas too far."

Mr. Scully's shoulders had relaxed, I noticed, so Davy clearly had not given away anything he was not supposed to. His eyes even seemed to have narrowed in thought, and I wondered if he might have guessed who Davy was describing.

"Did either of you see this gentleman? Or do you have any idea who it might be?" I asked the Scullys.

Mrs. Scully shook her head and glanced at her husband, who sat stonily. "I've not seen anyone strange about. Though I s'pose it could be someting to do wit the new school."

Gage's head lifted. "The day school?"

She nodded. "Some people don't want the nuns teachin' Rathfarnham's children." Her mouth twisted. "Afraid they'll never drive out their popery dat way."

I could tell from Gage's expression this wasn't the first time he'd heard such a complaint. Maybe the workmen he'd spoken with earlier had told him something similar.

I glanced toward the empty hearth, wishing I could make sense of all this. Kingfishers, Ribbonmen, strange gentlemen, and day schools—it was enough to make my head spin. And none of it explained why Miss Lennox had been killed.

CHAPTER ELEVEN

Upon our return to the Priory, by unspoken agreement we all retired to my and Gage's bedchamber. We were all too conscious of this being a strange house filled with curious ears belonging to a staff that was not our own to speak of private matters elsewhere. In fact, Bree admitted she'd been forced to dodge more than one prying query as she made her way through the servants' domain and up to us.

Anderley had not yet returned from the Yellow House, so it was only the three of us clustered together in a corner of the room. I reclined against the headboard propped up by pillows, my shoes and pelisse already discarded on the floor and the bed beside me, while Gage relaxed in the chair nearby, still respectably dressed but for his loosened cravat. Bree gathered up my pelisse and bustled over to the wardrobe.

"Before we hear from Bree," I said, sitting forward slightly, "will one of you please explain to me about these tithes, and secret societies, and Ribbonmen? Because I haven't the faintest idea what anyone is talking about."

Gage's lips curled into a smile. "The Ribbonmen are a secret society who seek to promote the interest of Catholics, particularly in regards to what they view to be the unfair practices of Protestant landlords toward their Catholic tenants."

I arched my eyebrows. "And I suppose the Protestants have a comparable society."

"The Orangemen. Named after the Protestant William of Orange, who, as you know, defeated the Catholic King James II of England's troops at the Battle of the Boyne in 1690, and became King William III of England, Scotland, and Ireland."

"Aye. The so-called Glorious Revolution. Granted greater liberties, so long as ye werena Catholic," Bree remarked dryly, shutting the wardrobe with a sharp thud.

Gage glanced at her, but did not comment. "The Orangemen are sworn to preserve Protestant dominance."

"And let me guess," I sighed. "The Ribbonmen and Orangemen don't like each other?"

"Not in the least. And their clashes have resulted in a number of innocent deaths and violent destructions of property."

That explained Chief Constable Corcoran's worry over them.

"Then the tithes? What have they to do with all of this?" I looked toward where Bree was bending over to pick up my shoes. "And Bree, for goodness' sakes, pull that dressing table bench over here and sit. Your bouncing around the room is making my head ache."

She dropped the shoes by the door and did as I asked without the complaint I knew she would have voiced had I kindly suggested she do so.

"The tithes are an enforced payment in cash or kind— livestock, for example—for the upkeep of the established state church, which, in this case, is the Church of Ireland," Gage explained. "We pay them in England and Scotland, too."

"Yes. I know that. But why is there some dispute over them?" I paused, suddenly grasping the implication. "The payments go to the Church of Ireland, but you said over eighty percent of Ireland is Roman Catholic."

"Precisely. So they are being forced to fund the maintenance of churches they don't attend, and clergy who do not serve them. Then in order to provide for their own mass houses and priests, they must make another voluntary contribution, which is simply too much for many of the subsistence farmers, who barely grow enough to survive as it is."

"Which is why they're revolting?"

"Yes. Refusing to pay their tithes, I gather."

"But won't the government seize their property then, to account for the tithes?"

"They'll try."

"But that doesn't mean the Catholics will let them do so peaceably."

Gage tapped his fingers on the arm of his chair. "I suspect that job falls to the constabulary, which accounts for Chief Constable Corcoran's frustration."

"I overheard some o' the day women talkin' aboot it at the abbey. Mrs. Scully and the like." Bree had wrapped her arms around her middle as if her stomach ached. "They spoke as if the protest was s'posed to be peaceful. That they're s'posed to let the tithe men take their property if they come to collect it when they dinna pay. But when the government puts it up for auction, no one was to buy it."

Gage tilted his head. "Make it more costly for the government to enforce the collection of the unpaid tithes than the tithes were worth. It's clever. If it works."

"Aye. They were worried their husbands wouldna be so good at the peaceable part."

I shifted so that I could lay my head back against the headboard more comfortably. "Well, seeing Mr. Scully's reaction to Gage's questions about the Ribbonmen and the activity in that field behind the abbey, I can understand why."

This surprised a grim smile from Gage. "Yes. He wasn't exactly subtle, was he?"

"The only way he could have been any clearer is if he'd stated outright that he was a member." I looked to Bree, who was staring at the bedside table, seeming lost in thought. "Did you discover anything else today?"

She blinked, focusing her gaze on me. "There was one thing. But I'm no' sure we should give it credence."

"What do you mean?"

She frowned. "Do ye remember the girl I told ye was weepin' a river yesterday?"

Goodness. Had we truly only arrived in Rathfarnham yesterday?

"The simple one?" I replied, fighting my own weariness.

"That be her. Well, she told me that Miss Lennox had a suitor."

I glanced at Gage to see what he had made of this comment.

The lines around his eyes tightened. "Why did she think that?"

"I couldna get a clear answer from her, but she kept insistin', and mutterin' something aboot a boys' school."

Gage sighed in exasperation, uncrossing his leg from over his knee and letting it fall to the floor with a thunk. "Nutgrove. It lies to the east, about a mile or two beyond that pond. One of the men I spoke to today mentioned it. How many potential groups of suspects are we to be given?"

"Do you really think it's worth exploring merely on this girl's suggestion?" I argued. "Miss Lennox joined the convent to become a nun, after all. She was renouncing the possibility of marriage. Why would she be meeting a suitor?"

"I don't know, but I find that to be a much more believable explanation for her being outside the abbey walls than that she was chasing a bird."

"True." I paused to consider the possibility, but then shook my head. "But it still doesn't make any sense. After everything she'd risked, the ostracism from her family, from everyone she'd known and loved, why would she enter a convent only to sneak out to meet a boy?"

"Maybe he wasna a suitor," Bree suggested. "Maybe she did go to meet a man, but the interest wasna romantic, but something else."

We all fell silent, evidently finding that scenario much more plausible. Though that still left any number of unanswered questions. Why? And who? Was he the gentleman Davy had seen near the pond? Did he kill her?

Gage scraped a hand through his hair and sat forward. "Whatever the truth, we've much more investigating to do before this inquiry is any clearer. I want to hear whether Anderley overheard anything at the tavern today, and I should look in on Marsdale." The corner of his mouth quirked. "There's always some chance he's stumbled upon something important in his usual fashion."

I smiled, thinking of our first inquiry together, and Marsdale's unwitting assistance in breaking a crucial alibi.

"I propose we proceed as we've begun. You both remain at the abbey and discover what you can from there, while Anderley and I try to convince the villagers to share what they know with us. Maybe if we're persistent enough, we can wear them down."

"Good luck wi' that," Bree remarked dryly, one of her dimples peeping out.

His eyes lightened at her jest, though frustration still marred his brow. "So I've noticed."

With that decided, they both left so I could rest before dinner. When I awoke, the shadows in the room had deepened, and the sky outside the window had taken on the muted glow of evening. I rolled over to find a folded piece of foolscap resting on the bedside table—a short note from Gage. Apparently, Anderley had returned and wanted his opinion of a suspicious patron at the Yellow House. He told me not to hold dinner for him; that he would return as soon as he could.

I felt a moment's irritation he had not woken me to tell me why this patron was suspicious, or asked me to join them, but then discarded it. If it had truly been important, he would have done so. This was probably a minor matter he'd elected to pursue now rather than sit twiddling his thumbs waiting for tomorrow. Besides, the mother superior had been right. I'd needed this nap.

Pushing upright, I stretched and rang for Bree. I asked her only to repair my appearance, feeling it was pointless to dress for dinner when I would be eating by myself. It had been some months since I'd done so, and the first time since my marriage. I found I did not like it, and elected to take a book down with me to help pass the time and distract me from the silence. Of course, it didn't stop me from noticing the ticking of the clock on the mantel behind me, or the clink of my silverware against the plate, but it did give me something to look at besides the long, empty table.

By the time I'd finished, I was more than eager to escape, telling Dempsey I would forgo my tea until later, hopefully after Gage returned. Instead, since it was such a lovely evening, I elected to take a stroll. Bree brought down a shawl for me, and I set off through the front door and around to the beginning of a trail I'd seen this morning before our departure. Somehow I felt less lonely if I kept moving. I'd noticed this long ago, and, perhaps, so had Miss Lennox. Perhaps that was the key to her roving. Not birds or assignations, but pure lonesomeness.

The trail led farther into the property, under the deep shade of the trees. Here and there small woodland creatures scurried across the path, seeking their burrows, dens, and nests for the night. The air swelled with the chill of evening as it gathered in the dark places beneath the trees and spread outward. With it came the crisp scent of night—the sharp earthiness of evergreens, the musk of peat fires, and the fullness of the nearby sea. I followed the path as it wound through the woods, with no real destination in mind except to breathe in the stillness.

Since the moment we'd received Lord Gage's letter, we'd been scrambling to apprehend what was happening, struggling to catch up. It was disorienting and maddening. And wholly unnecessary. If he'd merely given us a bit more information—a better summary of Miss Lennox's death, the people involved, and the fraught political and religious climate—we would have been better prepared to dive in. Instead, I felt like we were always one step behind, and never fully comprehending the cues in front of us.

I paused at the edge of the forest, to stare out across the fields of crops that rolled away toward the horizon. The neat rows of low-lying plants hiding the potatoes growing beneath the surface, the waving sea of golden, knee-high barley, and

even a small pasture where cattle grazed amid the sweet
green grass on the opposite side of a stream, its water sparkling in the last rays of the dying sun. To the south, I could
see smoke from a chimney curling up away from a cluster of
trees to join the mare's tail clouds trailing overhead. The
shrill *"chee-kee"* cry of a kingfisher brought my gaze back to
the trees surrounding me just in time to watch it lift off from
a perch on one of the highest branches and beat its wings
north toward the abbey and then on to its burrow in one of
the surrounding riverbanks. Unlike Miss Lennox and the
other sisters, he was not restricted to one patch of sky.

Had Miss Lennox come to realize that? That she couldn't
follow the birds wherever they led her? Had she been reconsidering her decision to become a nun? Though if it came to
that, I couldn't imagine the reverend mother begrudging
her choice. After all, she was merely a postulant. No vows
had yet been professed. I supposed that was why they had
these stages. To allow time for the woman to be certain of
her decision, of her calling, before it was too late.

It was such a monumental choice. I imagined they all
must doubt their conclusion at one time or another, as we all
did with important decisions. Mother Paul had said she'd felt
guided by the Lord into her profession as a nun, that many of
the sisters did, but was His will so easy to tell? I had rarely
felt certain about what path I was to take, the direction I was
meant to go. Even now, I still struggled with guilt and doubts
about my past at times, worried they were indications I'd
chosen wrong. But perhaps the sisters were different. Perhaps
their answers came clearer.

It was an unsettling thought somehow, and it left me feeling cold and a bit bereft.

I wrapped my shawl tighter around me against the chill
of a stray breeze trailing its fingers along my neck, fighting
back my dark thoughts, and retraced my steps to the point
where I had seen the path branch, this time turning toward
the south. The light was dim beneath the trees in this part

of the woods. The leaves rustled overhead in the growing force of the wind. Bree had been right this morning. A rainstorm was coming, but not for another hour or more.

Even so, I thought it was better not to dally. Something under these trees made the hair on the back of my neck bristle and my eyes dart to catch every moving shadow. I tried to dismiss it as my own melancholy, except I felt almost as if someone was watching me. Who, I didn't know. At one point, I thought I saw the retreating figure of a woman in a dark skirt, but when I hastened forward, I realized it had been a trick of the light.

I scolded myself for my ridiculousness and pressed on, noticing that my surroundings had begun to change. Here the trees were younger, their trunks thinner, their height shorter than those closer to the house, and there also appeared to be more of an order to their planting. I soon understood why.

A stone slab lay before me on the forest floor just off to the side of the path. Glancing around me, I could see that the trees had actually been planted in concentric circles around it, as if shaping the very grove around something. I slowly approached to find my impression hadn't been far off, for affixed to the slab was a brass plaque. I leaned forward to read.

HERE LIES THE BODY OF GERTRUDE CURRAN
FOURTH DAUGHTER OF JOHN PHILPOT CURRAN
WHO DEPARTED THIS LIFE OCTOBER 6, 1792
AGE TWELVE YEARS.

I stepped back, staring down at the solitary grave and wondering what had happened to poor Gertrude. Who was this father who had been so moved by her death that he'd positioned her final resting place almost within view of the house? Had it been out of love, or guilt?

So absorbed was I in my contemplation that at first I didn't hear the man coming down the trail until he passed through into the inner ring of trees. I looked up at him in surprise at the same time he spotted me and slowed to a stop. He was dressed in dirt-streaked clothes and a broad-brimmed hat. A pair of leather gloves tucked into the pocket of his coat flopped against his side with each step. If that hadn't been clue enough, the large, round basket brimming with bright red fruit, which proved to be wild strawberries, clutched in one hand and the large pruning shears in the other gave him away. This must be the Priory's gardener. And almost certainly the reason I'd felt someone was watching me. I'd probably sensed his approach from some distance off and just not been able to see him.

"Found ole Gertrude's grave, did ye?" he remarked, moving closer.

"Yes." I stared down at the plaque. "Though she wasn't old. Not truly. I was wondering what happened to her."

He nodded, setting the tip of the pruning shears down in the dirt and allowing the handle to rest against his leg so that he could reach up to remove his hat and rub the crook of his arm over his head of thick, mostly gray hair. "Fell out a window, poor lassie."

"How awful."

"Aye. And they say her da weren't never the same."

"How very sad."

"It is, m'lady."

I glanced sideways at him. "You must be the gardener."

He removed his hat again, and made a little bow. "Homer Baugh at yer service, m'lady."

I arched my eyebrows. "Homer? That's quite an auspicious name."

He grinned broadly. "Aye. Me mam worked as a maid at the castle. Used to study the books in the library when she dusted. Decided if she e'er had a son, she'd name him Homer. Married me da, the castle gardener, soon after. An' for sure, here I am."

I smiled, imagining his mother, who as a maid had probably had a limited education, carefully reading the spines, choosing the name printed on one of the thickest books. "You must have grown up following your father around the castle's gardens then?"

"That I did. An' a grand place it was. Then."

"It isn't anymore?"

"Nay. The Ropers, the family who inherited after the ole earl died, they've let it go to ruin. 'Tis used for various tings now. 'Twas a dairy farm for a short while."

"You're jesting. That beautiful building I saw through the trees beyond the main street?"

He nodded. "'Twas weed-choked, grown over, an' scattered wit cowpies last time I saw it. A time or two, I tot about sneakin' in through one o' the tunnels to see what's become of it for meself. But for sure, it'd only make me sad."

I had to agree. Just imagining it in such a state made me sad, and I hadn't grown up there. However, something else he'd said, had caught my attention. "There are tunnels leading to the castle?"

"Oh, aye. Put there durin' the wars betwixt the Round-heads an' the Royalists." His eyes sparkled at the telling. "Just one o' the castle's quirks, along wit the ghosts, an' tales o' the Hellfire Club parties, an' a missing lassie."

I narrowed my eyes skeptically. "Are you having a pull at me?"

"Oh, nay. If'n I was goin' to do dat, I'd be tellin' ye all about me buried treasure."

I laughed, and he rocked back in pleasure, delighted to have amused me. His eyes slid back down toward Gertrude's grave, and he seemed to cock his head in thought.

"Though I should be tellin' ye some believe there's treasure here, buried next to Miss Gertrude. Figuratively speakin', dat is." When I didn't respond, he leaned toward me as if imparting a secret. "Robert Emmet's bones."

I cleared my throat. "Who's that?"

His head reared back in shock. "Ye don't know?"

I shook my head.

"An' you sleepin' in his sweetheart's home." He shook his head and clucked his tongue. "For shame. Well, I'll tell ye. Robert Emmet was a patriot who led the 1803 Rebellion."

I held up a hand. "Wait. Different than the 1798 Rebellion?" My head was beginning to cloud again with confusion. How many rebellions had this village taken part in?

"Aye, but 1803 was much shorter. Just one night. Though it resulted in Emmet bein' tried for treason and executed."

"And his sweetheart?"

"Sarah Curran. Miss Gertrude's younger sister. She and Emmet fell in love an' became secretly engaged because Mr. Curran didn't approve. Emmet was captured 'cause he were tryin' to see her one last time afore he fled to France."

"That's terrible," I exclaimed, imagining how distraught Sarah must have been. "But why would Emmet be buried here beside Sarah's sister?"

His heavy eyebrows lifted. "Because he knew Sarah was wantin' to be buried here. So he made his friends promise to dig him up from the grave the government stuffed him in an' rebury him here. 'Cept Mr. Curran wouldn't let Sarah be laid to rest here." He leaned closer, his eyes alive with speculation. "'Sposedly because of all the criticism he'd received for buryin' Gertrude in unconsecrated ground, but I tink the old devil guessed what their plans were an' he wouldn't have it. Not while he still lived."

I sighed, staring down at the empty ground next to Gertrude's grave. "Well, that's sad. You would think he could have at least given them that. Though I suppose this is all conjecture anyway." I gestured toward the earth. "There's no proof that Emmet is really buried here."

"No, there isn't."

But I could hear in his voice, in the roll of that lovely Irish brogue, that proof or no, he believed it.

As if sensing my thoughts, he looked up at me and smiled. "But I've kept ye long enough," he declared, and I glanced around to see how dim the light had grown. "It'll be full dark soon. Do ye tink ye can make yer way back alone?"

"Yes. I think I can manage." I pointed down the trail leading to the left. "Would this way be shorter?"

"Aye. 'Twill lead ye in through the gardens proper an' round to the side gate."

"Thank you," I replied, and then offered him a smile of my own. "I enjoyed talking with you." I meant it. His storytelling and easy, avuncular banter had cheered me immensely.

"Ah, go on wit ye now. Ye'll be given me a big head."

But I could tell from the twinkle in his blue eyes that he was pleased.

CHAPTER TWELVE

True to his directions, within a few short minutes I found my way into the formal gardens of carefully laid out fruits, vegetables, and flowers, and around to the side gate that opened onto the front drive. Dempsey informed me that my husband had not yet returned, so I took my tea alone in the front parlor and then went up to bed.

Though it was silly considering how often in the past I'd sought my own solitude, I found myself almost wishing Bree would dawdle over my nighttime preparations, but if anything she seemed to be more hurried. I could tell by the dark circles under her eyes and the tight lines at her mouth that she was tired. So when she rebuffed my third attempt at conversation, I fell quiet, allowing her to finish her tasks and seek her own bed. After all, the past few days, with packing and unpacking and modifications for travel, had been more wearying for her than me.

But even with her own preoccupations, Bree was not unobservant. She paused at the threshold to glance back at me where I still sat on the dressing table bench, absently fiddling with the handle of my hairbrush. "I'm sure they'll return shortly."

I didn't pretend not to know who she meant. "Yes, I'm sure you're right. Good night, Bree."

"Good night, m'lady."

I puttered around the room, opening and closing drawers,

studying the paintings—though they were by no means worthy of even a minute's contemplation—deciding what dress I would wear the following morning. Eventually, I found myself reclining in bed with a book, listening to the rain tapping against the windowpanes, but even that couldn't distract me. When finally I heard the sound of horses' hooves on the drive outside, the hands of the clock on the mantel were inching close to midnight.

I waited impatiently, following Gage's progress through the house by the sound of his voice and footsteps. Finally the floorboards outside our door creaked, and the door opened to allow him to slide into the room. He closed the door softly and turned, only to stop short at the sight of me watching him.

"I thought you would be asleep," he admitted, pulling his arms from the sleeves of his frock coat as he moved toward his side of the bed.

I watched as the coat fell to the floor and he sat on the edge of the bed to remove his boots. "I was too restless. This house is strange and . . ." *And it felt wrong lying here without you beside me.* I didn't say the words. I was worried they sounded too needy. But he glanced back at me as if I had.

I dropped my gaze to the coverlet, running my fingers over the lace. Out of the corner of my eye, I saw his cravat drop from his hand. "I take it Anderley won't be attending you tonight."

"No. I sent him to bed."

I closed my book, trying to ignore his waistcoat being added to the growing pile. "Did you eat dinner?"

"At the Yellow House." His lips quirked. "Marsdale was there again."

When his trousers joined the pile, I found I couldn't keep silent any longer. "You know, you could drape all of that over the chair or the end of the bed. It would make less work for Anderley."

Gage paused in unbuttoning his shirt to look at me, and I wiggled my toes, fighting the urge to squirm. "I assure you, Anderley doesn't mind. But would *you* rather I did so?"

I shrugged and looked away, trying to stifle the irritation I felt at his even asking that question. "Do as you wish." I reached over to set my book on the side table, and turned back to find Gage still studying me.

"You're cross with me," he remarked in disbelief.

"Of course, not," I lied, and then asked to distract him, "Was your excursion successful?"

He stared at me a moment longer before sinking down onto the edge of the bed in nothing but his shirt and small-clothes. "Not in the least. That patron Anderley wanted me to observe did prove to behave suspiciously, but only because he was a pickpocket." His shoulders slumped as he shook his head. "Gossip here flies faster than in any London ballroom. It appears that everyone already knows why we're here, and none of them will talk to us."

To you, I thought. I'd yet to be given the opportunity to speak with anyone outside of the abbey. Unless you counted the chief constable. And I didn't. It was true, Gage's charm normally proved to be quite effective in getting people to talk, but this wasn't a London ballroom or a Scottish village. This was Ireland, and I wondered if in this situation his polish and natural charisma didn't work in his favor.

"Though I intend to return to the constabulary tomorrow and have a word with Constable Casey. I would wager quite highly he was listening to our conversation with Corcoran earlier today, and that he's to blame for some of this stubborn silence." He glanced at me, hesitant all of a sudden. "I'd ask you to join us, but I suspect matters may grow quite unpleasant."

"And I have my work to do at the abbey," I finished for him in a taut voice.

"Kiera," he cajoled, leaning toward me. "You *are* cross. Because I left you here?"

It was then I noticed the rouge smeared near his collar, though Gage wasn't finished talking.

"It was a perfectly dull and infuriating evening. I can't even begin to count the number of glares and cold shoulders I suffered. I half expected to discover I'd developed chilblains."

"Oh, I suspect Colleen would've blown on them for you."

Gage's face creased in confusion. "What?"

I arched my eyebrows and nodded toward his collar. "Or was she just blowing on your neck?"

He reached up to pull his collar aside to see it better, and then turned back to me with a tight furrow between his eyes. "Surely you realize this means nothing. The girl was hovering about us all night, trying to bring me more pints. And Marsdale, as you can guess, was absolutely no help in discouraging her."

It was wrong of me, but I rather enjoyed seeing him sweat for once. After an evening spent fretting over him and his absence, it was somehow satisfying to turn it back on him, spiteful though that may have been. Of course, it helped that I had already witnessed Colleen's small bids for his attention the night before, and how he'd ignored her, offering her not even a polite smile.

When I didn't reply immediately, he hastened to add, almost in affront, "Tell me you're not actually doubting me in this, Kiera?"

I turned to stare at the ceiling above the door with a sigh, ignoring his query. "I must say, I can't blame her for trying. She must live a hard life, and I don't imagine many of the men that frequent the Yellow House are much to look at." I tilted my head. "Although I have noticed a few rather good-looking lads. That Celtic dark hair and those bright blue eyes are quite a potent combination."

"Kiera," he growled, for an entirely different reason.

I bit my lip, trying to hide my mirth, but he saw it anyway. My amusement ended on a squeak as he pounced on me, planting a sound kiss on my mouth.

"That was rather poorly done," he murmured, staring down at me.

"Yes, well, you deserved it," I replied pertly. "Serves you right for coming home smelling like another woman."

"I do not smell like another woman."

"No," I admitted, smiling again at his affront. "But you do

smell like a tavern." I wrinkled my nose and tugged at the shoulder of his shirt. "Get rid of this."

The look that flashed in his eyes then had nothing to do with anger or annoyance. "Gladly."

I awoke the next morning rather more tired than I would have wished, but far from vexed by that fact. Not when Gage's apology had been so delightfully thorough.

We discovered it had rained most of the night, but although a few dark clouds still lingered in the east, the sun was already peeping through, setting the water droplets still clinging to the grass to sparkling life. In that moment, staring across the countryside of impossibly rich greens iced in tiny dancing crystals, I found it difficult not to entertain the actual possibility that this land was magical, populated by fairies and pixies and other assorted sprites, who both caused mischief and spun such beauty.

I made no protest as Bree and I were delivered to the abbey and Gage and Anderley set off for the constabulary barracks. Gage was right. There would undoubtedly be unpleasantness and more than a few curses exchanged, and I decided I didn't need to be part of that. Constable Casey was unlikely to tell me any more than he would tell Gage, and though it could be hoped he would at least remain civil if a lady were in the room, from our encounter with the man the day before, I would not wager on it.

I spoke briefly with the mother superior, this time in a small room next to the abbey's modest library, which I assumed to be her office. She appeared wearier than she had during our previous encounters, but that seemed only natural given the strain she must be under. I had little to tell her that she didn't already know, though I did ask if any of the sisters or the students had reported a gentleman lingering near the abbey in recent weeks.

Her brow furrowed in concern. "No. Do you think he might be the culprit?"

"I think it's rather too soon to speculate, but he is some-one we would like to talk with, if he can be located."

She nodded. "I will see what I can find out. If this man didn't try to enter the abbey grounds, perhaps the matter was never reported to me. I do encourage the sisters to use their discretion in such matters."

I could only imagine. If every small detail or difficulty was brought to her attention, she would never accomplish any-thing. I began to rise to my feet to take my leave when she spoke again.

"Mother Mary Fidelis mentioned you would wish to speak with her again this morning." Her eyes were under-standably inquisitive, but I had no way of knowing how much of our conversation the day before Mother Fidelis had revealed to her, or whether she had made known my frustra-tion with her.

So instead I answered simply, "Yes, I would."

"She's taken her drawing class out to the gardens. She said you were welcome to look for her there."

I thanked her and took my leave, eager to discover what Mother Fidelis had to tell me. Had her prayers been answered? If so, what had the answer been?

However, another thought occurred to me as I passed through the abbey's cloak room to the back entrance out onto the terrace. The sisters' and students' outdoor shoes were all lined up in pairs along the walls, except for those belonging to Mother Fidelis's class. In their case, their indoor shoes were placed on a shelf above the accumulating dust and dirt on the floor.

Why had Mother Fidelis chosen to take her class outside today of all days? This early in the morning, the ground and plants would still be wet from last night's rain. I supposed there was always the possibility that she wished for them to attempt to draw the droplets of dew trembling on the petals and the reflection of the water in the sunlight, but both techniques were quite difficult to capture accurately and rather advanced for such a class. Had she another reason for coming out here? Had she hoped we would be able to talk more privately with her students scattered about the garden?

I descended the terrace steps, staying to the central walk for the moment, trying to spare Bree the necessity of repairing the hems of my walking dress and reddish fawn corded silk redingote. It was one of my least favorite ensembles, purchased for me by my sister, who was far more aware of fashion than I. Apparently, the puffed upper sleeves and close-fitting lower sleeves from elbow to wrist were extremely stylish. I just thought them uncomfortable. Though I didn't mind the simple bonnet of rice straw trimmed inside the brim with lilac gauze ribbon.

At first, I didn't encounter anyone, though I peered down each of the lanes that branched off into the various sections of the garden. I assumed I would hear them before I saw them, but if Mother Fidelis was monitoring them closely, I supposed that might not be the case. I began to wonder if the reverend mother had misunderstood, and Mother Fidelis had elected to stay indoors. Or perhaps she'd taken the students down to one of the meadows at the southern end of the grounds. Until I saw a flash of movement ahead near the summerhouse.

As I moved closer, I spied a trio of girls perched on the steps. Though they were spaced apart, one of girls, the bold Miss Walsh from the day before, kept leaning forward to pester the girl in front of her, making their third companion giggle. This third girl was the first to notice me, and her eyes widened in alarm, as if she'd been caught putting spiders in the nuns' beds. Miss Walsh, on the contrary, sat straighter and offered me an innocent smile even though it was quite clear I had witnessed her tugging on the other girl's blond braid. The subject of her torment glanced up at me with a frown and returned to her sketching.

I moved a few steps closer, also bringing into view the pair of girls who were perched on a bench farther down the path to the left. There was no sign of their teacher.

"Mother Mary Fidelis. Where is she?" I asked the third girl, not about to give Miss Walsh the stage.

I glanced down at the blond girl's drawing as I waited for the giggler to find her tongue, recognizing it to be a credible effort. Though I could see she had not been able to resist including the two girls on the bench in it rather than just sketch the flowers. She glanced up at me, almost defensively, and I knew without her having to say a word that she would resent any compliment I tried to give her. So I decided to offer her some assistance instead.

"Don't forget which direction the sun is shining in," I murmured, trusting she would understand what I meant.

She dropped her gaze to examine her sketch, then compared it to the scene in real life and nodded.

In the meantime, the other girl seemed to have gathered herself. "She went toward the orchard," she told me, her eyes cutting down the path.

I started to thank her, but she surprised me by stammering more.

"But she's been gone a long time." She glanced around at the others. "We . . . we were just wonderin' how soon it was 'til our next class. Whether we should go back inside."

A tingle of uneasiness began at the base of my spine. "I imagine she's just helping another student," I replied calmly.

"Jane, most likely," Miss Walsh remarked under her breath, and one of the girls on the bench tittered.

I ignored them. "I'm sure she wishes you to continue working on your sketches. I'll see if I can find her."

The girl nodded, her shoulders lifting, happily passing the burden on to me. However, I noticed the blond student had looked up, and she was observing me more closely. I offered her a reassuring smile and turned to go.

I passed several other pairs of students, seated on benches tucked in about the flowers, and they all pointed me in the same direction. None of them expressed concern, and I didn't wish to alarm them by asking too many questions, so I continued to stroll toward the orchard. There at the end of the trail, just before the arch, sat one lone girl on a blanket spread on a bench in a patch of sunshine. Her eyes were clouded with worry.

"Are you here alone?" I asked.

"No. Molly . . . Miss O'Grady . . ." she corrected herself ". . . went into the orchard to look for Mother Mary Fidelis to ask her a question. But they've both been gone a *really* long time."

I didn't know this girl well enough to guess whether her emphasis meant they had actually been absent a significant amount of time or merely a few minutes, but I decided it was best not to dawdle asking questions. Instead, I turned my footsteps toward the arch. "Do you want to search with me?"

Her expression made it clear she did not, so I told her to wait there. I set off, calling each of their names in a normal manner, hoping one of them would answer. That tingle at the base of my spine had begun to crawl upward toward the base of my neck, making the tiny hairs stand on end. I forced my feet to move at a sedate pace, my voice to remain even, though I wanted to rush forward and demand they answer me.

I wove through the trees toward the back corner, concluding they must have headed in that direction. I don't know how or why I decided that. There was as yet no indication that anything was wrong other than the ambiguous statement of one girl. But I didn't stop to analyze my decision. I simply moved.

The closer I drew to the wall, the more certain I was that something bad had happened. It hovered in the air, like a falcon waiting to strike. No one was answering my queries. No sound was being made at all, not even by the birds. I quickened my steps, rounding one of the last rows of trees when out of nowhere something flew into me.

I gasped and stumbled back a step, barely keeping myself from being knocked to the ground. My arms had instinctively wrapped around whatever had lunged at me, and I realized on an exhale of relief that it was a trembling girl. Her words were stuttered and incoherent, even as I tried to calm her. Eventually, I was forced to grab her by the shoulders and shake her.

"Miss O'Grady," I snapped. "You must calm down."

Her eyes were still wide with fright, but her stammering words stopped.

"Now, try again. *Slowly.*" I searched her face. "Where is Mother Mary Fidelis?"

She blinked once, twice, and then pivoted to glance toward the last tree standing between us and the gap in the wall. "There," she croaked. "She . . . she . . ." She swallowed. "She's dead."

CHAPTER THIRTEEN

Her words were like a punch to the abdomen, driving the air from my lungs. I stared down at her tear-streaked face as dozens of questions formed in my mind, and most of them were just as quickly discarded. My eyes lifted to stare over her shoulder at the fluttering leaves, a kaleidoscope of greens, blocking my view through the gap in the wall to what lay beyond.

The girl hiccupped on a sob, recalling my gaze and my attention. I opened my mouth to ask her my most pressing questions, but then I realized it was pointless. She was in no state to respond, and I would discover the answers to most of them myself in a moment.

Instead, I grasped her shoulders tighter. "Miss O'Grady, I need you to listen to me. I need you to go and tell the mother superior what you've just told me. I need you to do so now, and I need you to do so calmly." I stared into her glazed eyes. "Do you understand me?"

She nodded.

"Then repeat what I said."

"Ye . . . ye be wantin' me to go tell the mother superior what I j-just told ye."

"I'm counting on you," I added for good measure, hoping this weight of responsibility would help her gain better control of herself. "Now, go."

I watched her disappear beyond the trees, wishing for a moment that I could go after her. Then I forced myself to turn and face what lay outside the wall.

My steps felt strangely sluggish even though my thoughts were sharp and piercingly clear. Almost without being conscious of it, I drew my reticule forward and slipped my hand inside, feeling the comforting chill of cold metal. I slid my fingers down over the barrel to the smooth wood of the handle and repositioned the pistol I now almost always carried, pulling it closer to the opening. Whoever had killed Mother Fidelis was likely gone; otherwise they would not have allowed Miss O'Grady to escape unharmed, but I'd learned it was always best to be cautious.

I pressed my other hand to the rough, gritty stone at the gap in the wall, gazing out over the field. Her body lay a short distance away, closer than even Miss Lennox's had lain, the black of her habit a pool of darkness against the sea of green. My heart pounding loudly in my ears, I cautiously leaned forward, looking to the left and then to the right. Seeing no one, I released my grip on my gun, letting it fall back into my reticule, and stepped through.

The grass here was still damp, lying in the shadow of the wall, but the ground near Mother Fidelis was drier, passing in and out of cloud and sunshine. She'd fallen in a patch of clover, the bright red of her blood splattering some of the pale white flowers. She had also been struck by a stone, but this time the blow had come to the side of the head, above the temple, and the rock which had done the damage had been cast aside just a few feet away. I could see blood marring the surface closest to me.

Why? Had the killer had less time to escape, and so he had not wanted to be caught removing the stone? Or had he more time to think since the first murder, realizing that by leaving it he created more confusion? Whatever his reasoning, it seemed clear we could now rule out the possibility that Miss Lennox's death had been an accident.

I moved closer, slowly lowering myself to my knees beside

her, uncaring now if the skirts of my dress were ruined by dew or something much worse. Mother Fidelis's eyes stared blankly off into the distance, and the first thing I did was to close them. There was no reason to wait. I could examine her while we were alone, and then she could be removed and laid out properly in the abbey's small chapel. A minimum of fuss. I suspected that was what she would have wished.

I carefully removed her veil and linen cap and prodded the wound, finding bits of dirt and grit and small bone fragments, some of which I removed and set aside in my handkerchief to be examined more closely. Then I scrutinized the rest of her scalp for further injury, an effort made easier by the short length of her fair red hair. Once finished, I rolled her flat on her back and inspected the rest of her from head to toe. There were no other wounds that I could see, not even a bruise or a small cut. I rolled up her sleeves to check her arms and lifted her habit to view her legs to just above the knees, but seeing no visible marks or reason to suspect I needed to continue, I spared her the indignity of any further examination. It appeared that the only damage to her body had been that fatal blow.

I couldn't help but wonder if she'd seen it coming. Had she turned her head? Is that why the blow fell to the side and not the back, as with Miss Lennox?

"M'lady?"

I glanced up from my contemplation of Mother Fidelis to find Bree standing at the gap in the wall. Her eyes darted back and forth between my face and the corpse lying before me.

"I was comin' to find ye when tha' girl came runnin' by. I couldna make heads nor tails o' what she was sayin', except it was somethin' awful." Her eyes dropped to the body. "Is it . . ."

"Yes," I replied wearily. "One of the sisters. Mother Mary Fidelis."

She nodded, her eyes wide. "What would ye like me to do?"

"Stay there for now, and keep back anyone else who comes this way." I picked up the veil and draped it over Mother Fidelis's head, hiding the wound and her face. There was nothing I could do for Miss O'Grady, but I could spare everyone else the sight.

When that was done, it seemed appropriate that I should say some sort of prayer, even just a short one. It was undoubtedly not the correct one according to Catholic tradition, but it was the best I could do. Then I pushed to my feet and picked my way across the field, conscious of the fact that the damp ground might have preserved footprints of some kind. I leaned down to look at the stone which had been used as a weapon, but other than the blood there were no other discernable markings. I decided it would be best not to move it until Gage arrived, and to allow him the dubious honor.

It wasn't long before the mother superior and Mother Paul arrived, peering around Bree through the gap in the wall. From my position standing solemnly next to Mother Fidelis's body, I could see the pale wide-eyed strain on their faces, the lines of grief.

"It's true then," Reverend Mother exhaled.

"I'm afraid so. I'm sorry," I offered after a pause, feeling as if those two words were wholly inadequate.

She nodded in acceptance. "I know, child." Her eyes stared at the veil covering her sister's face. "Is it the same?"

I knew to what she referred—the same wound as Miss Lennox, the same method of murder, the same killer. "It appears so."

She wavered on her feet, bracing herself against the wall to keep from falling. Mother Paul and Bree both reached out to steady her.

"Reverend Mother, perhaps you should sit," Mother Paul suggested.

But she held up her hand. "No. I'm fine now. 'Twas merely the shock." She inhaled shakily. "In any case, someone should say a prayer over her."

"I said something," I murmured and all three women turned to look at me. "I . . . I'm sure it wasn't the correct words . . ." I added uncertainly.

"I'm sure they were sufficient," Reverend Mother assured

me. "The Lord understands what we mean to say with our hearts, even if our words fall short."

I nodded, grateful I'd not unwittingly insulted them. "At any rate, it would be best if we kept everyone away until my husband arrives."

"Mother Mary Paul has already sent someone for him." She straightened, regaining some of her strength now that the worst of the shock was over. "Once we could make sense of what Miss O'Grady was trying to tell us, we realized that was certainly what you would wish."

"Yes. Thank you," I replied, grateful she'd thought to do so, and grateful we would have less time to wait until Gage reached us. "I suppose you sent Mr. Scully for him."

"Or Davy," Mother Paul said. "Whomever Mrs. Scully could locate first."

"The students have all been taken to the refectory with the other sisters," Mother Superior added, reciting as if to be certain herself that she had thought of everything. "Except Miss O'Grady, of course. I thought it best not to excite the other students. Sister Mary Xaveria will know how to comfort her."

Having seen Miss O'Grady's panic and distress, I concluded she was right. Some of them would have seen her frantically fleeing toward the building, but one could hope they had not understood precisely why.

She shook her head. "The poor lass. That she had to be the one to find her and witness such a sight."

I was more concerned with the fact that she and the rest of her class had been so close by when the attack occurred, but that could be addressed later.

I turned aside, wondering what else could be done as we waited. I stared awkwardly off into the distance, trying not to think about the body that lay at my feet, or the blood staining the leather of my gloves. A sudden chill breeze sent a shiver through me, and I noticed for the first time the gray clouds gathering again in the west. The morning's sunshine had been a lull between storms then. Within another half hour, I gauged the rain would be falling in earnest again.

Not willing to risk the possibility that the shower would wash away what little evidence might be there, I decided to begin pacing the field myself rather than wait for Gage.

"Bree, can you assist me?"

"O' course."

"Come closer, but mind where you step. That looks like rain blowing in and I want to examine these footprints before it's too late. Start near the wall . . ." I pointed ". . . and look for steps that were made after the rain, smashing down the grass and leaving a muddy impression."

"What precisely am I lookin' for?" she asked, her voice muffled from being bent forward. "A man's large print?"

"We can't yet say whether this was done by a man or a woman," I replied, keeping my eyes averted from the sisters. "So any impressions you find are pertinent. We can rule out those made by your and my shoes, and Mother Mary Fidelis's later." I refrained from mentioning what it would mean if we did not find any prints other than those made by the three pairs of shoes I mentioned, but anyone who was thinking logically would realize it. I'd noticed earlier in the mud room that all of the sisters wore the exact same style of outdoor footwear. If we found prints made by ours and Mother Fidelis's shoes and no others, then that must mean some of the prints attributed to Mother Fidelis's could be attributed to another nun. The rest did not bear thinking about until it was necessary.

I exhaled at the sight of the large print stamped in a spot on the ground where the vegetation was sparser, more relieved than I cared to admit by the evidence that at some point there had been an outsider present. The print was a few paces from the body, and decidedly large enough to indicate there had been a man here at some point between midnight and Miss O'Grady's arrival. I could not say for certain anything beyond that, nor could we discard the possibility that another sister had also been here, but the evidence was beginning to point toward a man being our culprit.

The gentleman Davy had seen? Miss Lennox's "suitor"?

There was no way yet to know for sure whether they had anything to do with it.

"I've found a man's footprint," I called out to tell Bree as I opened my reticule to rummage inside. "Let me know if you find any others." At the bottom lay a blue ribbon which had fallen out of my hair at some point probably months ago that I'd tossed inside and forgotten. I pulled it out and carefully laid it beside the impression to measure it. Then I folded the ribbon to mark the length and clamped it between the pages of a small book I also found inside my bag before resuming my search for more prints.

Between us, we located three credible prints made by what appeared to be the same man's shoe. We also identified which prints were ours, as well as four that matched those from Mother Fidelis's shoes. There were any number of smashed or scuffled areas, but without a definitive impression, they were unhelpful to our efforts. I also paused to remember to examine the substances on Mother Fidelis's shoes, ignoring the looks the sisters undoubtedly sent my way as I leaned forward to smell them.

It was in this undignified position that Gage, Anderley, Marsdale, Davy, and several members of the constabulary turned the outer corner of the wall a short distance away to find me. My face flooded with color as Bree helped me to my feet.

"Stop!" she called, and I was grateful she'd had the presence of mind to do so while I was fighting embarrassment.

The men looked to her in surprise and confusion, but followed her order. She stood stiffly beside me, looking slightly horrified that she'd raised her voice to Gage and Marsdale and some of the others.

"We've found several footprints that should be examined more closely," I hastened to explain. "So before you trample them, let us point them out."

Several of the local men, including Chief Constable Corcoran, seemed caught off guard by this pronouncement, but Gage and Anderley took it in stride.

"Show us," Gage said.

Bree moved to do so at my direction, while I stood over Mother Fidelis's body. I felt somewhat protective of her, not wanting any of these men to touch her. A quick glance at the concerned expression in the reverend mother's and Mother Paul's eyes told me they were having similar thoughts.

Gage left Anderley to deal with the footprints while he and Corcoran crossed to see the murder weapon where I'd gestured to it. I looked up as they moved away to see Marsdale come to a stop to stare down at Mother Fidelis lying between us. His face was pale, the whites of his eyes very clear as he gazed down at her.

"Is this . . ." He swallowed and tried again. "Is this how they found Harriet?"

I didn't answer. I couldn't. And I didn't have to. For when he looked up to see why I hadn't, the truth was stamped across my face. He blinked several times and then dropped his gaze back to the nun, but his eyes snagged on my hand. More specifically, on the pair of gloves now cradled in my left hand that I'd removed to search inside my reticule. I knew the blood was not starkly evident against the dark leather, but he obviously understood why I'd taken them off. He stared for a moment and then turned away abruptly, moving off to gaze out toward the cottages in the distance.

Bree, Anderley, and a constable I hadn't met stood next to the impression which had been most distinct. Though I noticed Bree continued to glance across toward where Davy and Constable Casey stood, their feet firmly planted where they'd stopped when she had called out for them to do so. The look Casey gave me, while not outright hostile, was certainly unpleasant, and from time to time he rocked back on his heels, as if anxious to be gone from this place. Given the conversation Gage had intended to have with him that morning, I was surprised to see him present, but I supposed an explanation would have to wait.

Beside him, Davy looked almost sick, and it was no wonder why. I wanted to tell him he didn't have to stay here, that his task was done. But I suspected, as any young man, he would not appreciate me doing so in front of the other men. Fortunately, I was not the only one to recognize his distress.

"Casey, Somers, find something to transport the body with," Corcoran barked.

Mother Paul gestured them through the gap in the wall, clearly having something in mind, or expecting Davy to. Perhaps the same thing they'd used to remove Miss Lennox.

That being dispensed with, Gage and Corcoran turned to me. Facing the chief constable's scowl, at first I felt a bit tongue-tied, but the gentle assurance and confidence in Gage's eyes helped me find my words. With my assessment finished, both men crouched to view the head wound themselves, but to my relief, they did not ask to see anything further, even trusting my examination of the objects I'd collected in my handkerchief to be thorough enough. Ordinary chips of rock and soil transferred from the stone, along with the skull fragments, would hardly prove to be useful in this situation.

"Well," Corcoran declared, rising to his feet. "I don't know what dis villain's reasons be, but I'd say yer stakes have just been raised, to be sure."

"Then maybe some of these mulish, closemouthed people will start talking instead of glaring at us as if we meant to lock up their women and children," Gage remarked in clear frustration. "If they'd spoken sooner . . ." He bit back the rest of the thought with a sigh, knowing it was useless to speculate. "Let's move her inside then. Before this rain begins in earnest." He glanced up at the sky as the first drops began to fall, and reached a hand out to gather me closer.

I didn't object, grateful to have his warmth at my side while I stood watching the heat slowly leach from Mother Fidelis's body forever.

CHAPTER FOURTEEN

Despite the rain and Gage's protests, I insisted on waiting until Mother Fidelis's body had been loaded onto the boards they'd found and carried before us through the abbey grounds to the infirmary and into Sister Bernard's capable hands. Corcoran and his men then took their leave, while the rest of us adjourned to the parlor with the mother superior and Mother Paul. At first, I was surprised the constables did not wish to join us until Gage explained that the chief constable was still determined to leave the entire matter to us. He had only agreed to come to the abbey because Davy had been unclear about what they would find when they arrived, and Gage had thought it prudent to have extra assistance should they be needed.

"And Marsdale?" I asked, huddling deeper into the blanket I'd been given to help stave off the chill and dry my garments.

Gage reached an arm around my back to rub it, eyeing Marsdale where he sat at the edge of the opposite settee, staring into the meager fire Anderley had finally managed to coax to life, and was even now feeding bricks of peat into. "He arrived at the constabulary just as we were setting out for the abbey. He must have overheard me at the Yellow House last night when I relayed my proposed plans for the day to Anderley. Insisted on making himself a nuisance, and I hadn't time to argue with him over it."

"And Constable Casey?"

"Denied it all. Listening to our conversation with Corcoran, telling tales about town, all of it. I decided he should come with us because I hoped whatever we found here would encourage him to stop impeding us and assist us instead."

I nodded, understanding now how they'd all come to be there, if not precisely why. The fire burning steadily, Anderley rose to his feet, allowing the heat of the flames to better reach me. Then he crossed the room to sit in the corner with Bree, who looked just as cold as I felt, wrapped tightly in her blanket. I thought about ordering her closer to the fire, but I knew she would resist. She had elected to remain upstairs with us rather than escape belowstairs because Anderley could not venture that far into the building. I suspected she also wanted to avoid answering questions posed by the day staff and lay sisters.

Mother Superior looked wretched, seeming to have aged a decade before my eyes. She sat rigidly in her chair, blind to Mother Paul's ministrations as she draped another blanket over her shoulders to match the one in her lap. As if by unspoken agreement, we waited to address the horribleness of the topic at hand until the tea had arrived and we had all taken our first fortifying sip. Even so, it was Reverend Mother who spoke first, shaking her head.

"I had no idea he would harm another of my sisters. I . . . I thought this was something to do with Miss Lennox herself, not the abbey. But it appears I was wrong." Her eyes closed almost in pain. "I have been egregiously blind. Father, forgive me."

"I'm not sure any of us expected this," Gage told her. "At the least, it was extremely rash for this person to harm another sister on such a morning, when the damp would leave footprints, with a class of students so nearby."

"Oh, yes. The girls," she gasped, as if that detail had either not occurred to her or slipped her mind. "If he had harmed one of them." She inhaled swiftly, closing her eyes again as if to settle herself. "I'm sorry," she uttered in a calmer voice as she opened them. "My exclamations are not helping matters. What is to be done?"

Gage leaned forward to set his cup down on the table before us. "Well, first of all, I think you should have the workmen begin repairs on that wall immediately."

"Yes, of course. Matters have most certainly changed, and if this sets behind work on the day school, then so be it. We can always open a few weeks late if necessary. It is more important to seal off access to the abbey from such an importune position." Her words grew stronger as she spoke, grateful to focus her thoughts and energy on what needed to be done.

"What of the girls?" I murmured. "Wouldn't it be best if they were removed from the situation and sent home for their summer holiday a bit early?"

She shook her head at this adamantly, though her eyes were troubled. "I can't do that."

I blinked in surprise. "I don't understand. Whyever not?"

"Are either of you familiar with the 1798 Rebellion?"

Gage and I shared a telling glance, remembering what Mrs. Scully had told us.

"We've heard something of it," he replied.

"Well, doubtless what you know is much more from an outsider's perspective, but I remember the uprising and its aftereffects intimately. There was great civil unrest for many years following the conflict. It was not safe to travel about the country, particularly outside Dublin to the west and the south. In fact, that is why I and two of my sisters were educated in York, England, rather than risk the journeys south to Cork, where our oldest sister attended school and then joined the Ursuline Convent there. Though, my mother, sisters, and I did make the trip down for her Profession in 1809. We had to travel by copper-lined stagecoach escorted by two dragoons of armed guards."

My eyes widened at this admission.

"And you fear that because of the secret societies and the resistance to paying tithes, even nonviolent as that's supposed to be, the same thing may be happening again?" Gage guessed.

A spark of wry humor lit her eyes. "I do not know how

familiar you are with the Irish people, but we are a rather passionate and fervent race overall. We are not adept at remaining passive when something we care deeply about is being taken from us." She tilted her head. "I suspect you English are much the same; you simply hide it better."

I lowered my head, stifling a smile.

"That, and you are currently in the role of conqueror. But someday someone will be in the position to challenge you, and we shall see how you react then."

Neither Gage nor Marsdale, who was listening quietly, had an answer for that.

She sighed, as if recalling herself. "But that is all beside the point. What I do know is that there have already been several small skirmishes over the matter to the south, particularly one in County Kilkenny, where a priest there had encouraged his people to place their livestock under his ownership prior to sale in order to resist the tithe collection and the yeomanry tried to enforce a seizure order on them. And just a few days ago in County Wexford, the Irish Constabulary either killed or injured thirty-two people resisting a seizure."

Gage's expression was grim. "I heard something of it myself last night in the tavern."

"Then you understand that people are not ready to accept matters as they stand. There will be more clashes, more injuries, more deaths in the coming days and months, and I do not intend for any of those to be one of my students." Her voice was firm. "I will send letters to each of their parents, and if they are willing to send bullet-proof vehicles and armed guards to collect their daughters, I shall let them go. But otherwise, they shall remain here."

Neither Gage nor I could argue with that assertion. If in fact the civil unrest was growing, as she feared, then she needed to do what was best to protect her students. Closing off that gap in the wall and keeping them inside the abbey seemed to be her safest bet, even with a killer prowling just outside the walls. One could only hope he didn't find a different way in, or another way to draw them out.

I took another sip of my tea, which had since grown too cold to relieve the chill that had settled inside me, and then put it aside.

"Do you think this tithes rebellion could have anything to do with the sisters' deaths?" Gage ruminated.

"I suppose anything is possible." Reverend Mother lifted her hands in bafflement. "But why would they kill a nun and a postulant? They have nothing to do with the tithes or a rebellion."

"But can we truly be certain of that? After all, you just mentioned how a priest had aided those in County Kilkenny."

She frowned and glanced to Mother Paul, who sat placidly listening except for a tiny line which had formed between her brows. "Yes, but they were not allowed to leave the abbey grounds."

"But they did. Miss Lennox at least twice—that we know of—and Mother Fidelis did so today."

Both nuns appeared momentarily flummoxed by the possibility that their fellow sisters might have disobeyed their vows and orders in such a way, venturing farther afield more often than they realized.

"How long has the wall been down?" Marsdale murmured, speaking for the first time since we had stood over Mother Fidelis's body, but for a brief greeting when he was introduced to the sisters.

"Several months. As I mentioned, it happened because of a particularly cold winter and wet spring. We had to wait for the ground to dry before anything could be done. And then with trying to finish the day school . . ." she trailed away ". . . well, it's been some time."

Gage sat forward, removing his arm from around me. "What other ways are there to leave the abbey?"

"There is an exit on all four sides, for safety reasons, you understand. The front gate, of course, and the door which leads to the gardeners' cottages, which I believe you've seen. Another to the south, which shall allow the day students in when the school is opened. It stands open during the day now to admit the workmen. The last, which is rarely used, is hidden in the wall behind a pair of holly trees down near the playing fields."

Which meant neither of the latter two were easily accessible, or convenient to the spot in which Miss Lennox's and Mother Fidelis's bodies had both been found. The door by the playing field was perhaps closest, but it meant a long hike along the wall and fording the stream which led down from the pond above the abbey under an arch in the wall into the grounds. The door by the gardeners' cottages was nearer, but depending on the time of day, it would be much more difficult to avoid being seen.

"Will you show them to us?" Gage asked and then, with a quick glance at the rain still streaming down the windows, added. "Or perhaps have Davy or Mr. Scully do so?"

"Of course."

She made to rise to her feet, but I stopped her. "And while they do so, perhaps Mother Mary Paul could show me and Miss McEvoy . . ." I nodded to Bree ". . . to Mother Mary Fidelis's room."

Gage turned to look at me with approval.

"Of course," she replied.

While the men traipsed back out into the damp, Bree and I followed Mother Paul up the staircase to the upper floor. However, contrary to the day before, I did not attempt to question the sister as we climbed. Though Mother Paul had not said or expressed much about Mother Fidelis's death, I sensed she was seriously aggrieved by the loss. For it to be done in such an appalling way, that would upset anyone.

Even I, who had witnessed dissections and murder by varied unsettling methods, was having difficulty acclimating to this one. Perhaps it had been the sight of her lying there in her nun's habit, a garment that seemed to mark her as removed, untouchable, and yet someone had approached and battered her. Or maybe it was that impermeable persona she had displayed, unruffled by what happened around her and resolved to do what she believed was correct. Even when it meant that she risked taking information which might have told us who had killed both Miss Lennox and herself to the grave.

I wanted to howl in frustration. If only she'd spoken to me yesterday. If only she'd answered my questions. Maybe her death would not have occurred. Maybe the sorrow I saw reflected in Mother Paul's eyes as she opened the door to Mother Fidelis's cell would not be there.

This room was slightly larger than the cell Miss Lennox had been assigned to, though nearly as austere. There was the same bed and dresser, but also a small desk positioned before a window. Mother Fidelis had more personal possessions as well. In addition to her grooming items and Bible, there was a small clock, the wood surrounding its face carved with roses; a number of books on various religious subjects; a sketchbook with a set of charcoals; and a sizable stack of correspondence tossed almost carelessly into the bottom drawer of her dresser. I asked Bree to flip through the books to be sure nothing had been placed between the pages while I opened the sketchbook.

The drawings inside were neither interesting nor particularly inspired. The artist understood composition and shading and all the other techniques one was taught, but they were flat and lifeless. Nothing more than wallpaper reproductions of flowers and trees and various locations within the abbey walls. There were a few scenes I couldn't place, but once I'd shown them to Mother Paul, she was able to recognize them all.

Except one. This one also stood out from the others because it wasn't as sharp and concise, making me wonder whether it had been drawn from memory rather than real life. But why? Was it a place from her life before she had entered the convent? Or was it found somewhere outside the abbey walls? Somewhere she had seen, but not wanted to dawdle near to sketch.

I closed the book and glanced at Bree, who was replacing

the last of the texts she had been perusing on the corner of the desk. "Anything?"

"Nay. No' even a page marker."

I knelt to gather up the letters in the bottom drawer of the dresser, estimating there to be at least twenty missives in all. Rising to my feet, I turned to look at Mother Paul. "I would like to take these and the sketchbook with me to peruse later, if I may?"

She hesitated a second and then nodded. "Whatever you need. Though when you're finished, we would like them back to send to her family along with her other personal belongings."

I promised to handle them with care, and then made one last cursory glance around the room. Staring at the humble wooden cross hanging on the wall at the end of the bed, I couldn't help but wonder how complicated the seemingly simple lives of these women could be. Were we trying too hard to make something out of nothing, or had they been better at concealing the truth than anyone realized?

The only thing I knew for certain was that you couldn't hide the truth from God. And Lord willing, it wouldn't remain hidden from Gage and me either.

By the time the men returned, it had long passed the midday hour, so we all elected to depart in search of sustenance rather than ask the abbey to provide for us. In any case, I wanted time to think and to finish reading Mother Fidelis's letters before I attempted to ask any further questions. So Gage, Bree, and I all squeezed onto the front bench of the phaeton so that she would not get soaked sitting on the uncovered footman's bench behind, and set off toward the Priory with Marsdale and Anderley riding on horseback behind us.

Upon our arrival, the parlor was swiftly made ready for us while Gage and I changed out of our wet and soiled garments. Marsdale would have to be content with drying himself before the fire since he'd invited himself along on this excursion. Though I'd noticed that other than the damp wrinkles, he was impeccably turned out in a new set of clothes, making me assume his valet had been able to follow our trail to Rathfarnham. Gage used the adjoining room, while Bree assisted me, providing me a moment alone with her as we wrestled with the stiff, damp fabric.

"I never had the chance to ask," I said over my shoulder as she tugged at a stubborn button. "Why were you seeking me out earlier? When you passed Miss O'Grady?"

"Oh! I completely forgot. Mrs. Scully wanted to have a word wi' ye. Wouldna tell me why. Said it was best if she talked to ye herself."

I exhaled in relief as the button finally came loose and the gown dropped to pool at my feet. "Well, I suppose she'll understand why I failed to come see her. I'll be sure to speak with her tomorrow."

Bree pulled a simpler maize yellow morning dress from the wardrobe and dropped it over my head and fastened me up before sitting me down in front of the dressing table to repair my hair. Fortunately, my bonnet had preserved most of my unruly tresses from the rain.

"What of you?" I murmured, watching her in the mirror, her own strawberry blond curls matted against her head. "Have you heard from your brother?"

Bree removed and replaced pins, and reshaped a few curls with her fingers, all of which she focused on with a great deal more attention than was warranted. "Nay, m'lady. But he were always slow to respond, if at all."

I frowned, unable to figure out why she seemed to wish to avoid this topic of conversation, but I decided it was not my place to press her.

"It's good enough," I told her as she continued to fidget with one stubborn curl. "Go get yourself dry and warm." She bent to retrieve my gown from the floor but I told her to leave it. "It will keep while you repair yourself and find something to eat. If the stains have ruined it, then so be it.

I don't think I'll ever be able to wear it again without thinking of Mother Mary Fidelis anyway." I rubbed my hands over the lower part of my arms revealed beneath the puffed sleeves of my gown and nodded toward the corner of the dressing table. "The same goes for those gloves."

"Aye, m'lady."

With an ivory shawl draped around my shoulders, I joined the gentlemen in the parlor, where a tea tray and an arrangement of assorted sandwiches and cakes had been laid out for us with commendable speed. I was surprised Gage and Marsdale had not fallen onto them like ravenous wolves, for that was how I felt, but they'd shown admirable restraint, waiting for me to appear. I didn't waste time with conversation, but instead sank down to pour out everyone's tea. They hurried forward from their positions standing near the large stone hearth to sit around the low tea table, and we all ate happily in silence.

The only accompaniment to our contented chewing was the sound of the rain still drumming against the windows beyond the faded chartreuse drapes. Next to the puce cushions of the furniture and the silk goldenrod throw pillows, they would have seemed horribly out of place if not for the patterned Axminster carpet which featured all three shades. Even so, I was glad the remainder of the furniture and décor were rather staid in design so as not to completely overwhelm my senses.

Unsurprisingly, it was Marsdale who spoke first as he reached across to fill his plate with more food. However, he did not open with a flippant gambit, as expected, but a sudden, unexpected insight. "I wonder if that nun went to confront my cousin's killer herself."

I paused with a sandwich lifted partway to my mouth.

"It's possible," Gage said around a mouthful of cake, before swallowing. "Why else would she have been out there when she was supposed to be instructing her students?"

I hesitated, glancing toward the closed door. We'd been cautious not to speak of such matters anywhere the staff might overhear us, but with Marsdale present, there was really no other option. We couldn't exactly invite him up to our bedchamber. I could just imagine what the staff would say about that, not to mention the crude insinuations Marsdale himself would make.

"Actually," I murmured, lowering the sandwich. "She had asked the mother superior to send me to her when I arrived." I frowned. "But she only said in the gardens. I don't know if she meant to take me to that place beyond the wall, or whether she found herself drawn there for some reason." I hesitated to say the third option, but Gage had already gotten there himself.

"Or if she intended for you to both confront the killer together."

I stared at him, trying to understand why the sister would have wanted to do such a thing. Had she thought the culprit could be reasoned with?

"If not that, then why else would he have killed her?" Marsdale asked.

Gage lifted his tea to drink. "Pure opportunity. Reckless though, it seems, with a class full of students so nearby."

"But he may not have even known they were so close," I pointed out. "That could have been mere bad luck." I thought of Miss O'Grady and how terrified she had been. I hoped she would be able to sleep tonight.

He frowned into his cup. "Or maybe Mother Mary Fidelis knew something about Miss Lennox, something about her death that the killer feared would give him away, and so he killed her to keep her quiet."

"Something she refused to share with me yesterday," I added with an aggravated sigh.

His grim smile sympathized with my frustration. "Yes."

I dropped my eyes to the stack of letters I had laid on the settee beside me. "I suppose we may never know."

"What are those?" Marsdale asked.

"All of the correspondence I found in Mother Mary Fidelis's room. I hoped perhaps they might give us some insight into what is happening at that abbey."

His eyes flew back to the pile of missives, his Adam's apple bobbing as he swallowed his latest bite. I could see the thought stamped across his features before he ever uttered the words. "Did my cousin have any letters?"

"I'm afraid not," I replied gently. "At least, none that we could find."

He frowned and nodded, clearly wondering, as I had, why she had not.

Given the circumstances, it was only appropriate that Marsdale should be solemn, and indeed, anything else would have met with a scold from me. But this morose version of his normally irreverent self somehow seemed almost unbearable on a day when we'd already endured so much.

I left them to their discussion, finishing the rest of my food, and then settled back with another cup of tea to arrange Mother Fidelis's correspondence in some sort of order. The men did not offer to help, and for once I was grateful of it. There were not many letters, and it would be easier for one person to peruse them all to look for any context or connection.

Most of them were from various members of her family, so I elected to read all of those in the order they were written rather than separately, reasoning that some of their news would overlap. They seemed to begin almost a decade earlier, when the sisters—then just the reverend mother, a Mother Mary Ignatia, and Mother Fidelis—moved to the abbey. What had become of her letters before that date, I didn't know, but there were allusions to information in previous missives.

The early letters began cordially enough with the normal tedium, affection, and grievances veiled as concern which characterized any family, though I did notice that the Therrins perhaps squabbled more than most. I gathered that they had been a rather wealthy family, which had paid a large dowry to the convent when Mother Fidelis—or Anne, as her family continued to address her—joined. However, some members of the family seemed to refer to the matter as if there had been conditions set to it, though what Mother Fidelis could have done from inside the abbey other than pray, I didn't know.

Then at some point, the letters became rather less affable. Apparently, she had elected to limit her contact with her family even more than she had already done by living in a convent. There were rather spiteful references from some of the letter writers about her telling them that discourse with seculars was a challenge, and that they were an impediment to her religious life. What precisely she had written, I couldn't say, as I did not have access to the missives she had penned them, but from the repetition of similar language across the authors, I assumed some of the passages were direct quotes.

It also became painfully obvious that the Therrins had fallen on hard times. They were angry with her not only for what they called, "abandoning them," but also for paying such a hefty dowry to the convent when a smaller portion would have done, or none at all. There were allusions to something in her past, and accusations of selfishness and hypocrisy after all they'd done for her. In and of itself, this sounded suspicious, but when compared with the other language in the letters, it seemed like just one of those typical childish threats that siblings seemed to coerce each other with even after they became adults. I noted that the last three letters, which went on in the same vein, had not even been opened, their seals unbroken. The only change came in the final letter, which reported the illness and subsequent death of her father two months earlier.

Setting them aside to analyze them, I didn't know how I felt about Mother Fidelis's actions toward her family. In one sense, I could appreciate her desire for peace, and how their incessant pettifoggery could hinder her efforts to focus on higher things. However, they were still her family. If my sister were to have done the same thing, I would have been incredibly hurt, and perhaps felt a little betrayed. I had no delusions that I understood everything about the Roman Catholic Church or becoming a nun, and maybe that accounted for it, but I still found the entire situation bothersome.

Right or wrong, her actions in this didn't so much matter to our inquiry as those of her family. Would one of them have been furious enough to move beyond letter writing to physical confrontation? But then how did Miss Lennox become involved?

When I explained it all to Gage after Marsdale departed, he agreed the supposition was weak, and rather absurd. "And yet many of the rantings in these letters are also absurd and unreasonable," I told him, holding up a pair of them in illustration.

The furrows in his brow deepened as he skimmed their contents. "I see what you mean."

"Is it worth even looking into?"

He raked a hand back through his hair and sighed. "I suppose anything's worth looking into at this point." His pale eyes reflected the same fatigue and frustration I felt. "Though, in this case, perhaps first we should discover whether she had any recent visitors at the abbey. Then maybe find out if any of her family members lodged nearby. If they lived in County . . ." he lifted one of the papers to look at the address ". . . Monaghan, they would have had to spend the night somewhere."

I nodded, following his logic. "If we can't prove they were even near Rathfarnham, then they can't be viable suspects."

"Just so." He sank back against the settee cushions and lifted his arm to drape it over his eyes.

"I did have one more thought."

He grunted for me to continue.

"If Mother Mary Fidelis was so intent on separating herself from the world, with limiting her contact with secular matters, then it wouldn't make much sense for her to have anything to do with the rebellion against paying tithes. 'Render unto Caesar,' and all that."

He lifted his arm so that he could peer under it at me. "But tithes aren't like other taxes. They're money paid to the church and its priests for their maintenance and keep. So it could be argued that it *is* a religious concern."

"I hadn't thought of it that way." I bit my bottom lip in consideration. "So I suppose we must leave that motive on the table as well."

He shifted the stack of letters to the other side of him on the settee, and then pulled me toward him, settling my head in the crook of his neck. "We have too many potential motives, and none that makes much sense."

I had to agree, though it also reminded me of something else. "At least Marsdale has been behaving himself. Though, I admit, it's a bit disconcerting. Bizarrely so. I don't think I heard him make an inappropriate quip all day."

"That's because you didn't spend any time with him before we reached the abbey. I nearly ran him over with the phaeton after a particularly coarse remark he made about abbesses."

I lifted my head to look at him. "Wait. Isn't that . . ." I couldn't finish the sentence.

From the set of his mouth I could tell he didn't wish to explain it either, but he would. "An abbess is also a term to describe a female keeper of a brothel."

I pressed my lips together tightly, fighting a wave of anger. "Well," I murmured on an exhale as I lowered my head back to Gage's shoulder. "I suppose the world can't be going to complete ruin if Marsdale is still capable of being so crude."

His chest lifted beneath my ear on a huff of laughter. "Yes, there is that."

CHAPTER FIFTEEN

As a newlywed, when your husband wakes you in the middle of the night, you naturally expect it to be for a pleasant reason. So to then be flung aside rather cruelly is somewhat a shock to the body.

I lifted my head from the twist of covers into which I'd been thrown, blinking my eyes blearily at the sight of Gage tugging on his trousers. He crossed to the window in three quick strides and parted the curtains to peer out, a stray beam of moonlight striking his bare chest.

"Sebastian, what is it?" I mumbled.

Noises outside the window began to penetrate through the fog in my brain. It sounded as if there was half a dragoon of mounted riders stamping about in the carriage yard, the beat of their horses' hooves accented by their shouts.

I stared wide-eyed at Gage as he bent over searching for something on the floor. He stood, tossing my nightdress to me as he pulled his shirt over his head.

"Dress, and find your pistol. Do not leave this room." He paused at the threshold, staring back at me. "I mean it, Kiera." His voice was sharp, the lines of his body taut. "I'll send Bree to you."

Then he was gone with a slam of the door before I could utter another word. I swallowed the sour coating of fear which had filled my mouth, and forced myself to do what he told me.

With the nightdress over my head, I slid from beneath the warm covers to scamper across the room toward the dressing table. Once standing, I could see the light from the torches the men on horseback carried through the thin curtains, and my legs stiffened. Did they intend to burn the house down?

The crash of something below made me jump, and I turned back to my task. On the third try, I found which drawer Bree had stored my reticule in, but then had to struggle with the string closure on the bag to extract my percussion pistol. I inhaled deeply, telling myself the shot would do me no good should I need it if I could not get my hands to stop shaking.

I inched back toward the window, pulling the curtain cautiously aside to see. The opening of the door brought my head around with a start, but it was only Bree, huddled in a wrapper, her curls restrained under a mobcap. She shut the door and turned the key in the lock, before crossing the room toward me.

"M'lady, get away from there," she hissed. When I ignored her, she tried something harsher. "Do ye want to get shot?"

I scowled. "I am not going to cower in bed with no idea what is happening. Besides, if they set the house ablaze, it's best we know immediately rather than stand around being singed."

This silenced her. After a moment's hesitation, she moved forward to stand at the other side of the window. I peered across the space at her, the torchlight clearly illuminating her as it flickered in the reflection of the glass, and caught her eye in an instant of solidarity. Then the shout of voices below recaptured our attention.

I couldn't see Gage, but I could hear him, his voice rising above the tumult to speak to the men who seemed to be the leaders of this mob, their horses standing at the front, facing the door. I noticed the lower half of the cowards' faces were covered by some sort of kerchief, attempting to obscure their identity.

"All right, then. You've brought enough attention to yourselves. What is it you want?"

I was shocked by the bold defiance of his speech, and afraid of what they might do to him. It was clear he refused to be cowed by these men. Whether this was the right tactic to take, I didn't know, but my muscles tightened in trepidation.

"What we be wantin' is for ye to leave," one of the men sneered in reply. "We've no need of ye nor do we want yer help."

Several of the men voiced their agreement with shouts and grunts.

"We takes care of our own," a second man shouted.

"We don't need the bletherin' English muckin' in our matters, sure we don't," said a third.

At this, Bree's hand tightened on the curtain, making it waver. I glanced up to find her eyes narrowed on the third man.

"He does look familiar, doesn't he?" I whispered.

She flicked an uncertain glance at me. "Maybe."

The horses' hooves began stamping in the dust again, drowning out some of what was said. But I did hear quite clearly when the first man threatened us. "Consider dis yer warnin'." He raised his arm, as if in signal, and the mass of horsemen churning about the yard began to turn as one toward the exit. Even as they did so, two of the men broke off from the group to ride toward one of the smaller outbuildings across the drive, flinging their torches onto the roof. I gasped as the thatch caught fire.

As the last of the horsemen disappeared into the night, Gage led several of the male servants out into the yard toward the smoldering building, shouting directions. After watching their efforts to extinguish the fire for several minutes, I crossed the room to replace my pistol, picking up my wrapper as I stepped over it. Throwing it over my shoulders, I moved to unlock the door.

"But m'lady," Bree protested, hurrying forward to stop me. "Mr. Gage said no' to leave this room."

"Until the riders were gone, yes. But those men are going to need something when they return. Cold water to drink and more to wash in, at the very least. I'm not going to cower in this room when there's something that needs doing."

I didn't wait for Bree to respond, instead throwing open the door and marching downstairs. However, I noticed she quickly followed in my wake, and joined me in the task of organizing the remaining staff. If Gage should become angry at me for disobeying him in this, he would soon learn how little I intended to allow him to boss me around, particularly when it was unwarranted.

As it was, he was so exhausted and filthy when he returned to the house, I don't think he even noticed I'd disregarded his order. He attacked the tea and sandwiches with the same fervor as I imagined the men belowstairs doing, and then dragged himself upstairs to scrub himself as vigorously as he could manage in a hip bath. The Priory had no modern plumbing, or even a cistern on the roof, so in days past we'd had to make do with the servants carrying up buckets of heated water to fill the bathtub. Given the night's activities, I'd decided Gage could wait until the morning to take a full bath.

"Were you able to save the building?" I asked from my perch on the end of the bed as I watched him bathe.

"Yes. Thanks to the rain earlier. The wood was still damp."

"That's a relief."

He sighed. "Yes, but it still suffered significant damage. Which we'll pay to fix, of course."

"Why 'of course'? I'm thinking your father or Lord Wellington should be given the bill," I replied tartly.

He didn't even spare me a glance for that, his eyelids were so heavy. I slid from the bed to hand him a towel as he finished rinsing himself. I knew he was too tired to answer questions, but I had one more I could not go back to sleep without asking.

"Who were they?" I whispered as he rubbed the towel over his shoulders.

His hand stilled and he met my eyes, sensing the fright that still gripped me. "I don't know for certain, but I did notice two or three of them wore a green ribbon in their buttonholes."

I tilted my head in question.

"That means they're Ribbonmen."

My head spun in confusion. "But why?"

"They don't trust us." He scrubbed the towel over his damp hair again before dropping it to the floor beside the hip bath. "That and they're hiding something they're afraid we'll uncover."

I opened my mouth to ask what, but he forestalled me.

"I don't know what." His mouth flattened into a thin line. "But I intend to find out."

I tried not to yawn as I sat waiting for the mother superior in the parlor the next morning, but it was rather a losing battle perched on those soft cushions as I was after such an eventful night. We'd risen from bed later than normal, but those few extra hours had not made up for those lost in the middle of the night. So I pushed to my feet to wander the room, absently examining the contents of the shelves and paintings on the walls. She found me studying an embroidered verse hung on the wall over a small bookshelf, clearly a recent addition to the room. It read, *Go forth and set the world on fire with the love of God.*

"St. Ignatius Loyola," Reverend Mother told me softly. "It is what he told St. Francis Xavier when he departed to spread the Gospel in India and Japan. And it is what I shall tell my sisters when I send them out to establish convents further afield."

I turned to look at her more fully, her face still lifted to the ornate words. "Is that what you intend?"

"Oh, yes. There are so many who are in need of God's love. So many in the world who have thus far been beyond His message. So many girls who need our attention and guidance, and the education we can provide them. It is both our privilege and calling to take it to them." She led me toward the settees. "Plans have already begun for a convent in Navan. And someday we hope to move beyond Ireland. To Canada, and India, and Australia, and Africa."

I considered her words, thinking of how I should feel to be tasked with such an endeavor. "That must be a rather daunting undertaking."

"For the sisters who shall leave us? Yes, in some ways." She smiled gently. "But we cannot truly serve the Lord if we aren't willing to push past what is comfortable. We must let Him guide our paths, even when it frightens us."

I returned her smile with a rather weak one, her words cutting a little too close to the bone. I didn't think anyone could argue I hadn't pushed past what was comfortable. Examining dead bodies and chasing murderers were hardly easy or safe. Though perhaps that was not the Lord's will, but my own folly. A torment of my own making.

I turned aside to stare into the fireplace, wishing I could singe away these doubts as easily as the fire had consumed the brick of peat whose ashes now filled the hearth. I had begun to wish I'd never heard of callings. There were enough things weighing on my mind without the added worry that I was somehow wallowing in macabre earthiness with these inquiries when I should be focusing my thoughts on higher things. Or at the least, concentrating solely on painting portraits.

"You are troubled," Reverend Mother observed, interrupting my thoughts. Her voice rang with empathy. "How can I help?"

"It's just the investigation," I lied, offering her an apologetic smile as I forced my mind back to the matter at hand. "Two are dead, and we don't seem to be any closer to catching whoever did this than we were before. If anything, I'm more confused. And then there's the added worry of whether he intends to strike again." I rubbed a hand against my throbbing temple. "We also had some rather hostile callers in the middle of the night."

"What do you mean?"

"Masked men with torches who would rather we left matters alone."

She reached up to clutch her pectoral cross, shaking her head. "I'm sorry I brought you into this."

"No, please. That is not why I told you. I merely wished to explain my melancholy demeanor, and to warn you." I scowled. "Besides, those men are fools if they think their threats will work on us. We have encountered worse."

Her eyes swam with curiosity, but she did not ask. "Thank you for telling me."

I nodded. "There are a few things I need to know. You gave us a list of all the people who have been to the abbey, including visitors, but I noticed you've only listed those from the last month."

"Yes. I wasn't certain how far in the past you wished to know."

"I wondered if you might remember if Mother Mary Fidelis, or Miss Lennox for that matter, had any visitors even prior to that. Perhaps in the last three or four months?"

"Miss Lennox, no. She never had visitors."

I felt a pang for the girl, all but shunned by her family.

"But Mother Mary Fidelis did."

I sat taller.

"About . . . six weeks ago." Her expression was drawn. "I remember because she came to see me after they'd gone."

"Do you know who it was?"

"Her uncle and brother. They wanted to inform her that her father had died and . . ." She hesitated.

"And to ask her for money," I guessed.

Her stunned expression was confirmation. "Yes. How did you know?"

"Several of their letters to her inferred it."

"I see. Well, as you can imagine, she was distraught, and deeply concerned she'd done something wrong, that she'd sinned against them in some way." Her eyes dropped to her lap. "I tell you all of this in confidence, and yet there are some things I will not share. However, I think that if I tell you that Mother Mary Fidelis had numerous interior trials, you will understand enough. Her wisdom and perception were hard won, and her serenity even harder. Harsh as it seems to say, her family was a stumbling block to her, and their sudden reappearance here after many years was not done as a kindness, but an accusation."

Having read their letters, I thought I grasped at least some of what she was saying.

Reverend Mother met my eyes almost in challenge. "Do you think they had anything to do with this?"

"I don't know," I admitted. "But their reappearance is something to consider. Mr. Gage is asking at the local inns to see if they might have recently stayed nearby."

He also intended to visit the constabulary yet again, to inform Corcoran of our midnight marauders, as well as to ask about the gentlemen living in the area and the local activity in aid of the tithe rebellion. But she didn't need to know all of that. Not unless it became pertinent.

"I also hoped I might be able to speak with Miss O'Grady."

"Of course," she declared, rising to her feet. "I anticipated as much. She's waiting in the library."

M iss O'Grady was seated at one of the only tables in the room, her hands clasped before her, the knuckles white from clenching. She looked up sharply when I entered the room, as if frightened I would pounce. There were dark circles under her pale brown eyes and deep sadness etched in the line of her mouth.

I slowly crossed the room toward her and spoke in a soft voice as I touched the back of the chair across from her. "May I?"

She nodded, watching warily as I pulled the chair out from the table and sat down. I waited, letting her study me, grow accustomed to me, as I'd seen Gage do many times with anxious witnesses and suspects. He seemed to have a knack for setting people at ease that I lacked, but I figured his techniques were worth the attempt.

When she inhaled a breath slightly deeper than the ones before, I decided that was as good as I could expect. "I don't wish to upset you. I know talking about what you saw yesterday is difficult." Her breathing hitched again. "But I need your help. I need to know if you saw anything that could help us find whoever did this."

She shook her head. "I didn't see anyting."

"I know you think you didn't, but you may have without realizing it."

She shook her head again, close to tears.

I searched my mind, trying to think of a way to get her to talk to me. "Forget what happened outside the wall for a minute. Block that from your mind, if you can, and just tell me what you remember about when you were walking through the orchard. You went to look for Mother Fidelis because you had a question?"

"I did," she stammered, swiping away a tear. "About my drawin'. I . . . I didn't think she could've gone far."

"Is there a reason you set off in the direction you did, toward the wall? Did you see something that made you think she went that way?"

She frowned. "I don't know. I started walkin', and . . ."

"Did you call her name?"

"I did, sure I did. And den . . . I tot I heard someting. But I don't know what. Maybe a twig snappin'. Someting. And I started walkin' faster. I couldn't understand why she'd not heard me. And den . . ." She inhaled shakily. "And den I saw the wall, and the gap, and . . ." She couldn't seem to bring herself to say the rest.

"When you peered through the wall, did you see anyone? Did you hear anything?"

She shook her head, and then lowered it to her chest, wrapping her arms around her torso as if to burrow inside herself.

I didn't press her further, suspecting she was being as truthful as she could and more questions would not yield other answers. "Thank you."

She didn't respond. I turned in my chair to see one of the sisters whose name I could not recall standing next to the mother superior. At my look she came forward to comfort the girl, and I took my leave, figuring my presence would not help.

"I wish I could have spared her that," I told the reverend mother as she led me from the room.

"You did well," she replied, responding to the distress in my voice and not the words.

She guided our steps toward what I knew to be the art classroom, and I glanced at her in question.

"I thought perhaps you might wish to speak to the others in her class. They're supposed to be painting today, but without Mother Fidelis to instruct, I thought it might be best to have them draw."

"Who will teach the class now?" I asked, and then felt awful for even thinking of so trivial a thing so soon after her death.

She did not chide me, answering this as calmly as she did everything else. "I suspect we shall have to hire an outside instructor. I don't think any of the other sisters possess the necessary skills."

We paused before the open door of the classroom, watching as a girl dressed as Miss Lennox must have, in the simple gray dress and short white veil of a postulant, struggled in vain to convince the students to stop talking, and for two girls who had crossed the room to return to their seats. By no means would the scene before us be considered rowdy, but it was definitely not the abbey's normal standard.

I glanced at the mother superior to see her reaction, and was surprised to see that it was more resigned than angry. Even so, she clearly was not going to allow this behavior to continue. She moved toward the front of the room. One could not fail to note how quickly the girls hushed and found their seats then. Even the postulant seemed abashed.

The reverend mother turned to stare out at the girls, seeming to pause on each one of them. "From your response, I can see you understand your behavior is unacceptable. I daresay Mother Mary Fidelis would be extremely disappointed were she here to witness it. We are searching for a new instructor for this class, but in the meantime, you will respect Miss Finch's authority. Do I make myself clear?" Her voice never rose, but remained perfectly level the entire speech, and was all the more effective for its calm.

The girls responded as one, promising they would.

She searched their faces a moment longer, as if to be sure of their sincerity, and then looked to where I still hovered near the door. "Now, Lady Darby and her husband are here to look into the matter of both Miss Lennox's and Mother Mary Fidelis's deaths. I've asked her to join your class today, so that if any of you know anything pertinent, you may tell her. I also understand she is a rather renowned portrait artist, so perhaps she might offer you some assistance with your drawings."

I bit back a humorless smile, noticing how cleverly she had arranged this. I had not even realized she was aware of my artistic career, but I could not fault her maneuvering. Not only could I give her students some small amount of tutelage, but it also provided me a way to mingle with them instead of standing at the front of the classroom a bit like a statue.

I dutifully wandered through the desks, peering over the girls' shoulders at their sketches and offering what suggestions I could. Most of them were quite atrocious, as was natural, and so I made the broad statements any instructor must repeat for beginners twelve times a day. Try to draw what you truly see, not what you think you should see. Remember your scale—how big is that object compared to the one next to it? Where is your shading?

However, there were a few students who showed promise, in particular the blond-haired girl I had helped the day before. Her still life was well executed, if a tad lifeless, as still lifes tended to be. I praised her effort, learned her name was Miss Cahill, and offered some more advice on how to approach the manner in which she captured light and reflection on the clear glass vase. She listened intently and then dove in to attempt it.

The half an hour passed pleasantly enough, but it yielded no results in terms of the investigation. Several of the girls eyed me with a wariness that seemed unwarranted, unwilling to meet my eyes, and if they did, glancing away quickly. I was even more certain some of them were hiding something, and I felt increasingly sure it was pertinent to our inquiry. The difficulty lay in convincing them to confide in me before it was too late.

When the class was over, I made my way out to the gardens, waiting near the portico in sight of the doors leading to the kitchen, as I'd told Bree I would. The air was cooler that day, making me glad of the amethyst pelisse with black corded leaf designs and a triangular epaulette-like collar I wore over my gown. I turned my face up to the sunshine, enjoying the feel of its warmth on my cheeks until I heard the door behind me open.

I turned to see Bree and Mrs. Scully emerge, though the latter refused to come farther than the dooryard. Her eyes darted left and then right, chary of something. Yesterday's events had upset her if her sudden skittishness was anything to judge by.

I crossed over to where they stood. "We could talk somewhere else, if you like?" I told Mrs. Scully, trying to set her at ease.

"This'll do, this'll do," she replied hastily. "What I've to tell ye is short-like anyway." Her gaze again swept the limited view of the gardens we could see from where we stood.

"I'm listening."

Her fingers pleated the apron over her gown as if still uncertain. "'Tis only . . . 'tis only there are goin'-ons in town, goin'-ons I think Miss Lennox may've gotten herself involved in."

I glanced at Bree, who appeared just as baffled. "What 'going-ons'?"

She shook her head vehemently. "I can't say. But ye'd best be talkin' to Father Begley at the chapel. He'll tell ye."

Well, that was as ambiguous a bit of information as ever I'd heard. "Mrs. Scully . . ." I began, but she cut me off.

"I must go," she insisted and turned to hurry back inside the kitchens, leaving Bree and me to stare after her.

I opened my mouth to speak, but hesitated at the sound of

footsteps. A moment later Davy's copper head came into view, followed by Mr. Scully's gray one. They did not see us, and I took the opportunity to observe them. Had Mrs. Scully been worried about her husband seeing her speak to us? Is that what had made her so fidgety? But why? Did she suspect him, or Davy, for that matter, of something terrible? Or were they simply involved with these "going-ons" she referred to so obliquely?

Well, whatever the truth, I hoped this Father Begley would speak to us as Mrs. Scully implied. Otherwise, we were going to be left with yet another question we couldn't answer, and that was one more than I could already stomach.

CHAPTER SIXTEEN

Knowing Gage would not be returning for us until after midday, and certain he would be furious were I to go alone, I turned to Bree. "Are you willing to go for a walk?"

She turned to me with a twinkle in her eyes. "What? An' miss the chance to learn how to make boiled baby?"

I cringed, having never enjoyed that particular dessert, especially its appearance. "Have they been putting you to work?"

"No, but I volunteer. Makes 'em more comfortable talkin' to me." She followed my gaze toward the southern end of the abbey grounds. "Where did ye wish to go?"

I'd been staring off in the direction of the playing fields, where the fourth door to the abbey grounds stood hidden by those holly trees the mother superior mentioned. Gage had told me they'd found the lock had been broken, and the door easily opened and shut. However, I did not relish taking such a long trek, or having to ford the stream. So I swung in the direction of the gardeners' cottages. "This way."

Bree followed me across the upper gardens and around the side of the abbey to the northern section of the wall, but when I pulled open the door to step out, she stopped me. "Are ye sure this is a good idea?"

"Yes. There's two of us, so no one will bother us." I smiled in reassurance. "Besides, work has begun to repair the wall today, so there will be workmen about. If someone did wish to make trouble, they wouldn't do so with so many witnesses."

She reluctantly acceded my point, though she wasn't finished questioning me. "Where are we goin'? And why?"

The gardeners' cottages slept drowsily in the sun, the tiny glade silent but for the conversation of a pair of birds overhead. I turned right, following the wall toward Davy's cottage and then beyond.

"I want a closer look at the pond Miss Lennox was supposedly visiting. And I want to see what's over that hill beyond it, where the sheep graze. Maybe that will give us a better idea just what she was doing. Or who she was meeting."

"Why do ye think she went o'er that hill?"

I glanced at her as she fell into step beside me. "Because of her and Mother Mary Fidelis's shoes. If I'm not mistaken, both pairs had manure on them."

"So that's why ye were tryin' to smell 'em yesterday," she murmured in sudden understanding. "I wasna' sure what you were doin'."

I grimaced. "Yes, and neither was anyone else."

"Aye. Just witch doctorin'," she remarked cheekily.

I gave her the gimlet eye.

The trees beyond Davy's cottage gave over to an open field filled with clover and wild thyme, and even patches of pale pink bindweed, buttercups, and blue milkwort. It was a lovely prospect with the distant cottages beyond, and the rough stone wall of the abbey growing wild with creepers in some spots at our backs. The trail more or less followed the wall, except in one spot where a stand of hawthorns had taken root abutting the stone, forcing the trail to go around them.

As Mrs. Scully had said, within ten minutes we reached the corner of the wall at the far end of the abbey's property. We could hear the sounds of men at work as we approached, the low rumble of their voices, and the shuffle and clink of their tools against dirt and stone. They looked up as we strolled past, standing to doff their caps. I nodded in greeting, but did not dally to force them to make small talk. I could feel their eyes following us as we made our way toward the pond, but knew they would eventually lose interest.

Out here, away from the protection of the wall, the breeze grew stronger, whipping down across the meadow and rippling the still water on the pond and the tall grasses growing at its verge. The leaves of the beech tree clapped together like applause. We circled the pond as I tried to imagine what, if anything, could have drawn Miss Lennox down to it not once, but at least twice. Her bird excuse seemed dubious, even watching the whirling flight of a flock of meadow pipits. The beech tree was tall, and boasted a small hole in the trunk just above the height of my head, but not for a kingfisher's nest. It likely belonged to a family of squirrels or some other woodland animal.

The stream which flowed away from the pond down toward the smaller one that stood within the abbey walls was easily crossed by a series of flat rocks, which I suspected had been placed there for this very purpose. We paused on the opposite side of the water, staring back across at the abbey surrounded by its stone wall. The white peaked roof of the summerhouse was just visible above it. There was nothing there to be seen that would frighten or alarm, just a rustic wall and the blue sky speckled with clouds overhead.

Furrowing my brow, I turned to face the rising landscape dotted with sheep. From this vantage, I could see that the hill circled around the pond, cupping it within its palms. The stream which fed the pond flowed in from the north just before the rise of the hill, and the stream which trickled down toward the abbey meandered past the base of the other end of the semicircle. At the base of the hill, it was impossible to tell what was beyond, so I lifted my skirts and began to climb, doing my best to avoid any muck the sheep had left behind.

The hill was not steep, but the climb was far enough that my breath quickened, and my legs—too long cramped in boats and carriages, and seated in parlors—ached from the effort. I inhaled deeply in relief as I reached the top and surveyed the countryside around us. Toward the southeast, past an expanse of fields, I could see the roof of a large building surrounded by trees. The land south of there was filled with nothing but meadows and neatly ordered rows of golden and green crops, stretching all the way to the Priory, I imagined. I couldn't conceive of Miss Lennox or Mother Fidelis setting off in either of those directions, if they ventured any farther at all.

However, the scenery to the north showed much more promise. In that direction, the hill fell away a short distance before rising again, only to have our view blocked by a wall of vegetation. I could see that a road led in that direction, disappearing from our sight behind the trees and bushes. Curious what lay beyond, I set off down the rise to discover how thick the shrubbery was.

Unfortunately, as Bree and I drew nearer, I realized there wasn't simply foliage in our way, but a wall, and a tall one, at that. It was overgrown with creepers and vines, and dappled with moss behind the hedging and tall trees, whose branches overarched the stone. If Miss Lennox or Mother Fidelis had come this way, they would have had to go around it, for there was no door. None that I could see anyway.

I paced toward the west for some time, drawing closer to the cottages I had seen in the distance from the abbey, situated near the road. They could have walked up to the road and around, but that would put them at risk of being seen by anyone living in those homes. Instead, I retraced my steps, curious whether they could have found a way around or through toward the east. But once again, we were foiled. Where the high wall ended a low stone wall began, stopping us and the sheep from stumbling into a deep ditch on the other side.

I scowled. "I guess I was wrong. Maybe they didn't go farther than that hill above the pond." I planted my hands on my hips and turned to survey my surroundings, feeling like I was missing something.

"Isna that far enough? We've already two reports o' a gentleman hangin' aboot that pond."

"Yes, but . . ." I narrowed my eyes. "Didn't Mrs. Scully say this was the rendezvous point for one of the rebellions?"

"Aye. In 1798."

"It's a rather poorly chosen location, don't you think?" She followed my gaze. "There aren't many ways to escape if necessary."

"Not noo. But tha' low stone wall and ditch look new. I imagine the army built those aboot the same time they started construction on their Military Road that leads into the Wicklow Mountains, where all the rebels who got away went into hidin'. That begins just beyond the Yellow House."

I studied the low wall. "I suspect you're right." My gaze traveled back along the low wall to the high wall and its vegetation. "But I still wish I knew what was behind that."

The low branches of a crab apple tree growing next to the high wall caught my eye, and I began striding toward it. I had already leaned over to pull the back hem of my skirts through my legs and tucked it into the belt of my pelisse by the time Bree caught up with me.

"What are you doin'?" she demanded.

I grabbed hold of the branch which stretched out almost parallel to the ground, level with my chest, preparing to hoist myself up. "I'm going to see what's over this wall."

But before I could jump upward, she wrapped an arm around my waist to stop me. "By climbin' a tree! Are ye daft?"

I laughed and turned to look at her. "Bree, I've done it hundreds of times before."

"Maybe. But no' since ye were sixteen, I wager. And no' while ye were in this state."

I sighed. "What state?"

She glared at me as if I were a child trying to hide something from her. I lifted my eyebrows in challenge, letting her know two could play that game.

"I ken your courses are late."

I frowned, considering the matter, and then huffed. "By two days."

"Three."

I crossed my arms over my chest, aggravated we were even having this conversation. "You know as well as I do that my courses are irregular. Two or three days is nothing. Besides, I think I would know if it was possible I was expecting."

She arched a single eyebrow, and I felt a blush begin to burn its way up from my chest.

"Yes, I know it's *possible*. I mean . . . that Gage and I . . . we . . ." I broke off with another huff. "But I think I would know if it was happening. There would be signs."

"You've been exhausted, m'lady."

"Because we've been traveling, and investigating an inquiry, and Gage sometimes wakes me . . ." I sliced my hand in front of me, stopping myself before I said more. "The point is, there are any number of reasons why I'm tired. And none of those involves a . . . a baby."

Bree's brown eyes softened in the midst of this fervent defense, and I looked away, all of a sudden feeling quite vulnerable. I noticed my breathing was much quicker than I wished, and I inhaled deeply, trying to steady it.

"Aye, m'lady," she agreed. "But I'm still no' gonna let ye climb that tree."

Her stubborn expression told me there was no arguing this, so I relented, pulling my skirts from my belt and allowing them to fall back into place.

"I suppose we should start back. Mr. Gage should be returning soon." I felt a vague, uncomfortable stirring, wondering if Gage had noted anything, whether he would even notice if my courses were late. Which they weren't, really. Not yet, anyway.

I turned to scour the wall one last time, trying to shake the thought aside. I stiffened as my gaze snagged on something that looked startlingly familiar.

"A gentleman willna say anythin' until you do," Bree assured me, divining my thoughts, but misreading the reason for my surprise.

I ignored her, moving out into the field in an arc, still facing the wall. "There." I pointed. "Haven't you seen that somewhere before?"

Bree followed my finger, her head tilting in consideration. "Maybe."

The way that single word was drawn out told me she was seeing the same thing I did. That was when I realized why I recognized it.

"Mother Mary Fidelis's sketchbook. That drawing we couldn't place. It was clearly done in spring when this wild cherry tree was blooming. And these creeping cinquefoil flowers weren't depicted. But the rest is the same. The position of the rocks, and the blackthorn, and spindle."

She nodded. "Aye, I see it." She darted a glance at me. "So she'd been here."

I was having a hard enough time believing our luck in finding it, I hadn't even begun to grasp the implications. "Yes. She must have. But why?" I turned to look around me again, back the way we came. "Where was she going? And why did she make that sketch?"

"I dinna ken, m'lady. It seems to lead us nowhere."

"It does, doesn't it? Except at least we now know for certain Miss Lennox wasn't the only one venturing outside the abbey when she shouldn't have been. And Mother Fidelis had professed her vows."

"Her solemn ones." Her expression reminded me this was the most serious of all vows.

"Yes. So what was so important that she would risk, if not precisely breaking them, at least bending them by disobeying her mother superior's orders?" I wasn't well enough versed in convents and the Catholic canon to understand what Mother Fidelis had been jeopardizing, and I didn't need to be to know this wasn't a simple or flippant matter.

Bree shrugged.

"Well, we'd best hurry now. Gage will be waiting." My stomach growled. "And I'm famished anyway. Though, I think I prefer to skip that boiled baby and whatever else they were preparing."

I caught the look Bree was giving me and wrinkled my nose in a scowl. I was not about to attribute my hunger or my finicky appetite to anything other than the result of a vigorous walk and thoughts of a disgusting dish.

"Is that why you've been so mopey lately?" I asked.

Her expression turned wary. "What do you mean?"

I glowered at her, letting her know she wasn't fooling anyone. "You've been uncharacteristically quiet and withdrawn, and downright uncommunicative at times."

Her face went blank, and she stared straight ahead, refusing to look at me.

"Oh, come now, Bree," I pleaded more gently. "I know you're unhappy. Won't you tell me why?"

"I didna ken I was required to report my every thought to ye."

Her tart retort was like a slap in the face, and my head reared back as if it had been one. I was well aware that I was overly familiar with my maid. I certainly didn't need her to remind me of it. If she wanted it to be different, to be normal, then so be it.

"As you wish," I replied, lengthening my stride so that she would fall behind me, as was proper.

"M'lady, I'm—" she gasped.

But I cut her off. "Let's not dawdle now."

I was glad when she didn't try to speak again.

Gage was indeed waiting for us when we emerged through the door by the gardeners' cottages and rounded the corner of the abbey, but it appeared he'd only just arrived. He leapt down from the phaeton and paused at the sight of us crossing the front lawn.

"And where have you been?" he remarked with a smile.

"Out to the pond and over that hill dotted with sheep," I started to explain.

His grin quickly faded. "Beyond the abbey walls?"

I paused before answering, uncertain of his expression. "Yes. I wanted to see if I could figure out where Miss Lennox . . ."

"Why would you do such a thing without me when you know two women have already been murdered there?"

"Why wouldn't I?" I scowled in growing aggravation. "I was perfectly safe, Gage. Bree came with me and the workmen are there preparing the wall. No one was going to harm us."

"That may be so, but no one would have been able to see or hear you once you were on the other side of that hill."

"And how exactly do you know that?"

He tapped his hat against his leg, his eyes darting across my face, searching for some reason not to answer me. "Because I went to look there two days ago."

I arched my eyebrows in mock outrage. "Without me?"

He did not find my reaction humorous. "Yes."

"Well, I suspect you didn't find what we did because you wouldn't have even known to look." I blinked my eyes up at him. "So may I please tell you now, or would you like to scold me further?"

I took his silent glare as assent and swiftly informed him of Mother Fidelis's sketch and what we'd discovered.

His brow puckered in puzzlement. "That is interesting. Though I don't quite see yet how it fits with her murder or Miss Lennox's."

"*Yet* being the operative word." I moved forward so that he could help me into the carriage, and then I waited for him to hand Bree up to the footman's bench and take his place beside me. "I'm almost certain there's a road behind that wall, running west to east. Do you think we might drive down it? And then we should pay a visit to the priest at the Catholic Chapel. Mrs. Scully implied he might have some pertinent information for us about some 'going-ons' Miss Lennox had gotten herself involved in. Her words."

Gage sat quite still through this entire speech. "You've been busy today."

"Of course I have." I clutched my reticule in my lap,

staring over the front of the carriage at the Friesian black horses. "Someone tried to intimidate us last night, threatening to burn down the house we were sleeping in. If two murders weren't incentive enough, that certainly was."

I felt his hand steal into my own, the warmth of his touch reaching me even through our gloves. "If they decide to return, they won't find us so taken by surprise. Or quite so unarmed." His boot nudged a long canvas package lying at our feet in the front of the carriage. "I've seen to that."

I glanced up in surprise as I realized they were almost certainly guns. Rifles, if the shape of the bundle was any indication.

"Courtesy of Corcoran. And he's agreed to spare a pair of cadets to man the gate lodge."

"Well, that's somewhat of a relief." A thought occurred to me. "Do you think these cadets can be trusted?"

"I should say so. But if not, we'll not be defenseless."

I nodded.

He picked up the reins and prodded the horses with a flick of his wrist. "Now, let's go see about this road of yours, but I'm afraid the priest will have to wait until tomorrow." His voice turned wry. "We've been summoned to a dinner party by Mr. LaTouche. You remember him?"

"From the constabulary."

"Yes. Well, apparently all of the most eminent of Rathfarnham's citizens shall be there, and we simply *must* grace them with our presence."

I smiled at the sarcasm in his voice.

"In other words, I do believe we are about to face an inquisition of the village's Protestant elite."

"And we must attend?" It sounded like it would be about as much fun as an autopsy, and I'd had my fill of those long ago.

His demeanor turned sympathetic. "I'm afraid so. If for no reason other than it will give us a chance to question some men who have been dodging my visits."

I sighed. "All right. If nothing else, I suppose it can be hoped they won't be serving boiled baby."

He flicked a startled glance at me.

"You might know of it as roly-poly."

He shook his head as if to clear it. "I know what it is. My father still talks about how they served it on board ship when he was in the Royal Navy. He tells a horrid story about trying to explain the translation to a Spanish general, which, of course, he finds absurdly hilarious. But what made you think of that?"

"Oh, Bree told me they were preparing it belowstairs at the abbey."

"I see." He slowed the horses as we came to the crossroads. Left would lead into town, while to the right sat the cottages we had seen from a distance behind the abbey. Instead, he drove us forward, toward where it looked like the road ended, but in truth it only turned at a right angle to head east.

I could tell immediately this was our road. It was extremely narrow, crowded between two towering walls, the sky blocked by overhanging trees. It was not a road I wished to traverse at night, but in the midst of a sunny summer day, it was quite lovely. Light dappled through the leaves on the overgrown track, as the trees swayed in the breeze, singing an airy, shuffling lullaby. Here there was no birdsong, and no encroachment of humans, not even the thwack of an ax or the scrape of a hoe. Lichen had overtaken much of the stone walls, perfuming the air with its earthy scent.

I didn't have to ask Gage to drive slowly, for the lane was filled with more right-angled bends, directing the road on a crooked course between what must have been the boundary between two properties. Populated by people who didn't desire to mix, if the height of the walls was any indication. I guessed the wall to the south bounded the full domain which formerly belonged to the original owners of Rathfarnham House. But what demesne lay to the north?

When I asked Gage, he considered my question for a moment before replying. "If I had to guess, I would say Rathfarnham Castle. From what I understand, the estate and parklands attached to it were quite extensive. But that land has long since been divided and given over to different uses."

I nodded, remembering how Homer, the Priory's gardener, had told me that part of it was being used as a dairy farm a short time ago. Now that I'd seen the road and the second wall blocking off the castle's old land, it was even more difficult to believe Miss Lennox or Mother Fidelis had ventured beyond the other wall. I tapped my fingers restlessly against the carriage seat, trying to make sense of it all as Gage turned the phaeton around at the spot where the road widened beyond the walls and drove us back through the narrow lane.

Then something else Homer had said tickled at my brain. Something that could explain a great deal. It seemed fantastical, but it was at least worth considering, and paying another visit to the Priory gardener.

CHAPTER SEVENTEEN

Mr. LaTouche's country home, Eden Park, lay only a short distance from the Priory, though I daresay we could have walked there by a more direct route as swiftly as we drove there. In fact, I suspected the grove of trees and chimney smoke I'd spied to the south, half a mile from the border of the Priory's property, belonged to Eden Park. Mr. LaTouche had declared they kept country hours, so the sun was still high in the sky on this long summer day as we pulled up to the columned exterior of his home in our borrowed phaeton. I supposed the grand classical white marble façade might appeal to some, but to my eyes, it looked like someone had attempted to re-create the Parthenon in the midst of the Irish countryside. I found I much preferred the quaint, almost rustic appearance of the Priory, with its ivy-covered walls and chimney, and rough-hewn stone.

Gage leaned toward me with a grin as we pulled up the drive. "Rather suits Mr. LaTouche's perception of his consequence, don't you think?"

My lips quirked. "Rather. Let's just hope he doesn't have an obelisk or shrine tucked away somewhere in his garden so we don't have to speculate on his perception of that."

Gage snorted. "Just so." Then his voice turned wry. "Although I don't think you shall have to worry about voicing that thought, for he shall do it for you." He nodded toward the door and I turned to see Marsdale standing atop the steps speaking to our host and a younger man beside him.

I supposed I should have ceased being amazed at where Marsdale turned up. In any case, I was not altogether irritated to see him. I figured we could count on him as an ally, and that was better than none, even if his ribald humor could sometimes be disconcerting.

Gage had told me he'd encountered Marsdale on more than one occasion about Rathfarnham as he sought potential witnesses with helpful information they were willing to share. I'd been spared his presence as I'd spent much of my time at the abbey. Though Gage admitted, albeit somewhat begrudgingly, that Marsdale had been more useful than he'd anticipated. Together they seemed less like a lone man on a single-minded mission, even as charming as Gage could be, and more like a pair of gentlemen out on a lark. Somehow this had made a few people more comfortable sharing what little they had about the abbey, the nuns, and the town in the form of gossip.

Apparently Rathfarnham was of three minds on the Sisters of Loretto. One, they were happy the sisters were there, and grateful for the services they provided the community. Two, the sisters stayed to themselves and had no effect on them, so they were content to leave them be. Or three, the sisters were a scourge that needed to be driven out. The first group consisted of Catholics, just as the third was Protestants, and their answers to the other questions posed became quite predictable. Either the women who were murdered were saints, or they'd gotten what was coming to them.

However, the second group seemed to be a mixture of the more apathetic Catholics and tolerant Protestants, and as such, their other answers were more interesting. There was some hinting that the nuns didn't stick strictly to their proscribed duties, nor inside the confines of their walls. How or why they knew or suspected this, they wouldn't say, still being too mistrustful of us as outsiders. Others suggested there might be some resentment on the part of a number of Protestants in the community because they feared the sisters would attempt to convert their children. They admitted this made little sense because no one would be forced to send their children to the day school they proposed to open. There was already a Protestant-directed school in town their children could attend. But this proved how unreasonable people could be when it came to matters of religion.

So while Gage had little luck in finding out if Mother Fidelis's relatives might have stayed at a local inn, or uncovering which gentleman might have loitered at the pond outside the abbey—it seemed there were too many with residences in the area to differentiate—he had still had some fortune in gathering information. I had seen how frustrated he was growing at the villagers' refusal to speak with us, but now here was something he could point to, and I was grateful of it. Fear was no small motive, and fear for one's children even more so. If someone had been genuinely frightened for their children, irrational or not, would they have tried to do something about it? Would they have resorted to murder?

I couldn't answer that, but maybe one of the people here tonight could, even though I suspected most of their children had private governesses and tutors or attended elite schools in Dublin or England.

Mr. LaTouche grinned broadly as we climbed the steps toward him, looking as polished as ever, almost as if he'd been dipped in shellac. "Mr. Gage, Lady Darby, how good of ye to join us."

I didn't fail to note he'd addressed me by my courtesy title when I'd asked him to call me Mrs. Gage. I was quite certain he had not forgotten.

"Ye look lovely as the sunset, sure ye do," he added as he bowed over my hand.

I smiled tightly in response, feeling his compliment might have been a bit heavy-handed given I was wearing a dinner dress of golden yellow silk. It was one of my favorite gowns, in spite of its abnormal shade. The drapery crossed in front, allowing a hint of the blond lace chemisette underneath to peek out. It boasted short beret sleeves of a more moderate width than most current fashion, with longer sleeves of white gauze extended from the top of the puffed sleeves to end in a ruche of blond net. Even my headdress of dark violet with white ostrich feathers surprisingly suited me. At least in this ensemble, I knew that I complemented instead of detracted from Gage's impeccable appearance.

Mr. LaTouche gestured to the young man beside him. "May I present my son, Colin."

I could see the resemblance. He possessed the same raven dark hair, the same Irish blue eyes, but where his father was stiff, and rather too polished, Colin was relaxed and self-assured. In some ways, his demeanor reminded me of Gage—the careless, almost effortless charm and grace of a very attractive man, who both knows it and has learned no one likes a man who preens. However, Colin's manner was still colored by youth, and I couldn't help but wonder if ten years ago Gage had been much the same.

"Just returned from Oxford," Mr. LaTouche announced with pride.

Gage congratulated him and shook his hand. "Any plans to see the continent?"

Like many young aristocratic and genteel men, Gage himself had embarked on the Grand Tour after his graduation from Cambridge. Though he had also taken an extended detour in Greece.

Colin's eyes gleamed. "I leave within the week."

"Good man."

"Perhaps you've some tips for the lad." Mr. LaTouche's eyes were a shade less excited than his son about this undertaking, and I felt myself begin to soften toward him at this display of apprehension—a clear indication of his affection for his offspring. Maybe he was not entirely like Lord Gage.

"Of course," Gage replied. "I'm at your disposal."

Colin thanked him, and we passed through into the house, leaving our hosts to greet those who were climbing the steps after us.

The inside of the house was every bit as grand as the exterior, with high, soaring ceilings and wide rooms. No amount of gilding had been spared, and ornate moldings and cornices drew the eyes upward toward the murals painted on both the drawing room and the dining room ceilings. Why anyone should wish their guests to stare upward while they dined rather than conversing with one another, I did not know, but they were lovely, and I would have enjoyed examining them more closely at leisure. The drawing room ceiling depicted figures of Greek myth, while the dining room hosted angels, from strategically draped adults to small cherubs.

"You'd think the artist could have let just one of those togas slip."

I turned a quelling look on Marsdale seated to my left. We were not a large party, only about a dozen total, most of whom were men. Mr. LaTouche, I learned, was a widower, and so could perhaps be forgiven this awkward arrangement. The other two women were obviously good friends with each other, and though polite, neither of them had the slightest bit of interest in me.

In any event, I was the highest-ranking female, thanks to my late husband, and Marsdale the highest-ranking male, so we were given the dubious pleasure of sitting at the middle of the table across from our host. This nod to French etiquette made me wonder whether Mr. LaTouche had more of a continental connection than just his name, or if he simply wanted to be at the center so that he would not miss a word of what was said.

Thus far, nothing had been mentioned of our inquiry, our conversation rather being filled with inconsequential things, but I knew that would not last. And indeed, as the second course of salmon on rye and stewed soles was laid before us, Mr. LaTouche looked up with a smile of commiseration. "Tell us, Lady Darby, how goes your inquiry into the misfortune of those two nuns?"

I glanced toward where Gage sat several places down the table to Mr. LaTouche's right, uncertain how much to reveal, and caught sight of Colin's anxious frown. It was evident he didn't approve of his father's choice of conversational topic. "We're making progress," I replied obliquely.

"That's excellent to hear. But no suspects to arrest yet?" His eyebrows lifted in query.

"No." Then to stem any criticism, I added, "One has to be absolutely certain of such things before smearing a good man's name."

"Certain, though, ye are, that it is a man?" a gentleman, who I seemed to remember being another mill owner, asked while licking sauce from his fingers. "It couldn't've been another one of these nuns?"

"Well, nothing is definite at this point, but we are relatively certain, yes."

"I hear you've spent some time with the sisters inside that convent of theirs." Dr. Lynch, a professor at Trinity College in Dublin, leaned forward in interest. "What was it like?"

"Much as you'd expect," I replied, and then realized I had no idea what these men expected. "They keep to a strict schedule. Prayers, meals, classes, tending the garden and other areas of the abbey. It's very quiet, and for the most part peaceful, as are most of the sisters. The sort of place no one ever imagines murders happening."

"But they did."

I looked up into the hard eyes of Mr. Gibney, a man whose occupation—if he had any—I could not recall. He seemed to be the type of man who disapproved of anyone and everything, and delighted in nothing so much as correcting and belittling other people. "Yes."

Before anyone else could ask me a question, Gage leapt into the small silence, rescuing me. "Actually, there is one thing we could use your assistance with."

Mr. LaTouche perked up with interest. "What's that, Mr. Gage?"

Gage's mouth curled in a self-deprecating grin that still somehow managed to cajole. "We've been informed by several witnesses that a man dressed as a gentleman was seen ambling about an area behind the abbey which we're told is, or used to be, called The Ponds. This area is close enough to where both women were discovered to cause some concern." He raised his hand to forestall any arguments. "We know there might be a perfectly reasonable explanation for why this gentleman was there. Perhaps he's interested in architecture, or is a student of history. He could have been bird watching."

I nearly choked at this reference to Miss Lennox's dubious excuse, and then my hand tightened around my fork at hearing the lie he so easily delivered next.

"Whatever the reason, at this point, we have no proof he had contact with either of the women. But the fact that he has not come forward to explain his presence, you see, is cause for some concern." His eyes scanned the faces at the table, as mine did. "So if any of you know who happened to be there, please ask him to speak with us, that we might eliminate him from our suspect list."

"What's it matter if a gentleman was there?" the mill owner asked. "'Tis clear to me he has nottin' to do wit dis."

"You must be quite the prescient then, my good man," Marsdale remarked, raising his glass to him.

"I don't like any untidy loose ends in my investigations. They cause problems for the King's Counsel later," Gage explained. "And this gentleman may have seen something that could help us, something he may not even realize has importance."

"Could it be one o' the Ribbonmen?" Dr. Lynch remarked as the footmen entered and began to whisk our plates away to be replaced by the next course. "After all, some of dem dress and display the mannerisms of a gentleman."

I glanced sideways at the professor. That was as sly an insult as I'd ever heard pronounced, and from the look in his eyes, I didn't think he realized he'd even given it.

"Maybe. They're all up in arms about these tithes," one of the other men interjected, and the conversation dissolved into a discussion of politics.

Marsdale lifted a hand to his mouth and yawned, not even bothering to pretend to find the discussion interesting. It was rude and slighting, and he knew he could get away with it because he was a duke's son and a guest. His eyes twinkled as he flicked them sideways at me, letting me see he was doing it on purpose. This realization made me want to both kick him underneath the table and laugh behind my serviette. I settled for biting my lip and staring down at my plate of stewed beef steaks and potato pudding.

Mr. LaTouche meanwhile had stiffened as if a poker had been thrust up his back, and he tried to change the subject. His son appeared equally uncomfortable, picking at his food, his brow lowered in what almost appeared to be distress. However, some of the other men, fueled by the drinks their host had offered in the drawing room and his fine selection of wine at the table, were enjoying this opportunity to rant on what appeared to be a favorite grievance.

"I don't know what they're complainin' about. I don't attend church here more 'an once or twice a season, and I still pay me tithes," Mr. Gibney groused. His sallow face pinched with affront.

"To be sure," someone chimed in to agree.

"The stubborn sods already got their emancipation, thanks to Wellington and his lot yieldin' to their threats o' an armed rebellion. And look what good it did? More threats. Ungrateful wretches."

"Shoulda let 'em have their rebellion. And crushed 'em once and for all." The mill owner's eyes narrowed.

"I believe there was concern for the loss of life of British soldiers and innocent civilians," Gage chimed in. "Not to mention the cost."

"Let the papists pay for it," he snapped, defiant to the end.

"With what?" Marsdale drawled idly. "From what I can tell, most of them don't have two pence to rub together."

"That's because they bury it in the ground like their potatoes, hidin' it away so we don't know they have it." Mr. Gibney retorted.

The mill owner huffed. "If they bother to exert themselves to work at all. Most of 'em are as lazy as the day is long. They want everyting to be given to 'em."

I frowned. I'd heard these same complaints and thoughtless jests made about the Irish in London and Edinburgh and elsewhere for most of my life, and never thought twice about them. But being here, seeing how they worked in the fields and their shops and in service at homes, I'd seen no evidence of this being true.

Marsdale was right. I'd seen the old cottages and mud daub homes of the lower classes of Irish society, a large majority of which were Catholic. They didn't appear to have an abundance of extra income, nor did I believe they were burying it and saving it for a rainy day, or the moment they finally kicked the English off their island.

How could these men not see it? How could they not hear how ridiculous they sounded? They were wealthy Anglicans, part of the small majority controlling the island. Most of these men protesting the tithes were poor Catholic farmers.

Mr. Gibney forked a bit of beef steak, gesturing with it, so the juices splattered across the table. "To be sure. Ye don't see the Presbyterians and Methodists complainin'."

"Do their churches and clergy not share in the tithes?" Gage asked carefully.

"The Papist priests were offered the same, but they refused."

Marsdale sat back, waving a footman over to refill his glass. "Probably worried the government would expect them to lie on their backs and give them something in return."

It was a crude, but somehow effective metaphor. And managed to successfully silence the men at the table long enough for their host to distract them with a new topic.

Whatever hopes I might have held that the situation in Ireland was not volatile had been effectively crushed. Not everyone at the table had spewed the same vitriol, but they also hadn't spoken up to suppress it, which was almost equally disturbing. Gage's eyes reflected the same troubling thoughts mine did. Even Marsdale appeared slightly dyspeptic, as if the discussion as much as the food had not agreed with him.

So when Mr. LaTouche asked to speak with me and Gage privately as we left the dining room, I suspected he meant to apologize or soften the hateful words of his friends. Instead, he clasped his hands behind his back and frowned at the pedestal of the sculpture we stood next to in the rear of the entry hall where he had pulled us aside. He stared for so long that I turned to look, wondering if he wished us to examine it.

His eyes lifted and his mouth pressed into a thin, humorless line. "I'm the gentleman who was seen behind the abbey."

I stiffened in surprise, but Gage made no discernable reaction. I turned to look at him curiously, realizing he'd already known, or at least guessed. Had he seen something in his face tonight that I had not?

I turned back to Mr. LaTouche as he continued to speak. "I did not realize it was important for you to know, or otherwise I would have informed you earlier, of course."

"Why were you there?" Gage replied.

He inhaled deeply, seeming to force his next words out. "Miss Lennox contacted me and asked me to meet her there."

My husband's eyebrows lifted nearly as high as mine did. "She contacted you? How?"

"By letter."

"Do you still have it?"

"I don't. I . . ." He hesitated. "I burned it."

Gage's brow furrowed. "Before or after she was found dead?"

"After." I could tell that inside he was squirming with guilt even as his exterior remained rigidly still.

"I see." An entire soliloquy was contained in those two words. "And what did she tell you?"

I noticed Gage didn't waste time by asking if he'd ever managed to speak to her, for we already knew they'd been seen together. But Mr. LaTouche didn't know that. I could see in his eyes that he wondered just how much we knew, trying to calculate how much to say. When finally he exhaled, allowing his tight shoulders to relax a fraction, I thought we might get the truth.

"I suppose you could call me a family friend, and I assume that's why she contacted me and not someone else. She must have known I lived nearby. She . . ." He shifted his feet, frowning. "She wanted me to make contact with Lord Anglesey on her behalf, to warn him of a rebellion some Catholics in the area were planning."

A strange look entered Gage's eyes, and I couldn't tell whether he believed him or not.

"Did she say who?" Gage asked.

He shook his head, glancing back down the hall toward the room where the others were gathered. We could hear the low rumble of their voices. "She wouldn't be specific. Honestly, she wouldn't tell me much of anything. Expected me to just take her word for it." He wrinkled his nose as if he'd smelled something foul, and I thought of all the reactions I'd seen from him that night, it was the most genuine.

"Did you do as she asked?"

He lifted his nose into the air, almost in affront. "I did not. Frankly, I didn't believe her. Or at least, I didn't believe her words merited so drastic a measure as reporting them to the Lord Lieutenant."

"Then did you inform Chief Constable Corcoran?"

"I did not."

Gage's eyes narrowed, studying him. "So you told no one?"

Mr. LaTouche seemed to finally grasp how unimpressed we were with his actions. "Until now." As if that made up for his failure to do so before.

My husband's voice was sharp when he next spoke. "You claim to be eager to see Miss Lennox's murder solved, and yet you didn't stop to think this might be important for us to know? Why did you not tell us before?"

He stared at us, seemingly flummoxed, but Gage was having none of it. He arched his eyebrows, demanding an answer.

"I . . . I thought you might accuse me of something unsavory. Or try to blame *me*."

I wanted to roll my eyes at his display of affront.

"When did you meet her?" Gage demanded to know.

"Once. A few days before I heard of her death." He sniffed. "So even if I'd written Lord Anglesey, it wouldn't have made a bit of difference."

"Maybe not for her. But perhaps for the other victim."

He stared at us stonily, making it clear how little he cared about Mother Fidelis or any of the nuns.

CHAPTER EIGHTEEN

"Do you believe him?"

Gage flicked a glance at me before resuming his determined stare ahead into the gathering dusk. "I don't know." He pulled on the reins, slowing the Friesians for their turn out of LaTouche's drive. "He appeared to be answering us in a straightforward manner, but something wasn't right. I can't quite put my finger on what, but I'm not sure I trust his recounting."

I agreed. "There were times when I felt he was being honest, and other times when I was certain he couldn't be. For instance, why did it take him so long to explain why he hadn't told us about all of this sooner? It was almost as if he had to think up a reason then and there."

He grunted. "No one in this entire benighted place seems either willing or capable of telling us the complete truth." His voice turned dry. "Though I think we would rather have been spared the helping of bile we endured at dinner."

I pulled my shawl tighter around me against the chill of twilight. "How can people be so hateful?" I asked in a small voice I wasn't sure Gage could even hear.

He reached over to rest his hand against my leg in reassurance. I laced my fingers under his, trying to fill the cold spot that had opened up inside my chest with his warmth. I was grateful he didn't try to explain it away or tell me to forget it. Some things just couldn't be fixed with words, no matter how wise.

Neither of us spoke as we traveled the mile of roads separating Eden Park's drive from the Priory's. But as we turned between the entrance gates, and Gage nodded to the cadets Corcoran had stationed there for us, I voiced a question which had been nagging at me for months.

"Does it bother you that people still call me Lady Darby?" I stared ahead as I asked it, but when Gage lifted his gaze to me, I turned to meet it, knowing I would see the truth in his eyes even if his words said otherwise.

He slowed the horses as we traversed the narrow drive through the trees, his face tight as he measured his words. "I won't say that I'm not irritated that your former husband's name is still attached to you, especially knowing how he mistreated you. And I suppose a primitive part of me wants to stamp you with my name, to claim you. But I know you are just as much a victim of the vagaries of society's laws of decorum as I am. I hear how you correct people. It's not your fault if they will not listen. Nor would I blame you if you tired of asking, particularly when they're merely passing acquaintances."

He paused, stopping the carriage in the middle of the drive to look at me fully. My throat dried under the intensity of his gaze. "The important thing is that no matter what name you are called by—Lady Darby, or Mrs. Gage, or Dame Pumpernickel . . ."

I smiled.

"I know you are mine. I only have to see the way you look at me . . ." he drew me closer ". . . or hear the way you say my name when we're alone."

"Sebastian," I chided gently, feeling my skin flush.

"Yes, that way." His mouth captured mine in a kiss I felt singe me clear to the tips of my toes. Only the impatient stamping of the horses pulled him away. Even so, he kept his arm wrapped tight around me and my head on his shoulder.

He halted the phaeton in the carriage yard and one of the

stable lads ran out to grab the bridles of the steeds. Jumping lightly down, he came around to lift me out, grinning at the pink I could still feel cresting my cheeks. "I want to speak to the cadets and survey the area to be sure all is well before we retire. I'll only be half an hour or so."

"Then I think I'll take a short walk in the gardens. The night's so lovely. I won't go far," I promised, still smelling the ashes from the scorched outbuilding, courtesy of last night's unwelcome visitors.

He nodded and, with a swift press of his lips to my temple, set off back down the drive.

I knew it was more than likely that Homer had retired hours ago to wherever the gardener lived, but the fact that I had met him at dusk before made me hope he might still be about. I entered through the side gate and followed the path toward the place I'd glimpsed two nights past where four tracks seemed to converge together to form a small circle. Staring intently into the growing dark, I stood at the center and spun to peer down each of the trails, looking for any sign of the gardener. When nothing caught my eye, I sighed and stopped to tip my head back to look up at the last remnants of red tinging the undersides of the clouds above me.

It was then that I heard the sound of something scratching in the earth somewhere to my right. I pivoted, trying to see what it was, but it remained hidden behind a line of hedges. Lifting my skirts, I hurried down the path nearest to it, hoping to find another path which would lead off in that direction. From what I had seen from the windows above, the gardens seemed to be laid out in a linear fashion, making them easier to navigate. True to form, I saw the path almost immediately, slowing my steps as I neared the hedge row. The sound had stopped, but I saw a man was still there, bent over examining something. I tried to make as much noise as I could as I approached so as not to startle him, and soon enough, he flicked a glance over his shoulder at me and his mouth widened in a broad grin.

"M'lady, now wha' brings ye out on such a fine night?" he

remarked, rising to his feet. "Be wishin' to perfume yer dreams?" He opened his hands to reveal a shy little violet, its dusky purple petals washed gray by the lack of light.

I moved closer to better see.

"They likes to shelter among the other plants sometimes, like a lil' girl run off to hide. I could put 'er in a pot for ye to have in yer chamber, if ye wish."

"Oh, that would be lovely," I told him in delight.

His craggy faced was soft with pleasure.

"There's some in the shed there." He gestured. "Won't be but a moment."

"Actually, if you don't mind, I'll join you," I replied, falling in step with him. "There's something I wanted to ask you."

If he was surprised, he didn't show it. "Is there?"

"Yes. You told me about Rathfarnham Castle. How your father and mother worked there. About the peculiarities of the place."

"So I did."

"And you mentioned there were secret tunnels."

This finally caught his attention, and he glanced at me out of the corner of his eye. "Ah, now," he exhaled, as if this explained something. "I shouldn't have done dat."

"I'm not after some lark or chasing adventure." I stared up at him seriously as we reached the shed and he turned to face me more fully. "You've heard my husband and I are investigating the death of those two nuns?"

His expression turned grim, and he reached out to open the door. "I have. The poor lassies."

"Then you must realize why I'm asking." I stood by the door, speaking to his back as he searched for a small clay pot among the detritus on the shelves built into the opposite wall. "Would you tell me how many tunnels there are and where they lead? Does one of them lead toward the abbey?"

He crossed back toward the small wooden table set near the door and put the pot there before carefully placing the violet he had dug from the ground, roots and all, into it. I watched him begin to pack more dirt around it, allowing him to consider my request. When he'd finished, he nodded once and glanced up at me.

"There be three. One leads to the church—the old one, St. Peter and Paul, in the graveyard. The second goes to the cellars o' the Yellow House." He paused, as if grasping the import, and I held my breath. "The third opens in the meadow on the other side o' Nutgrove Avenue, near the abbey. There be a wild cherry tree growin' by a wall, and some blackthorn, I believe. It's been some time since I've been dat way. Behind dem be a set o' stairs leadin' down."

A thrill of excitement ran up my back at this confirmation that I had been right. Miss Lennox and Mother Fidelis must have known about the tunnel and taken it. That's where they were going. To Rathfarnham Castle.

"Thank you," I told him. "You have just helped us immensely."

"Wait, m'lady," he gasped, recalling me when I would have dashed off to tell Gage what I'd learned and suspected. He held the potted violet out to me.

"Oh, yes," I replied with a little laugh. "Thank you."

But instead of releasing it when I grasped it, he held fast. I looked up into his eyes, having no difficulty reading the worry stamped there at this proximity.

"Go wit care. Don't go blunderin' into someting ye don't understand."

Some of my enthusiasm dimmed at his display of concern. "I will," I promised him.

He must have been satisfied with my response, for he released the pot.

I tried to retrace my steps back through the garden, but being partially distracted by my excitement over what I'd just learned, I must have taken a wrong turn. By the time I realized it, I seemed to have strolled deeper into the gardens nearing the boundary between it and the forest beyond. I stared around me in confusion, trying to regain my bearings. I looked for a light from the windows of the house, but either there wasn't one, or the trees to my right blocked them. I decided to circle around them to see if that was the case, but then something to my left caught my eye.

It was difficult to tell in the soft darkness of evening, when the stars were only just beginning to appear in the sky, but I thought it had been the silhouette of a woman, her skirts swishing about her. I hurried in her direction, thinking she could lead me back to the house. Rounding a corner, I caught sight of her as she turned another bend.

"Wait." I clutched the pot against my chest with one arm, and picked up my skirts with the other. "Miss! Please. Will you wait?"

I didn't know if she couldn't hear me, or if I had merely frightened her, but her steps seemed to quicken. I caught a glimpse of her as she darted around another corner. But although I ran to catch her up, when my feet reached the spot where she had last disappeared, I could no longer see her.

I pressed my free hand to my side, trying to catch my breath. Who had the woman been? A servant, surely. But why had she fled?

Before I could contemplate the matter further, I heard the sound of voices coming from the opposite direction. Grasping my pot tighter to my chest, prepared to pursue lest I lose sight of them, too, I moved forward to peer around a hedge to see a woman and a man standing beneath a tree. I opened my mouth to speak, but something in the edge to their voices made me stop. They appeared to be arguing, and though I could not clearly make out what they said, I did recognize the female's strident brogue. It was Bree. And if I was not very much mistaken, the man was Constable Casey.

I shrank deeper into the shadows of the hedge, observing them as a sickening feeling twisted about inside of me. Not again. This had already happened to me once before. This betrayal. Lucy, my lady's maid before Bree, had been seduced by a handsome face into sharing private information about me. I had thought Bree to be wiser than that, more loyal.

I forced myself to inhale past the vine of thorns constricting my airway, reminding myself not to jump to conclusions.

I had not been wrong. Bree was different from Lucy. Confident when that girl had been perpetually anxious. Adaptable when she had been flummoxed by change. World-wise when she had been so naïve. At the least, Bree deserved a fair hearing before I assumed the worst.

I watched as she impassionedly argued something, gesturing with her hands and hissing sharply up at Casey. She certainly didn't seem enamored of him, though I still couldn't understand why she would be out in the garden speaking to him. Had she merely stumbled into him prowling about as she came to search for me?

No, there was something in their manner toward each other that spoke of some familiarity, and Bree didn't look the least afraid or alarmed by his presence. I wished I could move closer so that I could hear what they were saying, but to do so would reveal my presence. I considered surprising them both, but then decided that could turn an angry situation into something far more volatile if Casey panicked. Besides, I wanted to hear what Bree had to say without him looking on. I figured I owed her that.

Then suddenly the discussion was over. Bree snapped the words "Go now" loud enough for me to hear, and pointed in the direction behind him. He glared at her a moment longer and then stomped off with a grunt. She stared after him, her posture defiant, until I heard the sound of a gate click shut. Her shoulders sagged and her head bowed. Then she reached her hands up to smooth her hair behind her ears and turned her steps in my direction.

As she moved into line with the hedges, she looked up from her contemplation of the ground and jolted at the sight of me watching her from the shadows. For a moment, we both stood still, studying each other. I could almost hear the thoughts spinning in her head, wondering what I'd heard, how much I'd guessed. I didn't speak, wanting her to be the one to break the silence, to tell me how she intended to play this. Whether she would be defiant or rueful, deceitful or honest. I should have known Bree would cut to the heart of the matter.

"He's my brother."

I stiffened in shock.

"Well, my half brother." Her voice was resigned. "We have different fathers."

"Thus your different last names," I murmured, still trying to absorb this new information. I knew her last name was McEvoy, and that by the rules of decorum I should be calling her that, but when I met her, she had still been an upstairs maid known by her first name, and so I'd never switched when she officially became my lady's maid.

"Aye." Her voice tightened with remorse. "I wanted to tell ye. But when I saw him that first time, ootside the constabulary, he shook his head at me, makin' it clear he didna want me to say anythin'. So I decided to keep my mouth shut, least until I could find out why."

That was why she'd looked as if she'd seen a ghost, because, in a way, she had.

"So you didn't know he was here in Rathfarnham?"

She shook her head. "Nay. Nor that he was a constable. What I told ye afore was the truth. I'd no' heard from him in years."

"Did you recognize him among the riders last night as well?" I pressed, having realized while I watched them argue why one of our midnight visitors looked familiar.

She frowned. "Aye. And if I coulda, I woulda skinned him alive then and there. He's always had a way o' findin' trouble, and draggin' me into it. 'Tis why I didna ken if I wanted to write to him before I realized he was already here."

"You could have said something when I asked you if you could identify any of them."

"Aye. But then I wouldna had a chance to find oot what he's up to."

I arched my eyebrows. "Did you?"

Her feet shuffled the loose earth. "Nay. Though I do ken whatever it is, they're anxious for you no' to find oot aboot it. And I dinna think it's only aboot the murders."

"The tithe protest," I sighed.

She nodded. "I asked him aboot it, and he got verra angry. Told me to let it be."

I scowled. It seemed to keep coming back to that. Though the tithe protest was supposed to be peaceful, so why all the violent opposition to us finding out?

"There's more," she admitted somewhat hesitantly. "He asked me to put poison in your and Mr. Gage's tea."

I gasped in outrage.

"No' enough to kill ye," she hastened to add. "Just enough to make ye ill."

"How kind," I replied drolly.

"I refused, but someone else may no'."

I looked up into her eyes, grasping the implication. What were we to do? Hire someone to taste our food before we ate it? I pressed a hand to my brow at the worrisome thought.

"I'm sorry, m'lady," she pleaded. "I ken I shoulda told you sooner, but . . . he's my brother."

In words it sounded like the feeblest excuse possible, but in reality I knew how complicated the ties to our family could be. Even those you hadn't seen in years. Even those who were nothing but trouble.

"I told him that whatever it is he's involved in, you and Mr. Gage will figure it oot. I begged him to come clean afore it's too late. But I dinna think he will listen."

I searched her eyes, wanting to believe her, wanting to think it was that simple, but the memory of past betrayals reared its head, making it all so much more complicated. "That's all you told him?"

Her forehead furrowed in confusion.

"You didn't tell him anything about me, or my past, or the investigation . . ."

"Nay." She spoke quickly. "O' course not. I would ne'er do that."

Her indignation seemed genuine, so I nodded even though my stomach swirled with uncertainty. My eyes slid to the side to stare up toward the house, where I could now see candles burning in two of the windows, showing me which direction to walk. "I won't need you tonight," I said carefully. "I need some time to think."

She clasped her hands before her, her voice heavy. "O' course, m'lady."

"I shall see you in the morning," I murmured, setting off toward the lights without looking back.

Gage was waiting for me when I strode through our bed-chamber door, propped up in bed in his burgundy dressing gown, a piece of paper dangling from his fingertips. "I was just considering whether I should dress and come find you," he remarked lightly, and nodded to the potted violet in my arms. "I see you were still in the gardens."

I frowned down at the plant and then absently set it on the corner of the dressing table. "Yes. I . . . I got distracted by the sight of Bree speaking with Constable Casey." I whipped my shawl off my shoulders and turned to see his reaction.

"Where?" He leaned forward. "Here? In the garden?"

"Yes."

Gage's mouth flattened. "So much for our cadets."

I tugged at the fingers of my gloves, feeling aggravated he was more concerned about what this meant in terms of how effective our guards were than how Bree had possibly betrayed us. "He's her half brother."

"Really?" I could hear the speculation in his voice. "What were they discussing?"

"I couldn't hear. But she appeared to give me an honest accounting of it when I confronted her." I thrust my gloves at the dressing table, laying them on top of the shawl. "I'm afraid I was too cross with her to see her again tonight, so you shall have to play lady's maid." I turned my back to him, waiting for him to rise from the bed and cross the room. I heard him set the letter he'd been reading down on the table by the bed. "What was that?"

"I finally received a response from Miss Lennox's family,

who have absolutely nothing useful to add. In fact, I would rather not have read their careless, scornful words." He sighed. "But the less said about that, the better. Now, Bree. What did she say?"

While his long fingers fumbled with some of the tiny buttons, I recounted what she had told me, including Casey's request to her. "Can you believe he wished to poison us?" I snapped in indignation as my dress gaped open in the back. "That he still might attempt it?"

He reached inside to undo the fastenings of my corset. "We'll just have to be careful what we eat and drink," he replied almost absently. His voice had deepened.

"And what of the staff here? Do you think they can be trusted not to accept a bribe or work in concert with him?"

"Yes. When I tell them we're aware of his intentions, and that we want them to be vigilant. If they realize we know, none of them will take the risk." His hands slid up my bare back as he bent his head to press his lips to the place where my neck met my shoulder.

"And what of this matter he's so desperate to conceal from us? Do you think it has to do with the tithe protest?" I shivered as his mouth skimmed up my neck to the spot behind my ear which he knew was sensitive.

"Likely. Kiera, can't this wait until tomorrow?"

"No." I squirmed around to face him. "It cannot." I pointed toward the bed. "Over there. I've more to tell you. Tonight."

The corners of his mouth twitched upward, but he complied, crossing the room to relax back against the pillows as I pulled my arms from the sleeves of my gown. He gestured to me as a courtier might do to the king. "Pray continue."

I raised a single eyebrow at his teasing before draping my gown over the back of a chair. "Bree was not the only one I spoke with in the garden."

"Oh?"

I ignored his overawed tone, turning to face the mirror as I began to remove the pins from my hair, and explained who Homer Baugh was and what he'd informed me. Though it became increasingly difficult to overlook his half-lidded eyes staring at me in the reflection. Regardless, I could tell the information about the tunnels interested him.

"I suppose that's how Casey disappeared after eavesdropping on our conversation with Chief Constable Corcoran."

I swiveled around to face him. "I'd forgotten about that. He must have darted through the tunnel at the old church. To warn the others?"

He shifted position in bed. "Most likely."

I considered the matter as I combed my fingers through my hair, searching for pins I'd missed. "Did I tell you Mr. Baugh said part of the Rathfarnham Castle estate had been used as a dairy farm a short time ago?"

His eyebrows arched, but I knew only half his attention was on the inquiry. "Did it now?"

I dropped my arms. "Sebastian, stop looking at me like that."

His eyes lifted to my face. "Like what?"

"Like *that*."

"My dear, what do you expect me to do when you're standing there in only your shift with your hands in your hair?"

I glanced in the mirror behind me, noticing for the first time how fine the lawn of my shift was. I flushed, wrapping an arm across my chest. "Oh."

"No reason for embarrassment," he replied in gentle amusement. "You are my wife, after all. But I think you can grasp how distracting you are."

"Yes, I see." I stood stiffly, uncertain what to do. If I removed my shift to put on my nightgown, would that not be even more distracting? Should I reach for my dressing gown?

Gage chuckled, clearly divining my internal struggle. "Come here," he murmured, staring steadily into my eyes. "Kiera." He reached out his hand to me.

Had he dropped his gaze for even a second, I think I might have faltered, but he did not. Not even after he took hold of my hand and pulled me down to sit on the bed with him. The pale blue of his irises had deepened to that smoky color I'd become quite familiar with in the past two and a half months.

His hand slid upward to caress my cheek. "You are so beautiful."

My skin warmed with pleasure and my breath began to quicken, but before I could surrender to him, I still had to ask. "What about Constable Casey and the tunnels?"

"I think that will all keep until tomorrow," he replied, brushing his callused fingers over my skin. "Unless you propose we go stumbling through these pitch-black passageways now?"

I smiled. "No."

"Then I suspect we can also give Constable Casey at least that long to come to his senses and seek us out to share what he knows."

I nodded.

"Now, is there anything more you wished to tell me tonight, so I can avoid another rebuke? Though I have to say, I rather enjoyed you ordering me about."

"No, you didn't."

His eyes gleamed in challenge. "Try it."

"Kiss me," I demanded.

And he did.

Later that night, I couldn't sleep. Something had woken me, though at first I didn't know what. Until a cramp tightened my lower abdomen and I realized it was my courses. I rose to find the necessary supplies I knew Bree had packed, careful not to wake Gage, and checked the bedding. Then unwilling to lie back down, I went to peer out the window up at the bright moonlight shining down on the carriage yard.

It was true, the cramps still twisted inside me. I could ring for Bree and ask her to fix me a remedy. But that was not what had unsettled me, or caused this oddly hollow ache in the center of my chest. One I didn't want to examine, didn't want to analyze, and yet it couldn't be ignored.

I wished Bree had never said anything. That she'd never raised the prospect. Before our conversation, I'd not truly considered the possibility that I might be expecting. My courses were never a reliable distance apart, so I'd anticipated them to arrive any day within the next week. But her words had made me face something I had not yet been ready for, I'd not yet wanted to stir up inside me.

We were wed, and Gage was attentive. I knew it was only a matter of time. But somehow the thought of my having a child made it difficult to catch my breath. By all accounts I should have been relieved to see my courses had begun. But I wasn't. I didn't understand that. How could I be panicked by the prospect of having a child one moment, and then unaccountably sad that I wasn't the next?

I wished my sister Alana were there to talk to, but she was hundreds of miles away in Scotland. I could write to her, but it would take days if not weeks for my letter to reach her and then just as long for her response to return to me. Besides, I wasn't certain I wanted to commit this all to paper. It was too thorny, too difficult.

I sighed, lifting my hand to feel the cool glass of the window, the shock of its chill against my warm palm somehow bracing and comforting all at once.

That's when I saw her.

It was the woman from the garden. The one I'd followed, but been unable to catch. I was almost certain of it, though I'd never seen her face, and still couldn't do so from this vantage. I realized now how young she seemed. She stood at the edge of the carriage yard, staring up at the house almost wistfully, though I didn't know how I could tell that. I wondered if she could see me, and what she was doing there.

Memories from last night's disturbance flooded me and I turned to wake Gage. But something made me hesitate, and when I looked back, she was gone.

I stared at the spot where she had been standing. Had I imagined her? Perhaps she had been a mere trick of the shadows.

I shook my head. No, someone had been there. Just as someone had been in the gardens. But who? And why was she watching this house?

CHAPTER NINETEEN

At breakfast the next morning I asked Dempsey if one of the maids might have been out in the gardens or the carriage yard the previous night.

He straightened as if he'd been slapped. "I should hope not," he replied almost in affront. "Did ye see one o' dem?"

Gage set down his utensils as I described the woman I'd seen to him as well.

The butler gathered up a plate to be removed from the table, making a credible effort to appear unconcerned, but the pleated furrows of his brow gave him away. "Ah, now. 'Tis likely just Miss Gertrude."

"Miss . . ." I blinked. "You mean the girl who fell from the window?"

"That's her. She's buried in her da's favorite spot in the garden."

"I've seen her grave," I admitted.

"She likes to hang about the place. Shows herself to those who be sad or lonely, like her."

I stared after him in some amazement. I didn't completely discount the existence of ghosts—I was half Scottish, after all—but I found this claim to be a bit difficult to swallow.

I turned back to find Gage watching me, his eyes warm with consideration. He didn't speak, waiting for me to say something first. What there was to say, I didn't precisely know, so I offered him as reassuring a smile as I could manage and returned to my breakfast.

The Catholic Chapel was a rather unassuming building which stood a few hundred feet from the Yellow House, downstream of the Owendoher River. Compared to the Anglican Church next to the constabulary, it was almost severely plain and austere. Something I found surprising given the fact that it was the Roman Catholics who had built and worshiped in most of the great cathedrals of Europe, and certainly in Britain—Canterbury, Salisbury, York. That is, until Henry VIII stripped those cathedrals and much of the rest of their property away from the Catholics and made them part of the Church of England. Even so, I couldn't help but remark on its simplicity to Father Begley when he came forward to greet us.

"Ah, now, but yer forgettin' the penal laws o' the last century. Catholic mass was outlawed, and so those who kept the faith were forced to worship in secret in makeshift mass houses. Some o' which were naught more dan tents. There was one here in Rathfarnham, close to dis very spot, but nearer to the river. Once the laws were repealed, the people built dis chapel, but could not be affordin' to construct anything more ornate. Nor would they be inclined to do so. Not when it could be taken from dem again."

"That makes sense," I replied, somehow feeling ashamed that all this had happened to them, even though none of it had been my fault. Not directly.

Father Begley's eyes were kind. "Don't trouble yerself o'er much. The Lord still watches o'er His flock." He gestured toward a trio of pews, waiting while we took our seats before he sat in front of us. He shifted his black cassock so that he could turn to drape his arm over the back of the pew to look at us.

I heard Bree settle into the pew behind us, quiet and solemn, as she'd been that morning. Matters were awkward between us, and as I still didn't know what I wished to say to her, we both remained silent except for the usual communication between a lady and her maid. Anderley was off at the Yellow House or somewhere else, assigned to his normal task of attempting to blend in and listen for information that might be useful to us. Efforts that thus far had proved ineffectual.

"Now, what is it I can be doin' for ye?" the priest asked. He was younger than I'd expected, closer to Gage's age of thirty-three than the Scullys' contemporary, with close-cropped hair of sandy brown and sharp hazel eyes, which softened with a gentle, almost bemused smile.

Gage glanced to me, allowing me to take the lead. "You are aware of the investigation we're conducting into the deaths of Miss Lennox and Mother Mary Fidelis?"

He nodded. "Reverend Mother Mary Teresa wrote to me on yer arrival, and asked me to do all dat I could to help ye."

"That was kind of her. We've been given reason to believe that you might possess information that could assist us. Mrs. Scully, you are familiar with her?"

"I am."

"She said there were 'going-ons' in town that she feared Miss Lennox had gotten herself involved in, and dare I say, Mother Mary Fidelis, too." His expression tightened with concern. "She would not tell us more, but she suggested we speak to you. That you would be able to explain."

"I see." He turned away, staring up toward the altar, and the gold cross that held pride of place. "The reverend mother has been tellin' me she has great faith in ye," he said, sounding almost as if he were ruminating to himself. "She believes the Lord has sent ye to us."

I felt a tingle along my spine at this pronouncement, wondering at the reverend mother's conviction.

Father Begley's gaze swung back to us, studying our faces.

Whatever he saw there made him nod. "And so I will put my faith in ye as well." He tapped his fingers against the wood of the pew. "As Mrs. Scully put it, there are 'going-ons' in town."

"The tithe protest," Gage guessed.

The priest's smile was humorless. "It appears the reverend mother's trust in ye is well founded. It is the tithe protest. Or the tithe war, if ye prefer. Depends on who ye are talkin' to as to how they wish to phrase it. A large number o' the farmers here in Rathfarnham have refused to pay their tithes. A number o' dem have herded their cattle together an' attributed dem to me, so as to avoid the tithes since, as a clergyman, I don't pay."

"Like in County Kilkenny?" I asked.

His expression turned grave. "Our bishop encouraged us to use creative methods o' circumventin' the law. But after hearin' o' the violence that broke out o'er that attempted collection and the one in County Wexford, I've been fearful the same will happen here." He shifted in his seat, his voice becoming more strident and animated. "'Tis supposed to be a peaceful protest. No resistin' seizure. But the men have become riled. Some o' 'em seemed to be stirrin' for a fight. Not all," he assured us. "But some." He scowled. "Enough."

I curled my fingers around the smooth edge of the pew beneath me, inhaling the scents of wood and beeswax. Had Miss Lennox been right in what she told Mr. LaTouche? Were some of the protestors planning open rebellion? Is that why she was killed? To keep her silent? And Mother Fidelis as well?

"And Miss Lennox and Mother Mary Fidelis?" Gage prodded. "How do they fit into all of this?"

The priest leaned forward, clasping his hands in front of him. "I did not learn o' dis until a few weeks ago, or else I'd have put a stop to it, to be sure. Apparently Mother Mary Fidelis has been helpin' the men for some time. They keep the cattle at the castle. There used to be a dairy there, and there's equipment left o'er from dat time." He sat tall again, meeting our gazes. "There's also several tunnels leadin' to it

and plenty o' places to hide, should they be needed." His eyes narrowed. "But ye already know this, don't ye?"

I glanced at Gage. "We guessed."

He nodded. "A couple o' months ago Miss Lennox followed Mother Fidelis through the tunnel and uncovered their secret. She begged to be allowed to assist, and seein' no alternative, they let her."

No alternative *then*. But had they found one since? Something more drastic.

"How exactly did they help?" Gage shook his head in vexation. "Forgive me, but it seems an odd undertaking for a nun."

The priest lifted his hands. "I don't know, sure I don't. But he might," he added, nodding toward the man who had just strolled through the doors and stood blinking as his eyes adjusted from the bright sunlight to the dim exterior.

Gage rose to his feet, prepared to give chase if Constable Casey fled. However, any thought he might have had of running seemed to be obliterated in the face of his fury. He stomped up the aisle, curling his hands into fists while his face flushed an alarming shade of red next to the green of his uniform jacket. "Of all the rotten, underhanded, *traitorous* . . ." He broke off with almost a growl. "You're talking to them!"

The priest held up his hands, trying to calm him, but Bree talked over his soothing words. "Calm yerself, Mick. They'd already figured it oot. Didna I tell ye they would? Father Begley and I were just confirmin' some details." She eyed him disapprovingly. "Noo, stop bein' a fool, and tell 'em what ye ken."

"You great eejit!" he swung on her to exclaim. "They're not to be trusted. Didn't Granny teach ye better dan dat?"

Bree arched her neck, staring down her nose at him. "Granny taught me to measure a person by the worth o' their actions. Same as she taught *you*. And I'd say I ken my employers a sight better 'an you do. They're fair and reasonable." Her eyes narrowed. "And willin' to overlook the fact

that ye wished to poison 'em. So I suggest ye put yer prejudice aside, and start talkin'."

Rather than chagrin, his eyes flared with spite. "Do they
know yer a Roman Catholic, just like us? Or would ye be
hidin' that like the cross tucked inside the neck o' yer dress."

Bree pressed a hand to her collar, presumably where underneath her cross lay, as some of her anger drained away in the
face of her brother's nastiness. Indignation flared inside me.
Had we been different people—the people he thought us to
be—his careless words could have cost Bree her position, and
her livelihood if she'd been dismissed without a reference. For
a brother, even a half one, to say something so thoughtless
infuriated me.

"We know," I bit out, pinning him with my glare. "And
we don't care."

The corners of his whiskey brown eyes, so like Bree's, tightened in mistrust, glancing between Bree and Gage and me.
Seeing our ire and Bree's silent astonishment, his anger began
to thaw toward befuddlement. "Truly?"

"Truly," Gage replied steadily for us.

Casey turned away, scrubbing at his pale hair in thought.
For a moment, he seemed just as likely to stride out the door
as tell us anything. What made up his mind in those seconds,
I don't know, except that he gave an exasperated grunt and
tossed his hat into the pew beside his sister. "All right. I'll talk.
Seems I've no choice. What is it yer wantin' to know?"

I glanced at Bree as Gage quickly relayed everything
Father Begley had just confirmed for us. The light shining
through the thick leaded glass windows created a fiery halo
around her strawberry blond hair. Her eyes were fastened on
the floor while her fingers continued to fiddle with the necklace beneath her dress. I wondered how I'd never noticed it
before. She had it on under the high collar of the dress she
currently wore, but not all of her bodices were so concealing.
Seeing as I wore my mother's amethyst pendant always, I normally noted other people's jewelry, no matter how simple,

wondering if it held any significance. But in Bree's case, I'd never marked it. Of course, at a young age ladies were taught not to notice their maid's appearance, to almost look through them as the maid flitted about, dressing and undressing them. Perhaps, without realizing it, I did the same, even if the rest of my interactions with her were far from conventional.

I turned back to Casey as Gage reiterated the last question he'd posed to Father Begley. "What I'm curious about next is how Miss Lennox and Mother Fidelis helped you? Did they care for the cattle?"

Casey scowled at the floor and reluctantly began to speak. "When needed. But their main task was to be helpin' us from the outside. Gatherin' information we could never be gettin' from the mother superior on our own. Word of what the bishop—a great friend o' hers—and O'Connell be sayin', and what the protesters in other parts o' the country be doin'. They always knew more than the newspapers reported." He sank down in the pew beside Bree. "When Miss Lennox came, she told us she had an uncle highly placed in the government. That she could be gettin' information from him. Didn't tell us it was Wellington himself, though," he muttered under his breath.

Gage and I shared a look, and I could tell he wondered just as I did whether Wellington had been aware of his cousin's duplicity. If, in fact, any of this was true.

"How did she propose to contact him?" he asked.

"She wrote to him."

I frowned. Then why hadn't we found any of this correspondence? Had she hidden it somewhere we hadn't thought to look? Somewhere elsewhere in the abbey. Or maybe she'd burned the letters, afraid they would fall into the wrong hands. If we considered that possibility, then we also had to contemplate its counter. That someone had found the letters and taken them, either before or after Miss Lennox's death. Their discovery, in fact, could be partially the motive for her murder.

There was also one other option, and Gage had evidently already thought of it.

"Could she have lied about this contact of hers?"

Casey's mouth twisted, not liking that suggestion one bit. "'Tis possible. But she did bring us useful information she got from somewhere. 'Bout the government's plans to enforce tithe collections an' so forth."

Father Begley shifted abruptly, making the pew beneath him creak. It was obvious he was distressed by this new information. "What of all this talk of yer plannin' armed rebellion? Ye swore there was no truth in it."

"There isn't," Casey snapped. "Dat just be the Orangies tryin' to stir up trouble."

"And all the other men?" Gage prodded doubtfully. "They intend to remain peaceable if and when the government tries to collect their tithes?"

Casey's hands flexed in his lap and his eyes dropped to bore into the back of the pew behind Gage. "I'll not be claimin' we don't have a few hotheads who like to talk, to be sure."

If he was saying some of these men were even more short-tempered than he was, then it was no wonder people were concerned this protest could erupt into violence.

As if he'd heard my thoughts, one corner of his mouth quirked upward wryly. "We're all a bit enraged o'er dis matter. We may've got our emancipation, but at the expense of many o' us losin' our votin' rights when Parliament raised the county freehold franchise from those with forty shillings to ten pounds' worth o' property." He scoffed. "An' now wit all these tithes goin' to the Church o' Ireland." For a moment I thought he was going to spit on the floor, but he seemed to catch himself in time, remembering where he was. He inhaled deeply. "It's a lot to swallow, to be sure. But I took an oath to the British Crown when I accepted dis post as constable, and I'll not be dishonorin' it."

"In spite of your assurances, I would still like to see this place where you are keeping the cattle. To confirm for myself that you're telling the truth and not stockpiling weapons or worse." Gage's eyes hardened in the face of Casey's defiant glare. "I know they're at Rathfarnham Castle. I could go on my own. Take a few of your fellows from the constabulary. But I'm allowing you the opportunity to show me around instead."

I glanced out of the corner of my eye at Bree, who had folded her hands in her lap as if to keep from reaching out and smacking her stubborn brother. Her lips were nearly white from being pressed together in an effort to remain quiet.

Casey sat back with begrudging respect, folding his arms in front of him. "So be it. I'll take ye. But in exchange I want yer promise you'll not be interferin' tomorrow at the fair when we'll be bringin' the cattle to market."

"So long as I do not find any evidence that violence is planned, I'm agreed to that," Gage replied readily enough. "However, you do realize Chief Constable Corcoran is almost certainly already aware of your ruse? In fact, I'm certain he's counting on your voice being the one of reason in this matter." Gage's tone fairly dripped with skepticism, which made a smile flicker across Casey's features.

"Likely. But dat's my matter, not yers. I don't be intendin' to violate any laws, or lettin' anyone else do so."

"Just like two nights ago when you and your fellow Ribbon-men trespassed and set fire to an outbuilding at the Priory."

Father Begley sucked in a harsh breath, clearly hearing this bit of news for the first time.

Casey at least had the grace to look abashed. "The trespassin' was just to scare ye away. I didn't know any o' the men meant to take it further."

"Well, forgive me, if that means I don't have as much confidence in your fellow protesters' adherence to the law and willingness to avoid violence as you do." Gage turned away, lowering the knee he'd propped up on the seat of the pew as if to rise.

"What of Miss Lennox and Mother Mary Fidelis?" I pointed out before he could do so, not wanting them to lose sight of the most important matter at hand. "Do you think any of the other protesters could have harmed them?"

Casey shook his head. "They were one o' us."

"But what if they weren't? What if someone found out that one or both of them was betraying you? Are you confident they wouldn't have harmed them then?"

The grim expression that stole over his face was all the answer I needed, but still he shook his head insistently. "No. I'll not be believin' they betrayed us, and neither would the others."

I met Gage's eyes, seeing the same distrust of his certainty.

CHAPTER TWENTY

As Casey walked next door to the Yellow House to fetch Anderley on his behalf, Gage pulled me aside to ask me to remain at the abbey with Bree rather than join them. I could hear the concern in his voice as he explained how uncertain he was of what exactly they would find. There was every possibility they would be ambushed by a dozen men. Casey seemed reliable, but we couldn't be certain the other men would not be rash enough to shoot first and ask questions later.

None of this was in the least reassuring, and I was tempted to demand he forget the bargain he'd made with Casey and go speak to Chief Constable Corcoran now rather than risk it. But I knew he would never go back on his word, especially when such a raid could jeopardize so many more lives than Casey's. So I agreed, knowing Gage didn't need my pair of eyes, nor the distraction of worrying about my safety. In any case, much as I wished to see the castle, this wasn't a tourist excursion, and Homer's warnings about the derelict state it had fallen into made me suspect I would only be distressed by the sight.

Gage did, however, want us to show him the location of the tunnel which led from the abbey. Casey confessed he had not taken that passage in some years, and could not recall its exact placement, so Bree and I agreed to lead the way. It would have been quicker for Casey to guide them through the tunnel that began at the Yellow House, but since our main objective was to solve the murders of Miss Lennox and Mother Fidelis, Gage felt it was important to see which route they had traveled.

Leaving the phaeton and horses at the abbey, Bree and I led them through the door by the gardeners' cottages and along the abbey wall, past the pond, and up the hill to the wild cherry tree growing against the old stone wall. Now that we knew what we were looking for, it was easy to find the set of steps leading downward, shielded behind the blackthorn and spindle. Bree and I stood back to watch as they disappeared from sight, a lantern from the carriage guiding their way down into the dark tunnel. I felt a moment's uneasiness when all evidence of them vanished, but I turned my back determinedly on the prospect and began striding toward the abbey.

The ground was still soft from a downpour of rain in the early morning hours—not long after the girl outside the window at the Priory had disappeared—so we made our way carefully. The workmen who had labored on the wall the day before could not do so while the ground was so saturated. So rather than return through the door by the gardeners' cottages, we picked our way through the gap, attentive not to disturb anything. While I paused to wait for Bree, I glanced around me, examining the work that had been done.

It was then that I caught movement out of the corner of my eye, a swift flash of white against the brown and green of the orchard. Perhaps it had just been the startled flight of one of Miss Lennox's birds, but I didn't think so. Holding a hand up to forestall anything Bree might have said, I lifted the hem of my soft emerald green skirts and crept forward on the balls of my feet in the direction I had seen the white vanish, peering through the trees. Bree was at my heels, blindly following my lead as she did so often.

I reached up to brush a long branch laden with small yellow-green clusters of growing fruit. A bee buzzed past my hand, attracted by the sweet scent. Ahead of me sat a large rectangular wooden box on the opposite side of the next tree in line, positioned up against its trunk. I was certain I'd seen it before as we'd woven our way through the trees, but I'd not taken note of it. After all, it was normal to see such large trough-like containers as well as barrels spaced throughout an orchard. But I marked it now.

If one was in need of concealment, it was the perfect hiding spot. Particularly, if the people you were hiding from were not looking for you.

Was that why Miss O'Grady had not seen anyone fleeing from the murder of Mother Fidelis? She'd described hearing a noise, the reason why she'd set off in the direction of the wall in the first place. Had what she heard been the killer concealing himself? If so, did that mean our thinking was all wrong? Did the murderer not come from outside the walls, but within? Were they hiding here even now?

I felt a chill run down my spine at the prospect.

I glanced at Bree, pointing toward the box. She nodded and began to circle around the tree before us in the opposite direction even as I slowly moved forward. Reaching inside my reticule, I withdrew my pistol, ready to use it if necessary.

When we were within one step of seeing into the chest-high trough, we both paused, staring through the branches at each other. Then I cocked my pistol, and with a nod we sprang forward.

The girl inside shrieked at the sight of me leveling my gun at her. "Don't shoot me. Don't shoot me," she begged, clambering to the opposite side of the box. Old leaves and sticks crunched under the soles of her shoes.

I lowered my pistol to my side, uncocking it. My heart still pounded in my ears. "Miss Walsh, isn't it?" I snapped in exasperation. The troublemaker. "What are you doing here?"

"W-why do ye have a gun?" she demanded with false bravado.

"Because I thought you were a killer." I glared down at her. "Are you?"

"No! No. How can ye ask such a thing?"

"Then, I repeat, what are you doing here?"

She pushed unsteadily to her feet, brushing off the leaves and dirt clinging to her frock. Her eyes darted over her shoulder at Bree and then back to me as she rubbed her arm where she must have bruised it when she launched herself backward away from my pistol. "I decided to go for a walk."

"While you're supposed to be in class?"

She lifted her chin. "Aye."

"And *here* of all places, where you know a murderer has already killed two women?" Fury tightened my voice as I tucked my gun back into my reticule. "I didn't take you for a fool."

Her spine stiffened. "I didn't leave the walls. An' besides, he killed two nuns. Not the students."

Her callous retort made the skin on the back of my neck ruffle like a cat. "Yes, but Miss Lennox was dressed much the same as you, wasn't she? Are you certain, should the murderer return, he would know the difference?"

This silenced her, making some of the peachy color of her complexion drain from her face. I almost felt sorry for speaking so bluntly. Almost.

"Miss Walsh, please be straight with us. Lies will not help you." I stared daggers at her, letting her assume whatever she wished to think I meant by that statement. "*Why* are you here?"

Her shoulders drooped and her eyes dropped to the floor of the box. I followed her gaze to where a book lay half-concealed by leaves. The cover was nondescript, but it was obvious that whatever the contents were, she did not want me to see them.

"Do I even want to know what type of book that is?"

The fiery hue that suffused her cheeks told me all I needed to know.

I held out my hand, demanding she give it to me. She

hesitated a moment before stooping to pick it up and thrusting it into my fingers. I saved her the indignity of examining it.

"Where did it come from?"

"Miss Kelly's sweetheart snuck it to her durin' his last visit."

"Your sweethearts are allowed to call on you?" I asked in surprise.

She peered up at me through her lashes, some of her normal mischievousness sparking in her eyes. "If they say they're our brothers."

I didn't know whether to laugh or frown at this last pronouncement. No wonder the sisters had so many rules about silence in the halls and strict adherence to schedule. How else were they to keep these girls out of trouble?

"And is this where you all steal off to read it?"

"We can't be keepin' it in the dormitory, now can we?"

I arched a single eyebrow in scolding at the insolence that had returned to her voice. "Then one of you must have seen Miss Lennox and Mother Mary Fidelis leaving the abbey's property?"

Her rebelliousness swiftly fled.

I stared at her in expectation, letting her know I was not going to dismiss the matter.

"Maybe," she hedged.

"Tell me." I glanced at the book in my hands. "And maybe I'll fail to mention I found you with this."

She stared at the book, and then asked hopefully, "Will you give it back?"

"No," I snapped.

Behind her, Bree lifted a hand to her mouth and turned aside, hiding her amusement. The girl had cheek, I had to give her that.

She shrugged and sighed, dropping her gaze again. "We saw dem. Well, we saw Miss Lennox." Her voice dropped to a conspiratorial whisper. "We thought maybe she was just havin' a tryst, maybe wit one o' the boys from Nutgrove o'er the hill. One last fling before she gave herself o'er to the Lord's service." It was clear Miss Walsh was not destined to be a nun, for the manner in which she spoke of Miss Lennox's impending profession was akin to sending someone off to their execution.

"I see. And you girls didn't think to tell anyone?"

"We told Mother Fido after Miss Lennox was killed. But then she was killed, too." Her gaze drifted to the side.

Under the circumstances, I allowed her use of what must have been the girls' nickname for Mother Fidelis go without comment. "And you were afraid if you told anyone else, they might also be killed?" I guessed.

She nodded.

It formed a twisted sort of logic, particularly to impressionable minds. Except I knew that Mother Fidelis had already been aware of Miss Lennox's ventures outside the abbey, and that she had not left to conduct a tryst.

I studied Miss Walsh, wishing there was some bit of advice I could give her that I thought she would heed, but it was clear my words would be wasted. The dark-haired girl was too lovely and obstinate for her own good. I only hoped some small bit of the sisters' example and instruction influenced her for the better.

"Go on. But stay away from the orchard in the future," I warned her. "At least, until this killer is caught. And tell the other girls that if they know something, they should speak to me now, before it's too late for someone else." The last was a bluff. We had no idea whether the killer intended to strike again. But I hoped as an intimidation tactic it would prove effective.

Miss Walsh nodded and leapt out of the box, dashing off between the trees.

Bree shook her head. "That girl is gonna find herself in a whole pile o' trouble someday that she canna worm her way oot o'."

I was inclined to agree, until I opened the book we'd confiscated from her. One look at the title page and I burst out laughing. "Or maybe not," I managed to say, tipping the book for her to see.

"*The Canterbury Tales*. What's that?"

"A collection of stories from the Middle Ages. And not as indelicate as we might have feared." I glanced up toward where the girl had disappeared. "Perhaps there's hope yet for our curious Miss Walsh."

I n the end, I couldn't keep my encounter with Miss Walsh a secret from the mother superior. As we made our way through the gardens up to the abbey, I realized the girl had certainly been missed, and when she failed to appear in a timely fashion, the sisters would fear the worst. My suspicions were proven correct. For when the reverend mother and Mother Paul joined me in the parlor, their first concern was for the wayward girl. I hastened to reassure them that she was unharmed and should have returned to the abbey even before me. They exhaled a collective sigh of relief, and were further reassured by a message from another sister, informing them that Miss Walsh had finally appeared in class.

"What was her explanation for being there?" Mother Paul asked, irritation furrowing her normally smooth brow. "Curiosity?"

"Something of the sort," I replied, having told the girl I would try not to tell them about the book.

Even so, it was evident Mother Paul wasn't completely fooled, but she didn't press the matter. "In this case, I think it might be time you contacted her parents," she told the reverend mother.

"Yes. You may be right. It's no longer an issue of simple tardiness anymore, but safety—hers and the other girls. We cannot have that."

"She is rather willful, isn't she?" I asked, not wishing to

stick my nose into matters that didn't concern me, but curious all the same.

"She is the constant subject of all our prayers," she replied
tactfully, despite the evident strain in her eyes. She clasped
her hands together in her lap. "Now, I'm quite certain you
did not come to see us today for the sole purpose of saving
Miss Walsh from her folly." Her gaze focused intensely on
my face. "What have you uncovered?"

I should have known better than to think the reverend
mother would have missed the restrained energy vibrating
through me. Even so, it was not easy to deliver the news I
had to tell her about both Miss Lennox's and Mother Fidelis's involvement in the tithe war. I felt certain the shock that
registered across her face was genuine. However, Mother
Paul was more difficult to read. She accepted the news as
equitably as her mother superior, but her expression merely
tightened with each new revelation, her gaze turned aside.

"I feel as if I should have known, or at least suspected,"
Reverend Mother replied, shaking her head. "It is . . . troubling, to say the least." Her thumbs tapped together in her
lap. "I shall have to inform the bishop. He should be made
aware."

"What of you, Mother Mary Paul?" I inquired, turning to
the other sister. "Did you have any idea what they were doing?"

She frowned. "No. Not really. But . . . I had misgivings.
Unfounded, of course. Which is why I never said anything,"
she told her mother superior.

"How long ago did you begin to suspect?"

She considered my question. "Perhaps a few weeks before
Miss Lennox's death. I found Mother Mary Fidelis searching
for something in your office. A paper of some kind. But I
noticed your latest letter from the bishop was open on your
desk. You had shared some of its contents with me earlier
that day, and then folded it and put it in the drawer of your
desk. It talked about O'Connell, and the tithes protests, and
his worries that more clashes like the one in County Kilkenny

earlier that spring might occur. He asked for our prayers for the Lord's guidance."

"Yes, I remember," Reverend Mother murmured. "And I understand why you didn't say anything. But why did you suspect Miss Lennox was also involved?"

"I didn't. Not until she was caught outside the abbey wall. Then I began to wonder."

Mother Superior lifted a weary hand to her forehead. "Yes. That makes sense."

It did make sense. And if Mother Paul had noticed, she might not have been the only one.

Gage and I were mostly silent on our drive home from the abbey, the subject occupying our thoughts too sensitive to discuss while speaking loud enough to be heard over the clattering wheels. The men had said very little upon their return from the castle through the tunnel, but I noticed their clothes were rumpled, including Constable Casey's, and Anderley sported the beginnings of a black eye. He refused my attempts to examine it, mounting his horse and riding back toward what had become his customary post at the Yellow House.

I closed the door behind us as we reached our bedchamber, but Gage held up his hands, forestalling any questions. "Some of the men took exception to our visit, which resulted in a bit of a coat dusting. The worst of which you've seen. There's nothing more to say on the matter."

I arched my eyebrows at his testiness. "Did you locate any weapons?"

"No. Or they would have used them," he muttered under his breath, tugging at his cravat. "Everything else seemed just as Casey described. If they're planning a rebellion from that location, it will be a rather short-lived and slapdash one." He winced as he shrugged his dirt-streaked coat over his left shoulder.

"You're injured," I gasped, moving forward.

"No, I'm not," he snapped, twisting away. "Just a bit sore. I don't need you to coddle me."

I whirled toward the door. "Then I'll wait for you in the parlor, shall I? Seems someone needs to lick his wounds." The sound of its slam was rather satisfactory, but I paused halfway down the stairs, annoyed I'd forgotten to remove my pelisse. I set to unbuttoning it, pulling it from my shoulders as I rounded the newel post to find Marsdale standing in our entry.

At times, the man truly was a nuisance, showing up where he was least wanted and least anticipated. Though, in this case, I supposed his presence might prove to be helpful. He deserved to know what we'd uncovered about his cousin, and I was curious to hear his reaction to our revelation.

He caught sight of me standing there watching him and flashed me his usual impish grin, but something of my thoughts must have been reflected in my expression, for his humor faded.

"M'lady . . ." the butler began.

"It's quite all right," I assured him. "Could you have some tea sent up? Lord Marsdale, if you'll join me in the parlor."

I dropped my soft emerald green pelisse onto the back of the chair closest to the door and crossed over toward the windows which looked out onto the carriage yard. I rolled my shoulders to adjust the neckline of my matching gown, smoothing out the bows at the collar and brushing a hand down the skirt toward the decorative twists of fabric.

"You are distressed," Marsdale remarked with more gentleness than I'd yet heard him use.

I glanced back to find him still standing near the door, as if uncertain how to proceed. "Not unduly." I offered him a weak smile. "Do not worry. There won't be any tears."

He moved forward a few hesitant steps. "Is it about my cousin?"

I noticed then the pale cast of his skin. I didn't wish to lie, but I also thought Gage should be present when we told him. "Partly," I hedged. "But I suspect it's more the weight of this inquiry vexing me." I stared out the window at the brilliant afternoon sunlight. "It's bound to happen at least once during every investigation."

"Then why do you do it?"

I noticed he hadn't pressed me to tell him what I knew of his cousin. Perhaps he was in as little of a rush to hear whatever had alarmed me as I was to tell it.

"Because someone needs to. Because I'm good at it." Those words sounded almost trite, and I wondered if they were enough. But he didn't press that either.

The tea tray arrived then, and I settled onto one of the armchairs, grateful for something to do. Marsdale seemed equally relieved.

When Gage entered the room a short time later, he found us both sitting quietly, sipping our tea like two of the most proper members of the ton rather than two of the most scandalous. We must have made quite an incongruous sight, for he stumbled to a halt after taking just a few steps into the room. His eyes traveled between us several times before advancing.

"Did you tell him?" he asked as I set my cup aside to pour his.

"I thought it best to wait for you," I replied, dropping sugar into his cup and passing it to him.

He nodded, taking a seat in the chair next to mine. His hair at his forehead and around his ears and neck was still damp, and the collar of his jacket was folded up at the back. I reached over to brush it flat, and he gave me a quick smile.

"All right, out with it," Marsdale declared, draping his arm over the back of the settee. "I'm riveted in suspense," he drawled in a droll voice that did nothing to hide his nerves.

Gage took a sip of his tea. "It's not as bad as we have made it seem. But it is . . . worrying." He explained what we'd learned earlier that morning about Miss Lennox's involvement with the tithe protest, her supposed information gathering, and even Mr. LaTouche's somewhat contradictory claim the evening before.

Marsdale listened without comment until he finished, and

then sank back into the cushions of the settee, his expression one of astonishment. "So someone is lying?" he finally muttered.

"It appears that way. Though I suppose it's possible that your cousin was playing both sides, so to speak. She might have provided information to Casey and the other members of the tithe protest and, in the process, stumbled on to something that made her think there would be an armed revolt, and so asked LaTouche to warn Anglesey about it." I frowned even as I finished saying the words.

"Yes, but then why didn't she simply write to Wellington, or whatever family member was corresponding with her, and inform them of her fears? Why contact LaTouche at all?" Gage pointed out, and I could not answer him. He was right. It all sounded far too convoluted.

He looked across at Marsdale, who was scowling at the table before him. "Did anyone say anything pertinent after we left LaTouche's yesterday evening?"

"No. Though LaTouche was quieter than I've generally observed. Bowed out of a hand of piquet, when everyone knows he's mad for it. His son even seemed . . . puzzled by his behavior."

"What of your cousin, Miss Lennox? Do any of her reported actions make any sense to you?"

He shook his head. "No. But then again, when you told me she'd converted and decided to become a nun, I was also completely shocked. Nothing I ever knew of her led me to believe she was particularly religious, or that she would ever defy her family in such a way." He lifted his eyes toward the ceiling as if in remembrance. "Though as I've said before, she did often keep to herself, so perhaps I didn't know her well enough to tell." His brow lowered. "But I do know one thing. Harriet was fiercely loyal. Had she thrown her lot in with these protesters, she would not have betrayed them."

"Not even if they were planning some sort of violence that might see innocent people harmed?" Gage pressed.

"Even then," he insisted. "And certainly not to LaTouche, who is likely one of those Orangemen dead set against them."

With each new thing I learned, my understanding of Miss Lennox became less clear. She had been described as quiet, humble, and meek, yet she'd defied her family to convert to Catholicism and join a convent. Then she defied her religious order and joined in the efforts of the tithe war. There was something inconsistent, something unreliable, in all of this, though I couldn't put my finger on what it was. Her conversion seemed so precipitous, as did her decision to help the tithe protesters, and Miss Lennox struck me as a person who was far more considered than that. Mother Fidelis had hinted the same as well.

Marsdale sighed, suddenly sounding very weary. "But what do I know? I haven't spoken to Harriet in years. Not since my father tried to arrange a marriage between us."

I looked up, pausing in my efforts to gather the tea items together and stack them on the tray. Out of the corner of my eye, I could see that Gage seemed just as startled by this pronouncement as I was.

He sat forward. "You were engaged to Miss Lennox?"

"Not officially." He looked up from where he was plucking at the fabric of the settee, seeming to notice our watchful expressions for the first time. His scowl blackened. "What? I wasn't ready to stick my neck in the parson's mousetrap. And besides, I liked Harriet too much to wish to saddle her to my profligate ways. Being a duchess someday wouldn't have mattered a fig to her, and that's the only compensation our matrimony could have offered her."

"It sounds as if you cared for her," I said quietly.

"Of course I did. Harriet was a dashed fine girl." His face tightened with some intense spasm of emotion before he could bring it back under control. He cleared his throat and rose abruptly to his feet. "Excuse me."

Then before either of us could say another word, he disappeared from the room. His footsteps receded rapidly toward the entry and out the front door. We sat listening as he called for his horse and then followed the lad toward the stables.

"I think you broke him."

I turned to Gage with a glower, unimpressed with his quip. "Marsdale may be a scoundrel, but even scoundrels have hearts."

He smiled at me gently. "Ah. Even me."

I arched a single eyebrow, assuming he referred to his reputation when we first met. "You were never a scoundrel. Just a very poorly disguised rake."

Gage's smile broadened and then dimmed as he glanced toward the window, where the sound of horse's hooves riding off into the distance could be heard. "The question is, just how much of a scoundrel *is* Marsdale?"

I folded my hands in my lap, having no trouble following his line of thought, as the same thing had occurred to me. "His appearance in Whitehaven did seem far too coincidental."

"Was he truly fleeing Lord Skipton and his daughter, or was he just returning from a visit to Ireland and seeing us ready to set off in that direction decided to tag along?"

"But what of his valet and luggage? They weren't with him. He said they were trailing behind him."

Gage shrugged one shoulder. "Maybe that was a lie he told, thinking it would make his story more believable. Maybe they were already at the inn and the message he left instructed his valet to follow after us the next day."

"And so what? He traveled to Ireland to see his cousin in a convent and then murdered her? Why? What motive could he possibly have? And don't say religion, because I do not for one minute believe Marsdale cares enough about that to kill someone over it."

"No. But contrary to what he wants people to think, he does care about his family. You heard what he said on the boat about his brother, and you've heard the way his voice softens when he speaks of his cousins, especially Miss Lennox. Who, admittedly, it sounds as if he actually loved, whether or not he realizes it. Perhaps he only came to be certain she was well, but something set him off. Something to do with loyalty perhaps."

"He does speak an awful lot about that, doesn't he?" I considered what he'd said. "But then why didn't any of the sisters recognize him?"

"Maybe he never came to the abbey proper. Maybe he wrote to her and met her by the pond, just as LaTouche claimed he did."

"And Mother Mary Fidelis saw them together and confronted him, so he killed her, too?" I eyed him doubtfully.

His mouth flattened in chagrin. "It does seem rather far-fetched."

"Everything about these murders seems far-fetched," I remarked in discouragement, rising to my feet and crossing the room to stare out the window again. A squirrel sat in the middle of the carriage yard a few feet away, his red tail rolled up his back like a plume as he chomped away at some sort of nut he rotated in front of his mouth. Some sound made him still, glancing behind him, before he stuffed the rest of his meal in his cheeks and ran off into the forest.

A moment later I heard Gage rise to join me. His arms wrapped around me from behind. "I admit, when I joined my father in this private inquiry business, I never expected to be investigating the death of a nun, let alone two. But here we are."

I tipped my head to the right, pressing it against his chin.

"However, the longer we investigate, the more I'm reminded they were just people. Perhaps they'd devoted themselves and their lives to the service of the Lord and the church, or were about to, but that didn't mean their problems went away. I suspect whoever killed them, whatever their motive, we will find it is just as common as any other murder. Anger, jealousy, money, fear . . ."

"Love or hate," I finished for him.

"Yes."

"It seems the key lies in truly understanding what Miss Lennox, and consequently Mother Mary Fidelis, were doing. Was she helping or harming the protest?" I exhaled, feeling my frustration return. "Or does this have nothing to do with that at all?

"I don't know. But the cattle fair is tomorrow, and I suspect one way or another it will provide us with some answers." His arms tightened around me. "I just hope they're not answers we would rather not have."

CHAPTER TWENTY-ONE

Early the following morning I stood staring at the back of the phaeton as it receded down the abbey drive, feeling rather like an unwanted parcel dropped at its destination. Gage and I had argued since before sunrise about his intention to leave me and Bree at the abbey while he and Anderley ventured to the cattle fair. I was not pleased to again be left behind simply because he feared for my safety should the protesters turn violent if the constables raided the fair to confiscate property in order to collect unpaid tithes. It seemed a rather poorly kept secret they would. There were bound to be numerous opportunities to observe some of our chief suspects, and I would not be there to do so.

"Ye ken it's for the best," Bree murmured as the carriage slowed for the gate.

"Yes. But that doesn't mean I have to be happy about it." I whirled away to climb the stairs, trying to dismiss Gage from my thoughts. I only hoped he heeded his own advice, and refrained from jumping into the fray should the protesters and the constables clash.

The morning at the abbey passed quietly, though not serenely. It was almost as if the entire building were holding its breath waiting for something to happen, tensing its bricks and mortar for the next barrage. It was partially to do with the cattle fair and everyone's uncertainty over what would happen there, but that could not account for it all. Some of the sisters and students seemed naïvely unaware of what was happening outside the abbey walls, and yet the strain was still evident on their faces. I hoped the stress might compel someone to come forward with some previously unknown piece of information, but no one sought me out. In fact, a number of them still refused to meet my eye, as if I were the source of their ill fortune and not the person trying to remedy it.

The tension finally snapped around ten o'clock when a wagon came clattering up the drive. I had been seated in the parlor—hiding from the others' anxious stares for a few moments, if truth be told—but at the sound, I hurried toward the window. I could see Davy at the reins, and then as the wagon turned, Mrs. Scully in the back, leaning over someone. I dropped the curtains and hurried toward the door. At the banister, I leaned down to see Mr. Scully lying in the bed of the wagon, his eyes closed.

I rushed down the steps just as the door to the old servants' quarters and the kitchen burst open. At the sight of me, the women moving toward the wagon stopped short.

"What's happened?" I demanded to know as I rounded the wagon and pulled myself up onto the bed.

"The constables. Some o' 'em opened fire," Mrs. Scully shrieked through her tears.

I could see now that Mr. Scully's lower leg was soaked with blood, though someone had been smart enough to tie a tourniquet below the knee. He seemed unconscious, hopefully only having swooned from the pain the ride in the back of the wagon must have caused.

"Someone . . ." I glanced toward where Davy kneeled beside me. "Davy, will you fetch the surgeon?"

He nodded and leapt down to unhitch one of the horses from the wagon.

"We need to get him inside. Bring out one of the cots from the infirmary. We'll use it to carry him."

A few people scrambled to follow my orders as Sister

Bernard peered over the bed of the wagon at the man. "I'll gather the supplies we'll need," she declared before hurrying back inside.

An audience of sisters and students had gathered on the balcony and stairs above us, but I could not spare them a thought for Mr. Scully began to stir. He turned his head from side to side, groaning as his wife crooned to him.

"You're at the abbey now, Mr. Scully. We're going to move you into the infirmary and see what we can do about your leg until the surgeon arrives. Is the bullet still inside him or did it pass through?" I asked Mrs. Scully, but she shook her head unhelpfully. "Do you know if he's hurt anywhere else?"

"I . . . I don't know."

I patted her arm. "Mr. Scully, are you . . ." I broke off, already able to tell he couldn't answer me. Not yet.

The cot arrived and I urged several of the lay sisters and day women up into the bed to help me lift him, taking as much care as we possibly could with his leg. Regardless, he howled with the pain, almost making one of the youngest women drop the top left side of his body. Once he was on the cot, we slowly slid it from the wagon bed, and six women hefted him between them. The outside stairs were far easier to navigate than the narrow interior ones, so they carried him through the main door and through the corridors to the infirmary, sending onlookers scattering before them.

At the infirmary, Sister Bernard was ready and waiting for him, taking over the situation with such skill and aplomb that I was content to stand back and watch. She had a postulant to assist her, shooing the curious out the door, and pouring Mrs. Scully a glass of water. I crossed toward the basin of water to wash the blood from my hands, sparing only a forlorn glance at the stains on the cornflower blue fabric of my skirt.

I sat down next to Mrs. Scully where she perched on the edge of her chair, watching Sister Bernard and the postulant attend to her husband. Her hands clutched the glass so tightly I worried it might shatter.

"Why on earth did the constables fire?" I asked as much to

myself as her. After what happened in County Wexford, I felt
certain Chief Constable Corcoran would have given them strict
instructions not to shoot unless ordered to do so by him.

"I don't know," she sniffed. "One moment they were
tryin' to seize a pair o' cows and the men were shoutin' at
'em, and . . . and the next they were shootin' 'em."

There must have been more, but I did not press her. Not
like this. "Mr. Scully was one of the protesters?"

"Against dose odious tithes? Aye."

"Was anyone else injured?"

"To be sure."

"Do you know who?"

She shook her head. "Once I saw my Sean go down, I
couldn't tink o' anyone else." She flicked a distracted glance
at me before turning a more thoughtful one my way. "But
yer tinkin' o' yer own husband an' his man." This time she
was the one to reach over and pat my arm in comfort. "They
be fine, lass. Yer man be the one who tied off Sean's leg and
hefted 'im into the wagon."

I exhaled the breath I hadn't known I was holding and
offered her a tight smile of gratitude. She looked as if she
wanted to say more, but then the postulant approached to
say she could speak to Mr. Scully if she wished. I stayed
back, allowing her to talk to him alone. From the mellow
tone of his voice, it was evident they'd dosed him with some
form of morphine, likely laudanum.

There was little Sister Bernard could do except keep the
wound clean, his blood from draining out of him, and
attempt to minimize his pain. The surgeon would have to
decide what was to be done next—whether the leg could be
saved, or if the lower portion would have to be amputated.
If he didn't arrive soon, there might not be much of a choice.

"The Englishman's wife. Where is she?"

I glanced up in surprise.

"Mrs. Gage?" Mrs. Scully asked her husband. "She's right
here."

I slowly rose to my feet and crossed to where he lay.

"Mr. Scully, how are you feeling?" I asked politely, curious what he had to say.

"Forget that." He waved his hands as if to bat it away. "Ye need to know that they was one o' us. Do ye understand?"

I nodded. The few remaining hairs on his head stood on end, and his pupils were large black dots, dilated from the laudanum, and making him look wild.

"The tree 'll tell ye." His eyes fell shut. "For sure, it will."

I stared at him in consternation, uncertain how to respond, or what he even meant. If he meant anything at all.

Mrs. Scully's eyes were wide with the same confusion. "Sean, perhaps you should—"

"Remind Davy those bushes won't prune demselves," he snapped suddenly before beginning to ramble about roses and beetles.

"Laudanum will do that to people sometimes," Sister Bernard murmured in a low voice, trying to reassure us both.

"Of course," I replied. "I'll go see if Davy's returned with any word from the surgeon."

I slipped away, grateful to escape. In any case, I wanted to think, for Mr. Scully's words were not as odd as they sounded. There was only one tree I could think of that would mean anything to Miss Lennox, kingfisher's nest or no.

Eager to test my theory, I turned toward the mother superior's office to discover if there was any news and almost collided with Davy. I pressed a hand to my chest over my pounding heart. "Mr. Somers," I gasped. "So sorry. Were you able to locate the surgeon?"

His hand lowered from where he'd gripped my arm to steady me. "On his way, m'lady. 'Twas stitchin' up a wound. Said he'd be comin' here when he finished."

"Good."

"And Mr. Scully?"

"Is resting as comfortably as Sister Bernard can make him until the surgeon arrives. He's being well cared for," I assured him.

He nodded, shifting from foot to foot.

I studied his young face, the darting shyness and evidence of strain, wondering if he was part of the protest as well. "Mr. Somers," I began slowly. "Did you see what happened?"

He hesitated and then gave another nod, lowering his eyes to the floor. "Ole Mr. Devlin started wavin' his cane. Angry, he was, the constables was tryin' to take one o' his herd. Startled one o' the horses, which bumped into Kelly, who bumped into Mrs. O'Brien. And some school lads threw a few rocks, and . . ."

"So it was general chaos?"

He inhaled a quick breath and bobbed his head. "Everyone was yellin' at everyone else, and afore we knew it, the Peelers was shootin'."

I shook my head at the senselessness of it all. "Was anyone killed?"

"I don't know, m'lady, sure I don't."

I pressed a hand to my stomach where it clenched in dread, sending up a little prayer that no one had paid the ultimate price for today's inanity. "Thank you, Mr. Somers." I began to turn away, but his voice stopped me.

"M'lady. If I may?" He cleared his throat. "I've somemat other to tell ye."

I turned back to face him, some new tension in his already anxious disposition telling me this wasn't a passing comment. "Of course."

"I . . . I saw yer husband at the fair."

"Yes. Mrs. Scully mentioned he helped load Mr. Scully into the wagon."

"Before dat. Before the trouble. I . . . I saw him speakin' wit a man. A gentleman."

I waited patiently for him to work his way around to making his point.

"He's the man I saw in the field, out by the pond."

"Then he must have been talking to Mr. LaTouche. He's tall, with dark hair, dresses impeccably?"

"That's him," he confirmed.

"He admitted to us that he'd been in the field near the

pond." I decided it was best to keep his confessed reasons for that to myself for now. "Did you see anyone with him?"

He ran his fingers back and forth along the brim of his hat. "Once."

My eyes widened at this new information.

"I . . . well, I remembered after ye asked dat I might o' seen him earlier dat day Miss Lennox died. I didn't mark it at the time. Seemed almost like anotter day after all dat happened later. But I tot ye should know." He paused. "An' I know I saw him the evenin' afore Mother Mary Fidelis . . ." He inhaled. "I saw 'er speakin' to him."

"Mother Mary Fidelis was speaking to Mr. LaTouche?" I reiterated in surprise.

He nodded. "Right near the wall. Where . . ." He stopped, the words seeming to stick in his throat.

"Yes. Quite." I frowned. "But why didn't you say anything about this earlier?"

He hunched his shoulders. "I didn't know who he was. And I tot ye was already lookin' for him."

Seeing the way he squirmed just talking to me now, I suspected it had more to do with his wanting to avoid any discussion of the matter whatsoever. I sighed heavily. "Well, thank you for telling me now."

He scurried toward the door leading belowstairs while I waited, not wanting to follow him directly and cause him more discomfort. Fortunately, one of the lay sisters bustled past at that moment, carrying an armful of sheets, and I asked if she would be good enough to ask Bree to meet me in the gardens. She dipped her head, and I set out toward the back door.

A light rain had begun to fall, though the sun still shone through the wispy clouds to the east. It was the type of weather it was foolish to hide from, sunny one moment and misting the next. Particularly if one was prepared for it. I slipped my arms into the sleeves of my blue pelisse with scalloped trim and wrapped it about me, before adjusting my bonnet on my head. Bree appeared in similar attire, handed down from me and altered to fit her slighter figure.

"I need to take another look at that tree by the pond," I explained as she joined me.

Despite the light, sporadic rain, the workmen were almost certainly toiling away at the wall, so we used the more circuitous route through the door by the gardeners' cottages. The men looked up as we passed but, after a tip of their hats, ignored us as before. The ground near the pond was soft with mud, adding more stains to the hem of my skirt along with the blood.

Bree hung back as I approached the tree. It appeared much the same as before, but then I had not looked inside. I was curious whether my hunch was correct or if I was about to risk being bitten by a squirrel. An exposed root rounded upward adjacent to the hole in the trunk, allowing me to step up on it to cautiously peer inside rather than reaching in blindly over my head.

At first all I could see was darkness, though nothing appeared to move, but as I shifted my head around, the gleam of something pale caught my eye. I slowly slid my hand inside, conscious there could still be a creature calling that hole home. My fingers brushed something smooth and crisp, and I reached in farther, grasping a bundle tied with something. I almost shouted in triumph when I pulled out what appeared to be a stack of correspondence held together with string.

"Are those letters?" Bree asked, moving closer.

"It looks like it." I grinned down at her. "Belonging to Miss Lennox, I presume." I rose up on tiptoe to check inside the hole one last time to be certain I hadn't missed any before stepping down from the root.

"Why on earth did she decide to hide 'em in a tree?"

"Why else? She didn't want anyone to read them."

Bree tilted her head in acknowledgment.

I stared down at the little packet, scolding myself for not searching the hole in the beech tree sooner. This wasn't the first time I'd found something important hidden inside a tree, but it would be the last time I underestimated its value as a place of concealment.

There had been a lull in the shower of misty rain, but I knew it was only a matter of time before it began again. Even so, I couldn't resist the temptation to read one or two of the letters to assuage my rapacious curiosity. What sort of information could these missives possibly contain that Miss Lennox would believe it necessary to hide them outside the abbey walls in a tree? Whom had she been corresponding with? Was it Wellington or another of her well-placed family members, like Casey alleged, or someone else?

I slipped one of the letters from the packet and unfolded the paper addressed simply to "HL." I frowned at the absence of any address, and then thumbed through the other missives, finding them to be much the same. Had they contained an outer sheet of paper with her full name and direction? How else would the postmaster have known where or to whom they were to be delivered? But none of the sisters could recall her receiving any mail, and yet this stack was evidence of quite a regular correspondence. How else had it been conveyed to her? I glanced up at the tree, wondering if it served as more than a hiding place.

The letter was brief, as were the second and third ones I quickly perused, but given what I already knew, it was not difficult to infer what they meant. I was stunned. Nothing was as we'd been led to believe. Not even Lord Gage's insufferable assertions.

"I . . . I need to find somewhere dry and quiet to sit and read these," I told Bree, feeling as if I'd stumbled into a labrynth.

"What is it, m'lady? What do they say?"

I glanced up into her concerned gaze. "I think Miss Lennox may have been a British spy."

CHAPTER TWENTY-TWO

I sat on a divan in the summerhouse, staring out through the large rounded open windows at the rain falling more earnestly. It tapped against the roof overhead with almost a musical quality, and softened the garden landscape beyond into a misty watercolor scene. However, far from charmed, I felt cold and stiff. Partly from the chill weight of my damp clothing drying in the breeze, which I suppose could have been remedied somewhat by closing the folded shutters of the windows. But that would have meant shutting out the light to leave us sitting among the dank, musty stench of the furnishings that the draft helped to mitigate as it stirred it with the scent of the rain and blooming flowers beyond.

In any case, most of the cold and stiffness I felt came not from without, but from within. I glanced toward the stack of Miss Lennox's letters piled between us and then up to Bree, who was perusing the last of them with a scowl. I wanted to rise, to force some movement into my limbs, some clarity into my mystified thoughts. Instead I sat rigidly staring out at the rain, trying not to feel what I was feeling.

Bree lowered the last of the letters, crinkling the paper as it touched her lap. I thought she was just as much at a loss for words, but she found them more quickly than I did.

"The poor lass."

"Caught in a mess not of her making."

Her gaze turned fierce. "Aye. By a lot o' men who seemed to care naught for her."

I began to gather up the correspondence to bind them together. "I suspect they cared. But not as much as they should have."

She folded the last of the missives and passed it to me. "Still. This task o' hers was eatin' her up inside. Ye can tell tha' from the way they berate her. And they did naught to help her."

I gazed down at the letters held together by the bow I'd tied in the twine, perhaps the last evidence of Miss Lennox's mind and thoughts the world would ever know. "It's no wonder her nails were bitten to the quick. Keeping secrets to oneself is difficult. But one this massive, particularly when she seemed to genuinely care about these women, these students . . ." I lifted my hand before me ". . . this village." I inhaled swiftly. "I've kept my fair share of confidences." I glanced at Bree. "As have you. But nothing like this."

It was as much an acknowledgment as I could give that her keeping her brother's identity a secret had been forgiven, and I could see in her eyes that she understood.

"Makes one wonder what some o' those people would do if they found oot," she remarked.

"And how exactly Mother Mary Fidelis fit into all this. Did she know, or was she as fooled as everyone else?" Recalling how perceptive the sister had been, I had difficulty believing she was completely blind to Miss Lennox's deception, but she may not have known all. "Well, we do know one thing. Mr. Scully was aware of her secret. He knew of her hiding spot, and he said, 'She's one of us,' which leads me to think he was privy to at least some of her thoughts. Otherwise, how could he be so certain of her not betraying them?"

The sound of footsteps on the stairs leading up into the summerhouse made us both turn in our seats.

"Gage," I exclaimed as he strode through the open door, shaking water from his hat and greatcoat. I hurried toward him, more relieved than I realized to see him safe and unharmed, despite Mrs. Scully's earlier assurances.

He gathered me into his arms, under the sides of his sodden greatcoat. "Now, what's this?" he murmured as I buried my head in his cravat, inhaling his familiar scent. "Not that I mind such a greeting, but it would be good to know what's brought it on."

I stepped back to look at him. "Davy and the Scullys told me about what happened at the cattle fair. They said you were well, but until I saw you for myself . . ." I broke off, not sure how to explain.

Thankfully I didn't need to. He nodded. "I'm fine. Both Anderley and myself." He dipped his head toward his valet, who stood a discreet distance away with Bree, giving us as much privacy as the small octagonal building allowed.

I smiled at the dark-haired servant, the skin around his eye an ugly constellation of colors. "I'm glad of it."

"The Scullys arrived safely then?"

"Yes. We moved Mr. Scully to the infirmary and Sister Bernard made him as comfortable as she could. When I left them, they were still waiting for the surgeon, but he should have already come and gone." I studied his face. "I assume you called at the front door. Did they not tell you how he fared?"

"One of the younger sisters answered. All she told us was that you had gone out to the gardens." His eyes traveled over our rather drafty and sparsely furnished surroundings. "What are you doing out here? Wouldn't the abbey parlor be far more comfortable?"

"Perhaps. But Bree and I found something." I explained how Mr. Scully's words had led us to the location of Miss Lennox's long-lost correspondence. His eyes watched me carefully, and I knew I was not doing a very good job hiding my shock and dismay. Rather than tell him why, I urged him to sit and read the letters himself. There were only about two dozen, most of which were short, and sometimes terse. I suspected Miss Lennox's letters had been much more voluble, but none of those were included in the stack.

I paced before the windows, fidgeting with the buttons at the wrists of my gloves while he perused them. The thunderous expression which fell over his features left no doubt as to how he felt about their contents. Even Anderley and Bree, who had been chatting in the far corner of the summerhouse, fell silent, conscious of their employer's building fury. Periodically, I shared glances with Bree, both of us mindful of what was to come.

Gage lowered the last letter with such a snap of his wrist that I was afraid he'd ripped the paper. "I cannot believe my father knew about this and did not see fit to inform us."

I lifted my hands in entreaty. "We don't know that for certain . . ."

"Of course we do. If Wellington knew, and he clearly did, as he penned some of these missives himself . . ." he rattled the paper he still gripped in his hand ". . . and likely put the poor girl up to this ridiculousness in the first place, then my father knew."

I lowered my arms, unable to argue with that.

His eyes narrowed to slits on the floorboards a few yards in front of him and then, with a scoff of disgust, rose to his feet. "He must believe we're idiots! How could he possibly think we wouldn't figure this out?"

I glanced toward where our servants stood, unable to help listening to us, though they tactfully looked away. I doubted he wished for them to be privy to this part of our conversation.

He scraped a hand back through his hair and followed my gaze, his chest still heaving with anger. Then he strode toward the window farthest from Bree and Anderley to glare out at the rain as he spoke in a lower voice. "I knew he cared little for some of my choices, that he was infuriated by my refusal to bow to his will, but *this*."

I inched forward, past experiences making me wary of approaching a man bristling with anger even when rationally I knew I had nothing to fear. Gage spoke to me very little of his father, but I knew there was more behind this sudden vehement rage than his father's failure to share pertinent information with us about this investigation. But the best I could do at the moment was try to diffuse some of it, to help him refocus on the matter at hand.

"It certainly would have helped us conduct this investigation faster," I replied measuredly. "And possibly spared Mother Mary Fidelis's life."

He whipped his head around to stare at me. "How are you not angry about this? The man just unforgivably insulted us."

"Oh, I am. But I already know your father does not like me, or think highly of me. So I suppose I'm less shocked. In any case, just at the moment, one of us should keep a level head, and I figured it should be me since you have more of a right to your outrage."

This explanation seemed to take some of the fuel out of his fire, for the hard line of his mouth softened. "Quite right." He inhaled deeply, calming himself, and then turned to face us all. "Well, then. What does this mean for our investigation?"

Anderley stepped forward, clasping his arms behind his back. "Excuse me, sir. But seeing as I seem to be the only one who hasn't read those letters, would anyone mind telling me what they say before we discuss it?" He glanced at Bree. "Miss McEvoy said you've discovered Miss Lennox was a British spy?"

Gage nodded. "It appears that the British government— or at least Wellington and his cronies, since he's no longer prime minister—were more concerned than they publicly wished to acknowledge about the organized efforts begun to conduct this tithe war. Part of the reason Wellington and Peel and their government finally relented and pushed for the passage of Catholic Emancipation was because they feared the Irish Catholics rising up in armed rebellion, and the danger that would pose to British lives and British sovereignty. However, with that achieved, the Catholics in Ireland are now rallying around a different cause.

"For some reason—the letters aren't clear—Wellington seemed to fear these seeds of rebellion were being sown in Rathfarnham. Because of the history of the area, I imagine.

There have already been two revolts with their leadership partially centered here, in 1798 and 1803. And any rebellion after the government's capitulation would be an embarrassment, particularly to Wellington and his legacy. The letters do mention that previous attempts had been made to position men here in the village, to worm their way into the heart of the protestors, all of whom failed.

"Which is why they next decided to use a woman. One who'd not only converted to Catholicism, but decided to become a nun." Gage's voice was sharp with disapproval.

"Except she hadna. No' really," Bree chimed in.

"Though it's obvious she came to sympathize with them to some extent." I stooped to gather up the letters where Gage had laid them. "She started to believe it was not the Catholics who were intent on causing disorder, but the Protestant Orangemen. The later letters from Wellington and two other men, who must have been part of the arrangement, tell her to stop speculating on matters she cannot fully comprehend and focus on the Ribbonmen."

Gage pointed over my shoulder at the letter I was refolding. "The last one makes reference to something she wrote to warn them of, dismissing it as nonsense. But we don't have Miss Lennox's letter, so we don't know precisely what it was she was warning them of."

"It obviously couldn't have been some sort of trouble the Catholics wished to cause, for then it wouldn't have been brushed aside," I reasoned. "So it's probably something to do with the Orangemen."

"I've heard talk of their planning a parade," Anderley suggested. "The proprietor of the Yellow House and a few of the other shop owners are worried their businesses might suffer damage. Apparently, it's happened before."

"Of course," Gage gasped. "The Twelfth. That's the anniversary of the victory of Protestant King William III, William of Orange, over Catholic James II at the Battle of the Boyne. The Orangemen hold marches that day every year."

"But that's only two days from now," I pointed out.

Gage's expression turned grim.

"So ye were doin' something worthwhile hangin' aboot the tavern all day," Bree teased Anderley. "No just avoidin' work in that way o' yers."

He narrowed his eyes.

"Could she have somehow discovered that the Orangemen intended to make trouble during this parade of theirs?" I asked, ignoring them both. "But when she tried to warn Wellington and the others, they dismissed her suspicions," I ruminated, trying to puzzle this out. "So she contacted Mr. LaTouche, an old family friend who she knew lived in the area. *That's* why she wrote him. To warn him of the Orangemen, not the Catholics."

Gage's eyes gleamed in agreement. "But he also refused to help. He told us so himself. *That* he wasn't lying about. So what did she do next?"

I frowned, recalling what Davy had confided in me. "She tried to persuade Mr. LaTouche a second time. Davy just told me he's almost certain he saw him earlier the day she was killed, though it could have been the day before. He also saw him talking to Mother Mary Fidelis the evening before she was killed."

Gage tapped his hat against his side. "Mr. LaTouche has been in some awfully suspect places at suspect times."

I had to agree. "But would he have killed them? Why? To keep Miss Lennox quiet about the parade, and Mother Mary Fidelis quiet about the first murder?"

"It's reason enough if you're devoted to the cause. Especially if he still believed Miss Lennox had converted to Catholicism."

I sank down on the bench behind me, staring down at the stack of letters clutched in my hands. That hollow ache I'd been feeling for days began to throb again, seeming to open a hole up inside me. Sometimes it was difficult to accept the terrible lengths people would go to for their beliefs, particularly when they fooled themselves into thinking they were acting in the Lord's name or for the public's good when they were truly reacting out of hatred and fear. I had some personal experience with this beyond our other inquiries. I'd witnessed the wild panic and fury of the mob outside the magistrate's court when I was brought up on charges of unnatural tendencies after my involvement in Sir Anthony's dissections came to light. But that had been because of the rumored crimes they'd believed I'd committed—luring people to their deaths so we could desecrate their bodies—not because of who I was as a person. These people, these neighbors, both Protestant and Catholic alike, who spat at each other with such hatred that it sometimes erupted into violence, did so because their faith was slightly different. Because they couldn't be bothered to learn the truth about each other.

Had Mr. LaTouche killed Miss Lennox simply because he believed her religious beliefs were different than his? I didn't know, but the very idea, not to mention the fact that he would have been acting under a faulty assumption, made me despondent.

"Either way, a visit to Mr. LaTouche is in order," Gage said, concern shining in his eyes as he looked down at me. "And since Mr. Scully led us to the letters, it would be good to speak with him again as well. As soon as he's able to speak lucidly, that is." I hadn't told him about the laudanum, but it was a good bet that any man who'd just had a bullet extracted from his leg or an amputation would be dosed heavily. "If he knew about the letters, someone else also might have."

"It would also be good to try to figure out who picked up and delivered Miss Lennox's correspondence." I explained my observations about the lack of address on the letters, and the sisters not recalling her receiving any mail.

"Whoe'er it was might no' even live in Rathfarnham," Bree observed. "He coulda just as easily rode doon from someplace like Dublin, havin' been told where to convey his missives an' collect what been left." She shrugged. "'Tis how I'd do it."

"Bree's right," Gage agreed. "The probability of us finding that man is slim. He's not likely to show up bearing another message when everyone involved already knows Miss Lennox is dead. And if Wellington and the others . . ." his eyes hardened, making clear which others he was talking about ". . .

had been worried about collecting their correspondence to her, they would have done so by now."

"Or sent us to do it." I arched my eyebrows, wondering if that had been Lord Gage's intention all along.

We all fell silent, considering the implications of that while the drumming of the rain against the roof continued, though noticeably slower than before. I turned to stare out through the curtain of mist toward the abbey in the distance.

"Would someone in the British government have killed them?" I murmured, daring to say what we were all thinking. "Would they have killed them for disobeying orders, for knowing too much? Perhaps more than we even realize."

Gage crossed his arms over his chest. "If so, they did a rather slapdash job of it. Leaving Miss Lenox on the outside of the abbey walls. Not positioning the rock so that it could easily be explained as an accident. And then sending us to investigate. That was a rather unnecessary risk. Especially when most people in Britain, including us, had heard nothing of her death." He shook his head. "No. There would have been easier ways to manage the problem. They could have removed her from the situation, taken her back to her family."

"Where if she'd wanted to voice her discoveries, to cause problems for them, no one would believe her."

"Quite. Killing her would have caused them more problems, not less. And I cannot believe Wellington would condone it. I might question the wisdom of his decision to involve his cousin with this affair, but I feel certain he would have removed her if he'd known she was in immediate danger."

I hoped he was right, but I'd seen men do far worse things for the sake of protecting their power and good name when they should have been more concerned with protecting others.

"What if one of the nuns had found out her secret?" Anderley spoke up, rocking forward on his heels as if he was anxious to be away. "Could one of them have killed her? For playing them false?"

"I don't think . . ." I began, but then stopped, a thought having occurred to me. "Not unless . . ." I lifted my gaze to meet Bree's and I could tell she was thinking the same thing. I hated having to consider any of the sisters, doing so felt horridly wrong somehow, but experience had taught me to keep an open mind when considering suspects. That even the best of people could sometimes do terrible things.

My shoulders sank as I considered the unthinkable. "Mother Mary Paul. She was also a convert, something I thought she had in common with Miss Lennox. If she discovered Miss Lennox had not really converted, that she was staying at the abbey under false pretenses . . ." I furrowed my brow in disbelief. "I don't think she would be capable of violence, but I also don't *want* to believe it."

"She was in charge o' Miss Lennox's room." Bree's face showed the same pained incredulity. "The lay sisters told me they had to get permission from her to go in an' clean or even strip the sheets from the bed."

I gripped the packet of letters tighter, feeling the bite of the papers' edges. "I'll speak with her."

I lifted my eyes to meet Gage's and he gave a little nod, knowing me well enough not to press. I would do what was needed, even if I didn't like it.

CHAPTER TWENTY-THREE

Because of Mother Fidelis's death, a number of sisters had been required to take over her former duties, including Mother Paul. So rather than wait for her to finish instructing her Italian class, we elected instead to pay our visit to Mr. LaTouche to discover why he had lied to us. Our explanations to the mother superior about Miss Lennox's letters could wait, as well as our interview of Mr. Scully, who, as predicted, was heavily sedated after having the bullet extracted from his leg. I was relieved the surgeon had not thought it necessary to remove the lower half of his leg. There would still be some concern about infection setting in, but with proper care, hopefully the wound would heal adequately. It was fortunate the Scullys and the abbey had Davy to handle matters while he recovered.

The rain slackened and then stopped as we drove south from the abbey toward Eden Park. The sun even began to peek out from the clouds as we turned up the long drive to Mr. LaTouche's home. We had taken a gamble that the man would even be in residence, but it paid off. The butler gathered up my and Gage's wet things and showed us into the drawing room with its painted ceiling. I'd forgotten about Mr. Scully's bloodstains on my skirts, but I hoped by folding them strategically while I sat, our host would never notice.

It was not long before Mr. LaTouche joined us, not

appearing in the least surprised by our visit. He greeted us cordially, offered tea, which we declined, and then gestured us toward a grouping of furniture near the low-burning fireplace.

"I suspected I might be seein' ye yet today after our conversation was interrupted at the cattle fair," he proclaimed, settling back against the coffee leather of his wingback chair. By interruption I supposed he meant the violence that had erupted between the armed constables and the tithe protesters. What a quaint way to put it.

A shrewd glint entered Gage's eyes as he clasped his hands before him. "Yes. Some new information has come to light."

"Oh?"

"We located Miss Lennox's correspondence."

Mr. LaTouche blinked hard. "I see."

"Do you? Good. Because I would like you to explain why you lied to us." Gage's tone was perfectly casual, except the hard edge to it when he uttered the word "lied." How or why Mr. LaTouche had not heard it and heeded it, I do not know.

"Lied?"

Gage's eyelids lowered in derision. "You told us that Miss Lennox wanted you to warn Lord Anglesey about a rebellion the Catholics were planning, but that's not true, is it? She wanted you to warn him about the disturbance and potential violence the Orangemen intended to cause during their parade in two days' time."

LaTouche's jaw clenched in anger and he sniffed. "There's no disturbance planned. If the Catholics cannot be keepin' the peace, dat is not our fault."

"It is if you're deliberately provoking them."

"Who says they'll be provoked?"

I wanted to reach across and smack the haughty condescension from his brow.

"Why did you lie?" Gage demanded. "Are you incapable of honor or honesty?"

As insults went, it was just about the worst thing he could accuse a gentleman of, and for a man like LaTouche—who clung to the pretensions of a distant relation's noble birth—it would be unforgivable. But I suspected Gage knew this, and had incited him on purpose.

LaTouche shot forward in his chair. "How dare ye! Why, I should be slappin' yer cheek wit me glove for such an insinuation."

Gage was unmoved. "And yet we've already proven you lied."

LaTouche scowled. "Only because I knew ye would turn yer suspicions on the Orangemen when it's clear a papist killed her."

"You don't believe a Protestant is capable of murder."

"'Course," he spat. "But not like this. Superstitious nonsense. Served her right for abandonin' her rational thought and joinin' 'em."

"Except she hadn't," I replied, furious with his callous remarks.

"What?" he barked belligerently. "'Course she did. Why else would she be in that nunnery instead o' . . ."

I narrowed my eyes, wondering what he was going to say when he stopped himself in time. "Because Wellington asked her to keep an eye on the tithe protesters here in Rathfarnham."

If it were possible for a person to swallow their own tongue, I thought Mr. LaTouche just might have. He made a horrible sound in the back of his throat, and his eyes widened in shock. "Yer serious?" he managed to gasp.

"Very."

"But she . . . Why didn't she tell me?" he snapped, his anger returning.

I shook my head. "We're not privy to those details. But we do know you spoke to her on the day she was murdered."

He stiffened in affront. "I did not."

Gage's mouth tightened in aggravation. "Someone saw you."

"Well, that's a lie. I did not speak wit Miss Lennox for at least three days before she was killed."

I frowned. He seemed awfully certain of himself. "You're sure?"

"Of course I am."

"And why should we believe you when you lied to us before?" Gage pointed out.

"I don't have to stand for dis." He shot to his feet, striding furiously across the room. "You can see yerselves out." With that, he slammed the door.

I turned to stare at Gage, who was scowling at the closed door. "Could he have been telling the truth? About the last?"

"I don't know," he admitted. "I don't like him. I don't trust him. But that doesn't mean he wasn't being truthful."

If he was, did that mean Davy had lied? Or had the young man become confused? He had seemed somewhat uncertain on that point, and LaTouche had stormed off before we could question him on the matter Davy was clearer on. Well, it was too late now, unless Gage wanted to go after him, and I suspected not. Not without more proof. But this was not the last Mr. LaTouche would see of us. That was at least one thing of which I could be certain.

I glanced up as the connecting door between our bedchamber and the room next to it opened to see Gage emerge in dry, clean clothes, his hair placed back in order by Anderley, and then I returned to the list I was making. Bree had come and gone, sighing over the stains on my skirt as she helped me change into a simple dress of lavender silk.

He crossed the room to stand behind me where I sat at my dressing table, resting his hands on my shoulders. I could smell the crisp lemon verbena scent of his soap. "What are you doing?"

"Making a list of the facts we know about this inquiry and how our suspects fit."

I caught sight of his smile in the reflection of the mirror. "Organizing your thoughts. I was considering doing the same thing."

"It feels as if we're missing something, something just at our fingertips, but we can't seem to grasp it. I hoped by writing everything down, I might figure out what it is."

He nodded, reading over my shoulder as I continued to write. I started with the bare facts of each murder, added in the evidence and observations we'd made, and then inked in the information we'd been told, placing question marks by those things that had not yet been proven. Some facets which had previously puzzled us were now explained, such as the fresh manure on their shoes and the lack of correspondence in Miss Lennox's room. Others still made little sense. Had Miss Lennox removed her veil? Why? And what of the man's footprints? Was it proof that the murderer was a male, and therefore could not be Mother Paul, or had they been left behind by Mr. LaTouche the night before?

I sat back to stare at the page. "What do you make of the fact that the killer took the stone with him or hid it after Miss Lennox's murder, but left it nearby after Mother Fidelis's?"

"Perhaps he panicked. It seems evident from everything here that the first murder was unplanned. Maybe he seized an opportunity that was presented to him or was driven to it out of anger and then was shocked by his own actions. He could have panicked after he'd realized what he'd done and, not thinking, taken the stone with him."

"But he was more prepared, more experienced when it came to the second murder. Having had time to think, he realized it would be better to leave the stone." I pointed toward an observation I'd written on the page. "Mother Mary Fidelis said that she and Sister Mary Maxentia had called Miss Lennox's name as they searched for her. Maybe the killer was still with her body and only ran off when he heard them."

Gage nodded. "That makes some sense, though I'm not sure it can be proven."

I set my pen aside and picked up the list, swiveling to face him. "What do you suppose he did with the first stone?"

He backed up several steps to sit in the armchair near the bed. "If he was smart, he got rid of it as quickly as possible. Where? I don't know."

I sat studying the list, but rather than having any sudden insight, I felt my exasperation grow. "None of our suspects fits everything we know." I pressed a hand to my temple. "I suppose LaTouche is the most promising, unless you prefer to blame an unidentified Orangeman."

He closed his eyes and tipped his head back against the chair. "I agree. This inquiry is maddening. Perhaps if we'd been able to arrive sooner. Or if Mother Mary Fidelis had seen fit to confide in you rather than take matters into her own hands." He scoffed, raising his hands in entreaty. "Or if people in this bloody village would stop being so dashed suspicious, we could have caught the villain by now."

Gage almost never cursed in front of me. It was obvious how sick and tired he was of this investigation. He rarely lost his temper with an inquiry, so I knew there had to be more to his sudden aggravation than merely our lack of compelling proof. His philosophy was to keep doggedly working the elements involved until something turned up. That took intense patience and perseverance.

Setting the list aside, I crossed the room toward him, sinking to my knees. Before they could touch the floor, he pulled me into his lap instead. I didn't speak. He knew why I had approached him. He would tell me what was bothering him in his own time. Instead, I rested my head against his shoulder and shared my body's warmth.

"I'm a loyal British subject," he finally said, his voice rumbling against my ear. "An English gentleman. I should reject any notion of treason, of breaking the rule of the law, of promoting civil discord. And yet, I can't help feeling sympathy for these men and women, these Catholics." He tilted his head back to stare at the ceiling. "I've heard the rhetoric all my life, the hateful jokes and slanders bandied about in London, but to see what happened today." He exhaled heavily. "The taunting and angry words were on both sides, but the Protestants have all the power, and from what I could see, today they also had all the guns."

So Constable Casey had told the truth. The tithe protestors had not arrived armed, even if they had forgotten to leave their tempers behind as well.

"Does it remind you of Greece?"

"Yes. In some respects. The same passion, the same defiance." He sighed. "The same conflict over religion. Though Turkish and Christian beliefs are far different from each other than Catholic and Protestant."

I could almost hear the recriminations spinning in his head, refrains similar to those that still plagued him from Greece. I lifted my head to look into his eyes. "Do not take this burden on yourself. Perhaps you turned a deaf ear to the slights made against Catholics and Irishmen in the past, but you did not create the problem. You cannot be blamed for your ignorance."

"But don't you see? Yes, I can. I could have asked questions. I could have sought the truth. But I was content to let it be."

"You cannot know everything, Gage. You cannot champion every cause. But now that you know, perhaps you can do something about it. You're not without influence, even if you aren't yet a peer."

"True."

"Sitting here castigating yourself will not help matters." I grimaced wryly. "Nor will it solve this inquiry."

His mouth quirked at the corners. "Also true." He lifted his head, and sat taller. "But perhaps I can make strides toward both tomorrow." He scowled. "I plan to pay a visit to Chief Constable Corcoran to let him know how displeased I was with his officers' behavior at today's fair, as well as to be certain they're prepared for this Orange Day Parade. Then I believe I should call on Lord Anglesey in Dublin. Perhaps he knows something about Miss Lennox and her efforts here in Rathfarnham. And if not that, he might at least be able to send some additional troops here to help keep order during the parade."

"That seems like a sound plan."

He lifted his hand to brush a stray strand of hair back from my face. "Yes. Except I hate to leave now with all the growing tensions and potential for violence."

"I shall be perfectly safe. There's no cause to worry," I assured him.

"You may think so, but to be certain, I would like you to remain close to the Priory or inside the abbey walls."

"Is that really necessary?"

"I don't care if it isn't. I want you to listen to me in this. And I'm going to ask Anderley to stay with you."

I frowned. "So you're going to ride to Dublin alone? Now how do you think I feel about *your* safety?"

"No one is going to harm me on my journey to visit Anglesey. Any trouble is far more likely to occur here. And I do not want you left without protection." His eyes searched mine before they briefly dipped to my abdomen.

I flushed, feeling that sickening swirl of sentiments rise up inside me. "Sebastian, I'm not . . . That is . . ."

He pressed a hand to my cheek. "I know." His eyes were soft with unspoken things. "I'm merely thinking of the future."

I swallowed. "Oh."

His smile was gentle. "It will happen in time. There's no need to rush."

I could feel that my answering smile was somewhat brittle as I tried to hold back a tide of emotions. My mind churned with doubts and questions, none of which I could utter.

He pressed a kiss to my brow. "Which is why I want you to listen to me. Please."

I laughed breathlessly. "Well, when you ask that way. All right. I'll stay at the abbey or near the Priory." After all, his request wasn't unreasonable, just irritating.

CHAPTER TWENTY-FOUR

The following day, the mother superior and Mother Paul were both waiting for me when we arrived at the abbey. I tried not to feel alarmed, but after everything we'd learned the day before, I'd begun to anticipate the unexpected.

Gage had departed for Chief Constable Corcoran's house and then on to Dublin a few hours earlier, but it being Sunday, those of us going to the abbey dawdled, waiting for mass to end. After all of the difficulties of the week, rather than risk offending either religious faction further, we'd elected not to attend services at the Anglican Church, instead observing our own prayers and devotions at the Priory.

Once we'd learned that Mr. Scully had been moved to his cottage the evening before, I sent Bree and Anderley to call on him. At first, Anderley resisted, but I'd argued I was safe within the abbey walls and it was more important they discover if Mr. Scully was coherent enough to explain what he knew about Miss Lennox.

Fortunately, the reverend mother's opening comment was not unsettling news of another dead body or trouble from the previous day's unrest spilling over into the abbey. Instead, her words were ones of concern.

"In light of everything that's happened, I wonder if we haven't placed you and Mr. Gage in danger," she said after we'd settled ourselves on the settees facing each other before the hearth. "You told me about those riders threatening you in the middle of the night, and then the violence yesterday at the cattle fair. I do not wish to see either of you harmed."

"I appreciate your concern, but we've taken precautions," I assured her. "We're not going to be driven away so easily. Not when we're closer than ever to solving these murders."

"You've uncovered something." Mother Paul's voice was colored by surprise, and I found myself studying her face, trying to discern what that meant.

"Yes. We found Miss Lennox's letters."

She didn't even flicker an eyelash at this revelation.

"You did?" Reverend Mother remarked. "Where had she been keeping them?"

I turned back to her, watching Mother Paul out of the corner of my eye. "In a hole in the beech tree that stands next to that pond beyond the abbey's walls."

Both nuns' brows furrowed, but Reverend Mother was the one to voice her confusion. "I don't understand."

"We believe she was using the tree as a sort of letter box, leaving and receiving messages there rather than at the abbey. Which obviously means she had been leaving the abbey grounds far more often than you realized, even given her activities with the tithe protestors."

The nuns exchanged a look of what seemed to be mutual puzzlement.

"Did Mother Mary Fidelis know about this?" Mother Superior asked.

"I don't think so," I replied hesitantly. "Not given the letters' contents." I informed them of Miss Lennox's deception, of her true reasons for being here, and her connection to the British government. Mother Paul stared at the floor in stony silence, displaying little reaction other than a taut frown.

However, Reverend Mother's heart was clearly in her eyes as she shook her head. "I suppose that explains the uncertainty I sometimes sensed in her. All postulants display it to some degree. After all, joining a religious order is not a decision to be taken lightly. But Miss Lennox's insecurity was different. It's why I asked Mother Mary Fidelis to pay her particular attention, to help her discover the truth of what she was meant to do." She glanced at her assistant. "Did you have any inkling of this?"

Mother Paul lifted her head. "I suppose, in a way, I did," she replied softly. "Not the part about her being here at the behest of the government. But I didn't feel the passion from her that I expected in a convert. I wondered if perhaps her zeal was simply more self-contained than mine had been. I worried I misjudged her."

Reverend Mother offered her a gentle smile that spoke of private matters to which I was not privy, and then turned back to me. "In any case, I would not have allowed her to move forward, to be clothed, until I felt these . . . inconsistencies had been addressed, had she even tried to. But I must admit, I am troubled by all of this." She pressed her lips together. "I shall have to think and pray on this."

I didn't suppose there was a precedent for such a thing as being intruded and spied upon by one's own government.

Her dark, solemn eyes lifted to study me. "Has this new information allowed you to uncover who the killer is?"

"Not precisely. But it has given us a different angle to pursue, with a different set of suspects." I shifted uncomfortably in my seat, trying to figure out a tactful way to question Mother Paul's potential involvement. I needn't have fretted, for she proved to be as astute as ever.

"Such as me," she replied calmly.

I glanced up in surprise, and her lips curled into a tight smile.

"I'm also a convert. Perhaps you're wondering if I found out Miss Lennox's secret and took offense at her betrayal of our trust and care. If I sought to handle matters myself."

I felt myself begin to flush, discomfited by my having entertained those exact thoughts, even if they were necessary.

She shook her head. "I did not know. This is the first I've learned of it. And I would never have harmed her. It is not my place to sit in judgment of such things."

"Besides, Mother Mary Paul was at chapel and then in the refectory with the rest of the sisters and our students," Revered Mother interjected. "The only one absent that evening was Miss Lennox. And before chapel, Miss Lennox met with Mother Mary Fidelis. So you see, Mother Mary Paul had no time to confront her, even if she wanted to. No one at the abbey did."

Somehow I had forgotten that fact, perhaps because I had not made certain of the times when she first informed us. We'd not suspected the sisters or students then. I nodded in agreement. She was right. No one at the abbey could have committed the crime without their absence being noted.

"I'm sorry," I told Mother Mary Paul. "I did not want to consider you a potential suspect, but when one deals with such delicate matters, one cannot give one's personal wishes credence over facts and logic."

She graciously accepted my apology, and then excused herself. I supposed even nuns had difficulty forgiving someone for suspecting they were capable of such a heinous act. Who could blame her?

I slouched lower in my chair, feeling the weight of this inquiry, and all the other ones I'd assisted Gage with, settle on my shoulders. We sat silently for so long as I contemplated the empty fireplace and all the unattractive things I'd been forced to confront, I almost forgot the reverend mother was still there.

"Something else is troubling you," she murmured. "And do not tell me it's merely this inquiry. I can perceive the difference between mere frustration and the uneasiness of the spirit." She tilted her head. "Will you tell me what it is?" Her voice was calm and measured, inviting my confidence.

So much so that before I could allow myself to reconsider, I found myself confessing. "As nuns, you speak of being called to your vocation, to devoting your life to Christ by living in a convent, and professing vows, and performing acts of faith and charity. Noble aspirations."

She waited patiently as I struggled to find my words.

"I wonder . . . I wonder if what I do—examining corpses, and questioning people's motives, and delving into the sordidness of murder. I wonder if I'm treading where I was not meant to. Whether . . . my involvement is displeasing to God." As soon as the words were out of my mouth, I wished I could snatch them back. They were so raw, so private, and once I voiced them, once I put shape and definition to them, they became very real, tangible. They sat on my chest, pressing down, until I felt I couldn't breathe.

She frowned. "Why do you say that?"

"As women, we're taught that our calling is to hearth, and home, and husband. That we should wish for nothing more." I dropped my gaze to my lap, where I was worrying my hands. "When I first began assisting with these inquiries, I had none of those things. But now I do. Now I'm wed and . . . and someday soon I'll likely have children to care for. To cherish and protect." I blinked up at her. "Does that mean I should give up the rest? Is that what is sensible? Is that what the Lord would want of me?"

Her eyes were kind. "First of all, what does your husband say about all of this?"

I swallowed. "He says he's happy to have me assist him. That he understands it is part of who I am."

"Then I should trust he means it."

"Yes, but once I'm expecting, doesn't that change things? Won't he expect me to stop?"

"That is something you will have to ask him."

I exhaled a shaky breath. "Yes, of course. You're right." I had known that before I'd even asked her. But part of me was afraid of what his answer would be, of what that would mean.

Her mouth creased into a gentle smile, clearly reading my thoughts. "Mr. Gage seems to me to be an astute, considerate man. I'm sure he will take into account your feelings on the matter."

"Yes, but I don't know what they are," I argued.

She sat taller, her gaze turned doubtful. "Don't you?"

"No," I insisted. "I said it is part of who I am, but is that true? Is it who I am? I didn't want to learn all of these things about anatomy. My first husband forced it on me. And yet, I cannot deny how helpful it has been at times with our inquiries. But I still feel guilty for using what I know."

"Perhaps it was forced on you, but it has certainly been used for good. 'But as for you,'" she began to quote from the Bible. "'Ye thought evil against me; but God meant it unto good, to bring it to pass, as it is this day, to save much people alive.'"

I hesitated, considering the verse as she rose to her feet. "That's what Joseph said, isn't it? To his brothers when they were shocked to see him alive and prosperous in Egypt after they'd beaten him and left him for dead so many years before?"

She nodded and moved around the table to perch on the settee next to me, taking my hands in her warm ones. "Mrs. Gage, I will tell you what I tell the sisters, what I tell my students, and what I have learned myself."

I looked up, listening carefully.

"The Lord calls us to simply trust and seek. He will show us the way. But when that way is shown, we are not allowed to say, 'Enough! Let me settle.' We must go even where we think it is impossible, do those things that we think we are incapable of. For the Lord will make it possible; He will make us capable." Her eyes gleamed softly. "You may be called to a home and husband, but that does not mean He doesn't also have more for you to do. The Lord does not say, 'Go this far, only this far, and no further.' He does not only call men to do His good work. Like our institute's founder, Sister Mary Ward, I believe women are equal to men in intellect. So why would He not also call women to broader things."

I had never heard anyone espouse such beliefs, let alone a woman of such stature as a mother superior. It went against everything I'd been taught in church, among society, and even by my parents. And yet her words rang true, for I had contemplated the same thoughts. However, we weren't talking about running a charity or even painting my portraits.

We were talking about actively pursuing criminals, men and women committing the gravest of sins.

"But these inquiries . . ." I clutched her hands tighter. "They are sometimes dangerous. What . . . what if something happened to me?" I forced the words from me. "What if I died too young, and was not there for my children?"

Her eyes searched my face. "Like your mother died too young and was not there for you?"

I stiffened in surprise. "How did you . . ."

"'Twas merely a guess," she replied. "How young were you?"

"Eight."

She nodded. "A difficult age to lose one's mother. Though is there any good age?" she added with a frown.

I smiled tightly, conceding her point.

She pulled one of her hands from my grasp to rest it on top of them. "I cannot speak to the danger of what you do. But I can remind you that avoiding it does not guarantee you a long life. Illness, childbirth, accidents. You can live your life wrapped in swaddling clothes and still not escape danger. So it seems silly to me to deny doing that which you enjoy, through which you can do the most good, as long as you are sensible."

Her words were logical and sound, and though they couldn't completely erase my fears, they did help me think more clearly. However, I couldn't help voicing one more argument.

"But our investigations are so base, so of this earth."

"And those things that we as sisters often address are not? Poverty and sickness and ignorance." She arched her eyebrows in gentle chastisement. "We do not only pray and study and sing requiems."

I grimaced, acknowledging her point.

"All our efforts cannot be in the pursuit of beauty, of higher things. Sometimes it is because of our struggle with earthly matters that we are able to aspire to beauty, to higher things at all. To provide our children the opportunity to aspire to them."

"I've never thought of it that way," I admitted, contemplating what she'd said. I'd begun to feel so worried about the ugliness of what I did, that I'd forgotten some of the good that was wrought from it.

"As for your guilt, you need to let it go. Once and for all." She leaned forward, staring intently into my eyes. "Holding on to it after you've already asked for forgiveness is like saying you don't trust in the Lord's ability to wash us clean of our sins. Perhaps that will help you to see it in a different perspective. It's not a badge proving how sorry you are, but a weight pulling you into further sin."

That certainly gave me a new outlook. She was right. I had been carrying it around like a heavy badge of honor, as proof that I hadn't wanted the knowledge Sir Anthony had forced on me, but what good did that do? Some people were always going to look at me askance whether I felt bad about knowing the things I did or not. Possessing that knowledge in and of itself was not shameful, particularly when put to good use. So why not stop apologizing for something that was not my fault, and be grateful for the greater understanding it gave me. Why not accept the good that had been made from my first husband's cruelty.

I looked up as the reverend mother's hands released mine. "Thank you."

She nodded. "Sometimes the truth of our actions eludes us. Sometimes we require others to point it out."

Her words caught at a thread in my mind, unraveling it from the rest of the facts and questions stored there. It must have been reflected on my face, for she lowered her head in concern.

"You've thought of something. What is it?"

"Miss Lennox," I began slowly. "I was just wondering why she agreed to come here. To play out this farce and gather information for the government. From what I've learned about her, she didn't seem the type of person to do such a thing. So why?"

"I would agree with you. That's one of the reasons I found it so shocking. Quiet and considered. Not out for adventure." She pressed a hand to her chest over her pectoral cross. "Maybe her family had been wronged by a Catholic in some way, or she believed they had."

I shook my head. "I don't think this was about revenge, or anything of the like. I don't think she would have been able to hide her feelings so well had it been that. But something definitely motivated her. I only wish I knew what."

The promised blue skies of earlier that morning continued to prove true, I noted, as I descended the steps of the back portico into the garden. It was the type of day Gage and I would have spent lounging on some lower fell, watching the clouds stream by had we still been on our honeymoon. It was nearly as lovely here in Rathfarnham, except for the weighty matters that occupied my thoughts.

I turned my steps toward the orchard, wanting another chance to search the box we'd found Miss Walsh hiding in. If all of the students and sisters had alibis for the time of Miss Lennox's murder, then it was also unlikely that any of them murdered Mother Fidelis since it was a logical assumption she had been killed by the same person. Which meant that if what Miss O'Grady had heard while searching for the sister was someone scrambling to hide in that box, then it was someone who knew the abbey grounds well, but was not a sister or student. Perhaps one of the hired staff.

I frowned at the thought as I hurried down the central walk toward the summerhouse. I wasn't far from the white wooden structure when I heard the sound of voices. Were the students out here sketching again for their drawing class? Except it was Sunday, and I believed the reverend mother mentioned that this would be the girls' recreation time.

Almost immediately, I recognized the distinctive pitch of Miss Walsh's taunt, but this time it was not aimed at Miss Cahill or any of the other girls, but Davy. He stooped over to pick up a pile of cuttings which must have fallen out of the wheelbarrow before him, clearly flustered by the cluster of girls seated on the steps of the summerhouse. Miss

Walsh stood next to the wheelbarrow, twirling a length of thorny stem she must have plucked from his pile.

"Who's goin' to be yer sweetheart now, Davy?" she teased with a cock of her hip.

His face burned a bright ruddy shade. "She weren't my sweetheart," he bit out in a rough voice, his mouth contorted with discomfort.

"No? Well, if you'll be bringin' me flowers like ye used to bring Miss Lennox, *I'll* tink about it, to be sure."

I opened my mouth to interrupt, but Miss Cahill surprised me by speaking up first. "Leave him be, Eliza. Yer bein' cruel."

Miss Walsh swiveled toward the girl where she'd emerged from a spot farther down the path. Her eyes narrowed maliciously. "Oh, I see now. Yer sweet on 'im, too."

Miss Cahill glared at her over the sketchbook she clutched to her chest, while Davy hurried to push the wheelbarrow restacked with its burden away. As he was about to see me anyway, I decided it was best to make my presence known.

"Miss Walsh," I snapped in a cool voice, which made everyone but her jump as they turned my way. I nodded at Davy's wide eyes as he scooted by. "Have you nothing better to do with your free time?"

"Not since you took my book," she declared cheekily.

I arched a single imperious eyebrow, refusing to be spoken to in such a manner. Before I could deliver her a setdown, Miss Cahill spoke again.

"She's s'posed to be workin' on her drawin'." She shot a defiant glare at Miss Walsh. "Since she missed class the other day."

Miss Walsh's gaze promised retribution. "'Tis finished." She lifted her chin into the air in challenge.

I held out my hand. "Then let me see it."

She hesitated a moment, and then climbed the stairs to the summerhouse to snatch her drawing from where it lay on the top step. I noticed none of the other girls came to her defense. The sketch she triumphantly handed me was an abominable mess. But as much as I wanted to tell her so, I bit my tongue, recognizing I would be behaving no better than her if I humiliated her in front of her friends.

"You need to add some shading. I cannot tell from which direction the sun is shining." I lifted my gaze to glare at her. "And do not simply draw a circle in the top corner and call that done." The mutinous gleam in her eyes told me she had been prepared to do just that. "These proportions are also off. That flower is as big as your classmate's head. Fix it." I passed her drawing back to her, ignoring her scowl. I waited for her to take her seat on the summerhouse steps, not trusting her to do a thing I said once I turned my back to her.

However, I also did not have time to stand about monitoring troublesome girls. Were any of the sisters keeping an eye on the students, or was this their recreation time as well? I lifted my gaze to survey what I could see of the gardens from where I stood.

It was then that I caught Miss Cahill's eye. She was watching me through her eyelashes, but she did not flinch and look away as she had done so often before. I glanced at the ever observant, ever spiteful Miss Walsh, and the other girls who were now whispering with one another, their anxious gazes on me. If Miss Cahill wished to speak with me, this was certainly not the place to do it.

I pretended to ignore Miss Cahill as she strolled past me, but I saw which path she disappeared down. Then I fastened one final glare on the girls at the summerhouse and turned to walk off. Miss Walsh was not cowed, I knew that, but perhaps some of her friends would think twice before laughing at her mockery of others again.

I did not have to go far before I rounded a bend in the path and found Miss Cahill perched on a bench among hedges dappled with Japanese roses. She looked up at me, still clutching her sketchbook to her chest.

"Might I sit with you?" I asked lightly, and she nodded. I arranged the skirts of my deep charcoal riding habit next to her on the stone bench, and watched a pair of bees flitting through a patch of yellow irises across from us. "I thought maybe you had something you wished to tell me, and you didn't want to do so in front of the other girls."

She lowered her book to her lap and stared down at it, clearly struggling with herself over something, perhaps gathering the courage to speak.

"May I see them?" I asked, gesturing toward her book, thinking this might distract her from her anxiety.

She blinked at me and then slowly handed me her sketches. I flipped through the pages, making casual remarks of praise as well as a few helpful suggestions. Though she still didn't speak, I could tell she was listening intently, while at the same time her mind worked furiously, deciding what, if anything, to say to me.

Finally, she licked her lips and gasped. "One of the girls, she . . . she told us we shouldn't talk to ye. That you and yer husband were no friends to Catholics." Her eyes lifted to meet mine, as if she was afraid what she would see. "Are you?"

I met her gaze squarely, trying to decide how best to answer. "Miss Cahill, do you trust the reverend mother?"

Her eyes widened. "Of course."

"Then do you think she would have asked us here, allowed us inside the abbey, if she did not trust us to conduct these inquiries into the deaths of Miss Lennox and Mother Mary Fidelis with integrity?"

She stared up at me as if this realization had escaped her.

I smiled gently. "She could have demanded we leave at any time."

"I didn't know that."

"It's true." I glanced back toward the irises. "Is that why all of the girls have been afraid to confide in us?" I tilted my head. "Other than the fact that when they confided in Mother Mary Fidelis, she was then killed."

She gave a small hiccup of surprise. Apparently, Miss Walsh had not relayed my message. I sighed, unsure why I was surprised by this.

Miss Cahill's hand tightened in the folds of her dull gray skirt before she suddenly blurted out, "Miss Lennox, she told me she'd been engaged to marry before she came here. Before she decided to become a nun."

My heart kicked in my chest at this revelation. Marsdale had mentioned he'd gotten the impression she was engaged the last time he'd spoken to family members about her a year earlier, but I'd dismissed it as nothing. Even Marsdale had admitted to being confused on that point, and neither Lord Gage, nor Wellington, nor even her parents in their letter had mentioned anything about a broken engagement.

"When did she tell you this?" I asked.

"A few weeks ago, she confided in me because I'm facin' a similar choice. Me parents have arranged a marriage for me, but I don't know if I be wantin' to go through wit it." She glanced up at me with eyes that pleaded for me to understand. "She was tryin' to help me, and I didn't want to be betrayin' her trust by tellin' her secrets when I'd no right to do so."

"What made you change your mind?"

Her eyes dropped to her lap, where she was worrying the fabric of her pinafore.

"Her fiancé, her former one. He lives here in Rathfarnham."

I blinked in shock. "You're certain he lives here? He didn't just pay her a visit?" But then I remembered that the mother superior had already said she'd never had visitors to the abbey.

She nodded resolutely. "She said he lived in a great house not far from here, wit tall white pillars like a Greek temple."

I caught myself just in time before I gasped. There might be more than one home in Rathfarnham with white pillars, but at the moment I could think of only one. And there just happened to be a young man living there, recently returned from Oxford, who would be of the right age to wed Miss Lennox.

Knowing what I did now, I had to wonder who had broken the arrangement. Had the wedding already been canceled, or had Miss Lennox jilted her fiancé in order to join this convent and spy for Wellington? How had her ex-fiancé felt about that?

"Did I do the right ting by tellin' ye?" Miss Cahill asked anxiously. "Is it all right I shared her secret?"

"Yes. It most certainly is," I told her, pressing a hand to her arm. "You did the right thing."

I only wished she'd done so sooner, but I could not berate her for her loyalty to Miss Lennox. Not when this matter had clearly tormented her. The smile she gave me was filled with such relief, that I forced myself to smile back.

"Did she tell you anything else about her former fiancé or their broken engagement? Had she seen him?"

She shook her head. "I don't tink so. She just explained how she knew 'twas a tough decision, for me an' everyone involved. That whatever I did decide, I might have to live wit the repercussions the rest o' me life."

That statement sent a chill down my spine. For Miss Lennox had been speaking from experience, and whatever repercussions she'd been living with, they had been far shorter lived than she could have ever known.

CHAPTER TWENTY-FIVE

Despite Gage's wishes, despite Anderley's vehement protests, I was not going to sit about waiting for my husband to return before I spoke to Colin LaTouche. Not when
that young man could depart on his Grand Tour at any
moment, if he hadn't already done so. "Within the week,"
he'd told Gage, and that had been three days ago.

Bree knew better than to try to persuade me from a course
I was determined to take, but Anderley—his loyalty being to
Gage—did not understand he would have been better served
to hold his tongue. Most of his complaints I was able to ignore
as, rather than taking the phaeton that morning, we had
instead ridden on horseback, so I could drown out his natter-
ing beneath the canter of our horses. In any case, there was
nothing he could do to divert me from my path, not without
behaving well outside a servant's decorum. There were some
distinct advantages to being a lady.

However, I did not disregard his concern completely.
After all, I was not a fool. I was well aware of how dangerous
a man could turn when cornered. I knew that Anderley was
armed, as Gage had instructed him to be, so I told him to
accompany me inside and wait just outside the drawing
room door rather than join Bree and the other servants
belowstairs. Should I have need of him, I would call out.
This silenced his more heated objections, but I partially

suspected he was thinking of other ways to make his displeasure known later.

We were in luck. The butler informed us Colin was still in residence, though his father had gone to Dublin. I refused to allow myself to contemplate what that meant for Gage, and whether he was in any danger. Dublin was a large city. There was no reason to think their paths would cross.

The butler eyed Anderley askance when he followed at my heels and stood at attention outside the drawing room door, but he did not object. I was certain my remark about protective husbands and the coy glance I cast his way helped explain matters to his satisfaction. He needn't know my husband had no reasons to fear my infidelity.

"Lady Darby, this is a lovely surprise," Colin proclaimed, though I noticed there was a hesitation in his step as he entered the room before he approached.

"I know you weren't expecting me. But there's a matter I was hoping you could help me with."

"Of course." He guided me toward a yellow silk settee positioned near one of the windows and sat down beside me a proper distance away. "What can I do for you?"

I noticed that his grammar and elocution were closer to that of a proper Englishman than his father's. Courtesy of his time at school in England, I supposed.

"Some information has come to light. Information that concerns you."

His eyebrows lifted, but he did not squirm. "What information?"

"Were you acquainted with Miss Lennox, the postulant who was killed outside the Rathfarnham Abbey a few weeks ago?"

His face paled, and I knew I'd taken the right tact. To see what he would divulge himself before pressing him for the rest.

"Yes. Yes, actually I was." His eyes searched my face, perhaps wondering what I already knew. "We were once engaged to be married."

"Before she decided to enter the convent?"

"Yes." His voice was quiet, his gaze steady, though I detected some strain behind his eyes.

"Were you close?"

"I thought so." He fell silent, his brow furrowed in thought. "No, I know we were."

"It must have hurt you deeply when she broke it off," I guessed, seeing his reaction. "Particularly, when she told you why."

"Actually, in a way it made it easier. To think she was throwing me over for God instead of another man."

"I'd not thought of it that way," I admitted. "However, I suspect your father was furious."

He nodded tentatively. "He was. He wanted our match for political reasons. So to see her jilt me, well . . . yes, he was angry."

"Angry enough to hurt her?"

I could see in his eyes that he knew what I meant.

"No. Not in that way."

"Are you sure? Did you know she wrote to your father? Asked him to visit her?"

"Yes."

I studied him, trying to figure out what he knew, how to convince him to share it. "Did he tell you why?"

"Yes. Just as he told you."

So his father had told him of our previous conversations. In order to keep their stories straight?

"What about you? Did you hurt her?"

The corners of his eyes crinkled in remembered pain. "No. Never. I would have gone to the stake rather than harm her."

Something in this quiet young man's voice made me want to believe him. "You were seen with her the day she was killed." This was only a presumption, but a good one, seeing as Davy had observed a gentleman with her, and Mr. LaTouche had denied it so forcefully.

His eyes dropped to the carpet. "She wrote to me. Asked me to come. At first I didn't know what to think. I didn't yet know she'd spoken to my father. But I couldn't not go." He glanced up at me as if to see whether I understood.

Had I been in his situation, with Gage asking for me, I knew that I would have gone. No matter how he might have hurt me. I nodded and he exhaled in release. It was then that I realized he was almost eager to be telling me this story. To be sharing it with someone. It weighed on him, and whatever he'd told his father of it, it had certainly not been the full truth.

His smile was pained as he thought back. "She seemed so glad to see me. So relieved." His knee began to bounce as he struggled to suppress his distress. "She told me the truth. About why she'd ended our engagement and entered the convent. About the tithe war and her gathering information."

"She told you all that?" I asked in surprise. "Did you ask why she hadn't been able to tell you before?"

"She said Wellington didn't believe we would be able to keep the secret, or act accordingly. That he believed my father would give her away." He scoffed, looking upward. "He was right. My father hates papists. And to see the girl who jilted his son become one made him livid. He never would have been able to feign his hatred if he'd known it was all a ruse."

His animosity must have been very evident to the Ribbonmen, which was why the deception had been so effective.

"But to not tell you?" I argued, knowing how much that must have hurt.

He swallowed. "I understand. I know why they had to do it that way." He smirked in self-deprecation. "Or, at least, I accept it now."

"Did she tell you why she agreed to this scheme? Why she agreed to spy on the tithe protestors?"

His voice hardened. "Because of my father. Apparently, he was close to bankruptcy and started bribing officials to approve false manifests for his ships, so he could short his investors the profits they were due from those ventures. But Wellington promised to convince the government to overlook his past disreputable practices if she would do this for them."

I frowned, not pleased with this new piece of information in the least. That they'd used an innocent young woman's affection for her fiancé to further their own agenda, and gotten her killed in the process.

"I take it you knew nothing about your father's troubles."

"If I had, I would have told her not to give in to their threats. To let my father take responsibility for his own mistakes."

There was a wealth of history behind those words. History I did not have the time or the inclination to delve into. Not when there were more pressing concerns.

I leaned forward to capture his gaze. "Why didn't you come to us with this information sooner? Why did you make us search you out?"

His eyes widened. "You were sent by Wellington, so I assumed you already knew why she was at the abbey, as well as my father's troubles."

He was right. It was a reasonable assumption to make. If only it had been true. How much time would that have saved us?

"As for my visit to her, I knew it had nothing to do with her death. I certainly didn't kill her. So I didn't think you needed to know."

"What about your father? He certainly had ample reason to harm her. You've admitted yourself how angry he was, and how much he hates Catholics."

His shoulders drooped. "Yes, but he was with me the evening she was murdered. He couldn't have done it. I checked. It was my first suspicion, so I asked Chief Constable Corcoran, to be certain it could not have happened earlier."

I stared at him, feeling our best suspect slipping through my fingertips. "That doesn't mean he didn't hire someone else to do it."

His eyes were troubled, letting me know this was something he'd already considered. How far had matters deteriorated for this young man to suspect his father of such a heinous act?

"I know my father is not the best of men, but I don't think

he's capable of such a cold-blooded thing. Perhaps if he'd confronted her and lost control of his temper. But to plan it, premeditate it." He shook his head. "I . . . I don't think so."

The fact that he sounded as if he was trying to convince himself as much as me did nothing to reassure me.

Despite his son's obvious grief over the death of Miss Lennox, the question remained. How deep was Mr. LaTouche's hatred? And how far would he have gone to avenge the wrong he believed she had done to him and his son?

Whether Anderley heard anything of what was said inside the drawing room or he could simply read the strain on my face, I didn't know, but his touch was kinder than before as he hoisted me up onto my saddle. Or maybe he'd merely had time to plot his revenge.

I eyed him distrustfully as he helped position my foot in the stirrup. "If you put a burr under this horse's saddle, so help me . . ." I began.

He glanced up in surprise, and I realized I'd jumped to the wrong conclusion.

Pressing my lips together, I studied him as the horse danced sideways, sensing my agitation. "I know it was you who stuck the burr under Marsdale's collar. However, as humorous as I found that bit of maneuvering, should you ever try such a thing with me, you will have a very long time to regret it."

Anderley stared up at me, a small smile curling the corners of his mouth as he gave a swift nod.

"Saddle up," I ordered, rolling my eyes at his impudence.

The road to the Priory was no more than a mile, so we should have been able to make it back before Gage returned from Dublin. However, I had not counted on the trio of mounted men standing in our path. They were dressed in the dark green uniform of the constabulary, but I did not recognize any of their faces. They might have been from Rathfarnham or the village to the south of here, but they were plainly intent on something.

My fine riding habit and servant escort marked me as a woman of quality, so I did not expect trouble from them; however, their presence made me nervous nonetheless. They tipped their hats to me as we approached the crossroads where they stood, but they made no effort to move their steeds to allow us to pass.

"Good day," I said, drawing my mare to a stop. "May we assist you in some way?" I decided a breezy attitude might be best, and was rewarded when the middle rider's eyes relaxed from their narrowed suspicion.

"Not in particular, ma'am." His eyes swept side to side at Bree and Anderley. "Simply searchin' for those who might cause trouble."

"I see. Well, I wish you good luck in your task." I urged my horse forward, giving the man no choice but to move aside or deliberately confront me. For a moment, I thought he might actually attempt the latter, but was relieved when he reluctantly guided his horse to the side and nodded to his cohorts to do the same.

"Take care. There be blackguards about," he called after us.

I nodded. "We shall."

Anderley stayed close to my flank as we continued north, and I did not object. The constables should have made me feel safer, but instead they only made me uneasy. I was careful to keep my horse's pace steady, still feeling their eyes on our backs, until we rounded a bend in the road and passed out of their view.

"You can fall back a pace," I told Anderley then, exhaling a tight breath at the sight of the stone entrance pillars to the Priory in the distance.

When he didn't listen, I turned to follow his gaze, now seeing the same thing he did. The lone rider mounted on his steed at the head of the lane, watching us. My heart leapt in recognition, even from this distance. But, of course, I thought I would know him anywhere. After all, he was my husband.

I needn't have looked at his face to discover he was displeased. It was stamped in the rigid line of his body. When we drew close enough to see his scowl, it merely proved it.

"Have you just now returned from Dublin?" I asked, keeping my voice light.

"Yes."

And with such rotten timing.

He didn't speak again as he rode two strides ahead of me up the drive, though I was certain he had more than a few choice words to share with me. I was itching to tell him what I had learned while he was away, but I refused to speak to his horse's backside, even if I thought it might have eased some of the tension.

In the carriage yard he leapt down with far more spryness than a man who had spent several hours in the saddle should have been allowed, and rounded my horse to lift me down. I gasped in surprise at his swift movements, but did not think of arguing, even when he pulled my arm through his and guided me into the house and up the stairs. The hairs on the back of my neck stood on end, a recalled reaction from confrontations with my first husband, but I ignored them, trying to steady the accelerated beating of my heart.

He closed the door to our bedchamber with a sharp click before rounding on me. "Where were you?"

"Just now?" I replied calmly, playing for time as I crossed toward my dressing table, removing my riding gloves.

"You know when, Kiera."

"We were paying a visit to Colin LaTouche. I discovered . . ."

"After I explicitly told you *not* to go anywhere but the abbey."

"I hadn't planned to go anywhere else, but something I uncovered today made a trip to Eden Park necessary."

"So necessary that you couldn't wait an hour or two longer for me to return?"

I flushed under the scrutiny of his snapping eyes. "I had no way of knowing when you would return. You told me yourself you might not be back until nightfall." I slapped my gloves down on the table. "And Colin LaTouche said he was leaving for his Grand Tour within the week."

"He's not leaving until Tuesday."

I stiffened. "Well, I didn't know that. How did you?"

"He *told* me," he practically sneered.

"Not while I was present."

"No. But you could have asked me."

"No, I couldn't. Because you weren't *here*." I removed the hat pins from my hair and dropped them onto the table beside the gloves with a very unsatisfying ping. At least the hat made a louder thump when it joined them.

Gage's hands clenched and unclenched at his sides. "You should have listened to me regardless. I doubt anything you learned could have been so important that you had to disregard my wishes for your safety."

"I didn't disregard them. Anderley and Bree were with me, and Anderley and I were both armed. Besides, nothing happened."

"But something could have. And I might have been miles away in Dublin."

I could hear the worry behind his anger, see the concern in the crinkles at the corners of his eyes, but that didn't mean I was going to relent. "What do you want me to say? I made a reasoned decision to take the risk based on the information available to me. I won't be wrapped in cotton, Sebastian. I won't be cossetted. You knew this when you married me."

His hands lifted to clasp my elbows firmly. "I did. But you also promised to listen to me when I made a reasonable request."

"And I *did* listen to you. My visit to Eden Park wasn't some lark."

His jaw clenched, telling me he was not going to agree with me. "What was *so* important that you felt you needed to disobey me and go there? What did you uncover?"

I lifted my chin, staring into his eyes defiantly. "That Colin LaTouche was engaged to marry Miss Lennox." As he still gripped my arms, I felt his body jolt in surprise, and I nodded once in satisfaction. "She broke it off just before she entered the convent."

"How strange of Mr. LaTouche to neglect to tell us that."

"That's precisely what I thought." Then I proceeded to tell him everything I'd learned from Miss Cahill and Colin, not bothering to hide the frustration I still felt at not having any clear evidence to prove who killed Miss Lennox and Mother Fidelis. "Do you think Mr. LaTouche could have hired someone to kill both women?"

"It's possible," he replied, now perched on the edge of the bed. "But nearly *im*possible to confirm unless the man he hired confesses. At this point, I don't see that happening, as we don't even have an inkling who this mystery man is." His voice was sharp with irritation, and I stiffened, feeling as if he'd just dismissed my idea as being stupid.

"Well, I don't know what else to think," I countered, my words growing more and more strident. "Mother Mary Paul has an alibi. The Ribbonmen have no motive. Blaming Marsdale seems ridiculous, as we've absolutely no proof he was even here at the time of Miss Lennox's murder. The same goes for Mother Mary Fidelis's family. So who does that leave us with? The Orangemen and the LaTouches. But the LaTouches will vouch for each other."

Gage reached out a hand to rub my arm. "What of Mr. Scully? What did he have to say?"

I pressed a hand to my brow. "Anderley says he was far too heavily dosed with laudanum to speak, let alone make any sense."

He nodded as if he'd expected as much.

"What of you? Were you able to see Lord Anglesey?"

"I was." He sighed. "Little good it did us." He turned toward me as I lifted the train of my charcoal gray riding habit to perch on the bed next to him. "He knew nothing of Miss Lennox's activities, and was quite cross not to have been informed."

"I imagine so." It seemed we weren't the only ones who'd been left in the dark. Which seemed to confirm this task they'd assigned Miss Lennox had not been officially sanctioned by the government. It was merely Wellington's and his cronies' effort to prevent their embarrassment should the rebellion the Catholic Relief Act was passed to prevent become a reality.

"As for the Orange Parade tomorrow, he claims his resources are already stretched thin across the country. He said Rathfarnham will have to rely on its constabulary. That's what it was established for."

"Is Chief Constable Corcoran prepared?"

Deep grooves appeared in his brow. "He claims so. Took great offense at my suggesting otherwise."

"But you don't feel as confident as he does?"

"No. Not after yesterday."

I studied his handsome face. There were lines of worry now etched there that had not been present a week and a half before, and his shoulders seemed weighted down with a great burden. I leaned forward to wrap my arms around his torso, resting my head against his chest. His arms reflexively lifted to hold me back, as if he'd been doing so his entire life.

"What do you plan to do?" I asked, knowing he'd already contemplated this. Gage was incapable of doing nothing if there was even the smallest thing to be done.

"Much as I'd rather stay away, I don't think we can. We need to be there to try to keep the spectators calm, or help those who are injured, or simply be witnesses to whatever occurs. The government might actually listen to people like us."

I nodded against his shoulder, somewhat surprised he wasn't trying to keep me from attending.

Then he leaned back, forcing me to look up to meet his eyes. "But you must promise this time that you will listen to me while we're there. No questions, no hesitations. I need to know that I can keep you and Bree safe, and I can't do that if I think you won't listen."

I lifted my head to reply, but his words forestalled me.

"I mean it, Kiera. Should it be worse than the cattle fair . . ." His voice stopped as he clamped down on whatever troubling thought had sprung to his mind. "Well, let's just hope it's not."

"I promise," I replied, not hesitating this time. I knew he wasn't trying to be overbearing. He merely wished to protect me the only way he thought he could.

"I'll want you to stand near the corner with the constabulary barracks and the Anglican Church. The Orangemen are less likely to cause trouble there, but if they do, there will be some sort of sanctuary for you to flee to."

"Why *are* you letting me attend?" I couldn't resist asking, even if it meant making him reconsider his decision.

"Because the parade leads through all of Rathfarnham. Because I'm not sure I could get to you here or at the abbey if I needed to, and trouble has a remarkable way of finding you." His scowl turned black. "Because I don't trust that you would stay put. *Something* would impel you to leave."

I flushed with indignation. It was true. Trouble did seem to find me no matter the precautions taken to prevent it. Twice my life had been endangered by it. But I resented his implication that I couldn't stay put. The only times I'd ever disobeyed his wishes to stay safe had been for very good reasons. I wasn't some flighty hoyden, running about willy-nilly. I'd even saved *his* life once.

"That's unfair, Gage," I bit out.

"Is it?" he challenged.

I stood, and crossed toward the cord to summon Bree. I refused to listen to any more of this. But before I could pull it, he caught me from behind, twirling me to face him.

His voice was tense as he pressed his forehead to mine. "We're never going to resolve this, are we? My wanting to keep you safe. Your insisting you can decide when it's reasonable to ignore me."

"I suppose not," I said more softly. "Not unless you stop trying to protect me so much. But . . ." I frowned. "I suppose I wouldn't like that either. Because it would mean you cared less."

He gave a low laugh. "Well, I don't ever see that happening."

I pressed closer, absorbing the warmth of his arms before tentatively pointing out, "You know, before we married, you promised you would let me make these sensible decisions."

"Yes, well, what may sound rational and considered when making such a promise isn't so easy to accept when you're facing the very real prospect of your wife being harmed." He turned his head, speaking into my hair. "I rather like going to sleep with you beside me and waking to find you still there. I should hate for anything to change that."

CHAPTER TWENTY-SIX

The night was too quiet. Or at least, that's what I'd decided to blame for my sleeplessness rather than the worry spiraling through me, the facts of our inquiry tumbling about inside my head, the residual tension from my and Gage's earlier quarrel knotting my muscles. In the past, when I was feeling restless in the middle of the night, I would sit and sketch or work on one of the puzzles my brother-in-law had made for me. I'd not had much difficulty sleeping since our marriage, so I'd not packed any puzzles to bring with me, and just then I didn't feel like sketching. Instead, I lay staring at the ceiling, counting the divets in the plaster until I couldn't lie still any longer and got up to pace the room.

My husband slept on, heedless of my stirrings, and I moved toward the window to stare out at the cloud-shrouded moon. All was silent; all was still. That is, until the moment the moon peeked out from its pall to illuminate the girl at the edge of the carriage yard.

She stood in much the same place as she had before, half in shadow so that I could not see her face. Though what I could see of her looked older than that of the figure of a twelve-year-old girl. In any case, I didn't believe it was the ghost of Gertrude, or of anyone else for that matter. Her actions were too deliberate, too purposeful.

I slowly backed to the side, standing very still, and was

rewarded when the clouds swept their filmy gauze back across the moon and she moved. I watched as she dashed across the carriage yard toward the side garden gate. Dropping the curtains, I whirled around to wake Gage, finding him already risen up on his elbow.

"Kiera?" he asked blearily. "What is it?"

"That girl I saw before. She just dashed across the carriage yard toward the garden."

I didn't have to say another word; Gage was already up out of the bedclothes and pulling on his trousers. He thrust his feet into a pair of shoes and grabbed a white shirt, yanking it over his head as he opened the bedchamber door. "Ring for Anderley."

I did as I was told, hovering at the end of the bed near the door as Gage thundered down the steps. It seemed a decade before the valet appeared wide-eyed, but truly must have been only a matter of minutes. "Gage has gone after a girl who ran into the garden." Before I'd finished getting the words out, he was following after him, leaving me to stand there uncertainly in my wrapper, staring through the doorway.

I hoped the girl wasn't simply one of the Priory servants returning from a tryst. I frowned. No, if that were true, she would not have taken the route she did. The servants' quarters in this home were in a separate wing on the opposite end of the house near the stable and barns. It would have been far easier to sneak through the shadows at the end of the carriage yard.

I had just begun to cross the landing when Bree appeared in one of the doorways to the right which must have led to a hidden servants' stair. "M'lady?" she asked in question.

Ignoring her query for the moment, I moved toward the doors across from my and Gage's. "Do you know which of these rooms has the best view of the gardens?"

She blinked in confusion and I stepped forward to open one of the doors in impatience. "No' that one," she replied, hurrying to join me. "A tree blocks part o' the windows. The other one."

I hurried into the next chamber, ignoring the blurry shapes of the furniture draped in sheets as I crossed toward the windows. But before I could even lift the drape aside, we heard the crack of a gunshot.

My heart leapt into my throat, and I felt the sickening sensation of dread creep over me. I couldn't remember whether Gage had taken his pistol. I thought not. Or Anderley. So who had fired that bullet, and at whom?

Ignoring the windows, I urged Bree from the room. "Wake whatever staff you need. Get some water boiling and find me some clean cloths."

She did not need further instructions, but hurried off in the direction of the servants' stairs while I scurried down the front steps and into the parlor. I swept the room with my eyes, looking for the best spot to lay a gunshot victim. Though depending on the wound, the dining table might be best. I whirled around, undecided, and ultimately elected to wait and see.

Perhaps no one had been hit. Perhaps the shot had gone wide. But in my mind I kept seeing Mr. Scully lying in the back of that wagon, his lower leg a bloody mess. Except my imagination persisted in superimposing Gage's body in his place.

When finally I heard a door at the back of the passage open, I half expected to see a body being carried in. Instead, I saw the ashen complexion of Dempsey, the Priory's butler, trailed by Anderley and the sullen face of a young woman, whose upper arm was being gripped by Gage. I exhaled in relief, seeing no visible injuries.

That is, until Gage came fully into view. As he propelled the woman toward the parlor behind the other men, I could see that the other sleeve of his shirt was soaked with blood.

"Your arm," I gasped, rushing forward. But he would not let me look at it until he'd pushed the girl into the room after the man, where Anderley could keep an eye on them both.

"It's only a graze," Gage assured me in a tight voice. "Though they can still bleed like the devil."

"And become infected," I retorted. "We heard the gunshot. Bree is having water boiled."

He dismissed it with a wave of his hand. "Later."

"No. Now. You can question them while I clean the wound if it's truly so minor," I challenged and then glanced toward the occupants of the room. "Who shot you?"

"The woman."

I narrowed my eyes on her, but she turned away with a sulking twist of her head. "Who is she? I don't recognize her."

"I do." He did not elaborate, instead charging into the room with a restrained ferocity that had Dempsey quaking in his rumpled livery and seemed to have at least unnerved the girl. I had to admit, Gage did appear rather menacing, especially with half his shirt unbuttoned, revealing his rather impressive physique underneath and the blood covering his left arm.

He glared between them while Anderley stood to the side with his arms crossed. I had the distinct impression this wasn't the first time these two men had found themselves in such a situation.

"Now, which one of you would like to explain why Miss . . ." Gage arched his eyebrows at her, demanding her name. She kept her mouth defiantly shut.

"Hogan," Dempsey supplied, and she threw a venomous look his way.

"Who would like to tell me why she's been sneaking about the Priory gardens?" His eyes hardened to chips of ice. "And why she decided to *shoot* me tonight rather than explain herself?"

The girl turned away again, staring at the wall, but Dempsey squirmed in his seat. He was clearly the one who was going to talk, not her. In the hopes of saving his position, if nothing else.

Bree entered the room then with the items I'd requested as well as a cup of willow bark tea, and I was partially distracted while we set the items out on the sideboard behind Gage.

"Miss Hogan an' I've been . . ." Dempsey cleared his

throat ". . . courtin'. And sometimes she'll come to visit me in the evenings, when she can get away."

"From Eden Park."

I looked up at Gage's pronouncement, dropping the cloth I'd been wringing out back into the water with a splash.

"Isn't that right, Miss Hogan? You work for Mr. LaTouche."

Her eyes were worried now, but she still didn't speak.

Gage turned back to the butler. "Tell me, when did this . . . courting begin?"

He flushed. "'Tis recent."

"Since we arrived?"

"Well . . ." he cast a look of confusion at the girl ". . . yes."

"I see. I imagine she's been gratifyingly inquisitive about your work." Gage hissed in a breath as I pressed the warm cloth to his arm, dabbing away the blood so that I could see the wound. Other than that small sound, he continued on heedless, "How you manage the staff, what sort of hours you've had to keep, what your latest visitors discuss."

The butler's red face and sudden silence were answer enough.

Gage released him from his gaze, shifting his displeasure squarely to the real perpetrator. "Miss Hogan has been doing a bit of spying for Mr. LaTouche," he declared with finality, not bothering to ask her a question she wouldn't answer. "I recognize her from the dinner party the other night. Mr. LaTouche seemed to pay particular attention to her."

This time it was Miss Hogan's turn to blush, though whether it was from actual embarrassment or anger that she'd been found out, I didn't know.

"Would you like to speak now, Miss Hogan? Or shall I send for a constable?"

Her eyes widened, as if such a thought had never occurred to her.

"Surely . . ." the butler began to defend her, despite her duplicity.

But Gage cut him off. "She *shot* me. Perhaps the spying

bit was not her idea, but Mr. LaTouche cannot be held accountable for her pulling the trigger."

"But I tot ye was gonna strap me, sure I did," she gasped in a thick Irish brogue.

"I should hope you were afraid," he replied without sympathy. "You were on someone else's property, where you had no right to be, skulking about in the middle of the night with a pistol. How else was I to view you but as an intruder with malicious intent?"

This silenced her again, but her belligerent glare told me she didn't exactly agree.

Now that much of the blood had been washed away, I could see that Gage was right. The bullet had merely grazed him, leaving a nasty-looking gash. The shirt was already ruined, so I tore the remainder of the sleeve off so that I could clean the wound properly.

He glanced down at me distractedly, speaking to the girl. "If you tell us what you know, I'll reconsider sending my man . . ." he nodded at Anderley ". . . after the authorities."

"Reconsider?" she asked suspiciously.

Gage studied her. "If I believe you are being honest with us about what you know, then I will not call for a constable. Is that fair?"

"But I don't know nothin', I don't," she argued.

"Just try."

She sighed, lifting her eyes toward the ceiling, and then gave a jerky nod. "'Tis how ye said." She glanced at Dempsey. "Mr. LaTouche asked me to cozy up to someone here an' be findin' oot what I could about ye. 'Twasn't much." She pouted. "Least Mr. LaTouche wasn't happy wit what I could tell him. Kept tellin' me to be findin' oot more, but how could I?" She glanced at Anderley. "Tried to cozy up to dat'n, but he'd no' have it."

Deciding the wound was as clean as I could make it, I began to bind it with one of the clean strips of cloth.

"Did Mr. LaTouche explain *why* he wanted you to spy on us?"

She shook her head. "I don't know, sure I don't. But . . ." She hesitated. "He and Master Colin, they been talkin' 'bout the abbey. 'Bout a girl there."

Gage's eyes met mine in understanding. Mr. LaTouche was either guilty, or bound and determined to make himself look so.

He nodded to Dempsey. "Show Miss Hogan out. Though I do believe we'll be keeping her pistol." But he stopped the man with a hand to his shoulder as he passed. "I trust in the future you'll be a bit more circumspect."

"Yes, sir. I don't have to learn my lessons twice."

"Good."

I thrust the cup of willow bark tea into Gage's hands and watched as the pair slipped through the door. "Drink it."

He didn't argue, though I knew the drink was far from tasty. His wound must have hurt him more than he wanted to admit.

"Do you think it was wise to let her go? She's bound to tell LaTouche that we caught her."

He gritted his teeth, forcing down the last swallow as he passed me back the cup. "Maybe. Maybe not. But if she does, I don't think LaTouche will do anything drastic. After all, his sending her to spy on us doesn't prove anything other than that he's mistrustful. If he chooses to panic and run, he would actually be doing us a favor, for nothing would prove his guilt more."

"And if that maid turns up dead?"

He turned to me in some surprise. "She won't. That would sign his death warrant. He's impulsive, but not an idiot."

I hoped he was right. As sullen and foolhardy as the girl had been—shooting Gage and refusing to speak, even to save her own skin—I wanted no harm to come to her.

"No. LaTouche might lose a night's sleep, but he won't run. In fact, if I've read his character correctly, I expect he'll come to us." He scowled. "Which is all to my liking. The sooner we can uncover the truth and get out of this senseless mess, the better."

. . .

The Orange Day Parade was scheduled to begin sometime around midmorning, so we made certain to arrive long before that, positioning ourselves at the corner of the constabulary as planned. The officers of the constabulary forces had already taken up posts throughout the village, some on horseback and others on foot, including Chief Constable Corcoran, who tipped his hat to us, before returning his focus to a pair of his men. We'd noticed Constable Casey on our drive into the village, standing with another man in front of the Yellow House. Between the dark green of their uniforms, the green ribbons of the Ribbonmen, and the bright orange sashes and pins worn by those celebrating Orange Day, the gathering crowd became a rather colorful sight.

There was a great deal of shouting, and some minor scuffles and skirmishes, easily broken up, but nothing noteworthy to attend to. However, you could feel the throng's growing tension. It swelled along with their voices, making even the constables' well-trained horses whicker and shuffle in agitation.

I remained firmly at Gage's side, scanning the people who stood before the businesses lining either side of the road. Some of them, men and women alike, stood back against the shop windows with brooms and rakes. I wondered if this was how they intended to defend their property should it become necessary.

I recognized a few people shuffling among the crowd, though I imagined Gage and Anderley recognized more. A couple of the more soft-spoken men from Mr. LaTouche's dinner were present, conferring with each other a few yards away. As were a number of the servants from the Priory, including Homer Baugh, who stood solemnly across the street, his hands stuffed into his trouser pockets. I was surprised to see Mrs. Scully hovering not far to his left, her face drawn and weary. I wondered if Davy or one of the sisters was sitting with her husband. Marsdale sidled up to join us at one point, his usual sardonic manner on display in his garish orange and clover green striped waistcoat.

I stared at it in reluctant amusement. "Where on earth did you get that? Please don't tell me your valet packed it for you."

He preened. "Had it specially made, just for the occasion. I think the seamstress I hired thought I was a bit mad."

"She was right," I declared with aplomb while Gage merely shook his head.

The first discordant notes of a small band of musicians beginning to tune their instruments floated down the street, saving me from hearing Marsdale's response. I inhaled deeply, settling my nerves, almost relieved it was nearly time. Let it begin. Let it be over.

"Lady Darby, Mr. Gage, Lord Marsdale. How fortuitous to find ye here."

I knew I shouldn't have been surprised by LaTouche's approach. After all, Gage had predicted he would seek us out. But to see him and his son strolling toward us, LaTouche's mouth curled upward at the corners in a sheepish grin like a schoolboy caught in a naughty prank, was more disconcerting than I was prepared for. Especially given our surroundings.

"I imagine I owe ye an apology."

"You imagine right," Gage replied in a hard voice as we turned as one to face them, his arm still looped through mine.

LaTouche laughed as if Gage had made a jest. This made Colin glance at his father askance, seeming just as perturbed as I was by his rather careless demeanor. Meanwhile, Marsdale observed our exchange with piqued interest.

"Yes, well. Ye must see it was harmless," LaTouche declared, adjusting the fit of one of his gloves.

"Harmless for who? The butler with whom she trifled, who I gathered was rather fond of her? Or for Miss Hogan herself, whom I almost sent for the constables to arrest?"

LaTouche's jaw twitched in annoyance. "Now, was tha' really necessary?"

Gage continued on, ignoring his comment. "Had she known how to aim that pistol she was carrying, she would have put a bullet in my skull rather than merely winging me."

This startled him and his son, whose eyes widened to saucers. Even Marsdale's face creased into a scowl.

"Now, see here. I didn't tell the lass to be takin' a gun with her. She was just supposed to be findin' out what ye knew."

"Why?"

He blinked at the clipped tone of Gage's voice.

"Why did you so desperately need to know that you sent a young woman—who as your servant you are to protect, by the way, not corrupt—to spy on us?"

"She wasn't *spying*."

"I see. And what would you call it?"

"She was simply speakin' to yer servant, an' happened to be curious about ye and what ye were doin'."

Gage's expression was clearly unimpressed. "It doesn't matter what convoluted explanation you use, I still want to know *why* you did it."

A few members of the crowd clustered around us sent glances our way, but most of them ignored us in favor of the more exciting argument between two men who were shouting at each other across the street. A pair of constables jostled Colin in the back as they pushed past, hurrying across the lane to intercede.

LaTouche lifted his chin. "I wanted to be sure ye were doin' an adequate job with yer inquiry, o' course."

I frowned at this ridiculous fiction. Did he think we were stupid?

"Let's cut through this nonsense. You wanted to know what we suspected about you and your son." Gage nodded at Colin. "Who, I noticed, you conveniently forgot to mention was engaged once to Miss Lennox."

Marsdale jolted as if someone had stuck a knife between his ribs, and I offered him a tight smile of apology that we'd not delivered this news in a better way. His eyes cut to the young man, scrutinizing him closely as LaTouche snapped his explanation.

"Only because I knew ye would leap to the wrong conclusion. Just as yer wife did yesterday when she came chargin' in, demandin' to speak to my son."

I arched a single eyebrow at this description of my composed and courteous visit.

"That's not how it happened, Father," Colin objected, speaking up for the first time.

"Shut yer gob," LaTouche barked at him. "I'll not be takin' the blame for this, or lettin' you do so simply because you've been an eejit not to keep the truth to yerself."

"You do realize that the very fact that you've attempted to thwart us at every turn from finding out the truth has made you an even bigger suspect than you ever would have been," Gage pointed out in irritation. "If you'd explained your relation to Miss Lennox and your interactions with her and Mother Mary Fidelis at the very beginning, we would not have paid those facts as much heed."

"Mother Mary Fidelis?" For a moment I thought he was actually going to attempt to deny he'd spoken with her, but he grunted in annoyance instead. "I s'pose dat gardener boy told ye he saw us." He scoffed, dismissing him. "Well, dat was the evenin' *before* she was killed. I wasn't anywhere nearby when it happened."

"Why did you meet with her?" I asked, having wondered at this since we learned of it.

"She wanted to ask me if I'd seen anyone that mornin' I met wit Miss Lennox, the same day she died. But I told her like I told you, dat I didn't meet wit Miss Lennox dat day."

No, but his son had.

He glowered. "But if she wanted to know anyting, she should speak to dat gardenor o' theirs. He was always around." He narrowed his eyes in dislike. "Always watchin'."

And he had been watching that morning. He'd seen Colin with Miss Lennox, though he'd thought it was Mr. LaTouche when he saw him at the fair.

A sickening stirring began in my gut, just as the first trumpeted notes of a song from the band went up farther down the street. Everyone turned to see, even Mr. LaTouche and his son, but I grabbed at Colin's arm. He glanced over his shoulder at me in surprise.

"I know this is going to sound incredibly impertinent," I told him. "But I assure you there is a reason for it. Did you take hold of Miss Lennox's hand that morning when you met her, after she told you everything? Did you touch her or kiss her?"

The pain stirring in his eyes and the color cresting his cheeks seemed to answer for him, but I waited for him to respond. "Yes. All of it."

I nodded, releasing him, and glanced up at Gage, who was looking down at me in question. "I need to speak with Mrs. Scully," I leaned in to say over the noise.

His gaze lifted over my head across the street toward where she still stood, and then down the street toward where the parade could just be seen rounding the bend in the road. He nodded and turned to confer with Anderley and Marsdale briefly. Then clutching my arm close to his side, we hurried across the street.

Mrs. Scully's eyes widened as she caught sight of us coming in her direction. Her gaze darted to her left and her right, as if considering an escape into the crowd, but she held her ground, clutching her parcel to her chest. I glanced to the right just as we were stepping up onto the pavement, locking eyes with Mr. Baugh, the Priory's gardener. His eyes shone in curiosity, but he did not speak.

"Mrs. Scully, how is your husband?" I asked, opening with something I hoped would set her at ease.

"Ah, now," she exhaled almost in relief, and then nodded. "Much better, m'lady. Surgeon tinks he'll be able to keep the leg."

"I'm relieved to hear it."

"Me, too. Me, too. And I never got a chance to tank ye for all ye did to help him."

"Of course."

She shook her head. "Wit out ye an' the sisters, I don't know what I woulda done, sure I don't."

"They are wonderful, kindhearted ladies, aren't they?" I asked, seeing my opening.

"Oh, to be sure. The best o' us." Her eyes dipped to the pavement. "They don't deserve what's been happenin' to 'em."

"Then why haven't you come forward with what you know?"

Her head snapped upward and her eyes rounded in their sockets, but still she shook her head. "What I know? I don't know nothin'."

A few people nearby glanced at us distractedly, hearing the distress in her voice. "Yes, you do," I persisted, more certain than ever that I was right.

Her eyes began to fill with tears as she kept shaking her head.

"Mrs. Scully," I said as gently as I could while having to raise my voice to be heard over the band and the throng. "We already know. Your remaining silent will change nothing." I prayed the Lord would forgive that lie, as it was meant with good intentions. "But confessing what you know to us might alleviate some of your guilt."

She lowered her head and began to sob. "'Twas an accident," she gasped. "I know it was. He would never 've hurt her. Never." She sniffled loudly, making the women next to her glance at her and then glare at me. "Ye shoulda seen how upset he was. His hands were shakin' so bad, he almost singed 'em."

"And what of Mother Mary Fidelis? Was her death an accident, too?" I demanded.

"I don't know." Her voice rose frantically, and she reached out to clutch my arm with one of her hands. "But ye have to understand, he . . . he's like a son to me. Me own boy. I couldna' tattle on 'im. All I saw was him burnin' some clothes. Da-dat's no proof."

I lifted my eyes to meet Gage's, his own now bright with the same understanding. But at almost the same moment, the crowd parted and my gaze snagged on the tall man with a head full of brilliant copper hair weaving his way toward us. He saw us at nearly the same time and his steps slowed as his stare shifted to see Mrs. Scully gripping my arm, her head bowed as she wept.

In an instant, I saw the shock and horror and guilt flash through his eyes as his body slammed to a rigid stop.

"Gage," I murmured to be certain he'd seen him as well.

"I see him. Don't even think it . . ." he muttered, breaking off with a grunt as Davy turned to flee.

Gage took off after him, pushing his way through the bodies lining the street, impeding both of their progress. People shouted in affront and shoved back. Then Davy did the unthinkable. He dashed into the middle of the street, straight at the line of Orangemen riding on horseback.

CHAPTER TWENTY-SEVEN

I gasped and flinched as the horse nearest Davy reared, lashing out with his hooves. Somehow he managed to dodge to the side, evading them, but the rider was not so fortunate. He tumbled from the back of his steed onto the hard dirt with a sharp thud. The pole of the banner he carried struck the flank of a mare and snapped in half with a loud crack. The mare and two other horses panicked, and depending on the skill of their handlers, either shied under their reins or stampeded down the street toward the crowd.

Several shouts went up and a woman screamed, and then the crowd began to surge and writhe in every direction at once. I caught sight of Davy disappearing beyond the Orangemen, as one of the men marching on foot grabbed hold of Gage, slowing his pursuit. Gage shoved him aside, sending him careening into a man from the crowd who had moved into the street, and then resumed his chase.

In the blink of an eye, pandemonium seemed to ensue. The already roiling tensions of the Ribbonmen and Orangemen bubbled over in the chaos, and there simply weren't enough constabulary forces to contain it.

I moved forward to follow Gage, knowing he would never be able to make his way back to me even if he tried, but an arm shot out from behind to haul me back. Just in the nick of time, too. A man in front of me swung out with some sort of stick, narrowly missing my skull as he tried to hit one of the men in orange. My heart pounding in my chest from the narrow miss, I glanced upward to thank whoever had saved me.

"Mr. Baugh," I exclaimed in relief.

"Ye want to go after yer husband? Come wit me."

I didn't waste time or words by replying, instead allowing him to help me weave through the mayhem before us. Only once did my steps falter, at the sight of a man bent over rocking the body of a woman, his face a mask of anguish. But one glance told me the woman was already past my aid, so I let Mr. Baugh pull me away, sending up a swift prayer.

When we reached the other side of the street, we began to move more slowly, trying to figure out where the two men had gone, but still avoiding the fists and objects being hurled about. The scene was a deafening melee of shouts, thumps, shrieks, and the occasional clap of gunfire. The band had long since given up playing, their instruments turned into weapons. Even so, I heard Bree's voice rising above the tumult toward our right, and pointed Mr. Baugh in that direction.

She stood at the entrance to the old graveyard, one side of the gate gaping open. "They went in there," she explained. "Anderley and Lord Marsdale followed in case Mr. Gage needed help."

I felt a trickle of relief ease the tightness in my chest to know Gage was not pursuing a double murderer alone. "Then come on," I told her and Mr. Baugh, urging them through the gate. Inside had to be safer than without.

The metal clanged shut behind us as we made our way down the shaded path. I spared a glance for Bree, wondering if she was worried about her half brother out there in the chaos. Her expression was fixed and determined, but that didn't mean her stomach wasn't a mass of knots like mine.

Tall stone walls overgrown with ivy and moss lined both sides of the path, creating a sort of long channel through which one had to walk to reach the graveyard. Our feet crunched against the old leaves and other detritus which had built up over time, blocked from escaping by the walls and twin portals. The second of which was a sort of stone archway through which we had to pass to reach the cemetery proper.

There the walls were lower and easily leapt over in several spots despite the heavy vegetation filling the space. Towering trees, thick with leaves and vines, blocked out a great deal of the sunlight, giving the graveyard a gloomy appearance, filled with shifting shadows and the clatter of the limbs overhead in the wind. It was not the sort of place one wished to visit at night. In fact, even in daylight, I found it to be rather unsettling.

Many of the gravestones already leaned at awkward angles, as if the ground beneath had given way. One stone table monument had even cracked down the middle, collapsing in on itself. The crumbling remains of the old church at the center were overgrown with vines and shrubbery, so that much of what stone endured was all but swallowed by it. It was near this wreck that Gage, Marsdale, and Anderley stood with their hands on their hips, turning in circles, searching.

We crossed the space toward them, kicking up the thick musk of moss and mold which covered the earth. It coated my nostrils like a cloying miasma even though I snorted repeatedly, trying to clear the stench. The men looked up at our approach.

"He just . . . disappeared," Gage grunted in frustration.

"Could he have jumped the wall?" Bree suggested, glancing over her shoulder at the spot I'd also noticed near the entry arch, the place where Constable Casey had likely vaulted over to listen at the chief constable's window.

"No. We saw him run this way."

I turned to meet Mr. Baugh's eyes, seeing that he was thinking the same thing I was. "The tunnel."

"Yes," Gage replied impatiently. "But where is the entrance?"

"Dis way," Mr. Baugh said, striding past him to the other side of the church ruins.

Bree, Marsdale, and I followed them, but Anderley set off in the direction of the back wall of the graveyard where something must have caught his eye. Mr. Baugh halted about twenty feet from what had once been the corner of the building and reached down into the tangled vines of a patch of ivy growing near the base of the stone. With a hard tug, he pulled open what appeared to be one of two wooden cellar doors fashioned at an angle, and completely obscured by the vegetation. The smell that wafted outward, of rot and damp and earth, was enough to make my throat seize closed at the prospect of entering.

"The opening to the tunnel is in the far left corner," he explained as Gage moved closer to peer down inside the dark interior.

All that was visible was a half-dozen stone steps leading down into blackness, and none of us had brought a lantern or even a candle. Had Davy? Was he stumbling through that suffocating darkness even now?

I backed away. There was no way I was going to enter that hole, and neither was I going to let Gage go in. Not as unprepared as he was now.

To my relief, rather than attempting to advance, he straightened and shook his head. "There's no way we can follow. Not like this." He turned to Mr. Baugh. "This opens on the other end at the castle?"

He nodded, rubbing his chin. "Question is, where he'll be plannin' to go from there?"

Through the tunnel to the abbey? He must know we expected that. Did he hope to beat us there and leave again before we could reach him? Or would he take the other tunnel to the Yellow House or even set out from the castle? There was no way to know for sure which direction he would run.

Then Anderley called out from behind us. "Not that way. He leapt the wall over here." He skipped sideways, waving for us to follow.

Mr. Baugh dropped the door in place as we all hurried after the valet toward the back corner. The ground vegetation was thicker here, mixed with sweet grass and red fescue, some of which had obviously been trampled recently. Sure enough, there was a small gap between a scraggly bush and a tree where someone could squeeze through to escape the graveyard.

"There are tracks leading downhill from here toward the west," Anderley explained.

Gage's eyes narrowed in focus. "Good work. Take the lead," he told Anderley, before swiveling toward Marsdale. "I need you to wait here in case he decides to double back."

He shook his head. "No. I'm coming with you. If that sod murdered my cousin like I assume you believe since you're chasing him, then he's going to answer to me." He threw a glance over his shoulder at Homer. "Leave him."

"That's precisely the reason you should stay behind," Gage argued. "You're too invested in this. Your temper's too riled. Besides, Mr. . . ."

"Baugh," I supplied. "He's the Priory's gardener I told you about."

He nodded. "Mr. Baugh is a local man. He knows this land far better than any of us, and we may have need of him. I can't abandon the women here in case he returns or that mob spills over, so that leaves you."

Marsdale glared mutinously, but before he could complain further, Gage's patience snapped.

"Come now. You're wasting time, and allowing Somers to get away. If he doubles back, you can pummel him all you want with no witnesses to stop you." Something dark flickered in Marsdale's eyes, which made Gage add, "Just don't kill him."

"Fine," Marsdale barked. "Go!"

Having already helped me and Bree to scamper over the wall safely to the other side with Anderley's assistance, Gage hoisted himself over. His hand briefly caught hold of mine in reassurance before pushing me forward to follow the others.

Anderley led our progress down the hill as we all surveyed the open land around us, overgrown with tall grasses. The hill ended at the edge of a mill race, the water inside swirling and eddying its way south through a series of man-made rapids toward the next mill along the line. Several yards to the north, a narrow stone arch formed a bridge over the expanse. Still following the trampled trail of grass, Anderley didn't even hesitate before crossing the majority of its expanse, pausing at the end to reach a hand back for Bree and then me. The gap was crossed in the matter of about four steps, but the bridge was slight enough and the water flowing fast enough, that given time to pause and think about it, I'm not sure I would have managed the passage.

Once we were all over, we climbed uphill toward another thick swatch of vegetation, our steps slowing at the sound of what lay beyond. The muted roar of a swift-flowing river is not easily mistaken for anything else, and the rush of this one made the mill race seem like a gurgling trickle of bathwater. Even so, among the otherwise tangled underbrush, we could mark the distinct passage of a person or a large animal entering the trees. Was there some footbridge beyond? Or a trail leading down toward the river?

There was nothing for it but to proceed cautiously through the forest, though this time Gage insisted on leading. I stayed close behind him, but not near enough to hinder him should he suddenly need to move quickly. The woods were still and silent, but for the shuffle and crunch of our footfalls and, ironically enough, the shrill *"chee-kee, chee-kee"* whistle of a kingfisher somewhere in the boughs overhead, as well as that ever-present, ever-growing surge of the river. It must pass through a swath of stone or rock ahead for the sound to seem so amplified.

Sure enough, as we emerged from beneath the trees, we could see down into what appeared to be a shallow gorge. The water funneling through echoed off the cliff faces, turning the river into a roiling flume. The trees grew right up to the edge of the rock, leaving little if any room to skirt along the edge toward the rock that jutted out over the river. It was a sort of bare promontory with nothing but a scraggily tree clinging to its tip.

Gripping this tree as he leaned over to stare down into

the river stood Davy Somers. My chest tightened at his precarious position, and when he looked back, revealing his wild eyes and tearstained face, I began to fear just precisely what his intentions were for being there.

"Somers, come away from there!" Gage yelled to be heard over the pounding water below.

When he didn't respond, not even with a shake of his head, Gage picked his way through the trees to get closer, with me close at his heels, echoing his every step. However, once we'd reached the base of the rock, but a few steps from him, Davy yelled for us to stop.

"Don't come any closer," he threatened, leaning back over the river.

Gage held up one of his hands, while wrapping the other around my waist to hold me close to his side. "Somers, you don't want to do that," he shouted.

"Why? I deserve it." His voice was sharp, near the edge of breaking. "I'll be swingin' from a gibbet soon in any case, to be sure."

I inhaled sharply. "Yes, but to kill yourself . . ." We were told that suicide was an unforgivable sin.

"What does it matter? I'm goin' to hell anyway." He ended on a desperate whimper.

For a moment, I thought he was going to release the wiry tree and allow himself to fall over the edge, and I felt Gage's body tense against mine. But he righted himself at the last minute, shaking the leaves of the tree with the force of his grip. There had to be something we could say to convince him to come away from the edge, something to salvage this situation.

I focused on his face, the pain etched there. "Davy, we know it was an accident."

He closed his eyes. "I . . . I didn't want to hurt 'er."

I swallowed the sick taste that coated my throat at that sentiment.

"I know. You loved her."

He exhaled a ragged breath. "I did. But den I . . . I saw

her wit dat gentleman, dat LaTouche. And she *kissed* him. She . . . she was becomin' a nun, but she *kissed* him."

He looked away. Apparently, accepting her calling to be a bride of Christ was one thing—as a Catholic, how could he argue with that—but to see her with a man, to see her dishonoring those intentions, was quite another. Especially when it was clear he would have liked that man to be him. Except he hadn't known the truth. He hadn't known she had no intention of actually taking her vows.

"I . . . I just wanted to talk to her. So I followed her to the pond. But she kept sayin' I didn't understand. Dat I didn't know." His voice raised in disbelief. "But I did. O' course I did. Since the day she came to the abbey." He shook his head. "An' I tot she was different. I tot she cared. She just *couldn't* care how I wished. She lied. She lied."

He was spiraling into despair and anger, and I needed to bring him back. But we also needed the truth. We needed to hear his confession while he could and would give it.

"I was so *angry*. And she turned away, she dismissed me. So . . . so I grabbed her. I had to make her listen, to make her understand. But she pulled away. Made me rip off her veil. The way she looked at me." His face contorted in pain. "Told me not to touch her, and den she ran. I told her to stop. I just wanted to explain. But she wouldn't stop. Why couldn't she just stop?" he pleaded to the heavens.

"So you pushed her?" Gage guessed.

He shook his head, and I could see in his eyes that he was reliving it. "I . . . I caught her shoulder an' tried to turn her, but she pulled away. Her dress ripped and . . . and she tripped and fell backward. Onto that rock. I didn't mean for her to hit her head. I didn't know it was there. How'd it get there?" he demanded in rage, as if we had the answer, as if someone had played a cruel trick. Then his shoulders crumpled. "I didn't mean for her to . . . to die."

"But she did," Gage pointed out, though there was no recrimination in his voice. "So why didn't you tell someone what happened?"

"How? I . . . I knew what they'd tink. I knew what they'd say. Same as Mother Mary Fidelis did. I'm an orphan, an afore dat a bastard's son. Blood will show. Dat's what she told me. Said she'd prayed 'bout it. Dat she couldn't protect me. Not from such a wicked act."

Had Mother Fidelis truly been so brutal? From my short time with her, I'd discovered she was blunt and sometimes sharp, but I had not thought her merciless. Or had she known something Davy wasn't telling us.

"But Davy, you moved Miss Lennox's body. You dragged her closer to the abbey and removed the stone. Why?"

Had he left her the way she was, no one would have thought her death had been anything but a tragic accident. No one would have ever known.

His eyes were wide, almost blank. "I don't know. I wasn't thinkin'." He turned aside. "I couldn't leave her out in dat field. Not like dat. But den I heard dem callin' her name, and I . . . I ran."

"Taking the stone with you?"

He nodded. "I . . . I trew it in the pond the next day."

I tightened my own grip around Gage's torso, anchoring myself to him, trying to figure out how much of what Davy was telling us was the truth, and how much a lie. I didn't want to contemplate it at all, but we still had one more fact to face. He had killed Mother Fidelis. And I didn't believe for one second that both deaths had been accidents.

"So tell us what happened when Mother Mary Fidelis confronted you?" Gage said, saving me from having to pose the question.

Davy's grip tightened on the tree again. His mouth clamped tightly shut as he gazed down over the side of the rock toward the rushing river.

"Why did you kill her?" Gage persisted.

His eyes when he lifted them were hollow holes. "Don't ye already know?"

I stared at him dumbly, trying to understand, feeling I'd missed something very important.

"She spoke the truth. My da was a rotten blackguard. Hung at Gallows Hill." His jaw hardened. "She would know. 'Tis why she sent me away."

I sucked in a harsh, shocked breath, and I felt Gage stiffen beside me.

"Ah, now ye see. 'Tis her fault I was anywhere near Miss Lennox." His face tightened in pain. "'Tis her fault I could hurt her at all."

I could barely form the thoughts in my head, let alone speak them. This revelation made it all so much more horrifying. So much so that it was difficult to do anything but stare. I supposed I could see the resemblance—the height, the eye color, the red in their hair that I'd glimpsed briefly when I'd examined her wound—but Davy must have taken more after his father. Was this why Mother Fidelis had really distanced herself from her family? Was this the past they had referred to, that they would not let her forget? Was this why she'd insisted she have time to pray before she spoke to me?

While we stood there rigidly, stumbling over our own thoughts, Davy inched his way back toward the precipice.

"Davy, don't . . ." I gasped, taking an unconscious step forward, though Gage impeded me from going anything farther.

"It's for the best," he said, and I could see in his eyes that his mind was made up.

"But what of Mrs. Scully?"

If anyone had ever loved Davy, it was certainly her, and I could see in his face that he recognized that. He seemed to hesitate.

"Don't do this to her," I begged. "It will break her heart."

His eyes went blank. "No more than seein' me hanged."

"Davy . . ." Gage began.

But before he could utter another word, Davy released his hold on the tree and dropped over the side. I shrieked as he disappeared from sight.

From where we stood, we could not witness the impact, but Anderley, Bree, and Mr. Baugh were not so fortunate.

Their bodies jolted at the sight, flinching as they turned away. Bree moved deeper into the woods with her back turned while the men forced themselves to lean over and look again. Gage shuffled forward to see down into the gorge, but I stayed where I was, clutching my arms close to my body.

When he returned to my side, I couldn't help but look up into his grim face with a desperate hope. "Could he have survived?"

He shook his head and then gathered me into his arms.

CHAPTER TWENTY-EIGHT

The sun slanted through the abbey's parlor windows, casting long rays across the floor that almost touched the rug beneath the furnishings on which our disconsolate group had gathered, but not quite. Gage sat beside me, still clutching my hand after our retelling of the events earlier that day. Marsdale perched on the other side of me, his head turned away toward the empty hearth so that I could not see his face, but I felt the tension in his body. The mother superior and Mother Paul sat at either end of the settee across from us, their eyes round with shock, their brows etched with sorrow. It seemed no one knew what to say next. The weight of everything that had happened was still too much.

Then the reverend mother inhaled a bracing breath, seeming to steady herself to face what must come. "I knew Mother Mary Fidelis had had a child," she admitted. "But not that he survived, and certainly not that he was Davy Somers; otherwise, she would not have been eligible to profess. She was one of the first to join me, you know. When I was still in York preparing to begin this branch of the order. She was older than most postulants, more considered." She sighed heavily. "Or so I thought."

"When did Davy come here?" I asked.

"He already lived in Rathfarnham, doing odd jobs for the chapel and a few other establishments in the village."

She glanced upward around her. "When we took over this house, the gardens were in such a disarray. The orchard was essentially a bog, and the wall needed serious repairs. We thought Mr. Scully could use the help, particularly from a young, strong back. Davy was barely thirteen, but he was a good lad. And Mrs. Scully took an instant liking to him. She'd never been able to have a child of her own. I . . ." her gaze flicked to Mother Paul ". . . we never knew he was anything to Mother Mary Fidelis."

I nodded. Their bewilderment was genuine. Which left me wondering whether Mother Fidelis had carefully manipulated matters—joining Reverend Mother Teresa's order because of where they were bound, and finding work that would bring her son closer—or if their reconnection had been an extraordinary coincidence.

There were so many questions we didn't have the answers to. Some of which, given the content of their letters, I suspected her family would be happy to provide, along with a healthy dose of speculation. But in the end, they were answers that would make no difference.

Two women were dead because of a desperate young man's need for affection. Because one of those women had sent him away as a young child rather than raise him. I didn't know the circumstances involved, but I couldn't believe God would call a woman to do such a thing. Not like this. Not when it meant behaving in such a shameful, secretive manner.

My eyes strayed to where Marsdale still stared vacantly into the hearth. As for Miss Lennox, her death had simply been a horrible accident. A death that should never have happened, but could never have been foreseen, though that was little comfort to those who cared for her.

"So what's to be done now?" Reverend Mother touched the cross dangling around her neck. "What of Davy's body? Have the Scullys claimed it?"

"It was swept downstream," Gage replied. "It's yet to be found. Most of the authorities are still tied up dealing with the aftermath of the violence that exploded during the parade." From what we'd seen of Rathfarnham as we'd woven through the wreckage and debris, the smashed windows and toppled carriages, the pavement still splashed red with blood in spots, it would take weeks, if not months, for the village to recover. "His body may take some time to locate, or . . . it might never surface."

From the tone of his voice, I knew that Davy Somers was no longer the chief priority in Gage's mind. Speaking to his father, to Wellington, and giving them a piece of his mind were foremost. As was informing the government what a hash they were making of the situation in Ireland, and how foolhardy they were to allow these parades when they couldn't control them.

"Is that where you wish to go first?" I asked him later when we were seated alone in the parlor at the Priory after dinner. "To London?"

"Yes. I think it's best. We intended to go there anyway when our wedding trip was so impolitely interrupted. And that's where I shall find the men I need to speak to." His voice was brisk with purpose.

"Then that's where we'll go," I replied, using my finger to swipe around the top edge of the sketch I was finishing, smudging the charcoal. I lifted it to examine it more critically. "That will give me time to put my plans into action as well." I turned the drawing so that he could see it.

"That's Mrs. Scully." His eyes flicked to my face in question.

"Indeed. I think I shall use her likeness as part of my next exhibit. *The Faces of Ireland*." I tried to read his expression, but it seemed remarkably vague. "I know it's been several years since I've shown any of my portraits, but I thought it might be time. Perhaps . . . perhaps if I display portraits of these people, it will humanize them to those who think of them as nothing but a squalling mass."

He rose from his chair to cross toward me, taking the sketchbook from my hands.

"You don't mind, do you?" Perhaps he didn't want his wife exhibiting artwork. After all, painting a portrait commission was altogether different than creating a public display.

His eyes when he looked at me again were warm. "I don't. In fact, I think it's an excellent idea."

"You do?"

"Yes." He set the book aside and pulled me to my feet. "This inquiry was difficult for you, wasn't it? In a different way than the others."

I nodded, lifting my hands to straighten the folds of his dark cravat as I tried to find my words.

"I know something's been troubling you." He brushed a stray hair back from my forehead. "I haven't wanted to pry, trusting you would come to me when you were ready." His eyes searched mine. "But perhaps I should have."

"Maybe," I admitted hesitantly. "But I think it's likely I would have dodged the question."

"Is that what you're doing now?" he asked with a gentle smile when I didn't say anything more.

I shook my head, and then gasped a nervous laugh. "It's only . . . this has been the first inquiry in which I didn't have any personal motivation, and it's made me confront a few things I hadn't before. Well, that and our marriage."

He waited patiently for me to continue as I feigned great interest in his collar.

"You started to speak to me of it the other night." I swallowed, darting a glance up at him, hoping he might read my mind. Why was it so hard to say the word? "About children."

Gage rubbed his hands up and down my arms soothingly. "Yes. I said there was no hurry. It would happen in time."

"Yes, but . . . when it does. What then?"

His head tilted in confusion.

"I mean," I swallowed. "Will you still wish for me to assist with your inquiries? Or will you want me to stay home with the children?"

"Well, like most people of our station, I suspect we'll have a nanny. Though I anticipate you'll wish to be more present than most gentlewomen in their young children's lives, as your sister is. But beyond that, there's no reason you shouldn't be able to assist me." His eyes softened in reassurance. "I meant everything I said before we married. I want you to continue to pursue the things that interest you—your art, our inquiries. Perhaps we'll be a bit more selective in the crimes we accept to investigate. We have the freedom to do so. But there's no reason to stop altogether." His brow furrowed. "Unless you wish to?"

"But what of the danger?" I pressed. "You already fret when I must take any risk. How much more will you worry when I'm *enceinte* or we have a child at home?"

"The same."

I pursed my lips in skepticism.

"I will always worry, whether you are heavy with my child or not. Which doesn't mean I won't expect you to take more care. Though I don't believe I'll have to remind you to do so. I know you, Kiera. You might not balk at placing yourself in peril, but you would do so if our child's life was also at risk."

I frowned at his chin. The very thought of exposing my child to danger made my chest tighten and my stomach dip.

Gage's fingers tightened around my upper arms. "But where is this coming from? Why now?" He forced my chin upward with one finger so he could look into my eyes. "Do you wish to stop?"

"No," I admitted, and was gratified to see his shoulders relax in relief.

"Then what troubles you?"

"That . . . I should want to." I forced the words out even as shame scalded my cheeks. "That the fact I don't means I won't be a very good mother."

His pale eyes softened with a tenderness I didn't deserve, and I closed my eyes to it. "Kiera . . ." he began, and I cut him off.

"Don't."

"Kiera," he insisted, cupping my jaw with his hand, trying to make me look at him. "You have it all wrong. Don't you realize that the very fact that you even care to ask these questions already tells me you'll make a wonderful mother."

"That's absurd."

"It isn't. Just because you have a child doesn't mean you have to give up the other things that make you happy. Would you rather spend your time attending balls, and arranging charity functions, and paying calls on acquaintances you could care less to know?" The normal duties of a woman of my status.

He already knew the answer to that, but I replied anyway. "No."

His eyebrows rose. "Our investigations and your painting won't take up any more time than those other things, and at least they will be enjoyable and worthwhile." His expression softened. "You will still be able to be a good mother, Kiera. Perhaps a better mother for not stifling yourself because you think it's best for our children."

I hadn't thought of it that way, but his words rang true. They settled inside me like a warm blanket, loosening the stranglehold of anxiety, the dread of what was to come. I leaned closer, resting my head against his shoulder and pressing my nose into the folds of his cravat, inhaling his comforting scent mixed with starch and his spicy cologne. His arms immediately embraced me.

"Thank you," I murmured as I lifted my head. I wrinkled my nose. "Perhaps my worries are silly . . ."

"They aren't," he replied, cutting me off. His eyes were bright with sincerity. "I don't want you to ever feel hesitant about bringing them to me. Your worries are my worries, whatever they may be." He pulled me close again, his fingers absently toying with the closure of the caped collar on my dress. "I'm your husband. That's what I'm here for." His mouth curled into a charmingly rakish grin. "Among other things."

An answering smile tugged at my lips. "Yes. I should have known better. I may have been wed once before, but that was quite different, and I'm finding I'm rather new at this marriage business."

"We both are." He chuckled. "But we'll find our way." He pressed a kiss to my lips. "Whatever comes, we'll weather it."

"We have thus far. And we've endured far more storms than I suspect most couples do."

"In our line of occupation, we're bound to encounter a few squalls."

I laughed at his heavy-handed continuation of our strained metaphor, and he leaned in to kiss me again. Though it turned out to be shorter than either of us wished when we were interrupted by a rapping on the door.

He heaved a sigh, and turned to face Dempsey, who had been tiptoeing around us all day. "Yes?"

"I'm very sorry, sir. But I forgot to tell ye dat dis arrived for ye earlier." He held out a tray on which sat a thick letter, smudged and slightly bedraggled from transport.

Gage tensed, already anticipating the contents, but he thanked the butler and sent him away before addressing it. He flipped the missive over in his hands, examining all the sides. "Blasted letters," he grumbled, breaking the seal with a great deal more force than was necessary.

I recognized the handwriting as being his father's, and suspected he'd written to castigate us for not reporting our progress and findings as quickly as he wished. I knew Gage had sent him two letters already, one of which had expressed his fury over his father's failure to share pertinent details of Miss Lennox's presence at the abbey. However, there was no way of predicting whether either or both of those had yet arrived in London.

I began to sink back into my chair, but something on Gage's face arrested me. His initial annoyance had shifted to apprehension.

"What is it?"

He lifted another small tightly folded square which had been wrapped inside the first, breaking this seal more carefully. "My father. He's forwarded a letter from my grandfather." His gaze flicked up at me before returning to read the page. "My mother's father."

I blinked in surprise. Though he'd spent a considerable amount of time with his mother's family when he was young, while Lord Gage was away at sea captaining a ship for the Royal Navy, I knew that Gage had not seen his grandfather since his mother's death fifteen years prior. Their correspondence was almost as infrequent.

"It's my cousin Alfred." His pale blue eyes lifted to meet mine. "He's missing. My grandfather says he went for a walk on the moors one day and never returned. He's simply . . . vanished."

I wasn't familiar then with the dangers of Dartmoor. With the treacherous landscape of shifting bogs that could swallow a man whole, with the unpredictable weather which could shift in an instant, or the strange creatures which roamed its tors. I didn't know of the shadows which cloaked Langstone Manor, his grandfather's estate. Shadows which reached out to touch every life who intersected with its foreboding halls. But I would be. And life as Gage and I knew it would prove never to be the same.

HISTORICAL NOTE

A great deal of research went into this latest installment of the Lady Darby series, and it's always fun to share just what is fact and what is fiction. Many of the details of Rathfarnham, Ireland—the buildings, the roads, the waterways, the graveyard—were situated much as I described them, taking into account the difficulty of relying on mere descriptions and maps from around 1831. The three notable exceptions are the layout of the abbey grounds and its proximity to The Ponds, which were slightly altered to suit the story; Eden Park, which is listed on maps, but I could not find any definitive information on the property; and the Constabulary Barracks, which I placed at the location of the Royal Irish Constabulary Barracks built several years later.

Many of the buildings in Rathfarnham had fascinating histories, some of which I used, and some I didn't. Rathfarnham Castle truly did have tunnels running from its property to the old Protestant Church in the graveyard, and to a point to the west which is now part of a golf club. There are rumors that there was also a third tunnel leading to the Yellow House. These were built to protect the family and soldiers during the English Civil Wars of the mid-seventeenth century. There are a number of other intriguing facts about that castle. Such as its connection to the Hellfire Club, and the skeletal remains of a young woman found in the hollow walls in 1880. She was purportedly a young maiden who was locked in a secret compartment during a ball while her two suitors dueled for her affections, killing each other and taking the secret of her location to their graves. Some of the current cushions on the furniture are supposed to have been made from her silk dress.

The Priory was indeed the home of the Currans, and witnessed the tragic death of twelve-year-old Gertrude, whose father buried her in the garden with the exact epitaph listed in the book. The story about Robert Emmet and Sarah Curran is also true, though there is no evidence that Emmet's remains were buried on the Curran property. Several poems have been written about Robert and Sarah's doomed romance, including a short story by Washington Irving titled "The Broken Heart." The Come Here to Me! blog at comeheretome.com posts lots of absorbing historical tidbits about Ireland, including a wonderful entry about the Priory's history.

Loretto (now spelled "Loreto") Abbey, Rathfarnham, proved to be an enthralling place to research. I did my best to describe the nuns, the students, and the running of the abbey in that time period, though there were many gaps in my research I could not fill. Much of my information came from the Institute of the Blessed Virgin Mary and Irish Province of the Loreto Sisters Archives. They had a wonderful depth of information on some of the early sisters of that abbey, including Mother Frances Mary Teresa Ball. Most of the nuns I have utilized in the story were actual historical figures, with the exception of Mother Mary Fidelis and Miss Lennox. I was even able to weave in some quotes pulled from Mother Superior Mary Teresa's letters. A book which shed some light on the abbess was *The Life of Mother Frances Mary Teresa Ball: Foundress of the Institute of the Blessed Virgin Mary* by Henry James Coleridge. I also enjoyed reading *Abbey Girls* by Mary and Valerie Behan, a memoir written by two sisters who attended the abbey school in the 1960s, to give me somewhat of an inside perspective on what it was like to live there even 130 years later.

Miss Lennox is a fictional relative of the Duke of Wellington. Supposing that the duke's first cousin once removed, Lady Harriet Kerr, did not die, but instead lived to marry a man with the last name *Lennox* and produced a child, also named Harriet, who is the Miss Lennox from the story.

Many of the details I shared about the 1798 and 1803 Rebellions, and Rathfarnham's connection to them, are true, as well as the secret societies of the Ribbonmen and the Orangemen. The Orange Order still exists today, and still marches on or around July twelfth every year. Though after the violence which erupted in 1831, these parades were banned by Parliament the following year for a short period. The clashes between Catholics and Orangemen, particularly in Ireland, continue to this day, with some markedly historic incidences.

The Roman Catholic Relief Act of 1829 was indeed passed after a fraught campaign, and one of the chief reasons Prime Minister Wellington and his government did so was to avert open rebellion, though, of course, I have oversimplified the matter. Regardless, there was still a strong opposition and prejudice against Catholics throughout the United Kingdom. It would be many years before they were truly granted equality, but this was a great stride in the right direction.

The Tithes War lasted from 1830 until 1836 throughout Ireland. Much of it truly was a passive and nonviolent protest, punctuated only periodically with violent clashes. The first two skirmishes mentioned in the story, in County Kilkenny and Bunclody, County Wexford, did result in injuries and deaths. However, organized protestors' tactics were overall effective in costing the government "a shilling to collect tuppence." This resulted in the government suspending collections and eventually amending the law, though it was not completely repealed until 1869. For those interested in more information about the political situation in Ireland during the mid-nineteenth century, I recommend reading *Ireland 1815–1870: Emancipation, Famine, and Religion* by

Donnchadh Ó Corráin and Tomás O'Riordan, which contains excerpts from historical letters and legislation.

The colorful anecdotes I shared about Lord Anglesey, who was then Lord Lieutenant of Ireland, are quite true, at least according to him. He was an interesting character, to say the least.

Ready to find
your next great read?

Let us help.

Visit prh.com/nextread

Penguin
Random
House

P.O. 0005432133 20240115